SHE WOLF

BOUDICA'S LEGACY

BY
ALLAN FOX

Copyright © Allan Fox 2015
This book is sold subject to the condition that it shall not, by way of trade or otherwise, be lent, resold, hired out, or otherwise circulated without the publisher's prior consent in any form of binding or cover other than that in which it is published and without a similar condition including this condition being imposed on the subsequent publisher.
The moral right of Allan Fox has been asserted.
ISBN-13: 978-1518843983
ISBN-10: 1518843980

DEDICATION

To my children Kate, Helen, Hannah, James and Alex.

CONTENTS

PROLOGUE. BRITANNIA, 56 AD 1
PART I 8
    CHAPTER 1. ROME, 70 AD 8
    CHAPTER 2. BRITANNIA, 70 AD 15
    CHAPTER 3 19
PART II 35
    CHAPTER 4. BRITANNIA, 60 AD 35
    CHAPTER 5 44
    CHAPTER 6 48
    CHAPTER 7 69
    CHAPTER 8 74
    CHAPTER 9 82
    CHAPTER 10 90
    CHAPTER 11 97
    CHAPTER 12 105
    CHAPTER 13 111
    CHAPTER 14 113
    CHAPTER 15 121
    CHAPTER 16 130
    CHAPTER 17 134
    CHAPTER 18 138
    CHAPTER 19 147
    CHAPTER 20 159
    CHAPTER 21 163
    CHAPTER 22 169
    CHAPTER 23 177
    CHAPTER 24 182
    CHAPTER 25 187
    CHAPTER 26 206
    CHAPTER 27 214
    CHAPTER 28 224
    CHAPTER 29 231
    CHAPTER 30 239
    CHAPTER 31 256
    CHAPTER 32 264

PART III 270

CHAPTER 33. LONDINIUM, 70 A D 270
CHAPTER 34 280
CHAPTER 35 285
CHAPTER 36 294
CHAPTER 37 298
CHAPTER 38 319
CHAPTER 39 323
CHAPTER 40 333
CHAPTER 41 341
CHAPTER 42 346
CHAPTER 43 354
CHAPTER 44 360
CHAPTER 45 367
CHAPTER 46 372
CHAPTER 47 377

AUTHOR'S NOTE 381

ACKNOWLEDGMENTS

Many family members and friends have given me advice, support and encouragement to enable me to complete this book. In the task of bringing my first draft into being, four people were very significant. They were Sandra Hall who converted my horribly handwritten manuscript into a typed version that could be read by somebody other than myself. Peter Wight who was the first to read the story and make invaluable observations. Roy Friendship-Taylor who was a great source of historical background information. John Ward who carried out an initial proofread and edited it for me.

There followed others who took the time to read my early version and give me feedback. They included Marian Wells, Neil Bartram, Carole Fox and Linda McMutrie.

Then there were those who were a constant source of advice and encouragement. Amongst these were Kate Robinson, Hannah Fox, David Fernley, James and Alex Fox, Henry Southern, Bourne Robinson, Paul Kraus, Brenda and Brian Keeley.

And last but definitely not least there was Helen Davison who was involved from beginning to end in every aspect of the process.

Thanks to each and all of you for playing your part in creating this book.

Key
- **PLACE NAMES**
- TRIBAL AREAS

BRIGANTES

MONA   **LINDUM**

ORDIVICES   CORIELTAUVI

CORNUOVII   **RATAE**

VIROCONIUM   ICENI

CATUVELAUNI

TRINOVANTES

VERULAMIUM   **CAMULODUNUM**
LONDINIUM
ATREBATES

ISCA

PROLOGUE

BRITANNIA, 56 AD

It was important that she didn't make a sudden sound or movement. An excited Linona was looking beyond her own faint reflection into the depths of the icy-clear water of the broad, easy-flowing stream. The bright afternoon sun, which a few moments earlier had created a harsh, golden glare across the surface of the water, had been hidden by a dark, thunderous cloud. It enabled her eyes to adjust to the softer light, revealing her prey. She leant further forward in her crouched position.

"I can see one! Look, Olsar. It's hiding behind that rock."

She stabbed her short spear into the water, destroying her shimmering reflection. She felt the iron tip jar against the rocky bed of the stream.

"I can't believe I missed it," she cried. "Tell me what I did wrong?"

"What do you mean?"

"On the way here you were boasting that you're better than anybody else in your clan at catching fish in this stream."

Linona was speaking to a firmly muscled young man. He was crouching like her, but a few paces upstream. She was a princess of the Iceni tribe, daughter of Boudica. It was their custom that she would acquire the skills and knowledge of a warrior. Olsar was the son of the chief of their tribe's southern clan and considered to be one of the tribe's best young warriors. It had been no surprise to her, therefore, when her mother and father had decided to send her to spend some time with him and his family as part of her training.

"You didn't do anything wrong really from what I could see. You just weren't quick enough with your spear. Mind you, I wouldn't expect anything more from a mere girl, especially one who is only 15 years old."

The large pebble clutched from the stream hit him high on the back of his thigh, despite his startled attempt to turn away to avoid it. Linona bent down low, eyes fixed on his throwing arm, waiting for him to return her gift. It didn't come. Instead, he turned to face her and let out a loud contemptuous guffaw. If he wanted to provoke her further he had succeeded.

The difference in age and size mattered nothing to her. She leapt towards him turning her spear in her hands so that the point faced away from him. Raising it above her head she brought the slender wooden shaft down again, aiming at his head. He parried the first blow with his arm and stepped back a pace. Her next blow was directed at his already injured thigh. This time he stepped to the side to avoid being hit. As the third blow came he stepped back again. Too late, he realised he'd run out of solid ground on the edge of the bank. He stumbled backwards into the water, his arms flailing widely in a vain attempt to regain his balance.

It was her turn to laugh out loud, not with contempt, but with the humour of it. Olsar sat waist-deep in the icy-cold water, smiling broadly. He wiped his long yellow hair from his hidden face and shook his head to shed the water.

"You win. I surrender."

Rising slowly, he had some difficulty in finding a sure footing. Eventually he climbed back onto the bank to stand by her side. Still smiling, he offered her his hand in friendship. Linona nodded her acceptance of the gesture of peace and grasped his arm warmly.

"I'm sorry. I accept I should be showing you more respect, Princess Linona."

His next movement wasn't conciliatory, however. Gripping her arm more firmly he pulled her roughly towards him.

"But not today. You're still young and very naïve."

He spun her to face away from him, placing one arm around her waist and the other under her thighs. He lifted her struggling body off the ground and hurled her onto her back into the water. Her scream changed into a spluttering, choking series of gasps as she disappeared momentarily beneath the surface.

"You pig! You arrogant filthy pig! I'll kill you."

She stumbled to her feet and headed towards the bank.

"But I have the advantage of the high ground and I've got your spear. I won't let you out of the water until you apologise to me for losing your temper."

He waved the spear from side to side in low, broad sweeping arcs to make his point, and prevent her leaving the stream. The cooling effect of the water, and the obviously hopeless position in which she found herself, chilled her temper. She stood with her legs spread wide apart to help maintain her balance on the rocks beneath her feet. She planted her hands firmly and defiantly on her hips. The angry scowl on her face began to soften as the first traces of a smile appeared at her lips.

"I suppose you do have a point. Let me out and we can talk about it."

He didn't reply. His gaze had moved sharply from her to the heavily wooded area that covered the opposite bank.

"Did you hear me? Don't you dare ignore me."

"Quiet! We're in danger. Don't make any more loud noises."

Linona couldn't miss the complete change from the playful expression on Olsar's face. She acted quickly, moving beside him to peer into the darkness of the dense forest opposite.

"What have you seen?" she whispered.

"Not seen, but heard. Listen and keep quiet!"

Straining her ears she could make out a faint but increasing sound. It was one she wasn't familiar with. She turned her puzzled face towards him, not speaking.

"That, Linona, is the sound of Roman legionaries, dressed in armour and on the move."

"How do you know?"

"You're just visiting us for a while. If you'd lived in this part of our tribal lands for all your life, as I have, you'd recognise what it was immediately from a long way off. Your life could depend on knowing what it was."

"What should we do?"

"Withdraw quietly into the cover of the trees behind us to watch what happens. There'll be scouts moving ahead of the column. They may have spotted us already."

*

After a long anxious silence, Linona was the first to speak.

"It sounds as if they've passed us by and are moving away without coming down to the stream."

"Maybe. Let's wait a little longer," he murmured. "Why are you frowning?"

"I wanted to have a look at them. Let's follow the column so we can get a good look at what they're up to."

"It's too dangerous."

"My mother and father have often spoken about them, but I can't recall ever having seen a group of Roman soldiers close to. Please, Olsar."

"It's not a good idea. This stream is the boundary between our tribal lands and those of the Trinovantes. As long as we stay on this side the Romans won't bother us. Under the agreement with your father, they don't cross into our territory."

"That's the reply of a boring, fearful old man. I won't get another opportunity like this one to follow them to see what I can learn."

"You are our Princess and while you're with us your safety is the responsibility of my mother and father. I won't take such an unnecessary risk."

"Please, Olsar."

"There are going to be many more opportunities and reasons for you to get to know the Romans in the future."

"Not as good as this one."

"Get on your horse. We're going to leave quietly and return home."

Linona glared at him for a moment without replying. She gave a reluctant shrug of her shoulders, turned and mounted her horse. Unexpectedly, before Olsar could do the same, she moved her mount urgently down the bank and started to cross the stream.

"Don't worry! I release you and your parents from your responsibility for me."

She continued up the opposite bank, without a look back to see his reaction.

"I'm going to explore and learn about our visitors. I'll be fine. I'll keep a safe distance from them. I'm not the stupid young female you would prefer me to be."

Olsar made no attempt to call for her to return. His recent experience of her wilfulness would have taught him the futility of such a move. He mounted his own horse instead and headed into the water.

*

It hadn't been difficult to find and follow the route the legionaries had taken. Olsar estimated that the force was probably made up of a hundred or more. Even if the two of them had been in danger of losing the trail as they moved slowly along the recently disturbed ground they could not have missed the sight and smell of the smoke from several large fires ahead of them.

Cautiously they made their way through the trees until they approached the smouldering ruins of a small village. The main force of the legionaries had already left, but a small remnant was making final adjustments to several heavily laden carts. A group of sullen, resigned villagers was tethered behind the carts.

"Listen to me! We're in great danger. We mustn't go any further," Olsar whispered.

"I told you before that I won't do anything stupid," she snarled.

"What we are doing now is more than stupid."

"They're quite small men, really," she observed, ignoring his concern. "Why do our people fear them so much?"

Olsar didn't reply.

The legionaries finally began to move out, dragging the few

desolate villagers with them. After a short pause to make sure all the legionaries had left, the impatient Linona couldn't hold back any longer. She left the security of the trees, breaking out onto the broad dirt track that led to the burning houses.

Those villagers, who hadn't been able to escape and had been considered by the soldiers not to be suitable as slaves, lay in the dirt and mud of the village. Their bloodied and brutalised bodies showed no signs of life.

Linona dismounted before she reached the village, walking slowly by the side of her horse. Olsar was a few paces further behind, walking even more slowly and warily. His eyes, unlike Linona's, weren't on the devastation immediately in front of him, but on the track along which the legionaries had left with their captives. His fear of a sudden return of the soldiers would have been very evident to Linona if she had chosen to look at him. Her concerns were for those villagers lying on the ground. She began moving amongst them looking for any signs of life. A quiet groan and a waved arm from one of them captured her attention.

Kneeling on the ground Linona cradled in her lap the blood-covered head of a woman probably not much older than her own mother. A large chest wound made it difficult for her to speak.

"They've taken our sons and daughters to be slaves," she gasped. "Please help them."

"I understand. Don't upset yourself any more. We've brought many with us who can help," Linona lied.

"Some of you must go to rescue them. I beg you."

"When we've taken care of you we'll all go to free them. Please calm yourself and I'll bring you some fresh water."

"Thank you, my child."

These were the last words she uttered. Linona tried to give her what comfort she could, but the wretched woman's pained moaning weakened and she gradually faded away. Linona's tears fell gently onto the woman's face, merging with the fresh blood that was still moving down her forehead.

Linona couldn't speak. She turned her angry, desperate gaze onto Olsar, looking for answers to her unspoken questions. He shook his head and moved amongst the rest of the bodies in a vain attempt to find somebody who could still be saved.

"There's nobody left who can be helped," he decided. "We've got to return to my settlement now if we're going to get there before nightfall. Those who managed to escape will return later to attend to the dead. There's no reason for us to stay here any longer."

He grasped her arm and, meeting no resistance, he lifted and placed her astride her horse. She sat there still shocked, making no movement to take control of her mount. It had been her first sight of the slaughter of innocents on such a scale. It was also her first experience of the ruthlessness of the Roman army. Olsar, climbing onto his own horse, took hold of Linona's reins and began to lead her on the slow journey home.

*

They had reached a point within sight of Olsar's settlement before Linona brought her horse to a stop, causing Olsar to do the same.

"I'll never forget what I've seen today," she vowed.

"I'm afraid you've a lot more to learn about what the Romans are capable of."

"I'll leave tomorrow and return home to my mother and father. I feel I want to discuss with them the horror I've witnessed today. I'll be back with you in a few days."

Nothing more was said. She expected no reply. Olsar offered none. Side by side they covered the remaining distance to the houses. They heard the welcoming sound of their own people, who were happily and safely preparing for the approaching darkness at the end of what for them had been just another ordinary day.

PART I

CHAPTER 1

ROME, 70 AD

"Who would have thought it, Julius? Who could have predicted only a year ago that a rough-arsed old soldier like me would be standing here in the Royal Palace, the new Emperor of Rome?"

Vespasian, a heavily-built elderly man, had his broad back turned towards Senior Tribune Julius Agricola. He was gazing at the sumptuous furniture and exotic wall paintings in the main reception room.

"Not only that. In another year it's likely I'll be called a God, just like dear old Emperor Claudius." He chuckled and gave a dismissive shake of his head. "Do you suppose he's looking down at me at this very moment?"

Vespasian turned to face Julius with a broad smile and raised eyebrows.

Tribune Agricola, taller than Vespasian, but with a much younger seasoned soldier's muscular physique, had served under this powerfully built General in many campaigns. He could recognise his easy, excited mood. So, he had no need to be intimidated by him, even in these extraordinary circumstances. He avoided answering the questions asked of him in his reply.

"I confess I've called you a few things in addition to General in the past. I'm only relieved you never heard them at the time, especially now you've become the absolute ruler of Rome, with the power of life or death over us all."

Vespasian grinned at the less than respectful remarks of his junior officer. He moved to close the distance between them, holding a small document in his outstretched hand.

"Before I tell you why you're here I thought you would be interested in this."

Julius took hold of the document, reading it quickly.

"You'll see that it's a message from the Senate," Vespasian explained. "They're welcoming me, their glorious new Emperor, on my victorious arrival in Rome. They've humbly asked me to go to the Senate House so that they can demonstrate their new-found loyalty to me."

"Very wise of them," Julius added, "in the circumstances."

"You can say that again. That bunch of grovelling thieves and scoundrels must be wetting themselves at the sight of the Army camped outside the city walls They're sure to be wondering who amongst them are likely to be hanging from a rope before the day's out."

"Have I mentioned that as Emperor you now have the power of life and death over us all?" Julius asked.

"I know what your sarcasm is hinting at, Julius. You and I have delivered death in many ways in putting down revolts in Judea and elsewhere. Even so, I'll wager that these walls have seen horrors and depravity far exceeding what we've witnessed. The deeds of those monsters, Tiberius, Caligula, and lately Nero are known to all of us."

"I hope my old General, no matter how rough his arse is, is able to resist an urge to follow their examples."

"It's fortunate for you I prefer honesty to flattery in my officers. At least I still do at the moment. Perhaps in a year or two I might indeed start to behave like my predecessors and you may have to grovel before your Emperor begging for your life."

It was Julius's turn to laugh while he performed an exaggerated sweeping bow. Vespasian raised his arm and pointed in the direction of several chairs.

"Take a seat. It's time for us to be a little more serious."

They settled into heavily cushioned chairs, lounging and relaxing together as they had done often in the past.

"You'll have realised already that I've asked you to come here for a reason other than to wonder at this room and take part in a little light banter."

Julius nodded.

"Now the war is over, have you thought about what I might ask you to do for Rome?"

"These have been hectic times, Sir," Julius offered carefully. "I've not had much time to give it any real thought."

"I doubt that. I know you well and you're not a man to miss an opportunity when it arises, or to be reluctant to push for what you want."

"To be honest, I know one thing. I wouldn't make a very wise and servile counsellor in your court. I'm a soldier and warrior at heart. If I'm to be allowed a choice I would prefer to continue to serve you in that role somewhere in the Empire."

"You can relax. I agree with you. I need your skills as a soldier and more importantly as a leader for the task I have in mind."

Julius gave a grateful smile before choosing to try to direct the conversation.

"Let me guess. You want me to go to Judea to finish our work putting down the rebellion there."

"No! My son, Titus, can handle that for me."

Julius looked quizzically at Vespasian, who allowed a brief silence before continuing.

"What did you think of the Province of Britannia and those little Brits when you were a young Tribune there ten years ago?"

Surprised by the question, Julius shuffled in his chair.

"What can I say? The climate there is a constant challenge to a soldier, as are the Brits themselves. Both the weather and the tribes are violent and unpredictable at times. As a result, they both require you to take measures to protect yourself from their frequently changing moods."

"I know what you mean. I commanded a Legion there more than 25 years ago."

"However," Julius continued, "once you get used to them, the weather and the Brits, you find that there are times when they can behave quite reasonably."

Vespasian chuckled knowingly.

Julius, having lightened the conversation, became serious again.

"Why are you asking me now about Britannia? We've shared our memories of that Province with each other often in the past."

"I know! I know! I've asked you this time by way of introduction to explain what I need you to do for me."

"You want me to go back there, don't you?"

"Yes."

"You know I was recalled from there by Emperor Nero the last time, somewhat in disgrace."

"Yes."

"And you know it was because I objected to the Governor's policy of wiping out Queen Boudica's tribe in the months after our victory over her."

"Yes again. I also know it was a brave if foolhardy act by a junior officer. After all, you were opposing a victorious Provincial Governor, the new favourite of Nero."

"What the Governor was doing was unnecessary and just wrong for the Empire," Julius stressed. "The defeated tribe could've been spared and brought into the family of Rome to make a valuable contribution. Instead, most of that tribe were put to the sword or sold into slavery in the days and months after our victory. Their lands are said to be still empty and unproductive ten years on."

"And you paid a heavy price in your career, until you joined me. That strength in you is what I need now. Your willingness to do what you think is right for Rome is what you bring to me. It's a quality we share. It's why we've fought our way, against fellow Romans, to this place."

Julius nodded his acknowledgement of what was being said. Vespasian pushed his balding head forward so that his round, noble face jutted towards Julius to ensure his full attention.

"Britannia concerns me greatly. It's vital for the wealth it can bring. And yet, I'm being told that there's considerable unrest and indiscipline in the Legions based there. At the same time those unruly tribes, particularly in the north and west, continue to resist us and cause disruption."

"What's Governor Bolanus doing about it?"

"He hasn't been in the post for much more than a year. He's a career politician, not a soldier."

"Why don't you replace him?"

"At the moment he's doing just about enough to survive. I don't know him personally and I'm reluctant to risk aggravating things by putting my own man in just yet. There's enough change going on throughout the Empire following the civil war."

"What about the Legates commanding the Legions? Do they respect and support him?"

"As yet I don't have enough information and I don't have any personal knowledge of any of them to draw upon."

There followed a brief spell when neither man spoke, reflecting on what had been said. Vespasian broke the silence.

"Then there's my other concern. I'm led to believe by the clerks in the Treasury that there are problems with the flow of taxes and products, especially grain, from this Province. They're falling far short of the amounts expected."

"What do you think is the reason?" Julius asked. "It could be corruption, I suppose."

"Possibly. It could also be poor collection of taxes from the tribes causing trouble. Then again, lack of attention has probably allowed farm production to become inefficient."

"It could be all three in this case, if there's poor leadership," Julius suggested. "If you aren't wanting to replace Bolanus, what are you going to do?"

"That's where you can help."

"But I wouldn't make a very good tax collector or gatherer of grain for shipment to Rome."

"I agree. You would be the last man I would send if that was what was needed."

"I think you just paid me a compliment," Julius quipped.

"I did. So, let me tell you what I do want from you. You're being sent to assist Bolanus with the two main tasks I'm setting him.

Firstly, as you would expect, he'll be very firmly reminded by me that he has to meet the levels of tax and grain that the Province is being set. He'll be told that I won't accept any continuing excuses from him."

"How can I assist him in that, since we agree I wouldn't make a good tax collector or farmer?"

"You'll ensure, with the Legates that he has whatever help he needs from the Legions to allow him and the tax gatherers to overcome any resistance to our demands from the tribes. Lack of cooperation from the Army will not be an excuse he can use. At the same time you'll observe what is going on in all areas, military or administration, sniffing out where any corruption is occurring."

"And his other main task?"

"Military progress. As with any Provincial Governor, it's his duty to protect the lands we've already conquered, by maintaining our borders. He must then go on and capture more lands and people to expand the Empire. It's what you and I have been engaged in for years. In this case it is the regions to the north and west."

"My understanding, from what I've been told, is that not much territory has been gained since my time there," Julius observed.

"Precisely! So, he needs an efficient, disciplined army to change that. This is where you come in. You are to do whatever is necessary to end any unrest and indiscipline in the Legions. Bring them up to the standard you and I have always demanded."

Julius, who had been attentive but still relaxed until this point, sat upright in his chair, indicating a growing tension.

"Won't the Governor object to, probably even obstruct, a mere Tribune attempting to play such a broad role in the Army? And what about the Legates commanding the Legions? I know I wouldn't stand for it in their shoes."

"I'm sure you wouldn't. Even a weak Bolanus might try to cause you problems. That's why I am promoting you to General."

Vespasian paused, waiting for a reaction. He looked for any change of expression from the Tribune. Julius's face remained emotionless. He chose not to make a personal comment on his promotion. Instead he went straight to what he could see was still a difficulty.

"A General can command Legates but he's still subordinate to a Governor."

"Normally, yes," Vespasian conceded.

"He could easily overrule me if he disagreed with any action I wanted to take, if he found it inconvenient. He might even ask for my recall. It happened last time."

"Not going to happen! It's true you'll be subordinate to him in administrative and political matters. That's as it should be to maintain the authority of a Governor."

"I wouldn't want it any other way," Julius insisted.

"However, you'll not be subordinate to him in military matters. In those you'll have the freedom of reporting directly to me."

"What if he objects to that from the start?"

"Then he'll be the first Provincial Governor to be replaced during the reign of the Emperor Vespasian."

Julius could no longer hold back the look of pleasure spreading across his face. It was the acceptance Vespasian required.

"I shall put this division of responsibility in writing so that there won't be any confusion," Vespasian added. "Now, have you any further questions?"

"Only one. When am I expected to take up my new duties?"

"When you leave this room."

Julius stood up and saluted his Emperor.

"Thank you for my promotion and the trust you continue to place in me, Sir."

"And I thank you for your loyal service, past and future."

They shook hands. It was both a farewell gesture and a display of their respect for each other.

"We have interesting times ahead of us, Julius. May the Gods go with you. I suppose that should include me in the future."

CHAPTER 2

BRITANNIA, 70 AD

Marcus Vettius Bolanus, Governor of the Province of Britannia, lay on a long couch in the banqueting room of his official residence in Londinium. He rested on one elbow and stared at the large food-laden table in the centre of the room. He placed his other hand onto his ample stomach, letting out a long, deep rasping belch. His fellow diners chuckled. Some produced their own versions to rival his.

The mood in the room was light, aided by the wine which had been flowing throughout the meal. There was also an air of anticipation amongst those present because the banquet was the first part of the day's planned activities. After the meal they were to join the citizens of Londinium in the amphitheatre to watch the Games being provided by the Governor. The room buzzed with excited chatter each time the noise from the crowds reached their ears. The arena was a mere 300 paces away, and so the cries from several thousand people could be heard quite easily.

"That's the best wine I've tasted in many a year, Vettius. Where can I buy a cartful?"

The compliment came from the Town Magistrate.

"I'm afraid you'll have some difficulty my friend. It came with our honoured guest as a gift from the Emperor. However, I've provided the feast. I hope you're equally impressed."

"Indeed we are," the Magistrate added, patting his full stomach.

Vettius thought that they ought to be satisfied as he surveyed the remains of the meal in front of him. He had provided food of all kinds from many parts of the Empire, and it had cost him a good deal of money.

He raised his hand to beckon a slave, ordering her to bring more wine. He looked pleased with the result of his effort to impress his guests. A broad self-satisfied smile lit up his ruddy, plump face.

He hadn't been Governor of Britannia for long, not much more than a year, during which he had been very busy with the administration of his new province. Now was the first time he could relax a little. Fortunately two events had coincided to provide a perfect excuse for celebrations.

Firstly, it was ten years since Boudica and her barbarian horde had been defeated. Nevertheless, there were growing troubles with other restless and rebellious tribes, particularly in the North, and he needed to give to these tribes a harsh reminder of the power of the Roman army.

Secondly, General Julius Agricola had been appointed by the new Emperor Vespasian, nominally to be the Legate commanding the troublesome 20th Legion, but with overall responsibility for all military matters in the Province. He had just arrived from Rome and protocol required that he be granted a welcoming celebration of his appointment. He would impress the General by making him his special guest at the feast and later at the Games.

A loud roar from the arena made Vettius sit up. After a short pause he took a more formal control of the proceedings. He brought the relaxed discussions taking place around the room to an end by rising to his feet. A respectful silence followed.

"Gentlemen! Events in the arena are beckoning us. Before we depart, though, there's still time for one or two speeches."

A few playful loud groans followed, causing the rest, including the Governor, to chuckle quietly.

"To begin with, I have a pleasant, albeit formal duty to perform. You all know of the difficulties we've been having in the North with the Brigantes. That will soon be brought to an end by the appointment of a new General. He's been sent by the Emperor to assist me in crushing them. As you are aware, he's here today. I shall shortly ask General Julius Agricola to address us, even if only briefly now that you have just let your true feelings known."

Julius nodded his acceptance with a broad grin.

"Many of you will know him personally. Ten years ago he was here as a tribune on the staff of the Governor of Britannia, when Boudica was defeated by our magnificent army. He will be active throughout the Province as the two of us see fit so that we can stamp out rebellion once and for all. Let us all welcome General Julius Agricola."

Vettius turned to face the General. He gestured with his arms wide open, inviting him to speak to his guests.

Julius rose to his feet. He was greeted by muted applause. Some of those present did indeed remember the young, arrogant tribune who had upset many people in Londinium and elsewhere in Britannia with the way he had carried out his duties. His closeness to the Governor, Suetonious Paulinus, had allowed him to assume much greater authority than his formal junior status as a staff officer had warranted. This had been particularly evident in the period of reconstruction immediately after Boudica had been defeated, when high taxes had been demanded by Paulinus from some of those present.

He didn't begin to speak immediately. In the silence he moved his eyes around the room, momentarily holding the gaze of each guest in turn. When he did decide to speak he would have their certain attention.

He started speaking slowly and deliberately.

"Distinguished citizens of Londinium, My words to you will indeed be brief. My full stomach won't allow me to offer anything else. I recognise some of you here as the defenders of this province ten years ago. Some of you may recognise me in return. I know many of you suffered greatly in the rebellion. But, you had to move on and rebuild your lives, as did I. You can see that I'm not the young tribune of those times. I am now a General who has but one purpose. I will forge this army in Britannia into a force able and eager to crush any further rebellion by any tribe. If some of the Britons cannot work fully with us and recognise the dominion of Rome, accepting our customs and our Emperor, then they are against us. Either the grave or the slave market awaits those who actively oppose us. I give you my word that your future is safe. The peace that I will impose will bring even greater prosperity to you all."

He sat down to much warmer applause than before. Vettius graciously allowed it to continue for a while before getting to his feet again.

"Well spoken, Julius. Perhaps my friends here today will become rich enough to help me pay for future Games."

He appeared pleased with his remark. The laughter was allowed to fade away before he continued.

"And now for my last few words, you'll be pleased to hear."

"I'm conscious that today's events are well under way. It's time for us to leave for the arena. Before we go, however, I have one more thing I want to add. I've prepared these Games for the pleasure of the people here today in Londinium. They aren't just a celebration of our victory ten years ago and our continuing success since. They're also a demonstration of our future strength and determination. When news of what happens at these Games spreads throughout the tribes in the coming days, it will remind them of the consequences of challenging the might of our Army. You will soon see what I mean."

"By now the citizens will have had time to enjoy brave gladiators doing battle, not only with each other, but with wild beasts brought from all parts of the Empire. The crowd's appetite for blood will have been whetted by what has been taking place. I'm sure they'll be growing impatient for the main events; events requiring our attendance. Come, let's not delay matters unnecessarily. We're all in for a unique spectacle that will surprise and amaze you all."

Julius, with the appearance of a man not overly excited by what he had just heard was, nevertheless, the first to accept the invitation to accompany Vettius in leaving the banqueting room. The remainder followed. With much animated conversation and satisfied back-slapping, they began the short stroll to the arena.

CHAPTER 3

The guests in the Governor's party arrived at the huge amphitheatre and made their way up the stairs to their seats. They emerged from the gloom of the corridors into the bright sun-lit arena to find it filled to capacity with a crowd growing increasingly restless and impatient. The Games so far had been as expected. The excited spectators had been entertained by a variety of contests. Injuries had occurred and blood had flowed.

However, the promised thrill of a fight to the death had yet to be staged to bring the crowd to a frenzy of excitement. Except, that is, for the fate of one rather unfortunate, newly-trained gladiator. Armed with a short sword and large shield, he fought an opponent armed with net and trident. Failing to parry a thrust aimed high, in the way he had been taught, he took the trident straight through his throat. The blood formed a bright red pool around his head as he lay in the dust. His surprised but triumphant opponent withdrew his trident and stood over him, arms raised to the crowd. The kill had been greeted by a mixture of laughter and delight by the crowd, enjoying the thrill of such an unintended outcome.

Shouts for more had come from the more drunken, unsophisticated sections of the crowd, who didn't appreciate the intended finer and more artistic nature of events at this stage of the day's proceedings. The Master of the Games had been able to refrain from taking any obvious vigorous action against them. Nevertheless, he had begun to show some growing concern at the overall increasingly restless and unruly behaviour, which hadn't been helped by this unfortunate incident. He gave a signal to his soldiers, who were discreetly arranged in the background around the arena's terraces, to make their presence more obvious. Things had calmed down for a while.

Those sections of the crowd causing the trouble were despised by the Master. In training his assistants he described them as the low-born and the uneducated, incapable of understanding the art of ritual gladiatorial combat. He had explained that the amount of time, training and money needed to produce the best gladiators was beyond their comprehension. They'd be happy with a continuous flow of ill-trained, poorly equipped thugs, clubbing and chopping each other to death in every contest. The result was they needed to be kept under careful observation and strict control.

He had reassured his trainees that most of the crowd realised fights to the death were to be limited at the Games. They could be staged as a climax to a day's events or saved for special ritual occasions. Today was a very special occasion. Soon all sections of the crowd would have their lust for blood satisfied.

To his obvious relief the Master received a signal to tell him the Governor's party had arrived. A fanfare greeted them as they moved into their seats, waving to the cheering thousands on the terraces. The General took his seat next to the Governor, his eyes taking in the spectacle of the huge oval arena floor below him.

"What have you prepared for our pleasure, Governor?" Julius asked. "I'm intrigued by what you said earlier. What was it? 'A celebration of our success over Boudica and a reminder of our strength and determination'?"

"Patience, my friend. We will show you shortly."

Vettius stood up and moved forward slightly to let the whole crowd see him. An excited, expectant silence descended on the terraces. A few moments hesitation from him helped to add to the tension. He raised his arm in a sudden sharp movement. Trumpets around the terraces gave a single blast. The gates at opposite ends of the arena were thrown wide open. The crowd immediately gave an ecstatic mighty roar. They were showing their delight at two opposing 'armies' entering through the gates.

*

From the right, with the sun at their backs, a force of regular seasoned legionaries, about 30 men in total, strutted into the arena. They marched in arrogant precision before spreading out to form two lines facing the opposite gate. They stood with legs apart, swords drawn, with the bottom of their large shields resting on the ground. They had taken battle formation in readiness for the fight. The crowd gazed at them in total admiration. These were their guardians, their heroes.

*

In the gateway to the left, their opponents had been deliberately held back for dramatic effect to allow the legionaries to receive the adulation of the crowd. They were released and began to move slowly further into the arena. Leading them was a war chariot similar to those favoured by Boudica's Iceni tribe. In the chariot, standing alongside her charioteer, a strong-looking, thick-set woman was dressed in a simple grey woollen gown tied round the waist with a piece of cord. She'd had her hair dyed a vivid red colour. This was to ensure the citizens of Londinium recognised that she was representing Boudica leading the barbarian horde into battle. The crowd let their disgust and hatred be known.

Behind the chariot, a group of about 60 barbarian warriors formed a rough line of opposition facing the Roman enemy. The warriors wore no armour. In fact they barely wore any clothing at all. Some had their near-naked bodies covered in blue dye. Though they looked fierce they were in fact a collection of criminals, thieves and murderers, together with a mixture of unwanted troublesome slaves. They were well-armed as Boudica's warriors had been with swords, clubs and spears. To encourage them to fight, and provide the audience with a spectacle, they had been given this opportunity as an alternative to execution before this same crowd. They had been promised if they fought with courage in this battle, however inexperienced they were, it would bring them a pardon and freedom.

Behind them stood one of the Games Master's assistants. He was there to remind them of their duty and the promise they had been given.

"Remember," he shouted to the barbarian warriors "not all of you will die in this fight. Some of you will be spared, especially those who fight well. Freedom will follow. If you don't put up a fight you'll be brought back into the arena and executed. The choice is yours."

He looked to the Master and received the command to order the warriors to move forward to attack their opponents.

*

The 'battle' went according to plan. The chariot was at the front of the charge across the arena. The Roman lines parted to allow it through before immediately closing again. With little room left the chariot had to be stopped quickly before it collided with the far wall. It was being manoeuvred with some difficulty in the space available. Some of the legionaries, seeing an opportunity, left the rear rank to attack it. They easily took control and disposed of the charioteer. 'Boudica', on the other hand, had put up a fight, even though she was no match for experienced regular soldiers. She wasn't put to the sword, but allowed to remain standing on her chariot. A legionary held a sword at her throat while the battle continued.

The remaining barbarian 'warriors' charged the Roman line with some vigour but with little skill. By force of numbers they tried without success to break it. The legionaries, able to withstand the pressure, began to pick off those at the front. The barbarians began to fall, wounded or dead. Gradually the legionaries steered the battle back to the centre of the arena.

By this time, nearly half the barbarians were dead or badly wounded. They were left behind on the ground when the shield wall advanced. By contrast only one legionary had been slain, with two others wounded. To the delight of the crowd the Roman formation broke apart. A free-for-all began with individual fights taking place all over the arena.

Gradually the barbarians were either slaughtered or captured until the only one left standing was 'Boudica'. She remained on her chariot, her head bowed in shame at her capture and defeat. By now she had been stripped to the waist and her hands had been bound behind her back. Her humiliation was complete. At this point her chariot was released, steered by a legionary. Slowly she was paraded around the arena for all to see. Cries of derision and insults of every kind were levelled at her from the crowd until her chariot drew to a halt in front of the Governor. He turned to speak to Julius.

"What do you suggest, General? Should I grant her mercy or send her to her death?"

"Complete the message you want to deliver. Give them what they've come to see."

Despite his forceful words, Julius's reply was delivered with a wave of his hand to show his apparent indifference at what was happening.

Vettius rose to his feet, a triumphant sneer on his face. With a deliberately slow movement he raised his arm high in front of him and waited. The arena had grown quiet again in anticipation. His arm fell to his side in one sharp movement.

The soldier holding 'Boudica' had his short sword in his hand. Grabbing hold of her long hair he snapped her head back and quickly drew the blade across her throat. The blood gushed down her bared breasts. The roar from the crowd was deafening, indicating that for them the Games had clearly taken a pleasing turn.

There was a short delay as the floor of the arena was cleared. The earlier promise made to the few captured prisoners was ignored and they were led away to be used, probably executed at the next Games. The dead were dragged away using horses and taken through the gates. A quiet, tense murmur of expectation came from the terraces once again.

Vettius, seated again, was taking the opportunity of the lull in proceedings to talk with members of his party. Discussions were also taking place amongst members of the crowd who, no doubt, were speculating about what more could be planned that could follow and surpass what they had just seen.

"Now, General. We move to the final spectacular act." Vettius gloated. "What you are about to witness is very unusual."

"Please explain. Fights to the death by gladiators take place regularly throughout the Empire."

"That's true. However, I'm presenting something which you probably haven't witnessed before. In fact most of the Empire hasn't had the privilege of seeing it yet. Although this very unusual type of gladiatorial contest has been a regular and favourite part of the Games here for some time, it has only ever been a ritual act, not involving death before. For the first time today I've decided to take it to the ultimate."

The General gave a weak smile without comment, appearing content to let the Governor play his little game of secrecy and surprise. They would all know soon enough what he had planned.

The arena had been cleared and the blood stains covered with sand to prepare for yet more to be spilled. A signal from the Governor to the Master produced a long single blast from a solitary trumpet. The attention of the crowd had once again been seized, and silence fell. The Master stood up to speak.

"Fellow citizens, we now come to our final contest. It is one of a type which I know is a favourite of you all."

Though his voice was loud and clear, he was in danger of not being heard on all the terraces as the noise from the crowd began to swell. Raising his voice, he continued with his introduction.

"We have a special gladiatorial contest between two of your favourites. Because of the occasion it will be a fight to the death. No mercy will be given, none asked for."

The crowd roared with delight and approval. He raised his arms aloft, shouting out his final words to be heard above the din.

"Our gladiators are proud and honoured to be asked to be prepared for death. I ask you to greet these true warriors of Rome."

He lowered his arms and the main central gate opposite the Governor's seat opened. Two gladiators emerged, dressed from head to toe in long, blood-red woollen cloaks. On their heads they wore helmets with visors completely hiding their faces and identities. The welcome was rapturous. They gestured to the crowd and walked straight across the arena to halt before the Governor, saluting him as they did so. Silence fell once more, the crowd expecting a speech from him.

His words were very few. There was no need for any further delay.

"Gladiators, prepare yourselves so that the contest can begin," he roared.

Immediately the two unfastened their cloaks and let them drop. Uproar broke out again amongst the crowd. The people on the terraces, at first letting out sharp gasps in surprise, followed up with loud cries of approval. The two gladiators were females ready to fight to the death.

They weren't dressed as traditional gladiators in ritual armour and weapons. Instead they were both wearing loincloths. One cloth had been dyed green and the other had been kept white in order to distinguish between them, and to allow the inevitable wagers to be made on the terraces. They both wore a plain leather vest. Each vest was cut away to reveal the left breast, leaving no doubt that these were female warriors.

Each was equipped simply with a small round shield and short stabbing sword. In their belts they carried a short knife of their choice.

The Master, having joined them on the floor of the arena, took control of the contest. He spread his arms wide. The gladiators, understanding the gesture, began a slow stroll around the arena in opposite directions waving to the crowd and drawing the cheers and applause.

Wagers were being made throughout the terraces about the outcome. It didn't go unnoticed by the Governor. He turned to address Agricola once again.

"Do you care to follow the crowd's example with a small wager, General?"

"It would be a pleasure. I think the choice of gladiator and the amount to be set must be yours for providing such a unique event. It's the least I can do to show my appreciation."

He had been briefed by his staff officer that this small, rather insignificant little man had a weakness for flattery. His next comments showed he was taking the opportunity to use it.

"You've very kindly provided me with a welcome fit for an Emperor rather than a mere General."

An unexpected mild rebuke followed from the Governor.

"Don't become too self-satisfied my friend. Remember these Games were set for another reason in addition to your arrival. I will accept your suggestion on the wager, though. I have a liking for 'White'. I recognise her and have seen her in demonstration bouts. She has a style, strength and agility which may prove superior."

"I'm content with that. I think 'Green' looks bigger and stronger and she's displaying an arrogant self-belief parading around the arena. All of that should win her the day."

"As for our prize," the Governor continued, "six large amphorae of blood-red wine from Southern Gaul would suit us both, and be appropriate considering the event, don't you think?"

"As you wish. I'll enjoy drinking it when I win the wager."

*

When they had completed their walk around the arena the two gladiators came to a halt in the centre, where the Master was waiting for them. He took a final opportunity to remind them that, even though it was to the death, the rules of gladiatorial combat still applied.

"I particularly refer to the situation when a gladiator has been grounded. If that occurs, you must step back and allow your opponent to gain her feet before continuing. If she is unable to do so, any final thrust is to be delivered quickly and efficiently. I remind you we are not barbarians. Do you understand and are you ready to commence?"

Neither spoke. Instead they nodded their acceptance and readiness. Without breaking their cold stares at each other through their visors, they waited for their release.

"May the Gods choose a worthy winner. Begin the contest."

The two gladiators didn't react immediately. They had fought many times and they knew they had been chosen because they were the best. 'Green' was very tall, a feature shared by many of her tribe from northern Gaul. 'White' was not quite as tall and more slightly built. When she had paraded the arena, she had done so confidently using her sword to point to her white loin cloth and then to the crowd. She was letting them know who they should support with their wagers.

Watching each other closely, they slowly drew apart. 'Green' made the first attack and the contest had begun. Thrust was followed by counter thrust. Injuries, though none serious, were suffered by both. The excitement was building in those in the crowd. They competed in their cries of support for one or the other.

The end came suddenly.

As predicted by the Governor, 'White's superior skill and agility had begun to tell. A sudden quick thrust tore deeply into her opponent just above her loincloth. She staggered back and dropped to her knees. 'White' made an instinctive move to rush in and stab and slash in a blind angry frenzy. Just in time, she halted and withdrew to allow her opponent to regain her feet. 'Green' tried to force herself back up from her knees, only to stagger and fall backwards onto her back, her arms spread wide in surrender.

A tense silence descended on the crowd.

'White' held back, crouching slightly, her sword pointing at her opponent's breast. She looked to the Governor for his decision. He didn't keep her or the crowd waiting long before giving his signal. No mercy was to be shown on a day such as this. She took one step forward and thrust her sword straight down into the defeated gladiator's chest, sending her instantly to her Gods.

The crowd showed its wild appreciation. 'White' made her way towards the Governor as tradition required. She raised her sword to him in salute and dropped on one knee, head bowed, expecting a few words of praise on her victory. She was still some ten paces or so from him, below the raised terrace. He ordered her to drop her weapons and summoned her to come up from the floor of the arena to join him. She did as was commanded, but slowly, displaying some slight hesitation, even reluctance.

It was most unusual and unexpected for a gladiator to receive such an invitation to leave the arena in this way. Normally, she would have paraded in front of the crowd, before leaving through one of the gates. She would know that this man had the power of life or death over all present including her. If guards were ordered to act against her for some unknown reason, she would have no space or weapons to defend herself.

She reached the end of his balcony and began to move along it. Before she reached him she suddenly stopped and stared, not, as might be expected, at the Governor but straight at the General by his side. He returned her look appearing puzzled at this unexpected act. The Governor spoke, prompting her to continue moving towards him.

"Come and stand here! You haven't disappointed me or the people with your performance today. You were magnificent. I never doubted you for a moment. I know your identity, but I think the time has come for you to reveal yourself. Take off your helmet."

She didn't react immediately.

To disobey his clear instruction on such an occasion would be an open insult that punishment, even death could follow swiftly. To do as he commanded would lead to her identity being exposed to everybody. She moved her reluctant hands to her head to take off her helmet to reveal a face surprisingly beautiful for one who engaged in such a brutal occupation.

Her hair which had been cut short was a very pale ginger, almost blonde.

The Governor showed his pleasure with what he saw. He turned so he could address his guests from the banquet, especially Julius.

"To those of you not familiar with her, I would like to introduce our victorious champion. She is Lucia, daughter of the distinguished Quintus Tiberius Saturninus."

He turned back to face Lucia, raising her right arm high in the air for all to see and shout again their approval of her victory. When the noise died down he spoke excitedly to her.

"In my hand I hold this large purse of gold which you were promised for fighting today. The winner takes all since the loser appears unable to collect her part of it."

He obviously considered his remarks appropriate and humorous, laughing out loud and looking around for confirmation. Those in the surrounding group politely joined in. Not Julius.

Vettius continued with a growing air of self-satisfaction.

"The people will have enjoyed this unforgettable day, don't you think General?"

Julius didn't answer. His attention was fixed on the face of the tall, lithe woman standing in front of them. His failure to reply didn't matter. Vettius's own gaze and attention were also on the magnificent, bloodied woman waiting for his next words. His face had developed a broad, excited smile.

"I have something to give you, in addition to the winner's purse. It's something you won't have been expecting."

He half turned and looked behind at an attendant, who reacted immediately to approach him, carrying something hidden by a cloth in his hands.

She took the opportunity of the slight delay to turn her eyes back towards Julius, a look of growing concern on her face His expression, one of total surprise and disbelief had not yet disappeared since the moment she had taken off her helmet. They shared a lingering fixed stare but neither made any gesture or comment to each other.

The Governor was speaking again.

"Are you listening, young woman? You aren't hurt, are you?"

She shook her head, turning it back to face him.

"Good. I have here something which I had made for the winner of today's contest. It has been a day that needed a trophy to commemorate the uniqueness of the occasion."

He handed her a large knife with a strong, sharp shining blade. It wasn't the blade that was important, though, it was the handle. Made of bronze, it had been fashioned in the form of a female gladiator standing victorious over her opponent in the way she had done earlier.

"What do you say, Lucia?" a gleeful Vettius asked.

"I...I..." she stuttered, "I shall treasure this all my life. The Gods willing, I shall use it in the arena, where it will bring me many victories."

Vulnerable in these surroundings she was showing her gratitude, regardless of her apparent agitated state.

"Well said, young woman."

He turned to speak to his guests.

"That concludes the day's activities, gentlemen. It's time for us to leave."

As the others withdrew, Julius paused to give Lucia a last lingering sideways look, a glimmer of a knowing smile still evident to her around his lips. It was the nearest he came to letting her see he'd recognised her.

She, for her part, gave no obvious indication to him that he was known to her. She withdrew down the steps into the arena in time to see her opponent's body being dragged away, leaving a long red stain in the dust.

*

The wind had carried the roars of the crowd to the house of Quintus Tiberius Saturninus, not far from the arena. The noise had ceased some time ago telling of the end of the day's Games. Flavia paced across the floor, not knowing if her older sister Lucia was still alive. She was quite a bit smaller than her older sister and tended to live in her shadow. She idolised her and always had faith in her fighting abilities. Despite that, she knew a stumble, a momentary blinding by the sun, a brief lack of concentration in the arena could cause serious injury, even death.

Her look of concern disappeared the moment she saw the door open and Lucia enter. She went towards her sister, arms opened wide in grateful welcome, but before Flavia could reach her to express her joy and relief, Lucia spoke.

"He's back! We must consider our options and make plans."

"What are you saying? Who's back?"

Flavia looked confused. This was not the excited triumphant Lucia she would have expected. Her sister was very agitated, casting her cloak aside and quenching her raging thirst from a pitcher which had been left for her. She had obviously come straight from the arena, unusually with her wounds yet to be attended to. Normally, Lucia would not leave to return home until any wounds had been treated and she had cleaned herself.

"HE is!" she shouted. "That monster Tribune Julius Agricola is here in Londinium, only now it's General Agricola. He saw me up close and I know he recognised me."

"Are you sure it's him? Are you really sure he recognised you?"

"I'm very sure. What I don't understand is why he didn't arrest me immediately."

"We must leave without any delay," Flavia cried in panic. "We've got to flee, get away, go anywhere."

"That's not the answer you idiot," Lucia said harshly, still unnerved by events. "Even in those few moments when he recognised me, that evil man would have realised I couldn't just run away. He's a General and he could send the whole army to find me."

"Surely we could run and hide somewhere. We've done it before."

"If we ran and hid now he could kill hundreds in his search for us if he wanted to."

"That's too dreadful to imagine, just to take us prisoner." Flavia's voice was beginning to shake with emotion.

"It wouldn't bother him, even if he didn't find us. It would give him an excuse to accuse what is still left our tribe of preparing to rise against Rome once again."

"But those of our people who remain haven't the will or the means any more to resist. Surely he must know that, Lucia?"

"It will be irrelevant to him. As a general he's on course for greater things. The suppression of another Iceni 'uprising' in Britannia would do his political career no harm at all. Rome will always fear a repeat of the slaughter which took place ten years ago. No! We must stay here, if only to stop him using our flight from him as an excuse."

"And do what?"

"I don't know yet, but we must be very careful. We're in great danger."

"What do you think he'll do next?"

"At least I've had a short time to give that some thought already. At this moment he will be considering his options. Even though he'll be planning when to expose us, choosing a time and place to gain the maximum effect, I don't think he'll strike straight away."

"Can you be sure?"

"He's only just arrived. He will need time to assess the army under his command. Everybody knows there are urgent problems in the north with other tribes."

"We're in great danger and Quintus will suffer the same fate as us, even though he's never known our true identities." Flavia, as was typical of her, was already beginning to think of the plight of another.

"I know, I know," Lucia replied with a little annoyance evident in her voice. "I need time to think."

"We must tell him, tell him everything," Flavia pleaded. "We owe it to him for buying us both from the slave traders ten years ago. He gave us our freedom and adopted us, giving us our Roman names. He's been a true father to us. I have to tell him of the danger he's in and why." She sat down with the tears beginning to flow.

"I agree, little sister, I agree, although I don't know how he'll react. He is after all a Roman citizen who lost all he owned in Londinium, together with most of his slaves from this estate ten years ago."

"It'll remind him of things he's tried to forget," Flavia added.

"We know he's never really forgotten the horror of those times. How many times has he said he could never forgive Queen Boudica for his losses?" Lucia wondered.

"But he loves us. He'll understand."

"I'm not so sure. He still believes the death of his wife soon after our defeat was caused by the shock of the war. Things might never be the same with him when he knows."

They fell silent, reflecting on the dilemma caused by the day's events.

*

Old Quintus had done what he always did when he was troubled. He had retired to his bath house. Here, alone, he could reflect on what was happening. Today was particularly stressful. Lucia was in a battle, risking injury and her life. Amongst the many emotions he was feeling, the strongest was guilt. After all, he'd used his considerable charm and influence to enable her to do as she wished. She had decided to become one of a few women who were trained as gladiators for ceremonial combat. He had initially tried to dissuade her from taking such a dangerous course of action, but he had learnt in the past what a determined woman Lucia was. If she wanted something badly enough, she wouldn't let anybody stand in her way. She had a ruthless side to her character which at times in recent years had given him cause for concern. He was increasingly feeling the effects of the onset of old age and didn't relish anything which caused him stress.

On the other hand, dear, sweet Flavia had never given him anything to worry about, except perhaps his fears over her vulnerability. They both helped him to run his estate. He relied on them so much he didn't know what he would do if he lost either of them. He needed Lucia's strength and energy to cope with the daily demands of the estate and his other commercial interests. His own two daughters had been married and left, leaving him to run his estate alone.

He'd done all he could to help her today. He had sacrificed to the Gods even those who he didn't think would be inclined to help him. In the days running up to the Games he'd tried to keep away from wine to keep his head clear in case she needed him.

After his hot bath he was cooling down in the cold room when his personal body slave entered with a big beaming smile filling his face.

Quintus didn't need any words. He left immediately to dress to go to see his daughters.

*

Without thinking or looking to take in the mood of the two women he rushed to Lucia and embraced her gleefully.

"The Gods have heard me once again and I thank them for your safe return."

Lucia returned his embrace warmly. Flavia came over to join them and clung on desperately to both of them.

"But you're hurt," he said. "There's blood on you. I'll call for assistance."

"No!" Lucia said firmly. "I'm fine. They're only scratches. They can wait for attention. There's something…"

He didn't allow her to finish.

"Did your opponent suffer? Was the Governor pleased? You have to tell me everything."

"In addition to a very large purse, the Governor gave me this," she replied. Not answering his first question, she showed him the knife.

"My, my, my." He was obviously very pleased indeed. "Now you can retire. I've told you that you don't need the money from purses."

"Please, Quintus. Not now," Flavia pleaded.

"But your sister has stubbornly insisted on fighting to create her own wealth. Yet both of you know part of my estate and wealth will be yours when I die."

A determined plea for her to stop fighting in the arena was something he had decided to do while waiting in the bathhouse. Ceremonial contests were one thing. What she had been involved in today was too much.

Flavia winced at his last remark about his dying. Lucia straightened her back and replied.

"We've reminded you many times that in such a matter we are only your adopted daughters. What's more, we were previously your slaves. We wouldn't be allowed by your blood-daughters and their husbands to take part of your estate, nor do we want to. It rightly belongs to them. Now, please sit down, old man."

He recognised that look in her eye. It was better to do what she ordered.

"We have something to tell you. It won't be easy. It's a very long story to tell, and it will take a long time. You may wish to call for some of that Gallic wine you favour so much."

"There's a great deal we need to tell you, Father. Please be patient and let Lucia start."

"You originally took us into your household as your slaves ten years ago." Lucia began. "You asked us for our names and we gave you false ones to hide our real identities. Later, when you adopted us, you gave us our Roman names of Lucia and Flavia. My real birth name given to me by my mother was Linona. Flavia was named Cailan. Today, I've been recognised from the past by the new General, who has just arrived from Rome. He knew us and fought against us in the war ten years ago. We were Princesses of the Iceni, the daughters of Queen Boudica."

PART II

CHAPTER 4

BRITANNIA, 60 AD

Daylight had not long since arrived and revealed a light covering of snow on the ground and tops of the buildings. There were more than 50 houses forming the settlement which had been built on a slight rise in an otherwise flat landscape. It was surrounded by two large defensive ditches with a wide central causeway allowing access.

The excited sounds of children playing together in the snow were the loudest in the settlement. The rest of the inhabitants were slowly stirring, fighting off the morning chill. It was spring but, not too surprisingly, winter still had a sting in its tail with the arrival of the snow. Apart from the young, nobody would appreciate this inconvenience. It certainly wouldn't help the early morning preparations for the feast day ahead, even if the thin covering should have disappeared well before midday.

Regardless of the weather, the day set to welcome springtime would be a day of feasting and celebration. Offerings were to be made to the Gods, asking them for a bountiful year in the fields. In recent years the Gods had been good to the Iceni people. There had been ten years of peace and prosperity. Peace, because King Presutagus had made treaties with their powerful neighbours, the Romans. The men of the tribe had been left to tend the animals and crops in the fields, with very few being required to serve in the Roman auxiliary forces. The tribe had grown prosperous as a result.

The night before had been one of excited anticipation of the food, drink and dancing, that was to follow the next day. There were those few older ones who'd been worried by the cold north wind. It could have been sent because the Gods were unhappy with the tribe. Most people preferred to believe the offerings at the feast the next day would ensure that the Gods were aware of their gratitude. Warmer days would surely follow and the harvest would be good.

The offerings were to take place in the large open ground at the heart of the settlement. All the important events took place here surrounded on all sides by the houses of the most important leaders of the tribe. The whole of one side of the space was taken by the houses of King Presutagus and Queen Boudica.

The King and Queen lived in a large circular building. Immediately next to it, and only slightly smaller, was the house of their two daughters. Linona, who was 18 years old and Cailan, aged 16, had lived in their own house for some time. Their mother had decided that Linona particularly had reached the age when she should learn to run her own household. Cailan had begged to be allowed to join her.

Because Linona was the oldest child, the tribe would be expected to accept her and her chosen husband to lead them when Presutagus died. In providing Linona with her own house in the central square Boudica was making a clear statement to all the tribe's clans that she was preparing her daughter for leadership.

Inside the house Linona had woken early that morning, immediately rousing her sister. She was unable to contain her excitement at the thought of the day's coming events.

"What should I say to him if he asks me to sit with him at the feast today? I'll be so nervous."

She was speaking while dressing to keep out the morning chill.

"What? Who are you talking about?"

"You know very well who I'm talking about – Marac."

"Please be quiet Linona. Get back to bed and go to sleep. It's very early and cold, cold, cold," said Cailan with more than a little irritation in her voice.

"I don't want to get back into bed. I'm too excited."

"Be excited quietly then."

"Father has asked King Frigionus of the Trinovantes to come today to see how we can feast and celebrate the coming of springtime and the new year."

"Please shut up."

"The King is bound to bring his son Marac with him. I haven't seen him for a year. By now he will have become a full warrior of his tribe."

"So?"

"Late last night after you went to bed, early as usual, Father told me he wants me to marry Marac. He said he would like our two tribes to grow closer and stronger in these troubled times."

"What did Mother have to say?"

"By the look on her face I guessed it was her pushing the idea. Father would initially think that the Romans would view it as a provocative act, endangering our relationship with them and the peace he says it brings. He can be very weak at times."

"Marac is very handsome," said Cailan accepting it was time to get out of bed. "He will make a magnificent warrior. The last time he was here he couldn't take his eyes off you."

"I know, I know," Linona sighed.

The two princesses finished dressing in their simple woollen clothes, which were no different from the rest of their tribe despite their status. They made their way out of their house and into the larger one of their parents. Their mother and her two maidservants were tending the low fire in the hearth at the centre of the building in anticipation of preparing the day's first meal.

The King emerged from his sleeping area to be greeted warmly by his daughters.

"Father," said Linona, "you look pale. Come and warm yourself by the fire."

A few days previously she had confided to her mother and sister that she felt her father wasn't well. He had always been an energetic robust man. Lately she'd thought he was looking increasingly frail. For different reasons the other two didn't agree. Boudica wouldn't consider the possibility of anything happening to Presutagus until her daughter was older and married to Marac. Cailan loved her father so much that he always looked well to her.

By mid-morning the first meal of the day was over. There was a calm relaxed mood in the building with the usual coming and going of other members of the tribe. The mood changed with the arrival of a messenger from the south. He brought information that a large column of legionaries had entered Iceni territory.

Presutagus immediately cleared the house except for his wife and daughters. It would allow him to consider what his next move should be.

"We must call a meeting immediately of any of the Elders who are available to discuss our position," said Boudica. "Large columns like this haven't entered our lands in a long time."

"What are you suggesting?" Presutagus asked.

"The Romans never do anything like this without a purpose. We can't trust them." Boudica, as usual, was quick to react and decide what needed to be done. She considered herself to be her husband's equal in everything except their status in the tribe. Within the privacy of their house even this difference didn't prevent her from telling him what he needed to do. Linona, although she nodded to her mother, didn't openly agree with her at this stage. Presutagus looked and sounded irritated by his wife's aggressive comments.

"I accept we must have a meeting, but I have an understanding with the Romans. It has lasted years and I won't rush to assume anything has changed."

In a very short time most of the Elders had gathered inside the King's house. More information had been received to say the Romans had camped overnight ten miles to the south west of the settlement. The force was ominously large, consisting of at least 500 legionaries supported by cavalry.

Those in the room with the King were talking animatedly about the news. The views being expressed varied from fear that Presutagus was about to be arrested and taken to Camulodunum, to the possible destruction of the whole settlement. Presutagus, with Boudica seated next to him, was waiting quietly for the discussions to die down. Before he could speak to them a sentry from the main settlement gate was ushered into the room.

"There's a small troop of Roman cavalry coming towards the main gate. What should we do with them?"

"Let them in of course, and bring them straight to me. They're our friends and must be treated with respect. I will deal personally with any man who harms them."

The King barked out this order with such severity it shocked some of those present. It left nobody in doubt, including Boudica, that the King would handle this crisis his way. He draped his cloak around his shoulders, and spoke to those in the room.

"It appears we are about to find out what this is all about. We shall welcome our guests and see what we can do for them. Our dignified presence will soon be needed outside, my Queen."

She smiled her acceptance.

*

Standing in the cold air the council had been joined in the central square by everybody in the settlement. It was full, apart from a narrow strip right through the centre. The Romans, closely accompanied by two sentries from the main gate, approached the King on foot, halting just short of him. The Roman officer, a tribune, who was leading them spoke first, delivering his obviously prepared speech.

"I greet the mighty King of the Iceni, trusted friend and ally of our Emperor. All Rome knows of the long and true friendship between our peoples, one which has stood the test of time. I am Julius Agricola, Tribune and Staff Officer to the Governor of Britannia, Suetonious Paulinus. I bring you his warm greetings and a request he wishes to make of you and the Iceni people. He is sure, if granted, it will only build on the friendship we already enjoy."

Despite the diplomatic and respectful words which the young officer had used he couldn't disguise the arrogance in his stance and expression.

In the square the silence that had greeted the Romans ended as murmurings broke out amongst the people. Some were smiling with relief at the words. Others were staring suspiciously at the young officer.

The King replied to the tribune in a similar formal manner loud enough for all to hear.

"We welcome you, Tribune. The friendship between Rome and my people has brought peace and prosperity to us both. Long may it continue. We consider it would be an honour to receive and meet a request from the Governor. If it's within our power we will willingly grant it. Tell me what he wants."

The murmuring in the crowd continued, growing louder. Many were expressing their resentment at the words of their King to these foreign soldiers who had no right to be in their tribal lands.

"The Governor hasn't been in this Province of Britannia for long and wants to learn about your customs. He wishes to attend your feast as a guest to observe you carrying out your celebrations, and for him to pay ritual homage to your Gods."

Agitated discussions broke out in the crowd. Strangers weren't usually allowed into the settlement on days such as this. But to refuse such a request from the Governor would be considered a great insult to the Romans. The tribune ignored the commotion around him. The superior expression on his face showed he didn't expect to take back a refusal.

"It would be a great honour to have the Governor present here today. I shall provide a troop of twelve of my own mounted guard to ride back with you to your camp. They can provide a royal Iceni escort to the Governor."

The smug smile disappeared from the tribune's face. The offer of an escort by the King was one Julius could hardly refuse. It would, however, have the effect of demonstrating to the Governor that he couldn't just ride so deeply into the King's territory without being invited and escorted by his warriors. The Iceni still controlled their own territory.

"If you think that is necessary, then so be it," the tribune conceded.

"First, though, now we've done with the formalities, you can come to have something to refresh you before you must return to your camp."

The Tribune did as suggested, accompanying the King into his house. He left his own cavalry escort standing awkwardly amongst the 100 or more far from friendly people in the square.

*

Inside the King's house the tribune was introduced to the Queen, the Elders and the two Princesses. He would see from the cold glare the Queen gave him that she didn't welcome his visit. The Elders weren't showing any enthusiasm either. His focus soon centred on the elder of the two Princesses.

"I'm greatly honoured to be in the presence of such beautiful Princesses. As a mere tribune it hasn't been my good fortune to meet the daughters of kings before."

"Isn't your Emperor Nero just the same as a king?" Linona asked. "Doesn't he have daughters?"

The tribune gave a dismissive shrug before giving his reply.

"Emperor Nero is not a king ruling over a single people. He's the Emperor of many lands and peoples. Kings have the ears of gods whereas our Emperors can become Gods. The Emperor Claudius who brought Britannia into the Empire is now worshiped and has a temple dedicated to him in Camulodunum."

Linona didn't waste the opportunity to try to embarrass the pompous young officer.

"Are you suggesting that you've less respect for my father and mother who are just a king and queen, compared with your mighty Emperor?"

"Do I detect a touch of resentment towards the great Roman people in what you say?"

He had avoided her trap and was obviously enjoying her spirit and the lack of respect she was showing towards him.

"Why should I resent a people who have come to our land, defeated my people in battle and imposed taxes on us?"

Presutagus, looking uncomfortable, intervened.

"My daughter has a habit of being provocative to guests, with the intention of stimulating discussion. Unfortunately our discussion cannot continue. You must return without further delay to your camp to give your Governor my reply."

He took the tribune's arm and escorted him outside to avoid any further dangerous and potentially provocative comments by his daughter or anybody else.

"My people," he addressed the crowd again after the Romans had left, "we are going to have an extra unexpected guest or two today.

We have plenty to eat and drink. We will show them how we can enjoy our feasting and ceremonies. Let them see what a proud, strong, independent people we Iceni are."

*

As soon as the special guest, King Frigionus, arrived he was taken to one side by Presutagus to break the news about the imminent arrival of Suetonius Paulinus. He reacted angrily to this totally unexpected development. Unlike Presutagus he didn't have to be there to welcome the Romans.

"Camulodunum, as the Romans call it, is the town which they have built on my people's land. I won't rest until every Roman there is dead or driven back to Rome. I can't feast with such men as these."

"I understand how you feel but remember we have very important business to discuss for the future of Linona and Marac and our two tribes."

"I know what we were wanting to do. You don't have to remind me."

"Well then. Will you stay so we can talk?"

"For that reason I'll come back at a later date when the stench of the Romans has left your house. We can talk then."

"At least let Marac stay behind to observe these Romans and their leader. Who knows what he might learn about the man."

"He can decide for himself. He's his own man. If he wishes to stay I won't object," concluded Frigionus, moving away to look for his son.

Marac and the small band of warriors who had accompanied him and his father were in the square surrounded by a large number of people. They had brought gifts and were presenting them to some of the Elders of the tribe for distribution later at the celebrations.

Boudica and her daughters had been standing some distance away watching the excited welcome Marac and his men were receiving.

"He's become a fine, strong young man don't you think, Linona?"

"I know what you want, Mother. Fortunately for us all I agree with you on this occasion. However, I would like to talk to Marac before any discussions begin with King Frigionus." Her firm reply was a statement, not a request.

"Frigionus won't be staying," Presutagus declared angrily as he joined his wife and daughters.

"I would expect nothing less from him," said Boudica. "His people have suffered terribly in the past under the Romans, if not yet by this new leader of theirs. He has my full support."

"He will return later to complete our other business. Marac may be staying for our feasting. We shall know shortly."

A little while later Marac approached them as they watched his father ride away.

"May I join you? My father asked me if I wanted to stay for the feast even though he won't. I'll speak to your Elders to explain his decision to them."

"That won't be necessary. We all understand why he wants to return home," Presutagus replied. "I'm pleased you have chosen to remain here. You must be by my side at the feast tonight."

Boudica didn't miss the opportunity to further her plans.

"King Presutagus and I have been blessed by the Gods with two fine daughters, Marac. You've met Linona and Cailan in the past, but it's a while ago. You have our permission to renew your friendship while you stay with us."

"Your daughters have grown into fine beautiful young women. I'm sure we'll have plenty to talk about."

CHAPTER 5

"The Brits appear to have stopped following us, Sir," shouted one of the cavalrymen riding behind the tribune as they approached their temporary marching camp.

Julius Agricola raised his arm in a wide exaggerated arc to bring his column to a halt. If they were playing some sort of game, he could match them for sure. Slowly he turned his horse and looked down the slope which they were climbing. The dozen or so Iceni riders had formed a line across the track, facing straight ahead towards the camp. The lead horseman dug his heels into his horse and it reared in mock challenge.

Julius stirred his mount and trotted back, halting in front of the Iceni horsemen.

"Your escort duties will require you to make your presence known directly to the Governor himself. Does the sight of his camp fill you with such awe that you need to pause and gape with your mouths wide open? If you've a leader perhaps you could let me know what this is all about."

He was met with silence.

"In that case you can either continue with me through the entrance or return to your King. I don't care which."

He half-turned his horse to ride back to his men but was halted by the reply from the lead horseman.

"My name is Olsar. I speak for my men. We'll remain here."

"And why is that?"

"We prefer the open ground at our backs and to our side, to the enclosed palisades of your camp."

"You risk the Governor taking this as an insult."

"That's as may be. No offence is intended. I'm sure there can be little spare room in such a small place with so many tents and fighting men. We think only of your comfort. We'll wait here for your leader."

The Tribune gave a slight wave of acceptance, followed by a smile in recognition of the man's willingness to meet his own sarcasm in like manner.

He returned to his men and they rode on into the camp, watched by twelve slightly amused horsemen.

*

Julius jumped from the saddle and strode on past the sentry on guard outside the Governor's tent, ignoring a feeble attempt to stop him. Inside the entrance he was soon stopped by a raised hand and sharp glare in his direction from the Governor.

Suetonius Paulinus was seated at a small table on which were spread maps of Britannia. He was talking to two of his other staff officers. Julius looked surprised, since they had been left behind in Camulodunum by the Governor to deputise for him in his absence. Their grim faces alerted Julius to the fact that something significant had happened since they left. He moved backwards and to the side of the tent, his step quick and quiet.

"Officer Vidius! You've served some years in the territory of the Brigantes. What do you have to say about this news of these new skirmishes and unrest caused by this troublesome people?"

"The information has come from one messenger only, General," Vidius replied. "He comes from a small tribe to the south of the Brigantes territory."

"Is it the likely approach of warmer weather causing the sap to rise in a few warriors, filling their heads with thoughts of battle? Or is there something more to consider?"

"The small tribe is known to have been made to suffer by its much larger neighbour, Sir. It's possible their warning to us may be an attempt to try to get us to intervene on their behalf."

"Not a good move by them if we choose to ignore it and the Brigantes get to hear about it."

"Our spies, however, report an increasing presence of druids from Mona throughout the North, spreading their evil message," Vidius added.

"That's probably the more likely cause," said Paulinus.

"I think our planned campaign against Mona would benefit if we were to bring forward our departure date," Vidius continued. "I would recommend the speedy dispatch to the North of those units of the 20th Legion that could be ready within the next few days. News of that will reach the druids through their spies and may cause them to pause and reflect on whatever plans they may have to cause trouble."

"Agreed," Paulinus decided. "The two of you can return to get things moving. Julius will stay to tell me how he was received by our valued friend and ally."

Julius waited until the others had left.

"Well, Julius. What have you to tell me?"

"Presutagus was calm and very accommodating, Sir. If he had any surprise or concern at your request he was very successful in hiding it. His advisors and his family, particularly his queen, on the other hand reacted differently."

"How so?"

"They could barely conceal their initial hostility to our presence in their settlement. It got a lot worse when they became aware of our wish to attend their heathen religious rituals and drunken orgies."

"Did he look as if he was in full control of them, though?"

"He did. He had them by his side, in full view and hearing of his people, when he graciously and warmly accepted your request for an invitation today. I also think he is a rather crafty tactician."

"In what way?"

"He insisted that you be escorted into his settlement and into his royal presence by a band of his favourite warriors. They're outside our camp at this moment, waiting to carry out their noble duty."

Paulinus smiled broadly.

"Clever! Very clever indeed. At the same time as appearing to show me great respect he shows his people he controls his lands and who can enter them."

"Exactly."

"If we're to take our army north I must be sure our control here in the South and East is secure. If the King is still in control of his tribe they will continue to cause us no trouble. I need to be able to take as many legionaries as possible to end this druid problem once and for all."

"My impression, based on what I saw today, is that I don't think we have a problem with the King."

"While I'm occupied with the King and Queen later today I want you to talk to those advisers of his and the King's two daughters. Get under their skins. Find out their true feelings about us."

"The elder of the two sisters is a spirited young filly. A little attention and slight provocation might indeed bring results."

"You've done well. It's time to ride. We mustn't keep my royal escort waiting too long."

CHAPTER 6

Paulinus and Julius were accompanied by a small cavalry squadron of 50 horsemen and two centuries of legionaries fully armoured and equipped with provisions for an overnight camp. As the column approached the waiting Iceni horsemen, Julius could see they had maintained the same formation across the slope leading down from the camp. Such discipline was impressive, particularly if they had remained on horseback without resting. He nodded to Olsar who returned the gesture, an acceptance perhaps of the reluctant initial respect between the two of them.

"Your foot soldiers will be too slow for our purpose," commented Olsar. "You will need to move much quicker than walking pace to be able to take a full part in the feast. They will have to follow on after us. Some of your horsemen know the way from earlier."

Paulinus beckoned his cavalry officer to come to him. He gave him instructions to detach four of his horsemen with knowledge of the route to bring the legionaries with them at a full marching pace.

The Iceni horsemen, seeing the order to divide the column had been given, parted to allow room for Paulinus and Julius to pass through. As soon as the two men passed him, Olsar kicked his horse's belly and moved quickly in front of the next cavalry officer before he could follow his commander.

"Don't be alarmed, Roman. We only wish to give your General the respect he deserves. This will allow us to escort him as our King wishes."

The officer, his face showing a mixture of anger and alarm, looked ahead for direction from Paulinus who was by now a short distance away from him.

Paulinus pulled his horse round to see what was happening. He pushed his arm out in front of him, palm facing downwards. He lowered and raised it several times indicating the need to remain calm. It also showed that he accepted Olsar's words. The moment of danger passed and the Iceni horsemen took position behind Paulinus. Olsar rode ahead to take the lead and the combined group of riders moved on.

The tension and suspicion existing between the two sets of riders lasted throughout the journey to the settlement, but there was no further incident. After a short ride the column climbed an area of higher ground on an otherwise broad expanse of flat land. Ahead could be seen a large patchwork of fields, some dark green with pasture while others had been ploughed ready for seeding. These were interspersed with large areas of mixed woodland.

Paulinus's eyes stared straight ahead at the large outline of the King's settlement, clearly visible in the distance on a similar area of higher ground. He raised his arm and the column came to a stop. Only Olsar ahead of them continued for a short distance until he realised the rest had halted. Paulinus, turning sharply in his saddle to face his men at the rear of the column, beckoned his cavalry officer to approach him. Speaking softly so that the horsemen to his rear and Olsar in front couldn't hear him, he addressed the young officer.

"This rise in the ground will form the ideal place to set up our marching camp for tonight. It's close enough to the settlement and in view of our hosts."

"Are we waiting here for the rest of the legionaries, Sir?"

"I'm not, but you are, with half your squadron. Begin the preparations for the night. The rest will continue to accompany me."

He ignored the expression of dismay at being left behind, which the officer was unable to hide.

"It's important that the camp fires tonight are big and bright. Make sure the legionaries are even louder than they are normally. Our hosts need to be very aware of our presence. Do you understand?"

"Yes, Sir."

"However, whatever the provocation from any of their young bloods who might wish to challenge our resolve there must be no overreaction by our men. I shall hold you and the Commander of the legionaries personally responsible for ensuring discipline is tight tonight. Now go and divide your men."

By now Olsar, his face full of suspicion, had turned and ridden towards the Governor.

"I can see we're approaching your settlement. It was necessary to give final instructions to my own men," Paulinus said reassuringly. "I think it more fitting to reduce my numbers to reflect yours. It will reassure your King and people that we come as friends. Please let's continue our journey."

Olsar didn't say a word but his look of deep mistrust didn't change. He took position again at the head of the column and continued to make the final approach.

At the main entrance Olsar gave his men the order to dismount, indicating to the Romans to do the same. The Governor and the Tribune remained seated alongside him. Following Olsar's lead, they moved through the gates, heading towards the central area.

Paulinus and Julius exchanged a glance, but neither showed any concern they might have felt at the vulnerability of their situation. Their faith had to be in the knowledge that the King and his people would be aware of the retribution that would befall them, should the Provincial Governor die whilst in their care.

Moving between two houses, they broke into the large expanse at the centre of the settlement. There was no joyous welcome for the distinguished guests. They approached the King through a wide parting the gathering crowd had formed to allow them passage. The riders dismounted for their horses to be led away, and the crowd grew silent.

Paulinus spoke first before Presutagus, who appeared about to speak, could take the initiative.

"King Presutagus, you do me and Rome a great honour by your kind invitation to your festivities today."

"Welcome, my Friend. And you do us a great honour in return with your visit. We shall shortly move into my house to allow us to relax. I can then tell you what today has in store for us all. First though, I will get the festivities started."

The King, wise enough to know nothing would be gained by prolonged speech making in front of the restless hostile people, addressed them with very few words.

"Our great Goddess Nertha awaits the demonstration of the trust and faith we place in her so that she will continue to provide food for us in great abundance. Let the festivities begin."

The people in the crowd began chanting the Goddess's name as Presutagus turned to his left and the crowd moved back to reveal three large wooden spits below which fires had been lit. To the sides of the fires were large wooden tables covered with baskets of food, produce from the fields. They were the remains from last year's harvest and the great volume was to remind Nertha of how good she had been to the tribe and to show their great gratitude. Amongst the pile was a large basket of grain which had been raised higher than the rest of the food. It was to be used shortly in the celebrations. In front of the spits three farm animals, a goat, a sheep and a calf were tethered to small posts.

From the house immediately behind the display a tall elderly grey-bearded man walked slowly to where the animals stood. The crowd became silent, eyes fixed on the tall figure. He was dressed from head to toe in a pale grey loosely fitting, coarse gown. His hair, thinning with age, was long, nearly reaching his shoulders. Like his beard, it was wild and unkempt. His face was broad with a large nose showing evidence that it had been broken in the past.

A small group of men had approached the animals to hold them securely. One tribesman, holding a large knife in one hand and a large high-sided bowl in the other, moved to stand beside them.

The old man faced the crowd, raised his arms and looked to the sky.

"Nertha, we pay homage to your greatness and ask you to look kindly on us in the coming days and months. We bring to you our seeds from the fields, and the blood of our animals for you to feed upon, as you provide for us."

He signalled to the man with the knife to begin.

The goat, struggling against its tethers as if aware of its fate, was the first to have its throat cut. The warm blood, giving off a misty vapour in the cold air, gushed freely into the bowl. After a short while, during which the crowd remained silent with expectation, the goat was laid upon the ground and its body split open to remove the entrails. The steaming pile was placed in a dish held by a woman who was obviously pregnant. Accompanied by the man holding the bowl of goat's blood she carried the dish to the old man. He took the bowl of blood first and lowered his head, taking an exaggerated breath through his nose. Then, using his knife, he poked amongst the goat's entrails in the dish before moving a step back.

"Nertha will be pleased to accept this gift."

With the crowd murmuring in anticipation, he dipped his finger into the blood and made a mark on the woman's forehead.

"Let this woman who has been anointed with blood bring forth from her womb a strong healthy child so that our tribe can continue to grow in numbers and be strong and prosperous."

The crowd shouted and cheered with excitement. Silence soon returned as the ritual was repeated using the calf, with the same result. Another pregnant woman had received the blood mark and returned to the excited crowd, to be greeted warmly by her family.

Finally the sheep was dispatched to Nertha and its blood and entrails awaited examination. Firstly the blood was inspected as before except that the old man hesitated before taking a second large breath. His face demonstrated for all to see a mixture of puzzlement and concern. He turned his attention to the entrails, taking longer to study them than he had with the others.

With a step closer to the pregnant woman, he placed a gentle hand on her head. He ran his other hand over her heavily swollen body prodding and squeezing her, but with careful and slow movements. The woman was becoming increasingly concerned. She began to tremble under his touch.

"Don't be alarmed my child," he whispered in a soft voice, "Nertha is telling us something."

He spoke to the men who were assisting him.

"Bring me another beast for Nertha."

A second sheep was promptly brought and sacrificed as before. This time the blood and entrails received the old man's approval.

"Nertha is extremely pleased with us. She has demanded extra sacrifice to her to demonstrate the long lasting bond she has shared with us."

He turned to the pregnant woman with the knife in his hand. Grasping the woman's gown firmly in his other hand, he pulled her close to him.

Julius Agricola had had difficulty in displaying much interest in these events. So far they'd not been dissimilar to others he had seen in other religious ceremonies. Now he fixed a more attentive gaze on the couple at the centre of the action. He'd been told of the practice of human sacrifice carried out by barbarians, but had no experience of it. He and his fellow Romans considered it a disgusting and unholy act, long since banned by Rome. Were they about to witness such a monstrous act and, if so, to what purpose? His hand instinctively fell upon his sword handle and he moved close to Presutagus. Action might be necessary in a few moments if the sacrificial blood lust was to be directed at them.

The old man had paused, causing the crowd to grow silent in excited anticipation. With a swift movement of his knife he cut and ripped open the front of the woman's gown. Instead of thrusting the knife deep into her body he made a small cut across her stomach with the point. The woman winced but didn't move away, her staring eyes seemingly transfixed by the old man's. He dropped the knife and, still holding the woman firmly in his grasp, he dipped his finger into the sheep's blood. This time he made two gestures with the blood. The first, as with the others, was to place a mark on her forehead. However, this time he rubbed his finger into the open wound he'd made in her stomach, ensuring the two bloods ran together.

"This woman has been chosen as a special one by Nertha. She will shortly bless her with not one child but two," the old man jubilantly proclaimed to the crowd. "The second beast which she demanded was in return for her gift to us. She is telling us she will indeed continue to provide for us. She will do so with an even greater harvest this year."

Shouting to make his words carry above the cries of delight from the crowd, he drew the ceremony to a close.

"Let us escort Nertha to the fields and offer our gifts of blood and seed."

Had he looked in the direction of Julius he would have seen a cynical, knowing smile on the young man's face replacing the excited open-mouthed expression of a few moments before.

A large cart drawn by an enormous ox, itself apparently in the latter stages of carrying an unborn calf, made a noisy entrance into the square. Beside the driver a large effigy of the goddess Nertha was held aloft by a young maiden.

It crossed the square and stopped in front of the old man. He climbed onto the cart, touching the effigy with his forehead before taking a firm grip on the side of the cart. He gave instructions to the driver to leave the settlement and move the cart into the fields. The crowd formed an orderly procession behind them and the square gradually emptied. Only those preparing the feast remained.

"Aren't we going to follow them?" Paulinus asked Presutagus

"Not on this occasion. This day belongs to our holy man and the people. The absence of myself and the Elders of the tribe is demanded by Nertha. We mustn't appear to stand between our Goddess and her followers."

"Is your holy man one of those we call druids?"

"I've heard your word 'druid' before and it appears to cover a wide range of holy men. They have different names amongst the many tribes. We don't have a name for our holy men, only their birth names."

"How are they chosen?" Julius asked.

"From within our tribe by all our people."

"He looks very similar to druids I've come across in the past," Paulinus suggested.

"Maybe they do have similarities to other holy men from other tribes. Nevertheless, the rituals, teachings and beliefs we have are rooted deeply in our traditions and are unique to this tribe," Presutagus replied.

He searched his guests' faces for signs of acceptance of his explanation. He was well aware of the loathing the Romans had for druids. He had long since learned from other tribes that they were not tolerated and it was often assumed any sign of unrest was caused and led by them. He continued his attempts at reassurance.

"Later in the festivities I will introduce you to him so you can experience his wisdom and knowledge. I'm sure you'll find him not unlike your own wise and venerable holy men."

"I'm sure I will be in awe of such a man," Paulinus conceded with a forced smile.

"Let's go to my house and wait for them to return."

*

Linona had entered her father's house along with the others. Lost in her world of thoughts, she had observed the day's events as if from a distance. She had taken part in the springtime festivities for a few years now, but the involvement of the General and his arrogant Tribune on the one hand and Marac on the other had affected her emotions. She had always revered the earth Goddess Nertha. Her love and respect for her seemed to mirror what she felt for her mother. She hoped that one day, when she became leader of the tribe, she could combine the qualities her mother had of strength and determination with the power to provide for her people through Nertha.

Two very different men had suddenly entered her life and both had disturbed her heightened emotions. She already knew a little about Marac from previous short meetings. He was deliciously handsome and she thought he would make the ideal partner, providing her with sons and daughters to help lead the tribe in the future. She had decided he would be a loving, loyal, steadying influence throughout her life.

The Roman tribune was a very different man, except that he too, she had to admit to herself, was very attractive. She was looking at him and he stirred and excited her in a way that she hadn't felt with Marac. He was extremely confident and his apparent lack of fear earlier in the day attracted her even though the self-confidence had changed into arrogance.

"And this is my eldest daughter, Linona."

Her father's words brought her back to be confronted by the face of the Roman General. She reluctantly had to concede to herself that the Roman leader looked the part. He was not a physically imposing man, but he gave the impression of one who was very confident and sophisticated, always in total control of himself and those around him.

"Linona. It sounds like a Roman name," Paulinus suggested. If he thought his comments would be taken as a compliment, he was mistaken.

Linona's gaze had left the tribune's face, with its annoyingly amused, arrogant expression. However, because she had not yet fully let go of her previous confusing thoughts about him, she replied to Paulinus before she had time to take care in her choice of words.

"It is very much a traditional Iceni name and I'm proud of it. To be frank, I don't need a Roman name or anything else that's Roman," she snarled. "I am perfectly content to be Iceni."

Before anybody else had time to react to her provocative remarks, Julius intervened.

"It's a beautiful name to match the beauty of the bearer."

Paulinus shot a knowing glance at Julius.

Presutagus's worried look changed to one of relief at this last remark, and the apparent lack of any offence her words could well have caused. He quickly spoke up.

"I think we should all acknowledge that the bluntness of youth, both Iceni and Roman, can at times cause parents some embarrassment. I'm sure you agree, Governor?"

To avoid any further comment, he quickly moved on, introducing the two soldiers to the tribe's six senior Elders. They were the King's most trusted advisers.

Linona returned to her thoughts. Why had this Tribune helped her? She had seen her father's look of despair at her remarks and she wished she could have bitten her tongue off. It couldn't have been an act of kindness by the Roman. He wouldn't be capable of such an act. She would have expected him to use her outburst to belittle and humiliate her. Surely he was the kind of man to do that. She looked towards her mother and got a reassuring smile from her.

*

Once the introductions had been completed everybody except Linona had taken a seat. She had chosen to sit on the floor at the feet of Marac and to one side of Boudica.

"Tell me, my friend, what happened after the ox cart left the square?" Paulinus enquired. "Is there some deep, mysterious and secret ceremony which isn't for the eyes of strangers such as myself?"

His questions were light and unthreatening and Presutagus replied in similar fashion.

"The only thing deep out there is the mud in the ploughed fields. The cart will visit the land which is the closest to our settlement. The fields, which we've already prepared to grow our crops on, will have the grain thrown onto them. Our pasture lands will then have the blood poured on them. Finally, the woodlands will be given both to bring us the timber and animals so essential for our needs. Once all that has been completed, they will return to the square so the feasting and celebrations can begin."

"I'm interested in some of your other customs." Julius added. "One which I find particularly intriguing is the status of women in your society."

"What do you want to know?" the king enquired.

"I'm given to understand women are considered equal in status to men. For instance, I believe that dowries are received from both families, not just one, and property and estates are shared. Is this what happens?"

"Of course," Linona replied before anybody else.

"Am I also correct to believe that property and estates can be passed on to a woman when a man dies? And, is it also true that women can be leaders in all aspects of life including war?"

Linona's blood had risen. This was now the Tribune behaving as she might have expected. She considered the treatment of women in Roman society, as it had been described to her by her mother, was unacceptable. She was sure this man was a typically domineering, arrogant Roman male. Only her mother's pressure with her leg against her own stopped her from replying further. She was going to take over from her daughter.

"The roots of our two societies go back in time a long way and are very different," Boudica explained. "Our lands are situated a long way from each other."

"And separated by many different tribes and peoples," Julius added.

"I've little knowledge of your history," Boudica continued. "In our case, wars with neighbouring tribes have lasted over many years. We have learnt that the use of the strengths and skills of all our people has been necessary to survive. When I say 'all our people' I mean just that - men, women and children. Whoever has the greatest strengths, skills, or qualities of any kind has been required to put them into use for the benefit of all."

"Even in war?"

"Even in war! Whosoever is the best leader will take on this great responsibility. Whether it happens to be a man or a woman, they will be supported by the people."

She eased the pressure on her daughter's leg, who took it as a signal for her to continue.

"Tell me, Tribune," she probed, her heart racing with a mixture of rage and excitement as she met this annoying man's challenge, "do you feel we have something to gain by adopting your customs. If so, please enlighten us?"

She was pleased she hadn't overstated her case. She would be ready for him when he fell into her trap.

"Please don't misunderstand me, Princess Linona. I have no personal desire to force you to adopt our customs. I am anxious to learn about you and your people."

"With what purpose in mind?" she demanded.

"In this way the friendship between us can grow stronger in the future. I'm sure I could learn a great deal. Throughout the ages Rome has brought change to other peoples and at the same time absorbed many new ideas and beliefs from them."

Presutagus could see his daughter colouring red, either with rage or frustration at the young Roman's ability to sidestep her question.

"I draw great strength from my wife and both my daughters," he remarked, in an attempt to redirect the conversation. "This applies in all things both personal and in the broader matters of state. Do you each have families here or back in Rome?"

"I do indeed," Paulinus replied first. "My wife and three of my children live in my villa which is set in the hills behind Rome."

"Are they all daughters like mine?"

"Two of those three still living at home are strong sons who will be joining the service of the Emperor in the near future. My daughter is my youngest child. I also have another married daughter. I hope she'll soon provide me with grandsons."

"You have been blessed by your Gods."

"Like you, my children provide me with much joy and comfort. I miss them all constantly."

Linona saw for the first time a sign of humanity from the General, as his gaze lingered on the fire in the centre of the room. Perhaps he was remembering some treasured family event. She quickly dismissed the thought as the Tribune replied to her father's question.

"I've been serving away from home for a few years and not had the opportunity to give much thought to marriage and raising a family."

"And how does a young Roman soldier choose a bride?" asked Boudica.

"I'm sure my family will be considering what possible choices I have. They will wish to help and guide me to make a beneficial alliance when the time comes. I only hope their preferred choice is a woman who comes some way to match the beauty of your daughters."

"Perhaps we aren't too different in the way we do things after all," said Presutagus. "I'd like to talk some more but I think I can hear our people returning. Let's go to meet them. We can continue our discussions later."

"I would like to give a little speech to them before the celebrations begin, if that's acceptable to you, Presutagus?"

He nodded his agreement to Paulinus and rose to make his way into the bright mid-afternoon light, followed by all those in his house. A watery sun was bringing a little warmth to counter the light cool northerly wind blowing across the square.

"My good friends!" Paulinus began, addressing his silent, unwelcoming audience. "You should know that Rome values the friendship which exists with the Iceni people more than with any other tribe. We have gladly made it known to all your former enemies that you would have our support in any resistance against a repeat of the oppression your neighbours from the north and west, especially the Catuvelauni, have brought upon you in the past. Since we came to this land our Legionaries haven't allowed one attack on you by any other tribe. You have prospered because of this. We have benefited in return from your continued supply of grain and other goods to the Empire.

In the far distance you can see a small part of my army which I've brought with me. They aren't here to be a threat to you. On the contrary, I hope they will be a reminder to you of the strength and support we can bring.

You are privileged to have as your leaders King Presutagus and Queen Boudica. Already today I have learnt from them a lot more about this great tribe and your customs. I have seen the homage all of you have paid to Nertha, the earth Goddess, the Provider. Your devotion has greatly impressed me.

You have asked Nertha to look kindly on you again this year as she has done in the past. I am sure she will hear your call. I also add my pleas to her to reward such a great and glorious people. When I return to my camp tonight I will make sacrifices to my own Gods asking them to provide me with the power and strength to be able to continue to give my support to our Iceni neighbours."

Presutagus was glowing with satisfaction at Paulinus's words.

"Finally, there is something in my power and not dependent on the Gods which I can grant to you all. I shall arrange with the Imperial Procurator to reduce by one tenth the tribute you pay annually to Rome through him. In addition I shall reduce by one quarter the number of warriors contributed by you to the auxiliary ranks in our army."

The people in the crowd were hardly ecstatic at Paulinus's speech, but his last remarks were welcomed. After their initial surprise and concerns the day had gone well for them and the mood before the feasting began was improving.

Presutagus replied to the speech, making sure everybody could hear him. He thanked his friend and ally for his promise of continued support agreeing with him the existing peace would be guaranteed for some time to come. He was sure the tribe's prosperity would continue to grow.

Linona didn't welcome her father's comments. To her the visit today by these Romans was yet another demonstration of their power over her people. Gradually the tribe's need to be free of Rome was ebbing away. Freedom mattered less and less. She would change things when she became Queen and leader of the tribe.

*

The feasting and drinking began throughout the square. The drinks and the rest of the food were brought out and placed on the large platform especially erected for the day's festivities.

Paulinus and Julius joined in the feasting and were entertained by the spectacle of the dancing which followed. They still had their other objectives to achieve before the time for their departure arrived, but there was plenty of time for that to happen. A lull in the organised activities allowed them to move more freely amongst the crowd.

Paulinus had been watching the holy man who had remained to one side throughout the proceedings. Occasionally he had been approached by members of his tribe and appeared to be giving advice and receiving small gifts in return.

He made his way over to him and introduced himself.

"I think you know my name is Suetonius Paulinus and I've been told you are called Bodran."

"You've been told correctly."

"I've some questions which I'd like to ask you."

"I'm listening."

Bodran had spent his life talking to many of his people, and had learnt to be economical with words.

"Is it correct to call you a druid?"

"That's your word. It's not one that we use."

Linona had been standing close by with Marac and heard the discussion taking place. They joined the two men, without interrupting them.

Paulinus merely noted their arrival and continued.

"What do you call yourself then?"

"Bodran."

Linona smiled knowingly. She had had many conversations with Bodran. After all, he was one of her teachers. He had taught her the importance of listening carefully to what people were asking and to reply only with what was necessary, with thought rather than passion. He'd urged her to follow her mother's example.

"Are you part of a religious order?"

"I am not part of any group, druids or otherwise. I am addressed by my people by my name and they use no other."

"Do you have contacts with druids from other tribes?"

"Why would I need to do so?"

"Do you answer to a senior druid from any other tribe?"

"I answer only to the Gods and my people?"

"Do you have authority in other matters such as in battle?"

"My advice is sought in all matters of concern to my people."

A frustrated Paulinus moved away to seek out Boudica while Linona exchanged an amused smile with her old teacher.

"What was that all about?" Marac asked Linona as they moved towards the centre of the square. They were going to watch the wrestling bouts which had begun to determine the champion for the day.

"I don't know. But I'm sure they're up to something. I've probably asked him some of those same questions myself over the years when he was my teacher. Yet I just don't trust them in anything they do, even when they ask such apparently innocent questions."

Marac had stopped listening, his attention drawn to the wrestling. She suddenly became aware of somebody standing close behind her. She turned to look straight into the dark, deep eyes of Julius. She felt her heart race. Was it a nervous startled reaction to his sudden threatening closeness or was it something else?

"Leave Marac to enjoy the wrestling and come to talk to me," he whispered.

He withdrew, heading towards the table with the wine.

Linona thought for a moment about his request. It had surprised and excited her. What was his game? She had to find out. She left Marac, who by now was engrossed in the contest on the mats in front of him. Warily, she came alongside Julius who had a beaker of wine in his hand.

"Have you come to join me?" he asked, offering her wine.

Linona declined the wine and as forcefully as she could, demanded an explanation.

"What game are you playing with me and my people, Roman? Why have you come here? Why?"

"You know why we're here, to learn your customs and rituals and to reinforce our friendship."

"So you've said. I don't believe you."

"I will make a bargain with you. You tell me your secret, sweet Linona, and I shall tell you mine."

He made his offer with a broad smile which unnerved her again.

"I don't have a secret to bargain with."

"I've seen you with the young Prince. I think perhaps I'm witnessing the beginning of something both tribes will be happy about."

Her wintered pale face flushed with a mixture of anger and embarrassment.

"You're wrong," she spoke quietly, holding her head down to try to hide any sign of her stupid youthful embarrassed reaction. "It's required of me as the Princess to entertain Marac on a feast day like this."

"I understand and you need say no more." He was smiling with satisfaction at her embarrassment.

Linona tried to regain the initiative by suggesting she knew what his secret was.

"You are playing games and your purpose here today is different from what you claim. I suspect you have come here to impress and influence my father. The large bribe your leader offered to him and our people was part of some wider darker plan you have."

"That's not so, Princess. Our purpose is innocent. There are many tribes in this land with many customs. The Governor sees it as our duty to study them all in the interest of friendship and peace."

"I don't believe you."

"For instance, I was very interested in the sacrificial homage paid to Nertha by your holy man."

"In what way?"

"He was very impressive when he identified the Goddess's need for an extra sacrificial animal. It also provided some extra meat that I'm sure was welcomed by the large number of people and their unexpected guests waiting in the square for the feast to begin."

His words were mocking her, and she boiled with rage.

"I've heard enough."

"I do have a confession to make, though. I have now acquired another purpose which I need to share with you. I've been overwhelmed by your beauty and wonderful fiery spirit, a characteristic so often lacking in Roman women. I've been so smitten that I might consider taking you as my consort, perhaps even my wife. I would be a much more appropriate partner for you than any young tribal prince. Think of the benefit that would flow to your people from our marriage."

"You are a barbarian, a heathen and a fool. Go back to your army and your empire. You won't be welcome here ever again."

She strode off with the sound of his laughter in her ears to be immediately confronted ahead of her by the sight of Paulinus locked in conversation with Boudica. They parted just before she reached them. Paulinus headed off in the direction of Presutagus.

"That man is very dangerous," was Boudica's hushed, tight-lipped remark to her daughter.

"Why? What has he been saying?"

"We were talking about the future for our two peoples. He has made it clear he sees a problem for us in the future when we come to choose our next leader."

"What has it got to do with him?"

"He has more or less demanded that Rome will have some say in who is chosen. Whoever it is, 'he' will be required to honour and continue the treaties agreed by Presutagus. He made a point of explaining that Romans cannot accept women as leaders."

"What did you tell him in reply?"

"I was furious with him and I told him that he will have been recalled to Rome long before your father dies and the need arises to replace him. I left him in no doubt that the Iceni people must not be prevented from choosing their own leader, without Rome's interference. That was when he stormed off just before you arrived."

Linona's eye caught Presutagus calling to them. She grasped her mother's arm and they went to meet him.

"Our guests are leaving and I've asked Olsar to escort them. They want to leave without ceremony so as not to disturb the activities taking place."

The Romans expressed their gratitude for the hospitality shown to them before leaving with Olsar. Their departure was unnoticed by most of the people in the square.

As they left the square the three men mounted their horses and proceeded to the main gate where the small troop of Roman cavalry were waiting for the Governor.

"There's no need to escort me any further, Olsar," said Paulinus.

"I agree, since I could not approach a Roman camp twice in one day without attacking it at least once," Olsar replied, giving a crisp wave in the direction of his camp and grinning.

Paulinus sped off, showing his lack of amusement at the remark. His men chased after him, except for Julius.

"Farewell, Olsar, Commander of the Iceni cavalry. I think our paths may well cross again. I look forward to such an occasion."

He gave his horse a kick and rode after the Governor.

Olsar, no longer needing his taunting smile, stared expressionless as they rode away into the gloom of the failing light. The fires of the Roman camp shone brightly in the distance.

*

The Governor's tent, placed as normal in the centre of the camp, had been made ready for his arrival. The Senior Tribune who commanded the legionaries had been told Paulinus was approaching the camp and he had positioned himself at the door of the tent. He'd inspected the inside to ensure it would meet with his approval.

The Governor preferred to live simply when in an overnight marching camp. His furniture consisted only of a small camp bed, a campaign desk and several small chairs. He also allowed himself one luxury. He suffered badly from the damp cold weather in this remote northern land. The chill caused him great pain at times in his hands and feet. So, he had a small brazier inside the entrance of his tent. It would be kept alight throughout the night by his two personal slaves.

Paulinus dismounted in front of the tent, which was brightly lit by a large fire built closer than normal to his tent this cold night. The light from the fire was reflected by the brightly polished armour worn by the Senior Tribune who saluted and stepped aside to make way for him.

"Have some good Roman wine brought to me," he barked at the sentries, "and order my slaves to prepare hot water for me to wash the dirt of this miserable land off my body. I want to chase away the chill in my bones."

Julius stood to one side to allow Senior Tribune Camillus to enter the tent first. Although he himself was a favoured staff officer to the Governor he was still only a tribune. He had no wish to show any disrespect to this man, who was well regarded by both the Governor and the men under his command. He was a tall, bullish man and not one to cross. Paulinus had seconded him from his normal position as second in command of the 14th Legion to help him plan his campaign on Mona.

Paulinus warmed his hands by the brazier and signalled the two officers to be seated. Turning to allow him to face them both, but also to warm his broad backside against the brazier, he congratulated Camillus.

"You've carried out my instructions well. I particularly like the large fire outside my tent. I'm a little tired and want to rest early tonight so I won't keep you here much longer. I want you to carry out one more duty before you relax also. Double the normal guard and place sentries and patrols outside the camp perimeter throughout the night. It wouldn't surprise me if some drunken young bloods from our neighbours try to make a gesture or two following my visit."

Camillus rose from his chair, saluted, thanked the Governor for his remarks and left.

"That tribune is the sort we will need when we go to fight the druids on Mona. Unless, of course, you persuade me after today's events it would be unwise to continue with my plans at this time."

He moved to his desk where his slave had placed a large pitcher of blood-red wine.

"My view is quite clear, Sir. I see nothing to fear from good King Presutagus. Had their druid offered him as a third 'sheep' for sacrifice to his Goddess he would have met the requirement perfectly."

Both men laughed loudly.

"I think we couldn't say the same of that wife of his and her young female wolf cub," Paulinus added. "We may well have a problem in the future with those two. We must take more interest in deciding who we shall appoint to replace Presutagus as King when the time is right."

"I think they've decided already that Linona and the Trinovanti prince would make a charming couple to rule over both tribes. They would then have greater strength in numbers," Julius noted.

"I also suspected the same. It's a situation we will need to watch closely. I think a spell in one of our legions in Germania as an auxiliary might be of great benefit to Prince Marac. It would be a pity if he came to harm fighting those beasts."

Both men laughed again before Paulinus became more business-like. He lay back on his camp bed.

"We must put my plans for Mona and the druids into action without delay. Those plans remain unchanged."

"That's good to hear, Sir."

"Although we only have four Legions in Britannia, I've seen enough for us to be able to take most of the 20th Legion from these tribal lands and take them north to Mona to join the 14th Legion. The 2nd Legion will remain to protect the South West of the Province. The 9th Legion, based in our fortress at Lindum, will keep the North East quiet. The remainder of the 20th will occupy the forts between those two strongholds to protect our rear and to keep a watch on the rest of the Province."

"May I put one last question to you before I leave, Sir?"

The Governor, eyes closed, waved his consent and Julius responded quickly.

"You've told me previously about the Emperor doubting whether Britannia can meet his demand for more taxes."

"That is still the case."

"Yet today, you reduced the part supplied by Presutagus. Could I ask your reasoning for such a move?"

"What is easily given can just as easily be taken away. I shall defeat the druids on Mona and return with our full army. I shall point out to Presutagus that I will need a great deal of help in money and manpower after the campaign to restore our army and give him continuing protection from the Catuvelauni. A final solution to the druid problem and a restored contribution from Presutagus and his people will placate our Emperor. Now, I wish to rest, Julius."

CHAPTER 7

"My wife and the rest of the Elders tell me there's great advantage to be gained in our two families joining together through our children. I'm still to be convinced."

Everybody in the room was shocked at these totally unexpected remarks from Presutagus. He hadn't given the slightest hint of any reservations which he might have been having.

Two weeks had passed since the festival of Nertha, and life in the settlement had returned to normal. The weather had turned much warmer. Marac and Frigionus had returned and the two families had come together in Presutagus's house. They had seated themselves around the room and had been talking quietly and readying themselves to discuss the betrothal.

Linona had been impatient to begin with but she knew there was a way the old people liked to do these things. So she had bitten her lip and contented herself by looking at Marac and thinking how fortunate she was. It was going to be easy to carry out her parents' wishes. However, her patience snapped, provoked by Presutagus's comment.

"Father, I don't understand you? You can't treat…"

"Quiet, Linona." Her mother interrupted her, stopping her before she said words which she might regret.

Marac looked surprised and puzzled.

"Please explain yourself, my friend," Frigionus demanded, rising to his feet "You're very close to insulting me and my son."

Frigionus, King of the Trinovantes, was some years older than Presutagus, but he still displayed the energy and enthusiasm of a much younger man. At times his emotions got the better of him when he was frustrated. He was apt to lose his temper and speak without too much thought.

Linona began to feel anxious. She knew very well the two tribes didn't have any long history of friendship. She had been taught that there had been many occasions in the past when war had occurred between them. Many atrocities had been committed. When the Romans came they had weakened all the tribes, the Trinovantes in particular. Her marriage would help to ensure that fighting between the two tribes should never happen again. How could her father put this at risk? He didn't immediately answer her or Frigionus to explain his remarks. Instead he stared silently into his folded arms.

"I am waiting for an explanation," Frigionus spoke more aggressively, his anger mounting.

Presutagus's reply was delivered slowly. Linona thought he seemed to be searching for the right words.

"Calm yourself and I'll explain. Until the day of the feast I was convinced the coming together of our two tribes through the marriage of Linona and Marac was a chance to end the animosity which has existed between us for many generations. The arrival of the Romans has taken away our strength. We can no longer fight each other even if we wanted to. Now, by working together our peoples could become stronger and prosper, free from fear and suspicion of each other."

"I agree! I agree!" yelled Frigionus. "Why are you doubting it today?"

"Please be patient and allow me to continue to explain fully and carefully my reservations."

Linona thought her father was looking flushed. He wouldn't be enjoying what he was doing, so why was he putting himself through this.

Presutagus gathered himself and continued.

"The Romans have not only stopped our tribes from fighting they've weakened the Corieltauvi to our north. To the west the Catuvelauni who have often persecuted our two tribes in the past have been kept under control. They have pacified this land of ours and we need them."

"Not so. The Romans are savages. Don't try to tell me they are good for us."

"I'm not saying they are good for us. I know the Trinovantes have suffered more than anybody under their control. Yes! I understand your hatred. However, I warn you the Romans, if provoked, could do a lot worse to you."

"That would be difficult."

"In other lands they have destroyed tribes who have continued to oppose and fight them. Those who survived the initial slaughter have been sold into slavery."

Linona's worried expression showed her concern for her father. His face had become a bright red colour and his breathing heavy and laboured. She felt she hadn't often seen him as angry and agitated as this.

"Are you feeling unwell, Father?"

He carried on as if he hadn't heard her.

"Last week I saw that the hatred, which you have for the soldiers of this evil Empire, is still burning as brightly as ever inside you"

"You can be sure of that."

"But you had the chance to master the hatred as I have. You could have taken the opportunity to show us you can meet them face to face as equals. You could have shown them that you lead a proud people who should be treated with respect and not as slaves."

"Many have been taken as slaves already, or have you forgotten that?" Frigionus shouted.

"I haven't forgotten. Fortunately your son has greater vision than yourself. For this reason I am prepared for us to continue our discussion to see if we can reconcile our views to make sure these two young people can have a future together. It's what my wife and daughter want and I must try to help them."

He hesitated and his face twisted in pain. Frigionus seized his opportunity to reply.

"You are a fool if you think the Romans consider you an equal. How long do you think they will tolerate your so-called 'independence'? I shall answer for you. It will be until it suits them to change it. That's how long."

"That's not the case."

"For the time being it suits them to have you quietly go about your business as they pursue theirs. One day their full attention will be turned back onto you. We need to be strong, to join together."

"At least we both agree on that."

"Yes, but for different reasons. We should bring in other tribes and work towards a time when we can throw them back into the sea, back to wherever they came from. It seems we may both want our children to marry but your thinking is different from mine."

"That may be so, but you are the fool, not me, if you think we could ever defeat an army which has destroyed nations far stronger than we will ever be, even together."

Linona wasn't listening any more. Her father had clutched his chest as he uttered these words. He tried to stand but slumped back in his chair gasping for breath.

Boudica rose and stopped Linona as she rushed to help her father.

"Go and bring Bodran, quickly," she commanded.

"But what about father? I want to help him."

"You can do just that by doing what I say," she said and turned her firmly to face towards the door and pushed.

*

Presutagus still lived. He was weak but fully aware of what was going on around him. He lay on his bed and beckoned Frigionus to approach him.

"Let's not end our discussion like this," he whispered. "Perhaps we have both said things we didn't mean and used words we will regret tomorrow. Promise me we'll continue when I'm well again?"

"But of course," Frigionus replied. "For now I'll leave and return to my home. You can then receive the care you need without looking at my old troublesome face."

They both smiled and Frigionus withdrew making for the door. He was halted by Boudica who grabbed his arm firmly but didn't speak. Her gaze was firmly fixed on Bodran. He was at Presutagus's side instructing all present that the King must be allowed to rest and ordering everybody to leave.

"I will stay, Mother," Linona insisted.

"I want to stay also," pleaded Cailan who had become aware of the commotion and had joined the rest.

"Stay then. I will see to our guests."

Boudica withdrew with Frigionus and Marac. Outside she addressed both of them.

"My husband didn't speak for both of us earlier today. Mind you, I didn't get any comfort from your angry words. I think Linona and Marac may well have views of their own to express to us all on how they see their future and that of our two tribes."

"What are you wanting to say?" Frigionus asked.

"Bodran has told me that he thinks Presutagus isn't about to die but he will be bed-ridden for some time and weak for quite a while longer. I think I will be speaking for my people for some time to come. We'll meet again soon to continue with our plans."

"I agree, and I will be ready. Farewell."

Later Boudica addressed those who had gathered outside her house after Frigionus and Marac had left. News of the collapse of Presutagus had spread very quickly.

"Don't be alarmed. The winter chills have finally laid Presutagus low. Bodran has reminded me that we aren't as young as we used to be. The King will take a while to fully recover from his illness. The warm weather is coming and we'll soon see him back on his feet again. Please return to your houses. There's no reason to be alarmed."

*

Beside her father's bed Linona had begun to think about the two opposing arguments she'd heard earlier. Both men had been angry but both had made some sense in what they said. She needed to think the arguments through and talk to Marac about his view. Did he have one different from Frigionus? She wasn't sure of her own yet but she was sure it wasn't the same as her father's. She would try somehow to talk to Marac alone, and before the two families met again. For the time being she must do everything in her power to help her beloved father to become well again.

CHAPTER 8

"Divine Claudius, I ask you to grant me the strength to carry out my work in this damp and desolate heathen land."

The plea came from Catus Decianus. His massive girth was evidence that his work had nothing to do with hard manual toil in the fields. He was very proud to be the Imperial Procurator for the Province of Britannia, appointed by Emperor Nero himself. His task, one which he relished, was to ensure the necessary taxes were set and collected to be sent to the Treasury in Rome.

"I bring you this offering of the best wine which the Empire can produce as a token of my faith."

His words were spoken in a loud voice so as to reach the ears of the priests who stood by the altar. Their duty was to receive and take care of offerings from devotees of the God Claudius.

His thoughts were not quite as pious as his words.

"The old goat liked his drink when he was alive," he told himself. "Wherever he is now, a gift of wine would surely be appreciated and encourage the God to look kindly on me."

He placed the wine on the altar and stepped back with his head bowed. When he turned to leave he produced a large purse and gave it to the nearest priest. He was making sure his generous devotion to Claudius would be communicated to the citizens of Camulodunum and more importantly to the Emperor Nero's spies. He knew they were here in this town just as they were in Londinium, where he had his official residence.

His heavy tread echoed in the large empty marbled hall. Slowly and reverently, he made his way out of the inner sanctuary along the outer corridors. His mind was still on Claudius. He was smiling at the thought that this magnificent temple had been erected to pay homage to such a simple old fool. Claudius it was who had reluctantly accepted his nephew Nero's request for Decianus to be given his first role as a young administrator on the Imperial staff in Rome. The appointment of Decianus's father as one of the young Nero's tutors had proved to be of great advantage in his son's career.

Eventually he went through the wooden doors which opened onto the huge colonnaded front of the Temple and the large flight of steps falling steeply down to street level. Before descending, he halted in order to take in the view of Camulodunum that this raised vantage point allowed him. The dark threatening sky pressed down on the buildings and the thick grey smoke rising from them.

The town was growing rapidly. It was becoming prosperous because of the efforts of the legionaries who lived there. They had retired from the army and taken the fields of the defeated Trinovantes for their own use. The taxes which Decianus levied on them provided a significant part of the money he was required to collect and send to the Emperor to keep him satisfied.

He walked down the steps to be joined by the twelve guards who made up his personal bodyguard. Being the tax collector for the Province made him a target for the many who had suffered because of his enthusiasm for his task.

It was indeed a task which he enjoyed. It gave him a power in the Province second only to that of the Governor. He reported directly to the Emperor and didn't have to explain himself to Paulinus for his actions in carrying out his tax-gathering duties. He was allowed to recruit his own army of mercenaries to assist him. They numbered more than 1000 men. They were a mixture of former legionaries and auxiliaries capable of ruthless violence in the services of the Procurator.

Decianus and the small band of men completed the short walk to one of the town's administrative buildings and the meeting room, which he used as his temporary headquarters when visiting the town. Six of the guards remained outside while the other six accompanied him inside. Decianus liked the ominous presence of his men standing behind him when he met the citizens of the town. He considered it gave his demands more emphasis, hinting at the physical threat failure to comply would surely bring.

The unmistakable sound of soldiers' boots falling on the stone floor had brought a nervous young man running from a side room.

"You! You young fool. Bring me food and wine," Decianus barked. "I remember you from previous visits. If the wine's as bad as last time I shall have you flogged, you miserable hound."

It amused him to see the young man scurry away in terror. He knew from long experience that fear is an effective master. He was often reminded of the times when he had been beaten half to death by his father for the most trivial of matters. The beatings had sharpened his desire to avoid failure at any cost.

His document satchel had been placed on the large table which had been positioned in one corner of the room. The guards were familiar enough with the procedure to have moved the table into a position allowing the Procurator to dominate the room. He could glare fiercely at all those entering through the two large oak doors at the opposite end of the room.

Decianus took his seat at the table and opened the satchel. Taking out the baton of office which Nero had presented to him personally he placed it in front of him. It reminded those who he would be dealing with where his authority to levy the taxes came from. Then he took out his records of the payments required to be made by the citizens of Camulodunum. He kept meticulous records of every duty levied. His life, he fully appreciated, could depend on these records. Nero was not a compassionate or forgiving man.

He began to study the documents before giving his instructions.

"The officials of the town have been made aware of my visit, have they not?"

Part of him was hoping somebody had erred and his visit had been unexpected. It could have given him more pleasure if it were so.

"They have, Sir," Bestia the officer leading his guard replied.

He was standing stiffly at Decianus's side, his hand resting on the hilt of his sword prepared for anything.

"They are waiting for a call to join you."

"Good. Then call them, man! I don't wish to spend any more time here than is required to squeeze these pathetic farmers."

Bestia gave the signal and the soldier by the door withdrew.

"How many years have you been in military service, Bestia?"

Decianus would have a short time to fill and he thought he would amuse himself.

"17 and a half years, Sir."

"A whole 17 and one half years you say. It sounds as if you're counting down the days to your retirement. No doubt you will join these farmers when the time comes?"

"I shall be pleased to continue to serve your Honour until I'm no longer considered worthy. Retirement isn't something I think about." His reply was more considered this time.

"Good answer."

Decianus was slightly impressed. It was a careful answer for such an uncultured man. He hadn't chosen him to command his men because of his wits though. He was the tallest of his men, a strong, brutal man and his men feared him as much as they did any enemy. Since Decianus had appointed him on his arrival in Britannia he hadn't had any difficulty in collecting taxes.

Growing more impatient Decianus was reminded of his hunger and thirst from the journey earlier in the day.

"Where is that dog? You! Guard! Go and encourage him not to annoy me a moment longer."

The nearest guard withdrew to the side room as a small group of men entered the meeting room through the main entrance.

"At last, you've all chosen to come to see me."

It was always good to demonstrate his offence at any delay. It weakened any potential resistance.

"We came when requested," replied Varus Gerrinus.

He had been chosen by the people of Camulodunum to be the Town Magistrate. The decision had been helped no doubt because he had been a senior centurion with the 20th Legion before retiring with a distinguished record. He was known to fear no man, from barbarian chieftain to Roman general.

"I trust your journey from Londinium was a comfortable one without any incidents?" he asked.

The rest of the town's representatives were having difficulty hiding their amusement. Varus had made scathing comments while they were waiting to be addressed by Decianus. He had wondered how a man, as fat as he was, could get onto a horse and ride the hard miles from Londinium without killing the poor animal.

Decianus didn't answer. He would soon wipe any smiles from their faces.

"Gentlemen, I would offer all of you seats but it would appear they are in short supply in this building."

"We shall stand. We have no need of physical support."

The anger building inside Decianus found release as the young man returned carrying a large jug of wine and a dish of mixed meats, bread and some cheese. The hands of the young man trembled as he carefully placed the dishes onto the table and took a pace backwards. Decianus grabbed the jug and drank briefly from it before turning to the young man and spraying him with the wine from his mouth.

"Ox piss," he yelled. "I'll have you taken outside and flogged to teach you respect."

The contempt on Varus's face wasn't hidden.

"Have we been brought here to observe how the Procurator exercises discipline over slaves or are we here for some more appropriate business?" Varus taunted.

"Your insolence is noted, Varus," Decianus growled with an impatient scowl. "It won't be to your advantage or to that of the people of this town."

Decianus wasn't inclined to delay matters any longer. He wanted the pleasure of seeing their reactions to his news.

"Emperor Nero is losing patience with the Province and its failure to bring the wealth which his investment in this land deserves. He's authorised me to increase taxes as I see fit. Accordingly I shall double the taxes on land and on the people of Camulodunum. I've had the appropriate documents prepared for you so that my requirements can be put into effect."

He sat back enjoying the shock on the faces of those present. He noticed only Varus didn't change his expression.

"Has Governor Suetonius Paulinus had the opportunity to put his seal to your demands?"

"The Governor is elsewhere engaged in his springtime war game. I'm sure as a loyal servant of the Emperor he would give me his support. As you know he has no authority to object to my decision. If he does disagree with me he can make his views known to Nero, and may the Gods protect him if he should choose to do so."

"You are mad," shouted one of the citizens.

"Leave this to me," Varus cried sharply.

In doing so, he raised his right arm sideways, with his fist tightly clenched. It was a gesture to keep them in check but it also indicated to Decianus how angry he was at his dangerous and provocative action. He took his time before he spoke coldly and calmly to Decianus once again.

"What you are asking for is impossible. Because of the high taxes you already impose we've just enough left for ourselves and our families. This town is growing and it needs more money to spend on building facilities for our people. For some time now we've recognised the need to build a defensive barrier around the town. But such a structure needs money and manpower to build it. We are too busy manning the fields to do it alone."

"That, my friend, is a matter for you to consider and resolve. I can offer you a suggestion, should you have the courage to act on it. If you need to produce more, then take more land. If you need more manpower, then take more slaves. The Trinovantes have the land and they make good slaves if flogged often enough."

"If we were to do what you say we would cause more unrest amongst the tribe."

"So! What's your point?"

"Paulinus is in the North and he has left only a small part of the army behind. We have no support to call upon if we are met with a major uprising."

"There will be no major uprising you fool. They are a defeated remnant of what was, at best, a small insignificant band of barbarians."

"They are much more than that."

"If you aren't able to contain any new minor trouble you can count on the support of my men to come to your aid and defend you."

That, he felt, would leave them in no doubt of his contempt for these farmers.

"I'm going to return to Londinium immediately. I will leave you with one last thought. Should the Emperor finally lose patience with the Province and remove our Legions to control his more prosperous provinces, how long do you think you and your town would survive? Now leave me to find some decent food and drink in this town."

Bestia and the other five guards moved to come between the table and the group of citizens to escort them from the room. They stood in front of Varus whose icy glare moved from Decianus to Bestia. The two men glared at each other for a moment. Bestia, as before, had his hand on the hilt of his sword. Varus turned away slowly, staring at Bestia for as long as he possibly could. With a slow dignified walk he led his group outside.

Decianus roared with laughter. He hadn't had such an enjoyable time for ages.

"Bestia, let's go to celebrate. Bring the slave with us. He will take us to a more hospitable place than this. I'm sure we shall be very welcome wherever he leads us."

His joke was much appreciated by Bestia and the other guards whose dislike of the former regular legionaries turned farmers mirrored that of their Commander.

*

Outside, Varus was calming his group with some difficulty.

"We have no choice. Paulinus isn't here to help us, and even if he was, there's no certainty he would do so. We must meet these demands. Until Paulinus returns take only what we need from those smaller villages and hamlets and deal harshly with any resistance. I will issue written instructions to all citizens explaining the Procurator's demands."

The citizen nearest to Varus could contain his anger no longer.

"The pig should not be allowed to live. His dislike for the people of Camulodunum is well known. I say it would be easy for us to arrange for him to die on his way back to Londinium."

His words were being greeted with support until Varus spoke.

"I will personally deal with any man who foolishly tries to take such action. I for one don't want to focus the attention of that tyrant Nero on our town. The death of Decianus would be quickly put down to us. Paulinus would have no reason to take a risk with Nero by hiding that truth from him to protect us. We do as I say and carry out the Procurator's demands, for now."

CHAPTER 9

A short break in the clouds allowed the moon to shed its light on the narrow stretch of water lying between the mainland and the dark mass of the island of Mona opposite. In places it was no wider than many of the rivers which Julius had seen before in his travels.

The sight of the clear sky, dimly lit by the moon, had been a welcome change from the continuously clouded skies which he had experienced since the army moved into this mountainous country. The last time he'd noticed the moon was on his ride back to the marching camp close to the Iceni settlement. Then, it had been high in the sky, a thin strip of silver barely visible in the half light of dusk.

He stared into its mysterious glow and realised that he'd lost track of the days which had passed since the night of the feast. The days had gone by without notice because so much had happened as the army journeyed those many miles to the outer limits of the Province. He reflected on those hectic days while walking slowly back from the headland where he'd been gazing out across the calm waters of the sea.

With Paulinus and a large cavalry escort, he'd ridden ahead of the 20th Legion from Camulodunum to the fort at Viroconium where the 14th Legion was stationed. He thought of the awesome sight of those thousands of legionaries from the combined Legions marching out of that fort later, heading north to Mona. He had considered it the most thrilling moment of his life so far. Looking at Paulinus he had seen in his face the same exhilaration he himself was feeling. The difference was that the Governor, in his long military career, had done this many times before. It seemed to Julius that a true soldier must never lose so strong a feeling of power and excitement. One day he promised himself he would have his own army to lead in his search for the same glory the coming battles would surely bring to Paulinus.

Since their arrival at Mona, Julius had been occupied in working with the men and officers from the two Legions. They had begun to build the massive camp that would form the main base for the coming campaign against the island.

Making his way through the tents and fires of the camp he reached his own tent and entered to find several lamps had been lit and placed on his campaign box close to his simple camp bed. As a staff officer he merited these few luxuries together with the personal assistance of a young slave. He it was who had lit the lamps. He rose to his feet as Julius entered and with a wave of his arm directed the young man to retire to the sheepskins on the ground in the corner of the tent where he slept.

Lowering himself onto his bed, Julius extinguished the lamps and began to relax. Whilst his eyes adjusted to the darkness, he wondered if the moon's pale light still shone outside. His thoughts went back to the night two weeks ago in the Iceni camp and particularly to the time he had spent in the company of that irritating young woman.

The women he had experienced so far in his life had been from different parts of Roman society. There had been the occasional women in the brothels frequented by all soldiers. There had even been the slave women who had been offered to him for his pleasure from time to time by his wealthy friends. Those two groups of women were irrelevant and it was from the women from wealthy families that he would eventually choose a wife.

He couldn't recall anybody who had provoked his interest in the way she had. He was certain that part of her self-assured, opinionated manner was the result of her position in her tribe. From birth she would have led a relatively privileged life. She would have been educated to speak the language of the Greeks as well as his own, not unlike the women of Rome. Unlike them, however, she would have been taught the skills and attitudes necessary to be a warrior of her tribe. The fact that she was a female didn't matter to her people. It was an approach he found fascinating and alien at the same time. She would undoubtedly be a woman of great beauty in only a few more years.

What manner of woman did he wish to share his life with? There was great advantage in marrying a woman who could bring him a large dowry and influence in society through her family. Such a woman would have been taught the requirements of a good wife. Obedience, motherhood, management of the house and domestic slaves were all the skills necessary to enable a husband to fulfil his political and military ambitions.

He had met such women, and they were boring. What fun and challenges he could have each day with a woman like Linona. He would never be bored in her company. She would demand to be treated as an equal in all matters. What a silly thought he concluded. Such women were not made to be wives; consorts perhaps, but not wives.

His thoughts about Linona had made him restless. He wished the camp brothel had been higher on the list of priorities as the new fort was being created. He lay awake for some time before sleep eventually claimed him.

*

The meeting the following morning had been called in order for Paulinus to explain his strategy to invade Mona. It was attended by the two Legates commanding the Legions, their four senior tribunes, including Camillus of the 14th Legion, and Julius.

On the table before them lay a map which had been produced in preparation for the meeting. It showed the coastline of the mainland and the shores of Mona facing it. It covered several miles in both directions.

"Good morning, gentlemen," Paulinus began. "We all have a lot of other work to be getting on with so I won't take too long with this briefing. Keep your questions until I've finished what I have to say."

"The map we have been provided with is new to most of you. It's been drawn up in the last few days with the help of captured local tribesmen. Our own engineers have been making forays all along the coastline in both directions. As a result we have a good understanding of the depth of the offshore water and the strength of the tides. The ground on the island immediately opposite us is also well described."

"We can see that the stretch of water between the mainland and the island is only a narrow strip for some considerable distance in both directions, to the east and the west. What we have before us is very similar to a wide river crossing, with a few added complications. We shall approach it as such. We have carried out many crossings in the past under fire from an enemy, and can draw on the tactics we and others have used."

The eager group of officers were studying the map closely. Paulinus stood back for a while to allow the other more senior officers to absorb the details of the map.

"I shall continue, gentlemen. Our enemy will never have experienced an army our size assaulting their island. The leaders will be confident that we will have to cross at the narrowest point at low tide, and they will expect us to do it with our full force. It is, after all, how they fight their battles. They attack in large undisciplined numbers and try to overwhelm their opponents. We, unlike them, can be flexible. We can attack them in a number of ways. At first we shall confuse them, put other ideas in their minds to make them doubt their instincts. Then we shall go back to making them sure that the crossing will take place as they originally expected. That will be their undoing."

He turned first to Pontius Lubellus, the Legate commanding the 14th Legion, and his Senior Tribune Camillus Pecius.

"Some of the men from the 14th will survey the coastline to the west, taking boats with them to use in trial crossings. Legate Rufius Sempronius and Senior Tribune Lentullus Gratius will do the same in the east. Both Legions will make great display of our search in both directions for a crossing point. I want you to make several failed crossings in sight of the heathens. Lose a few boats and some men. Make them think we see too much difficulty in such a tactic. Then hide enough boats for our needs to carry out a later crossing before bringing the rest back in full view of our enemy. All the while I want you to decide on an actual place where we can cross with good numbers of men and horses in both the east and the west."

"When we are ready we will send men across at both these points to make their way back towards the centre on the opposite shore. Yes, our main thrust will be at the narrowest point in the centre but only as our two forces from the east and the west attack their flanks. I am ready for your questions, gentlemen."

Rufius was the first to react.

"The plan is brilliant, General. How long do we have to prepare the attack?"

"I think four days should see us ready, don't you think?"

No answer was expected and none followed.

"How is the command of the army to be divided?" Pontius asked.

"I shall command from the centre accompanied by you and Rufius. We shall be supported by my staff officers. The attack on the flanks will be led by Senior Tribunes Camillus and Lentullus."

Julius had observed quietly from the rear of the group as seniority demanded while other questions were dealt with. He could hold back no longer.

"General. I would like to be given the opportunity to take a field command in one of the three areas of the attack. Could I be granted a temporary assignment to one of the Legions?"

"What sort of question is that at this stage, Julius?" Paulinus asked. "You surprise me."

"It would give an opportunity for another tribune to gain experience as a staff officer if he exchanged with me for a short period."

He stared directly at Paulinus holding his breath. He wondered if he had overstepped the mark, chosen the wrong moment, angered the General with what he appeared to consider too trivial a request at such an important meeting.

Paulinus's eyes burnt into those of Julius's as he spoke to the others present.

"Any comment on the unprompted request from my staff officer, gentlemen?"

Nobody responded immediately. Julius began to think none of them had the courage to risk upsetting the General by taking up the request, without first knowing what the General thought. Then Camillus spoke.

"I think Tribune Agricola could prove an excellent addition to my command. I have a junior officer who would learn a great deal by providing the General with staff support."

"What do you say, Pontius?" Paulinus asked, his eyes still locked onto those of Julius. "It's your Legion after all."

"If the General feels the army and the assault would benefit from such an exchange I could have no objection, Sir," he replied cautiously.

"Let it be so then," Paulinus returned his attention to the map.

Julius could breathe normally again and exchanged a nod of the head with Camillus.

He now had a chance of glory thanks to this man. He was determined not to fail him.

"You all know my plans and I need not remind you how important it is that our own legionaries are kept as ignorant of them as our enemy across the water until we attack. Proceed and succeed!"

As the group left the tent Julius was told to remain behind by Paulinus.

"You choose the role of an ordinary front-line tribune to that of a staff officer alongside a mighty General in his moment of triumph. You disappoint me Julius. What have you to say for yourself?"

Julius hesitated before replying. Did the General mean what he was saying? Was he really disappointed? Julius thought not.

"I have learned a great deal in my time on your staff, General."

"And you have a lot more to learn yet."

"Indeed, Sir. In making my request I considered I needed to take an active part in this battle in order to prove myself worthy to continue by your side in the future."

"Go on."

"This will be the first battle and there will be others when we've taken the far bank. The druids will fight to protect their island with its sites sacred to them and their followers. With this extra experience I feel I will be able to give you better service in those future battles."

"Well spoken Julius, but I don't believe a word of it. You have a desire for glory and fame and you have an eye for the opportunity that could bring it. Still, I don't condemn you totally. At your age I was driven by the same ambition. Just don't get yourself killed. It would be a waste. Now go and prepare for glory."

Julius saluted and withdrew from the tent. Waiting for him was Tribune Camillus.

"Thank you for giving me the chance to join you," said Julius.

"No thanks are necessary."

"But why did you take such a risk without knowing how the

General would react?"

"Any junior staff officer, who has the courage and self-confidence to make such a request, asking a General to move him off his support staff on the eve of battle, won't fear a horde of screaming savages intent on splitting him from head to foot."

"I must admit there were moments when his eyes were burning into me that I didn't feel too brave."

"Nevertheless, I prefer such a man by my side rather than my young inexperienced officer who is only too eager to impress me. He'll carry messages for the General with great loyalty and daring."

"I agree he's likely to be more enthusiastic than I would be in that role."

"Come on, let's go and exchange ideas about what we do now."

Smiling broadly, he put his arm around Julius's shoulder and the two men headed for the 14th Legion's campaign tent.

*

Darkness had fallen on the eve of battle by the time the General had summoned his commanders to give them his final orders.

"They will expect us to cross at low tide and we shall not disappoint them. Tomorrow, low tide will happen during the morning. Let us keep their eyes and attention firmly on our centre. Let them see us preparing to cross."

He turned his attention to Camillus and Lentullus.

"The price we shall have to pay for victory will depend on your ability to bring your forces to the battle on the opposite shore by low tide. An attack from three directions will cause panic and flight in our enemies. The rear of their position is open and those who we can't slaughter will escape inland. Don't follow them! It's our first and only objective to secure the other shore so that the whole of our army can cross. We shall have plenty of opportunity to finish the task inland in the coming weeks. They've nowhere else to escape to from their island. Now, what are your final preparations for this night?"

He was looking at both senior tribunes but particularly Camillus.

"When we have your leave my men and those from the 20th Legion will move out silently in small groups," Camillus replied. "We shall move along the coast and wait for the dawn. The legionaries camped in the centre need to be a little noisier than usual in order to keep the attention of their sentries on the opposite shore while we're doing this. By the middle of the night our men will be in position, waiting for first light before we cross to the island. Then we'll make our way back along the opposite coastline to strike at the enemy's flanks. The next time you see us we'll be closing on the enemy facing you on the other shore."

"Excellent! And what about the centre?"

He turned to the two Legion Commanders who gave a summary of their deployment of the main central force of Legionaries and cavalry. They described how they proposed to get the army across the narrow strip of water to attack the druids and capture the far shore.

"I am pleased, gentlemen. Our plan has been put into operation efficiently so far. The whole of their forces appear to be gathered opposite our centre. I'm sure they are confident they can thrust us back. Let's teach those who survive the day what it means to resist Rome!"

He rose to his feet. His officers reacted by standing to attention to salute him. With a grand, exaggerated gesture he saluted in return. The assault on Mona had begun.

This time Julius had no intention of speaking at the meeting. His work with Camillus and Pontius during the past few days had produced a great deal of respect in him for both men. He was also in awe of Paulinus. The General had produced a battle plan for the assault and had inspired his commanders with a belief in it so strong that any suggestion of failure was unthinkable. He left the General's tent quickly following in the wake of his Legion Commander and Senior Tribune.

CHAPTER 10

It was a warm sunny day as Boudica and Linona rode into the land of the Trinovantes escorted by Olsar and 20 of his men. The suggestion to travel to the settlement of King Frigionus and Marac had appealed to Linona when her mother had first proposed it.

It was a while since her father had been taken ill. This had enabled him to make enough of a recovery to let him be seen going about the settlement, talking to his people. He had even carried out simple tasks which were suggested to him by the Elders. But any full recovery would take a long time.

Linona had been concerned at how much her father had aged in such a short time. She was very depressed but not surprised when he had taken to his bed again a few days ago. The need for the two families to talk had taken on a new urgency.

"We must finish these matters quickly, Linona," said Boudica.

"I agree, Mother."

"If Frigionus is agreeable there'll be an exchange of dowries. We'll grant Marac part of your father's estates. It's up to him and his father to declare his gift to you."

Linona wasn't concerning herself with any thoughts of dowries. Her mother's need for urgency was feeding her fears about her father's health.

"What has Bodran said about Father?"

"He fears he won't last until the return of winter."

Linona's face showed her pain at her mother's reply. She had expected as much but it still hurt to hear it confirmed.

"You must marry Marac as soon as arrangements can be made."

"I wouldn't object to marrying Marac tomorrow if it were possible. But why are you so keen for it to happen?"

"Your father has studied the ways of the Romans and he fears all his wealth and estates will be subject to taxation by them on his death. It's possible his wishes will be ignored and everything could be confiscated."

"But that's not acceptable. We've our own customs and ways of passing on our wealth to our children."

"We may have no choice."

"What do you mean?"

"If the Romans choose to attack us we are only one tribe. That man Paulinus made it clear that a kingdom which loses its king, without a male heir to succeed him, could cease to exist, becoming fully absorbed into their Province."

"But you are our Queen and would guide us as well as any man could."

Linona was very angry, partly because her mother and father hadn't previously mentioned these thoughts or involved her in their discussions.

"Even though I will be Queen and sole leader I won't be acceptable to the Romans. Women don't rule in Rome."

"Is there anything else I should know?"

"Since you ask me, there is more to tell you."

"Then please tell me."

"Your father considered that he might be able to manipulate events to get the Romans to accept and respect his wishes."

"What wishes exactly?"

"Firstly, if you are married, you and Marac might be acceptable to them as joint rulers of the tribe, bypassing myself. For that to be the case both of you would need to confirm your loyalty and friendship to the Emperor. You would have to commit to continue the working relationship your father has established with them."

"You said we might be acceptable. That's good of them."

"Secondly, your father has made a will in which he leaves half of his estate between you and Cailan, and the other half to Emperor Nero, an incentive to get them to accept."

"But that's monstrous. What do the Elders say? What does Bodran say? He normally advises my father on these matters."

"The Council as you might expect were split on this initially, but came to give your father's wishes their support."

"And Bodran?"

"Bodran thinks like you that it isn't acceptable to succumb to those he considers to be an unholy army of brutal savages. In addition he feels it will be an empty gesture doomed to failure."

Boudica's voice sounded depressed and weary to Linona, who realised her mother was against her father's plan. Even so, she knew her mother would remain loyal to her husband's wishes.

"I agree with Bodran," Linona said.

At the same time she realised what had happened on the night of the feast when she'd seen her mother talking to Paulinus.

"You were discussing the will with him that night, weren't you? What was said?"

"I was. You'll recall the mischievous questions by the tribune about the role of women in our society."

"That hateful man."

"My conversation with Paulinus touched on your father's will. I asked if he had looked at it and knew of its contents. It is after all in his possession at his headquarters."

"Had he?"

"He said he was aware of what your father wished to happen on his death. I pointed out to him that his predecessor had acknowledged the will. Not only that, he had placed his seal on it to show he was accepting its validity on behalf of the Emperor."

"What did he say to that?"

"He said his predecessor had no authority to do what he did and could have made an unfortunate mistake. He offered to do what he could to plead our case with the Emperor whenever the time to do so arrived."

"No wonder you were angry."

Boudica began to explain her assessment of what the future held for them.

"I realise now that Paulinus came to our feast for one thing and one thing only. He needed to know we weren't in a position to cause him any trouble. The Romans wish to conquer the vast lands and peoples of the north. We must make them feel it wouldn't be in their interest to have a rebellious people at both ends of their province. If that were to happen it would take many years to conquer the wild tribes in the north. This will allow us to bargain hard with this very ambitious man. With your marriage to Marac our bargaining position becomes much stronger."

"We must tell Marac all these things you've told me."

"Unfortunately Frigionus must also be told," Boudica added with a scowl.

"I can imagine his angry reaction to yet another example of Roman deceit and abuse of their power."

"We live in very dangerous times, Linona. Your father has been a wise man and he has protected us all for years. We've one thing in our favour that might get us peacefully through the coming years. They need our friendship more than your father's estate."

Linona was only half-listening. They would soon be reaching their destination and her thoughts and emotions were in turmoil.

*

"The last time I spoke to your husband I told him I thought he might be a fool. Now I'm sure he is."

Frigionus had listened in amazement to what Boudica had said.

"He's surrendering to the Romans what isn't his to give. The coward has no right to hand it willingly to these murderous savages."

"Please calm down, Father! You can see from the look on the faces of Boudica and Linona they don't agree with his actions."

Marac's interruption was an attempt to prevent him saying anything more he would regret later.

"He, like me, is only a guardian of his tribe's wealth. How can he do this?" Frigionus shouted.

"Sit down, please! Let's explore fully what they're telling us,"

Marac replied sharply. "We need careful consideration of the situation we find ourselves in. What we don't need is one of your wild tirades which you will be sorry for later. Linona and I need your wisdom and guidance not another display of your anger and hatred."

Frigionus stared angrily at his son. He muttered a few oaths before taking his seat again.

Linona had only met Marac in her own surroundings and he'd always been quiet, polite and respectful to his father. Here, in his own house, he showed that there was a different side to him. It was one she liked.

"Thank you, my King," Marac smiled, and bowed slightly towards him to show his gratitude and respect for the old man. He turned to speak to Boudica and Linona.

"I'm pleased you've been open and frank with us about the condition of Presutagus, and the difficulties you face with the Romans."

"You needed to know."

"What you've told us will make no difference to our plans. My family will provide the dowry which is expected for Linona and me to be married."

"Then we'll continue to make the necessary arrangements without waiting for my husband to recover," Boudica added.

"I want to talk privately with Linona. We have a lot to discuss," Marac added.

"You are a fortunate young woman, Linona," said a calmer Frigionus. "You're marrying a man fit to be a king."

"And Linona will be a Queen to match him," Boudica replied, taking hold of his hand. "Come with me, you old fool. Let's leave the young ones to talk about their future. Show me around your settlement. Your sister's cooking, I remember, is something very special."

*

"Can we forget everything surrounding us for a short while?" Marac began when they were alone. "Let's forget what duty requires of us and talk about what we want and need."

"Nothing would please me more. I feel I need to know much more about you. I like what I've seen, particularly today, but I still don't really know you yet."

"Thank you for liking me at least," he teased. "I for my part have wanted you from the first time I saw you two years ago. Yes, you were young but to me you were already a woman, a beautiful, proud woman."

He looked for her reaction to his words. She was showing none.

"Do I sound ridiculous?" he asked. "I've been practising these words for so long and yet they sounded less than natural, as if someone had told me what to say."

"And have they?"

She was teasing him now and she was enjoying it.

"No I swear to you," he said, taking her hand in his.

"I know, I know. I think your words were exciting. I have feelings for you as well and I think you are beautiful too."

She giggled nervously.

They moved tentatively to embrace and their arms held each other closely. Marac moved his head back and looked into her eyes before leaning in to kiss her gently on her lips. Then it was Linona's turn to lean her head back. Gazing into his eyes she returned his kiss. She brought her hand to the back of his head and forced his mouth onto hers.

They broke apart. She had startled both of them with her passionate response and they both laughed. Linona knew this was the man she would be happy to share her life with.

Holding hands they sat down and began to ask each other question after question before coming back eventually to their future together as leaders of their combined tribes.

"Do you think one day we will have to fight the Romans to remove them from our land, to send them back across the sea?" Linona asked. "It's what your father seems to think."

"My father is full of hate and understandably so. He was taken captive very early in their rape of our lands. He was released only when our people's will had been completely broken. Many of our warriors had either been killed or taken into captivity and forced to serve in their army in other lands."

"What happened to your mother?"

"My mother was similar to yours. She was a proud, strong leader amongst our people. She fought alongside my father and continued on her own after his capture. She died soon after our defeat. My father thinks she died of shame. I was only a small boy when it happened."

Linona saw the pain on his face and held him close.

"You haven't answered my question. Do you think we will fight them one day?"

"In my heart I hope not. Many would die. But I do think it will happen. If I'm correct and it does, we'll need both our tribes and perhaps the help of others. In the meantime, we must learn their ways of doing battle. Only then could we defeat them."

Linona listened to him with growing admiration. This man could one day be the great leader they needed.

Boudica returned without Frigionus, cutting short any more discussion. She stood in the doorway rather than enter the room.

"Have you finished getting to know each other better, then? We want you to come to join us. We think it's time we ate."

She turned and left, not waiting for their answer. Linona gave a shrug of her shoulders and a weak smile by way of an apology to Marac. She took a tight hold of his hand and they followed her mother out of the house.

CHAPTER 11

The druid-led army, anticipating that the assault would happen soon, had kept up a barrage of sound aimed at their enemy. Along the coast, some distance away, Julius sat in the forest amongst his men. He'd been given initial command of half the force. Camillus would cross the water first, followed closely by Julius and his men.

Julius rose to his feet and moved quietly amongst his legionaries, joking with the centurions. Some of the most battle-hardened amongst his men had managed to sleep. Others were nervously chattering, checking and rechecking their equipment.

Just as dawn was breaking he saw the moment to move out had arrived. Camillus and his men were creeping down to the shore, carrying the boats to take them across the water. The accompanying cavalry consisted of auxiliaries from Gaul experienced in swimming across rivers with their horses. His own men began to talk excitedly about what they could see before Julius quickly brought the noisy discussions to a halt. He watched Camillus and his men move silently across the water. Before long his own group lifted their boats and eased them into the night-black water. Like those before, they crossed unopposed.

*

It had been daylight for some time. Julius and Camillus had hidden the force of nearly 500 men in the woods behind the shoreline. The two men with their two senior centurions were discussing their position. The dilemma facing them needed some careful thought before a decision could be made.

Because they had been unopposed they would have time to reach their objective sooner than the plan demanded. If they left immediately and continued to make progress, meeting no resistance, they would arrive too early and the General's plan would become known and receive a setback. If they delayed their march, only to find their flanking approach had been discovered and a large force sent to deal with them, they could arrive too late at the battle.

Camillus sought the views of his three officers. He wasn't helped by the two centurions who were divided on what to do. One was for delay and the other in favour of marching immediately. He turned to Julius and asked him what his preference would be.

Julius didn't hesitate to stress the need to march.

"Please explain your reasons," said Camillus.

"We have no way of knowing if our crossing has already been observed. At this very moment an opposing force may be heading our way to find out what is happening."

"True."

"If it is, then the further away from our target the enemy meet us the harder it will be for us to overcome them and reach the General on time. If it isn't, and we get within one mile unopposed or unseen, we can pause and wait for the right moment to strike."

"Yes, but what if we're discovered later before we reach the main battle?" one of the centurions asked.

"If we are spotted much closer to the target and face a large force, then we stand and fight to the death. In doing so, we shall draw away from their centre many more who would oppose Paulinus. We would confuse their leaders and split their forces."

He stared at Camillus, looking for signs of agreement. He felt strongly that to delay could be a disastrous mistake. He was sure he had made it clear enough to him.

Camillus's studied expression appeared to show he was weighing his decision in the balance. He didn't need to rush it. He stared for a while across the calm water before deciding.

"Then there are three of us in favour of marching immediately."

He turned to the centurion who was in favour of delay, placing a hand on his shoulder.

"Your opinion, though it was different from mine, was truly valued. There've been other times in the past when we've not seen eye to eye, and you've been right."

"That's true, Sir."

"And there's no man I would rather have by my side, whether I'm right or wrong, as we go into battle."

Julius listened and considered he had much to learn from this man. All along, before he asked the other three for their opinions, he may have been intending to do what he had now decided upon. If he had, his tactic had worked. His question and the decision he made after they had responded, had bound all four of them together. Even the centurion who had dissented nodded his willing support. Camillus was also shrewd enough to realise Julius might put into words the reason to act now much better than he could himself. The thought that this could be the case pleased Julius.

"Move the men out quietly and send scouts ahead," Camillus ordered. "Our General is waiting for us."

*

From his position on higher ground behind his army Paulinus could view the barbarian enemy swarm as they were whipped into a frenzied state by their druid leaders. They were standing on the back of chariots to raise them above the crowds around them.

He was aware that low tide was still a short way off but he had been informed that the earlier crossings to the island had gone as planned. His men had been told to stand in silence and not to respond to the shouts and goading from across the narrow strip of water. Discipline was essential, particularly in men who may be about to walk to their deaths. It was discipline that would win the day despite the Army being considerably outnumbered.

His eyes moved over the scene and his attention was drawn to the left of the massed ranks opposite. The wild shouting and milling around had stopped in this area. The druid controlling those warriors massed there was talking to them in an agitated state. Immediately a section of the crowd moved off and left the battle scene. The druid remained and the rest of those near him once again took up their challenges to the opposing army.

Paulinus speculated about what could be happening. The 14th Legion must be about to meet resistance. Nothing of the kind had happened on the right so he decided he would continue to wait for the low tide.

*

Camillus and Julius had been warned by the scouts ahead that they had been discovered. They could expect an attack very soon. With Julius he had chosen some clear ground, arranging their men in ranks with the cavalry led by Julius to the rear. They didn't wait for too long. The first of the barbarians came out of the forest. The sight they met brought them to a halt. Eventually, when they had all arrived, they ran screeching without any apparent fear into the front ranks of the men of the 14th Legion.

The fight didn't last long but Julius had to admit to himself that the savages had shown suicidal courage. Perhaps the later battles would be long and hard.

When the fighting had stopped Camillus made certain his own wounded men were being cared for. The enemy wounded on the other hand were quickly dispatched.

"We can now expect to have a fight on our hands all the way to the main battle."

Camillus was again addressing his men.

"We must move quickly but with caution. Our enemy have shown great courage if not very much discipline in attack. Keep close formation as we move out. Look out for any possible ambush from our flanks."

It wasn't long before a second attack came. This time a more organised force had been sent to meet them. Camillus and Julius had been discussing their position as they rode ahead of their column. They had agreed they would soon be approaching the main concentration of the druid army.

The column halted as they came face to face with a large force of warriors standing in rows waiting for them to approach. Julius estimated their number at least matched their own this time. It appeared that they were intent on forming a barrier to protect their main army.

Camillus summoned the senior centurions to join Julius and himself.

"This time they won't charge us. They've formed a defensive line and it's up to us to break through if we are to meet the General. We shall form a wedge and go directly through their centre. Their flanks will fold around us. Then it will be up to Tribune Agricola with his cavalry to attack them on the flanks. They appear to have no horsemen of their own to help them. Take up your positions."

*

Julius, sitting astride his horse in front of his cavalry, was impatient to join the fight. But he knew the importance of patience and timing to maximise the devastation his horsemen could bring to the near-naked enemy opposing them. He watched as the legionaries moved off in a narrow tight column which broadened towards the rear. They had formed the wedge to punch through the enemy's lines.

The two opposing forces met and the pressure of the tight formation of legionaries, swords in one hand and shields in the other, pushed the middle of the enemy's ranks backwards. As anticipated, the flanks of the column of legionaries began to be attacked. The contact became static as the Roman shield wall was being held. It was time for Julius to act. He could see the right side of the column was faring the worst. He decided that was where he would strike first.

Leading the charge, he felt a thrill unlike any he had experienced before. He had no fear, only the overwhelming desire to take lives, to slash and thrust his way through the mass of savages ahead of him. As he reached the first of the warriors they turned in surprise to meet his sword.

The charge relieved the pressure on the Roman right as warrior after warrior fell to sword and lance. Julius was able to withdraw his force and move them to the other flank. This time the warriors were ready for them, watching and protecting their rear whilst continuing to press the Romans' flank. The impact on the warriors wasn't quite the same as the other side. The ferocious fighting raged on.

Julius, from his raised position on the back of his horse, became alarmed when he saw another group of warriors making their way to join onto the rear of their main force. He had to react quickly. With his horsemen he fought around to the rear to try to stop that happening.

*

Legate Pontius Lubellus had been watching the left of the far shore for any sign of the arrival of his legionaries led by Camillus.

What he had seen would have concerned him. A second larger group had moved away from the shoreline. The druid who had been directing them had headed into the centre of their main force to talk to the other leaders.

"Something is happening to our left, Sir. Camillus may be having a little difficulty joining the battle."

"I agree," replied Paulinus. "I feel the time has come to commit. The tide has still to fall a little more but we can't delay. Some of our men will just get a little wetter than they might like. Go to take command of your two Legions, gentlemen."

He waited until the two Legates had reached their positions before turning to his supporting staff officer.

"Give the signals and let us waste no more time."

The horns sounded and the boats were launched into the quiet waters in a long line. The boats were filled with men, leaving the rest of the legionaries and cavalry to enter the water behind them on foot. They held their shields high above their heads as the water in the deeper parts reached waist height. Slowly the waters became hidden as rank after rank of legionaries followed.

The wailing from the far shore reached a peak, accompanied by a variety of missiles raining down on the men in the water. Some of those in the lead began to succumb and sink below the waves.

Very soon the front ranks started to feel the ground beginning to rise again, allowing shields to be lowered and swords drawn. The boats kept close to those in the water to maintain one consistent line of attack.

Despite the difficulties being experienced, the men in the water were given heart by the hail of arrows and javelins coming from the men still on the shore behind them. More devastating to the enemy were the bolts that were being fired from the ranks of ballistas. They were proving crushingly accurate in taking out the leaders in the front line of the warriors on the opposite shore. In contrast to the heavily armoured legionaries the bravest warriors in the front ranks were totally naked.

The boats touched ground and the two armies clashed, hindered by the bodies of those who had already fallen. The shield wall was beginning to take shape and at first the legionaries made good progress inland. It didn't last. The continuous pressure from behind from both opposing armies caused the battle line to form and remain static for some time.

The stalemate continued and needed to be broken. It was. From the right the men from the 20th Legion appeared. Giving a mighty yell they joined the battle. The druid army was faced with attacks on two sides. At first they fell back on the right but then adjusted their numbers so that they were able to hold the attack by the 20th Legion.

"Now, Camillus, now! Where are you?" Paulinus was speaking softly to himself. "We need you now and the day will be ours."

His quiet plea went unanswered.

He continued to study the fighting, particularly where the druids were active and directing the action. He signalled to two of the nearest staff officers to approach him.

"Ride to the officers commanding the ballistas in each Legion and tell them to concentrate their bolts on those druids who are directing the fighting. Do you see them? There, and more over there. They're near the limit of the range of the ballistas, but they must take them out."

He pointed across the water and the two men confirmed they could see the targets. They saluted and rode off to take the message.

"That will give the heathens something from the heavens to take note of," he said to Pontius and Rufius.

Looking back to the battle his smile broadened considerably.

"And that will give them something else to think about." He was pointing to the left of the far shore where the men from the 14th Legion had begun to appear, locked in hand-to-hand fighting. Gradually they were forcing the enemy to fall back.

"Now we have them," said Paulinus. "Let's watch and learn how their commanders perform, if they can manage to avoid our gifts from the sky that is."

Whether it was the latest barrage that had begun to rain down on them or the realisation they weren't going to prevent the invasion of their island, the druids in the centre began to leave the battle. Only one remained to direct the start of an orderly withdrawal of their forces, preventing a mass retreat in panic.

Paulinus rose from his chair. With a last look across the water, he called for his horse. He turned to the staff officer nearest to him.

"I leave the rest of the battle to Rufius and Pontius. I shall inspect our new camp on Mona in the morning."

CHAPTER 12

"How many years have you served the Empire in the 14th Legion, Barus?"

Camillus's question was directed at a short stocky legionary who was trying hard to stand straight and tall, despite his bowed legs. The pain in his two broken ribs didn't help.

"18 years, Sir," came the clipped reply.

"And how many battles, large and small, have we fought and won together?"

"Too many to count, Sir," Barus answered, angling his head slightly and filling his lungs with pride.

"Then why at your age, man, are you getting into a knife fight with legionaries young enough to be your sons?"

Camillus had raised his voice to demonstrate his frustration with the man standing before him.

"I can explain if the General would allow."

"I'm not a General as you well know, so you can stop the flattery. Go ahead though. Let me hear what you say happened."

Camillus sighed and leant back in his chair. He glanced sideways to look at Julius, who had lowered his head to hide any uncontrolled grin which might escape.

"Well Sir, this is what happened. I'd been sent to the mainland to take an important message to the Legate of the 20th. On my return it was high tide and I found there was a delay in getting transport back across the water to the island. It's very busy down there."

"Keep talking."

"I will, Sir. Well, you know me. Do your duty and return to base. That's me. But this time I couldn't. I figured it would be some time before I could get a boat across. So I needed somewhere to wait."

"Come to the point Barus. I do have other work to attend to."

"I saw a group from the 20th playing dice. I thought it would be a good way to kill time. As it happened it was easy to win against those lads and they took exception. They began to insult me, my mother, the 14th and its officers including you, Sir. One thing led to another and I received a small flesh wound and one or two bruises, but it won't stop me carrying out normal duties, Sir."

"One of your better stories Barus and as usual I don't believe a word of it. If you only have a few cuts and bruises, and are ready for duty, you can go out on one of the outer perimeter patrols tonight followed by seven days latrine duties." Camillus waved him away.

"Thank you, Sir."

Barus let out a slow deep breath in relief, turned and marched swiftly out of the tent escorted by his centurion.

"You can see why the General has kept the two Legions apart since our victory. With the 20th staying on the mainland and the 14th here building a base camp on the island we keep the rivalries to a minimum. Can you imagine what Barus and his friends would get up to if we occupied a joint camp with the 20th for very long?"

Julius had arrived from the mainland and been invited to join Camillus in his tent just before Barus had been brought before them to start his lengthy attempt to keep his punishment a light one.

"All the same I wish I'd been there to see him carve up those men of the 20th if they were being free with their insults about our Legion," Julius replied.

"I am inclined to think like you, and I'm pleased to hear your support for 'our' Legion. I'm also glad to have the men of iron like Barus in my command. Enough of this though. What can I do for you? The General's staff officer, restored to his normal duties, isn't likely to be just paying us a casual visit. Is it a business call or is it personal."

"Both, I suppose. As you know the General and the two Legates have been drawing up plans for the movement out of this fort into the interior of the island. The General wishes to complete this campaign without delay."

"And you want to take an active part in that, I suspect?" Camillus said, grinning broadly.

"I feel I've only completed half the task in the invasion battle. I would like the experience of taking the rest of the island by your side rather than in the safety of the General's tent on the mainland. Opportunities such as this don't come too often."

"So what do you want with me, as if I couldn't guess?"

"It would help if you were to ask for me to join you again. I greatly admired your command of the men. I feel I can learn a great deal in the coming weeks."

"Please! No flattery. You sound like Barus. I'll speak to Pontius. With his support I think the General will agree, for a short spell at least. I think we could have some good sport hunting down those druids and their followers."

"Thanks. You're a good friend."

Camillus rose from his chair and asked Julius to sit in it.

"If its experience of leadership you're seeking, I've more legionaries just like Barus, waiting outside to receive my wise rulings on the various charges they face. The chair is yours."

"I don't know whether or not to thank you at this stage. I suppose it's a collection of thugs and scoundrels?"

"Maybe so, but you will recognise some of them as the men who fought with such courage by your side in the last battle, perhaps even saved your life. It will be interesting to see how you deal with them."

"How many men do we need for the night patrols?" Julius asked, lowering himself into the chair and asking the guard to show the next man in.

*

A few days later, early in the evening, a large force of legionaries led by Camillus had arrived in the territory held by the druids. Moving cautiously, they had made good progress marching throughout the day. The building of a temporary overnight marching fort had begun in readiness for the coming of night. Expecting attack at any time, the alarm was raised when a group of riders travelling at great speed approached from the direction of the main fort. Camillus recognised the lead rider. He was the young tribune who had temporarily exchanged places with Julius on the Governor's general staff. He came to a barely controlled halt, breathless and red faced in front of Camillus.

"Greetings, Tribune. The General has ordered me to return to duty with you and for Tribune Julius Agricola to return to his staff immediately."

"Did the General give you a reason?" asked Camillus before Julius could intervene and make comment.

"No Sir," he replied.

"It looks as if the General has had second thoughts about you having a further spell with the 14th. Take a small escort with you," Camillus said grasping Julius's arm in farewell. "I'm intrigued, as you must be. I hope we can fight together again before very long."

"It will happen. Of that I'm certain," said Julius, striding off to find his horse.

*

"I want you to undertake vital work for me."

Paulinus was pacing the floor of his temporary headquarters.

"I've just received word from Camulodunum that Presutagus is ill. He's taken to his bed and hasn't been seen by our spies for some time."

"That's not good news, Sir. How bad is he?"

"I don't know. Whatever state he's in, I'm concerned about the instability this will create amongst the Iceni. What do you think?"

"Obviously, things now will be less stable until we return, Sir. If the king dies his wife and daughter won't be as friendly to us as the King and could take advantage of our absence."

"That's for sure."

"But then again, they are realistic. The two of them know the weakness of their tribe. There's no urgent wish to fight us amongst their people. They know what they have to lose if they were to challenge us. They've seen what has happened to the Trinovantes."

Julius was pleased he'd been asked for his opinion, but this couldn't be the only reason for his urgent recall.

"I agree with your assessment. They do indeed know what they have to lose if they were to challenge us. But, unfortunately there are other matters to consider. I haven't told you about the King's will before, have I?"

"No, Sir."

"I had my reasons. Presutagus, with the assistance of my predecessor, Veranius, wrote a will in which he chose to leave half of his estate to his daughters on his death. The other half is to go to the Emperor."

"That cannot happen, surely. There's no male heir to Presutagus. The estate becomes the Emperor's in full. Your predecessor, if not Presutagus, would have been aware of that."

"Indeed he was and he knew that splitting it in two would not be acceptable to the Emperor, unless there were very special circumstances."

"It wouldn't be to the liking of the Iceni either."

"Agreed."

"Then why did he do it?"

"Veranius then, like me now, needed to contain the tribe through Presutagus. The King for his part needed to keep his people from any war which they couldn't win. I've seen the will which is kept securely by my staff in my headquarters. The document bears Veranius's seal indicating he gives his support to splitting the estate as Presutagus wishes."

"He had no authority to do that. Do you feel you're bound by it?"

"If I were back there with my full army the will wouldn't be an issue. We could crush any resistance and fully absorb the tribe into the Province as we have done with virtually every other tribe, large or small. But we're not there, which is why I need your talents."

"How can I be of service, Sir?" Julius asked, his interest and excitement increasing.

"I need you to return to Camulodunum as fast as you can. Use your recently acquired knowledge of their Queen and her people to bring calm. Buy us time. This will need to be done, particularly should Presutagus die. Let her know I'm on my way back, having achieved a crushing victory against a mighty force of warriors. Stress to her we have suffered very few losses to our own army, even gained many extra future auxiliaries captured from this island."

"When will you return, Sir?"

"I shall use both Legions to wipe out the druids. When that's done we will establish a garrison here. This should take me less than 14 days, at which time I shall start the march back. Nothing must happen with regard to the will until I return."

"I understand."

"Promise and do whatever you need to restrain and placate them. When I'm back we can deal with the death of the King, if it should happen soon afterwards. We would appoint a replacement king, generously donating to him some druid gold or Trinovanti land. Finally, we will gradually and peacefully absorb the tribe fully into the Province."

"I shall leave at dawn, Sir."

"Good. One more thing before you leave to plan your journey. Be very wary of that cunning fox, the Emperor's Procurator Catus Decianus. He's aware there's a will with a Governor's seal on it, but I've not let him have sight of it yet. Because of that seal he cannot see it without my permission. He won't act immediately without seeing what it says. Although he doesn't report to me directly he is wary of me. Tell him I am returning and because of the circumstances I will disclose the contents of the will to him on my return. Assure him I shall work with him to resolve any issues should Presutagus die in the near future. You must make him aware of the need for patience while I'm here with the army. Now go with all speed. Take with you whatever support you need to ensure your safe journey."

Julius gave Paulinus his firm salute and left. He was frustrated at the thought it would take him several days to make the journey, although he was full of self-satisfaction that the Governor should place such trust in him. He also regretted having to leave the 14th Legion at such an interesting and exciting time. It would be a long time perhaps before he could lead men into battle again alongside Camillus. His return home now rather than later did have one advantage. He would see Linona much sooner than he'd anticipated.

CHAPTER 13

The small, slightly built middle-aged man standing by her father's bed had been a big surprise to Linona. She had expected King Cadellin of the Catuvelauni to be a big, strong, threatening brute of a man. She had been taught that, as long as her people could remember, his tribe had been ruthless in their dealings with them and the smaller Trinovantes tribe. Since the Romans came, the Catuvelauni had been forced like the Iceni to live under Roman control.

Bodran had told her that unlike the Iceni they were abandoning their culture and beliefs, becoming 'Roman'. This was particularly true of those living with the Romans in the large town they called Verulamium.

When she had talked to Marac about the Catuvelauni he described his tribe's hatred for them. She learned of the pain and slaughter inflicted by them on the Trinovantes in the past.

Linona was standing on the opposite side of Presutagus's bed, holding on to his greying, almost lifeless hand. He was breathing quietly and shallowly, unaware of those present.

"Your father has been a wise leader. I fear his death will bring troubled times to all of us."

"Why should you think that?" Linona was having difficulty not showing her dislike of the little weasel who stood by the bed.

"The Romans will take the opportunity to increase their control over the Iceni. It's an opportunity they won't be able to resist. On the other hand we've learned there's great advantage to be gained in accepting the ways of the Romans rather than in resisting them."

"Why have you come here?"

Linona's patience had run out and she wanted this man to leave.

"I wished to pay my respects to a man I have greatly admired."

"But there's more, isn't there?" asked Boudica, who was standing behind her daughter.

"You're correct, Boudica. There is more. I've been made aware that you and many in your tribe are mindful to be less of a friend to the Romans when Presutagus dies."

"Really?"

"If an opportunity arises, then you might join with the Trinovantes in some adventure against them. It would be madness, bringing destruction upon all of you."

"You have been misled. When my husband dies we shall continue as an independent people living in peace with all our neighbours."

"I hear what you say. However, I'm here to tell you the Catuvelauni will not join you in any action against the Romans now or in the future."

"You've made your position very clear."

"We have a good prosperous life. We won't throw it away."

"I thank you for your visit to my husband. If he were able to, I'm sure he would thank you himself. I think it's perhaps best if we all leave him to sleep quietly in peace as he prepares to join the Gods."

She pointed deliberately to the door and gave a slight nod of her head towards it. This, together with the look she gave him, would leave him in no doubt his visit was over. Like her daughter her patience had run out and she was making it obvious to her guest.

Outside, the King couldn't resist a final parting comment when he had mounted his horse.

"Please pass on to King Frigionus the words I've spoken today. He, more than anyone, needs to listen to my words of caution."

CHAPTER 14

The document room was to Librarian Gamellus Tullius the most important room in the Governor's Palace. The whole of the palace took up one side of the Forum in the centre of Camulodunum. Gamellus knew that most rooms were larger than this. Others were certainly grander with marbled floors and elaborately decorated walls.

He didn't need any such things in this room. The concrete floor and stone walls were quite sufficient for the storage of the large number of the documents which the administration of the Province had generated since the conquest by the God Claudius.

Gamellus had obtained a junior position on the staff of the first Governor soon after the conquest. Since then he had served four others as they came and went, each one grateful for the service he provided. They were all ambitious men from the best families in Rome. He on the other hand had been born to a humble slave family in Gaul. Educated by his Roman master, he had been able to buy his freedom when still a young man.

Eventually, the loyal service he had given in the Province had been recognised and he had been appointed to the post of Librarian. His daily tasks now included the recording, sorting, storing and quite often the copying of documents covering all aspects of life in the Province.

These were simple tasks in the view of others, but not to him. It was vitally important they were carried out to the best of his abilities. Why, he wondered to himself, did young Gaius think of it differently?

Gaius was the youngest son of Tarquinius Marellus, a wealthy and influential landowner and trader from Londinium. His father's connections had led to Gaius being assigned to help Gamellus.

*

At this moment Gamellus was not in the library. He was lying awake in his bed. It was the middle of the night and he was thinking about that very decision to appoint Gaius. At first he had been grateful to be given the help he'd felt he needed so badly. Now he thought it had been a disaster. It was the worst thing that could have happened, and he didn't know what to do about it. He had soon discovered Gaius was a lazy, untidy youth who was apparently incapable of remembering anything he was told. He'd made it perfectly clear by his actions and the things he said that he hadn't the slightest interest in the work of a librarian.

The documents in the library filled the shelves covering the four walls of the room. Despite repeatedly explaining the system to be used in placing documents in the correct section of the shelving, Gamellus continued to find important documents in the wrong place. Only today he'd found that a report from the 2nd Legion to the staff officer in charge of troop replenishment had been put away in the section dealing with the 20th Legion. Tomorrow he would chastise the idiot again, even though he knew it would have little effect.

He took a decision. He would approach the Governor on his return from his campaign and request to have Gaius removed. In the meantime he would record in detail the dates and details of the errors which were being committed by him, highlighting the disastrous consequences that could result. This latest Governor had shown that he too shared an abhorrence of poor attention by staff in carrying out his instructions. He began to feel calmer now he'd found a solution. He rolled over onto his side and drifted off to sleep.

*

If Gamellus had been stressed the night before it was nothing compared with the turmoil of emotions the events of following day produced in him.

His day started like many others as he arrived at his post, except that he'd arrived a little later than normal. He allowed himself this one failure because there were two very acceptable reasons. Firstly, he had slept a little longer than he would normally because of his failure to get to sleep until the middle of the night, concerned as he was about Gaius. Secondly, he had felt in a good mood when he did wake up. It made him decide to go to bathe that morning, even though he wasn't due to go to the baths for another day or so. He doubted if his assistant had bathed for many days. On some days he smelt as if he'd ridden to his work on the back of a wet ox. He had made a mental note to add this to his list for the Governor.

By mid-morning he had been working steadily but Gaius still hadn't arrived. His concentration was broken by the sound of soldiers approaching his room along the corridor. However, it wasn't a soldier who entered the room first. His day started to go wrong from the moment he saw the Imperial Procurator, Catus Decianus, stride across his room to take a seat at Gaius's desk directly opposite him. As usual he was accompanied by his personal bodyguards, who took up positions both inside the room and outside in the corridor. Gamellus knew it was to prevent anybody else from entering the room whilst Decianus was there.

"Good morning, Gamellus. How are you today?" asked Decianus, showing his lack of any real interest in an answer by moving his gaze slowly along the shelves of documents.

"Good morning," Gamellus whispered.

."You look rather tired. I suspect the work you do is getting the better of you. I hear you were performing so badly they had to give you an assistant to help you to cope."

He looked at Gamellus's face to see what reaction his last remark had provoked.

Gamellus was trying hard not to allow this horrible man to upset him. He certainly wouldn't show it if he had. He made no reply as he tried hard to hold Decianus's gaze without looking away.

"And talking of your assistant, where is young Gaius? I should like to meet and speak to him again."

"I'm afraid I have no idea where he is. He hasn't arrived yet and may well not do so. It's not unusual for him to be very late or not to attend at all."

Gamellus was hoping that if Decianus was here to see Gaius, and if he could convince him he might not attend, it would be pointless to wait too long for him. He would quickly remove his repulsive bulk from his room.

"You sound agitated. Relax, man. He's probably recovering from a good night worshipping, giving offerings to the good God Bacchus. I'd like to think he was chasing women at one of the town's many brothels. In fact, just like you and I did at his age."

Decianus let out a little chuckle.

"Then again, thinking about it, perhaps not in your case. Certainly not the part about the women."

The guards by the door found this very amusing. One of them passed on Decianus's words to others in the corridor.

"Please state your business," demanded Gamellus indignantly. "I have a lot of work to do for the Governor."

The sound of raised voices in the corridor caused both men to pause. One of the guards in the corridor looked in at the door. He explained that a youth was trying to enter, claiming that he worked with the Librarian in this room.

"Of course he does," yelled Gamellus, "at least some of the time. Let him in at once, you oaf."

Decianus, laughing at these remarks, signalled his guard to stand aside. Gaius entered, his clothing even more untidy than usual after the rough handling by the men in the corridor. He smiled as he recognised the Procurator.

"Good morning young man," Decianus said, grasping Gaius's arm in welcome. "I hope you are well."

"Thank you, Sir," he replied, smiling smugly at Gamellus. "I am very well."

"I was dining only last evening with your father in Londinium." Decianus continued. "He certainly knows how to entertain his guests."

"I haven't seen him recently, myself."

"That's why he asked me to look in on you during my visit here today, and to pass on his best wishes to you. He's a fine man."

"I would be grateful if you would return my greetings to my father for me the next time you meet him."

"If you're here merely to see Gaius," Gamellus interrupted impatiently, "I will excuse myself and continue with my pressing workload."

"Hold fast, clerk. I have business with you also. You have a will here that I'm interested in."

"I can't just hand over such a document without the permission of the Governor or in some cases, a member of his staff," an indignant Gamellus replied.

"Don't be alarmed I have no intention of removing it from your care. I only want sight of it."

"Whose will do you want to see? When did the death occur and what's your interest in it? We may not have it here any longer."

"He hasn't died yet as far as I know, but it might happen soon. It's the will of the Iceni King Presutagus. I know it's kept in the Governor's Palace. Since this is where documents are stored, it's going to be in this room somewhere. I want to see it now."

"It is indeed here. It has been closed and sealed by both the King and by the former Governor Veranius."

"Good. Get it out for me."

"Those seals may only be broken by the present Governor and he is at the other end of the Province at his moment. I dare not release it to you."

"Yes I know all about that," Decianus said, showing his growing impatience. "But I have dealt with you enough in the past to know that you always retain a copy of every document you consider important just in case something unfortunate should happen to the original. That copy, which won't be sealed, is what I want."

"The copy, like the original, is still for the Governor's eyes only."

"That is only your opinion. I don't care what you say. I want to see the unsealed copy immediately, or I shall have you flogged until you let me have it. My patience is wearing very thin. You, like everybody else, know what sort of man I can be if I'm not given what I want. Where is the copy? Point out to me which shelf you keep it on."

Gamellus had started to tremble, clasping his hands together to stop them shaking.

"You wouldn't dare. I will repeat what I have said to you. The Governor has instructed me to let no man see or have knowledge of the content of the King's will."

Decianus slammed both fists fiercely down on the desk, his face growing a shade of imperial purple with rage. If he had intended to bluff this little man into complying with his wishes by hinting at violence, it hadn't worked.

He beckoned to his guards in the room. The use of violence, whether bluff or otherwise, was going to move a step closer. That was until Gaius spoke.

"Can I be of assistance, Sir? I know where the most important documents and their copies are kept."

"Keep talking, Gaius."

"They're contained in the large oak chests hidden under the Librarian's desk. The keys to the locks are kept on a cord hanging from his neck."

"Good man."

Decianus turned to Gamellus and put out his hand.

"I suspected you would be difficult, you silly little man. I knew Gaius would also be working in this little dungeon, available if I needed him."

"I can't let you have them."

"I will have those keys or they will be removed from your throat by my guard's sword. I must point out that he is a very clumsy man."

Gamellus was a loyal and stubborn man but one who lacked courage when faced with inevitable physical pain or humiliation. Fighting back the instinct to vomit caused by the terror he was feeling, he slowly met Decianus's demand. He removed the keys but couldn't bring himself to hand them to Decianus. Instead he placed them on his desk, head bowed.

"That was very wise of you. Now get out of my way."

He instructed his guards to withdraw the chests and place them on the desk. Eventually he found what he was looking for. He began to read through the copy.

"But this is preposterous. That imbecile Veranius had no right to put his seal of agreement to this laughable document."

He was talking to nobody in particular, merely thinking aloud.

"The Emperor will be very keen to speak to the former Governor about this. May the Gods help the stupid man."

Decianus read more of the document while continuing to speak his thoughts out loud.

"As I suspected the King has no male heirs. Needless to say he isn't a Roman. How could half his estate be left to his daughters in all seriousness?"

He looked briefly at Gaius.

"Thank you, young man."

He turned to look again at Gamellus. He had been pushed away from the desk by the guards and had slumped onto his knees in despair.

"You've just learnt a valuable lesson. It's futile to try to deny me anything I want. Although you were initially stupid in resisting me, I shall be sure to explain to the Governor how helpful you were. The Emperor would be very pleased with the support which you've given his Procurator today, even if you may have a problem with the Governor on his return. I'm sure Gaius will carry out your duties, should you be relieved of your post, even your head, for whatever reason in the future."

With a contemptuous grin on his face he rolled up the copy document. He made to throw it onto the ground in front of Gamellus, but hesitated momentarily. Instead he used it to tap him on the back of his neck in mock execution to emphasise his last comment. Only then did he cast the copy of the will aside. He turned and triumphantly marched out of the room, slapping the nearest guard on his shoulder.

It was some time before Gamellus rose from his knees to sit back in his chair. Gaius was completely ignoring him, standing in front of the shelves with his back to him.

"Go home," Gamellus whispered.

"I beg your pardon? I have work to do."

"Leave the building and go home," Gamellus screamed.

Gaius was so shocked by this sudden outburst he almost ran out of the room and down the corridor.

Gamellus locked his beloved scrolls in the protective chests before returning them to their place under his desk and placing the keys to them on his chair. Finally, he walked around his shelves, his hand lightly caressing the items stored there. He took one last look into the room before locking the door and moving slowly down the corridor, back hunched, arms hanging limply at his side.

CHAPTER 15

It was late in the evening when Julius entered Camulodunum. Although he felt exhausted from his long journey in the saddle he felt he needed to seek out the Governor's staff in the palace. The sooner he found out the disposition of the remainder of the 20th Legion which hadn't gone to Mona, the better he would feel. He was also interested in receiving a briefing on any build-up of tension in the surrounding tribes.

The most senior officer on duty was a fellow tribune who Julius knew well and liked.

Marius Lanatus spoke first.

"It's good to see you, Julius. You look as if you're in need of the bath house. Are the Legions and the Governor returning already?"

"They're not on their way just yet, Marius. I'll explain in a moment."

Julius had difficulty speaking, his throat dry from the dusty road.

"Before I go to bathe, I'd be your slave for life if you were to get me a large beaker of wine to wash away the rocks in my throat."

Having rested briefly and quenched his thirst, Julius began to brief Marius.

"The campaign's going well. Mona will be ours before very long. The Governor will be here soon, perhaps in a few weeks."

"Why have you returned before him? It's not like you to leave a fight, even when it's nearly over."

"That's true, but on this occasion the Governor has asked me to return to see if there's been any change in the humour of our native friends," Julius replied, anxious not to say any more than necessary.

"I thought the information we sent to him about Presutagus would shake things up in your camp."

"It certainly did. What's the latest news on his condition?"

"Nothing to add really from information we've received up to present. But if you want my view he won't last very long."

"Is it that bad?"

"We've been told that other tribal dignitaries have been paying visits to him and his family. To me it suggests the end is very near."

"If you're correct I must act quickly."

"Sure you must, but not tonight. Let's go to the bath house together and I'll tell you more about what's been happening. Afterwards we can have a meal. I'm sure you haven't eaten properly for days."

*

Julius was grateful to his friend for having insisted he rest. He was seated in the hot room to allow the steam to draw the sweat and aches from his body. He scraped away the moisture and dirt from his arms and legs, reminding him what a good way it was to relax and recover.

"Can you tell me if any of the Iceni tribesmen have been behaving differently since we left? Is there any build-up of tension amongst the hot-heads in anticipation of any major change?"

"Not because of the demise of the King. However, there is growing unrest amongst the Trinovantes in particular. It could easily be transmitted to the Iceni."

Marius's reply surprised Julius.

"Why should the Trinovantes become the source of any trouble when they've been quiet for years?"

"The Procurator has decided to take the opportunity, while the Governor is campaigning in the north, to raise taxes significantly for the people of Camulodunum."

"You are joking?"

"I'm afraid not. Faced with that, they've done what I might have expected."

"What exactly?"

"They've taken what they need from the Trinovantes to meet the new demands from Decianus. There have been killings amongst those who resisted and a few villages have been destroyed."

"But this is madness, particularly when the Governor is so far away. How many men remain in the 20th and where are they stationed?"

"There are less than 1,500 men. They're not the best either. Those were taken to Mona. They are spread out, stationed in the forts many miles to the north and west of Ratae, and almost half the way to Isca."

"What about retired legionaries?"

"Camulodunum has a lot of veterans. Decianus has offered them help from his large force of mercenaries if it's needed. I don't think the Trinovantes could cause any trouble which couldn't be contained by us."

"I'm not so much worried about the Trinovantes. It's the Iceni who would concern me if they chose to join their neighbours to demonstrate their objection to our rule."

"But they're unlikely to do that, aren't they? The history of the tribes suggests they dislike each other only slightly less than they hate us, as well you know."

"Perhaps," answered Julius, deciding to end the conversation there. "Come on; let's move to a cooler room."

*

The following morning Julius decided to speak to Magistrate Varus Gerrinus about the new taxes and the effect they were having on the citizens of the town. He knew Varus very well, considering him to be a capable man.

"We had no choice, Tribune. I understand your concern but we've become simple farmers since retiring. Many of us barely produce enough for our families. If the Emperor wants more from us we have to take it from elsewhere."

"Didn't you explain this to the Procurator?"

"Of course. He wasn't interested. We suggested he discuss his demands with the Governor first on his return, before insisting they were implemented. He flatly refused."

"Couldn't you have delayed things? You must have known the dangers we could be facing."

"We did know, but we had no choice. That man is very dangerous. He could do a great deal of harm to us. Our men are becoming very concerned. We are seasoned fighters and there are many of us, but we couldn't withstand a major revolt and attack on our own. The town doesn't have any defences built to protect it. I've reminded more than one Governor of this in the past. Finally, we're not as well armed these days as we once were."

"What do you want me to do for you?"

"Meet with the leech and get him to pull back with his tax demands."

"I give you my word I shall do what I can. Will you to do something for me in return?"

"I know what you are going to say."

"Ask your people to stop doing anything for the time being which will increase tension with the tribes."

"I'll see what I can do."

The two men clasped arms and Julius left for Londinium.

*

The smells from the river behind Londinium told Julius he would soon be arriving at his destination. The conversation the night before with Marius, followed by Varus, had made his visit to Decianus more urgent. It was also potentially very satisfying to have the opportunity to reprimand the pompous fool on behalf of the Governor. His actions had endangered the Province at a time when the Governor needed peace and subservience in the tribes in the south.

Londinium wasn't his favourite place in Britannia. The place had become a dirty, rat-infested port full of rogues and criminals. It had grown since the invasion to meet the requirement for a large amount of goods to be imported. It was also meeting the need to send out the produce from this rich land in return, satisfying the growing demand from Rome and the rest of the Empire.

It had attracted not only wealthy traders necessary for its development, but every sort of adventurer and rogue out to make his fortune. It was no surprise to Julius that Decianus had established his headquarters and his force of mercenaries here.

The large two-storey wooden building close to the waterfront housed Decianus in luxury. His private quarters were furnished with the best quality furniture and cloth from Rome and Gaul. He had many slaves to provide for his every desire.

His proximity to the ships, unloading their goods onto the river bank, gave him and his tax gatherers the opportunity to inspect and confiscate any item which took their fancy. He was hated throughout the Province for this and other corrupt acts. Few dared to challenge his power and his easy abuse of it.

*

The flight of wooden steps led to the first floor of the Procurator's headquarters, which had been built high off the ground in order to combat the occasional flooding by the river. As Julius reached the top he was met by four of the largest soldiers he had ever confronted. The first one spoke to him in an accent which Julius recognised came from Germania.

"You have business here today?"

"I do indeed. Tell your master that Tribune Julius Agricola is here to see him on the instruction of the Governor of Britannia."

"You will wait here," the guard ordered.

Julius wasn't pleased to be kept waiting but he wasn't going to argue with these men. He still didn't object when the guard returned to tell him to stand and wait outside.

Some time had passed before a clerk came to the door and beckoned for Julius to follow him. He eased carefully past the guards and was taken to a brightly lit large reception room. It was a room arranged for business with only two desks and several chairs.

Decianus was seated behind the largest desk. His clerk returned to sit behind the other and began to write.

"Please take a seat, Tribune. You don't mind if my clerk records the main points of our conversation, do you? I feel it would help to improve our memories at some future date, should it be necessary."

Decianus gave a forced smile which quickly fell from his face.

"Not at all Procurator. I trust we're both honourable men with no fear of the truth."

Despite his remarks he wondered what interpretation might be placed on his words. He decided to be very careful in what he said.

"Please continue, Tribune. You appear to have something to say to me on behalf of Paulinus."

Decianus's smug grin let Julius know he was beginning to enjoy himself.

"I'm sure you will be pleased to hear that the Governor is in the process of completing the capture of Mona and the druid stronghold. He will have pacified more tribes and expanded the Province hundreds of miles northwards to the glory of Rome. The Emperor Nero will be very grateful to the Governor for expanding the Empire in his name."

Julius had rehearsed these words carefully on his ride from Camulodunum He wanted to begin by reminding Decianus of the greater standing and authority Paulinus's victory would bring him.

"Nice start."

Julius ignored him and continued.

"It's come to Paulinus's attention that the King of the Iceni is close to death."

"Poor thing."

"If his death occurs before he returns, Paulinus has given me the authority to take possession of the King's will. It has the seal of a previous Governor. It must only be broken by Paulinus. The contents will be made known to you immediately on his return regardless of whether the King is dead or not."

"Have you finished?"

"Until the Governor returns he wants you to assist him by not taking any action which could prove to be provocative in these difficult circumstances."

"Get off your high horse. Have you taken possession of the document yet?"

"The King is still alive. There's been no need."

"Any idea what it might contain, Julius? Heard any gossip or rumours?"

"I've no need to listen to gossip. Paulinus will tell me if and when it's necessary to know the details"

"I find listening to gossip very informative. For instance I heard the King had left half of his estate to his daughters. Silly piece of gossip on the face of it, don't you think?"

"I don't know what you're suggesting."

"Come, come, Tribune, enough of this sparring. Let's get to the point."

Decianus leant forward on his desk.

"I have read the contents of the will. Before you accuse me of breaking the Governor's seal, it was a copy, which fortunately hadn't been sealed. It was provided to me by the librarian in Camulodunum. The King's will has no legal standing. I shall demand the forfeit of the whole of his estate the moment he takes his last breath. You can inform Paulinus that I'm sure the Emperor will be delighted with this large addition to the Imperial Treasury, maybe as much as he will be by the capture of Mona. What do you say now?"

He leant back giving a little chuckle and a glance towards his clerk.

"Paulinus must be allowed to give his ruling on it before it's implemented."

"Who says so? Nero? I don't think so."

"If you act before then you will be going beyond your authority. The Governor has the final decision in situations such as this."

Julius was trying to control his temper and his distaste for this man.

"Quite the little lawyer, aren't you, you young fool. Do you think the Emperor would give it a moment's thought? He will be very grateful to me for giving him money which he needs urgently for his adventures in other lands. Paulinus will be told to concentrate on what he does best, killing barbarians."

Julius had heard and tolerated this man enough.

"You are more than a fool. You are an imbecile with the brains of a goat. If you go against the wishes of the King by disinheriting his widow and his family you will cause great offence and anger in his tribe."

"So what?"

"I'll tell you what. This, together with the unrest your raised taxes have created amongst the Trinovantes, could cause the two tribes to rise up against Rome. This is a time of great danger for the Province."

"Nonsense, the two tribes wouldn't dare. After all these years they don't have the courage for a fight. Some of their young bloods might start something, but with the legionaries of the 20th and if needed the 9th, the veterans at Camulodunum and my magnificent soldiers, we would easily crush any disturbance. We'll do the Governor's job for him."

"I warn you once more. It's the specific instruction of Paulinus that you don't act on the will without his involvement. I also want you to delay any tax increases for the people of Camulodunum."

"A compromise! I'll offer you a compromise. Since you have been appointed as Paulinus's representative in dealing with this issue, I will make you an offer."

"I'm not interested in a compromise," Julius countered.

"If the situation arises - the death of the King - I shall delay acting upon the will temporarily until I have first discussed it with you. That is, as long as you are available and time permits. Accept what I say and go before I withdraw my offer. As for the tax increases, they are entirely my decision and they stand."

Julius rose to leave.

"I'll speak to you later. If the King dies I shall hold you to your word. You will take no action before we meet again."

He turned and stormed out of the room.

"I shall be here in this room waiting for you when the time comes. Don't keep me waiting too long."

Decianus was shouting after him as he left, looking pleased at having the final say. He was making it clear that the insolent junior officer should come to him when the need arose, not the other way round.

*

The ride back to Camulodunum was difficult for Julius. He needed more information if he was to succeed in keeping control of events until Paulinus returned. He would spend a few days assessing for himself the strength of the 20th Legion. He had to see what force he could muster either to suppress any tribal disturbances or, if need be, to challenge Decianus and his mercenaries.

CHAPTER 16

The death of the King was not greeted by signs from the Gods signifying his passing away as some had expected. No darkening of the sky, no storms, no earthquake, nothing came to herald his departure from this life.

Presutagus had died peacefully in his sleep in the middle of a starlit night when the rest of his family and tribe were asleep. His wife and daughters and others who were close to him had sat and waited night after night feeling as helpless as anybody else would as they watched a loved one slowly fade away.

Only Boudica was still awake sitting patiently by his side, perhaps suspecting the end was near for him. She had seen death many times before, seen it take people away in many different ways. Sometimes it happened quietly and peacefully. Sometimes she had been there when death came violently, taking a screaming soul on its way into the afterlife. Few had been as fortunate to die as simply as Presutagus did. It was perhaps fitting that someone who had schemed for so long so that his tribe could live in peace, should himself die peacefully and without pain.

His last breath was long and slow and Boudica recognised what she had witnessed before in others. She placed his arms across his chest before returning to her own bed. She slept deeply for the rest of the night. To her nothing would have been gained by waking everybody just to tell them he had died. They would all find out when morning arrived.

The pained sobbing of her daughter woke her soon after dawn.

At first Cailan had been devastated by the thought that her father was soon to die. Later, his days of slowly dying had begun to make her face the inevitability of it. It still came as a sharp shock as she had quietly approached his bed so as not to disturb him. His face, pale the previous night, was a dark grey. She had leaned closer to him not wanting to accept the truth before she let out a short, sharp cry of pain.

Boudica came to her side, followed soon after by Linona.

"Cry, my child," Boudica said soothingly. "Let the Gods know that today they have in their presence a great and wise king who has guided his people through troubled times."

Linona stood behind the other two, her unblinking eyes staring at her father's corpse.

"He was a good man," Boudica added. "Perhaps the Gods have taken him to make way for a different leader who will prepare us for what is about to come."

They were the last words of tribute she would make about him to her daughters. They were words she would want them to remember.

Linona clasped her sister to her. They stood for a long time, both of them holding onto his cold hands for the last time.

*

Sometime later, Linona nestled her face into Marac's shoulder. Unlike her sister but like her mother she had no need of tears. The strong arms which held her gave her great comfort as they stood alone in her house.

Marac had ridden to be by her side as soon as a messenger had arrived with news of the King's death. He would stay with her until the final ceremony took place, when the funeral pyre would take her father's body from her.

He raised her face and very gently placed his lips on hers, letting them linger there, breathing her breath, trying to take her pain away.

"I don't know if I can bring wisdom and strength to my people in the way my father did, when the time comes."

In her sorrow and fatigue her emotions were confused. She was full of self-doubt.

"You're not alone. The Queen will take on many of your father's duties for a long time to come."

"I know she will."

"We'll soon be married, learning from others and from each other how together we must lead both our tribes."

She held on tightly for a moment and then broke away.

"As usual when we meet we seem to talk only of serious matters and never talk about the two of us and our future."

"Good. I'm pleased to see you smile again."

Marac spoke as he sat down in one of the chairs close to the doorway of her house. She, on the other hand, began to walk around the room.

"I've decided this will be our house. I haven't told Mother yet. Cailan can move into her house. There will be room and they'll give support to each other."

"Will Cailan want to sleep in a house and in a bed where her father died? I haven't known her for very long but can see she is a sensitive, gentle girl. She is suffering very badly at the moment."

"We're not talking of her moving in today. There will be some time for her to get used to the idea before we're married. In any case I'm sure our mother will make many changes to her house to make it easier for her by removing memories of my father."

"Are there any alternatives?"

"None which I can accept. So they will do as I ask."

She halted her pacing but continued to speak.

"What? What is it? Why are you looking at me like that?"

"Like what, your Royal Highness?"

"You have a silly smile on your face. Have you something you need to say?" she asked as she approached him and sat on his lap.

"We really don't know very much about each other, do we? What I've seen today pleases me. If we're going to defeat our persecutors we'll have to be strong and ruthless with our own people as well as our enemies."

"I'm used to getting my own way with everybody, and it will include you in the future."

They laughed and kissed again, this time more firmly.

"When will you tell them what you want to happen?"

"What do you want to happen?" Boudica asked as she entered the house, followed closely by Cailan.

"Oh! We were just talking about our wedding plans. There'll be plenty of time for that later," Linona answered hurriedly. "How are you feeling Cailan?"

"She'll be fine," Boudica answered for her daughter.

"Marac, it's good to see you and for you to come so quickly," said Cailan. Her speech was shaking despite her attempts to control her emotions as her mother had demanded.

"Yes, it is," added Boudica. "We've learnt of the losses your people have been suffering recently at the hands of those thieves from Camulodunum. They will be made good from the savings promised to my people by Suetonius Paulinus."

"Thank you. It will confirm to us the great friendship between our two tribes."

"I agree. Let's go to my house. I've summoned Bodran and the Elders to talk about the ceremony tomorrow."

CHAPTER 17

The quick summary which Marius had given to Julius had proved accurate. The remainder of the 20th Legion which Paulinus had left behind was too far away, too thinly spread protecting other areas, and it was made up of too few, not very inspiring legionaries. It wouldn't be able to respond quickly or effectively to control anything but the smallest insurrection by the Iceni.

Julius had spent several days riding the roads and visiting forts occupied by the 20th Legion. He'd also sent trusted officers to the Legates of the 2nd and 9th Legions to inform them of his assessment of the situation Paulinus would be facing and what the Governor was intending to do on his return.

With growing concern he'd returned to Verulamium to rest for the night before setting off again to visit Presutagus. If he was to send a full report to Paulinus he needed to see for himself the condition of the King and learn the mood of the tribes. He knew he wouldn't be welcome.

As he approached the Iceni settlement an ominous sound greeted him. When he'd passed the site of the temporary camp from the previous visit he became aware of the sound of many voices being carried towards him by the wind. Coming closer he identified the sorrowful sound of the voices of women wailing and shrieking in grief. He feared the worst but hoped he was wrong.

"Stay where you are! You and your men dismount immediately or you will die."

It was Olsar, guarding the entrance to the settlement. He appeared to be in no mood to spar with him in the way he was the last time they had met.

Julius did as he was told. He could see the gates were closed, probably because his unannounced approach had caused alarm.

"Why have you come on this day? And no lies this time. Your lives depend on it."

"We've learned that the King is gravely ill and I wish to express the concern of the Governor. I can offer the help of our best surgeons if they can be of assistance."

"We've no need of your butchers. Go while you still can."

"I want to speak to your Queen and her daughter directly," Julius responded more aggressively. "You know I speak with the authority of the Governor. I demand that you allow me passage through those gates."

The two men stood in silence staring at each other. Nobody else made a movement or a sound. Only some of the horses moved, circling as they cooled down after their long journey.

It was Olsar who finally made the first move. He whispered to the man next to him who turned and moved through the gates.

*

Linona came running into her mother's house.

"What's going on?" she asked. "Why all the commotion?"

"We have a troop of Roman cavalry at our gate," Boudica answered.

"How dare they ignore our time of mourning with their threatening appearance?"

"They are led by the tribune who was with Suetonius Paulinus. Olsar thinks he doesn't appear to know your father is dead."

"It must be a trick. Don't trust him, Mother."

"If it is, they will all die, including Paulinus's ambassador. Bring only the tribune to me," Boudica ordered.

Her instruction was carried out and Julius found himself walking behind Olsar, his arms held firmly by two men at his side. His weapons had been taken from him and left at the gate. Julius had calmed his men by surrendering his sword and knife immediately and willingly when demanded.

As he came into the square he saw the large funeral pyre with a tightly shrouded body on the top. Only the face was exposed, the face of Presutagus.

Julius lowered his head, not in respect but in despair. What he'd feared most had happened. It would take all his efforts to stop events getting out of control. He must get away as quickly as possible.

Boudica left her house to stand in front of her people. She was joined by Linona and a group of Elders. She signalled to the men to release their grasp on Julius.

"Why have you dared to bring your soldiers to this place on this day of all days?"

"I can assure you I was not aware until I entered the square that the King had died. Had I known I wouldn't have dreamt of disturbing your grief."

"He lies," Linona shouted.

Julius ignored her, focusing on Boudica.

"I came here today to see the King, to see what help we could give. The Governor has won a famous victory in the North and is returning with his army intact. He has sent me ahead of him to prepare for his return."

Julius kept his eyes on Boudica. He would need to be careful in any further explanation.

"I realise and understand the offence my innocent if badly timed visit has caused you and I shall withdraw immediately."

"You will withdraw if and when I say so. Your Governor will need to know that when he returns I shall expect him to honour promises which have been made regarding my husband's wishes."

"I understand what you are saying."

"Secondly, from this time on our relationship with Rome will be between equals. Can you understand that also?"

"I do."

"Do you feel you can communicate to him not only the content of what I've just said but the sense of outrage my people, and especially the Trinovantes, feel at the way we've all been treated in the past?"

"I think you know the trust that the Governor has in me. I will report to him truthfully and accurately what I've seen and what you've said today."

Julius finished his attempt at reassurance and waited patiently as Boudica considered his reply. She was taking her time, perhaps for the benefit of those surrounding her rather than for him.

"Go then and tell him I shall wait for his return. I will expect him to come here to see me without any delay."

She turned her back on him and led away those who were closest to her. Only Linona remained, staring at Julius.

"I shall look forward with interest to our next meeting," she said.

"As will I."

"You can be sure I'll be watching you and your General very closely in our dealings with you from now on. I don't trust either of you."

"Please believe me, Linona. I came only to give any help I could to your father. I hope you'll give me the opportunity to explain my actions to you at some future time."

Staring fiercely at him she made no reply. Turning slowly she went to join the others.

It was then that Julius saw the sword that she had been holding closely at her side. He wondered if she had really been on the point of using it. It was intriguing to realise this young woman continued to excite him. When this delicate situation had been resolved with the return of the army, he would have to do something about her. He would have to deal with the effect she had on him.

*

"Each time we meet, Roman, I come closer to killing you. Perhaps our next meeting will be when it happens finally."

Olsar was smiling slightly, but it was clear to Julius his words had a deadly sincerity about them.

"Maybe so, barbarian. It will be interesting, that's for sure."

Julius and his men mounted their horses and galloped down the slope, away from the settlement.

CHAPTER 18

Several days had passed since Gamellus Tullius had last attended to his duties. His young assistant Gaius had begun to tell friends that if Gamellus didn't return to his post soon he would be dismissed and he would be appointed in his place. He was, after all, the only other person who knew where everything was stored, or nearly everything.

This particular morning he was sitting at his desk leaning back in his chair, struggling to keep his eyes open. His head frequently dropped backwards as he drifted in and out of sleep.

"You! Librarian, wake up!"

The young man shot out of his chair to see a soldier leaning against the door frame, arms folded across his broad chest.

"I'm sorry, Sir. I was only resting my eyes."

"I've been standing here listening to you snoring as if your life depended on it. If I were to tell the Tribune it probably would."

"What can I do for you, Sir?"

"Get yourself upstairs to the Governor's office now. Do you hear me? NOW!"

Gaius ran in terror past the soldier, heading for the stairs.

"Tribune Agricola wants to ask you a few questions, lad. Better wake up and have your wits about you. If you have any, that is."

The soldier looked back into the room and stared at shelf after dusty shelf of documents. He continued to speak as if somebody else was in there to listen to him.

"How could anyone who considers himself to be a man, think being a librarian could be any use in conquering this land?"

He shook his head several times, closed the door and quickly made his way back to the Governor's office to wait for further orders.

"Tell me again what your name is."

Julius hadn't been listening the first time. He'd been wondering how such a young man could have achieved this post at his age.

"Gaius Tarquinius Marellus, Sir."

"And tell me what your father's name is? For you to have gained such a position at your age he must be a man with considerable influence."

"His name is Tarquinius Marellus. He's one of the richest traders and land owners in Londinium. He's a close friend of the Imperial Procurator Catus Decianus, Sir."

"I see. Indeed I do see. And how long have you held your post in the Governor's palace? I don't recall having seen you around before."

"I haven't been the assistant to Gamellus, the Librarian, for very long, Sir. In fact it's less than a year. But you can rely on me. I know where everything is kept."

"I'm sure you do. Now don't waste another moment of my time. Go and find your master and bring him here to me."

Although he was talking to Gaius, he was glaring at the soldier who had been sent to fetch the librarian not his assistant. The soldier for his part stood and stared straight ahead at a very small spot on the opposite wall.

"I can't, Sir," said Gaius, beginning to tremble with fear. "He hasn't been seen since the visit of the Procurator."

"What precisely do you mean by that?"

"He acted very strangely after his argument with the Procurator. He left his post as soon as Decianus had gone and hasn't been back. I've had to do the work of both of us."

"Were you present when this argument took place?"

"Yes Sir."

Julius softened his expression and lowered his voice.

"I'd heard that my good friend Catus Decianus had been insulted by a member of the staff here in this building. It's made me determined to find out the culprit. Sit down and tell me all about it. Would you like some refreshing cold goat's milk? Very good for a bright young brain I believe."

Julius smiled and sat forward in his seat to hear the full story.

A short time later Julius rose from his chair.

"So! Let me summarise what you've told me. It was you who told Decianus where those special documents which he sought were hidden, after the Librarian had refused. You let him know where Gamellus kept the keys. But for you, his refusal to obey the Procurator may have denied him sight of the document he was seeking. Unless, that is, Gamellus had been taken out and flogged to loosen his tongue."

"That's correct, Sir."

"Do you have the keys to the oak chests with you now and, if so, please give them to me?"

"Certainly, Sir."

Proudly he took the keys from around his neck and handed them to him.

"Soldier, take this sow's runt outside. Have him flogged and thrown out of the premises. When you've arranged that, return to the library and make sure the door is locked. Remain on guard there until you're relieved."

"Yes Sir," the soldier shouted.

With obvious pleasure he took a few steps to grab the youth by the back of his neck and march him out of the office.

Julius placed his cloak around his shoulders. At least he now knew for sure Decianus wasn't bluffing. He really had seen the will and knew of its contents. It explained his confidence and eagerness to act on it.

It was time to make another visit to Decianus's wooden palace in Londinium.

*

A long table had been placed in the centre of the private reception room. Two young female slaves, who were Decianus's companions, had set dishes for the midday meal upon it.

Decianus's role as Procurator gave him every opportunity to sample the produce imported through Londinium from all over the

Empire. Nevertheless, he liked to keep his midday meal simple and light, at least by his gluttonous standards.

To help him enjoy the meal he had invited two guests from amongst Londinium's wealthy traders. He'd decided they were in need of some encouragement to hand over taxes more promptly than had been the case in the past. They could of course persuade him to accept delays, even reductions, if they were prepared to make contributions to supplement his personal income as a poorly rewarded Imperial Procurator.

The morning's discussions had gone well for him, and he reacted with good humour when his senior clerk came into the room, bringing news that Tribune Julius Agricola had arrived and was downstairs demanding to see him.

"I thought he might return sooner rather than later. Send him up here to see me."

He turned to speak to his friends.

"I think you might enjoy this."

"Is he alone?" Julius asked, following the clerk upstairs.

"No, Sir. He's had guests with him most of the morning."

When Julius entered the room his eyes immediately took in the three men who were lying on couches around the room. On the floor, propped against the front of Decianus's couch, were two pretty young female slaves.

"Ah! Tribune Agricola. It's good of you to come to see me again. I was half expecting you this time."

Decianus was allowing his fingers to play casually with the long silky hair of the slave nearest to him. He chose to remain sprawled across the couch rather than to stand to greet Julius formally.

"I'm sure you were. I would have been surprised had you not been, given the circumstances we find ourselves in."

"It's not a social visit then?"

"Don't play games. We've important matters to discuss privately. Ask your guests to leave. I can see you've finished your meal."

"I'm sure we can conduct our discussion in front of my friends.

They can be discreet about whatever you may have to say to me."

"Get them out immediately or I shall throw them down the stairs myself. What we have to discuss will have grave consequences for us all."

He started to move towards the trader who was nearest to him.

The two men didn't wait for Decianus to reply. They knew of the reputation of the Governor's staff officer. They rose quickly not caring to wait to see if Decianus won the argument.

"We will leave you to it, Tribune," the one nearest to Julius said. "Ships will have been arriving all morning and our presence will be required by now. Thank you for the meal, Decianus."

They crossed the room, avoiding any eye contact with Julius as they passed by him. Julius was the first to speak when they had left the room.

"If you were expecting me you must have heard the news."

"If by that you mean the death of Presutagus, then obviously I have. Before you say anything more, you have no need to remind me of my commitment to you that I would not take any action until we met again. I have kept my word."

"Good. You get to live one more day, at least."

Decianus raised his eyebrows in surprise at this last comment, but chose to ignore it in his reply.

"So, here we are, meeting. What do you want to say?"

"I'm here to tell you I've spoken to Boudica and her mood, although hostile, hasn't yet reached crisis point. She's prepared to wait for the return of Paulinus so they can discuss the implementation of her husband's will."

"Is she indeed?"

"I remind you that Paulinus has ordered that there must be no action to confiscate any of the King's wealth until he returns."

Decianus pulled one of his slaves towards him and whispered to her. She rose and left the room. He got to his feet, with bits of food dropping to the floor from his crumpled clothing.

"And I shall remind you once again that I answer only to the

Emperor and not the Governor with regard to collecting revenues and taxes. The Emperor is in need of money to fund his campaigns in more important provinces than this grey land at the edge of the world."

Decianus was speaking quickly preventing any interruption.

"You're a young inexperienced junior officer who concerns himself too much with a wrongly imagined threat from those subservient, demoralised barbarians. They aren't capable of any major act of resistance."

"Whereas you are blinded by your greed and can't or won't see the great danger we could be facing."

"Even if they were to gain enough courage to cause us some trouble they would be crushed very quickly."

"Not if the two tribes join together against us," Julius insisted.

"I shall repeat what I told you when we met the last time. Altogether we could muster a formidable force. We don't need the entire Province's army. I'm sure Paulinus wouldn't be panicking as you are if he were here."

Picking up a large piece of cheese from the table he couldn't resist one further provocative remark.

"So, sit down, stop worrying and let's see how together we can proceed to seize what is rightfully the Emperor's."

"You are an ignorant fool. I suspect you are about to take an unnecessary gamble which could have terrible consequences. I won't allow you to roll those dice."

"And how do you propose to prevent me? By the way before you do anything foolish turn around and make way for Bestia and his men to join me."

In his fury and concentration on what was being said, Julius had not heard the approach of the slave girl accompanied by Bestia and three of his men. They moved from the doorway to stand by Decianus's couch.

"I shall repeat my instruction to you. Don't take any action before Paulinus returns."

"I'll tell you what I shall do for you in order to ease your sense of panic."

Decianus was grinning and obviously enjoying himself.

"I shall visit the family of the deceased to offer my condolences. I shall ask them to provide me with details of the full wealth and the estates held by the late King in readiness for your General's return. If they co-operate I shall delay my plans for acquiring it all. This will give your General the opportunity to make whatever case he may wish to me regarding the King's will. If he takes too long to get here my patience may run out."

"Such a visit would not be welcome and would be seen as extremely provocative. It must not take place. I warn you, you miserable clerk, if you cause any more trouble before the army's return and Romans die because of it, I shall eventually hold you to account. These pathetic mercenaries you employ won't save you then."

Julius remained motionless. He had said all he needed to. His unblinking eyes were fixed firmly on Decianus who gave a laugh, lowered his head and sank his teeth into the piece of cheese.

Julius managed to restrain himself and left. As his footsteps thundered down the hollow wooden stairs, Decianus spoke quietly to Bestia.

"We go to the Iceni settlement the day after tomorrow. Prepare to take a force with us from Camulodunum soon after dawn on that day. How many men can we raise to ride with us? I want to make a quick surprise visit, so we cannot afford to take foot soldiers."

Bestia thought for a few moments before replying.

"We have at least 150 of our own horsemen and we could easily double the number with volunteers from retired cavalrymen at Camulodunum."

"Make sure they can be trusted to do whatever is necessary."

"I'm sure they'll jump at the chance to teach the Iceni a lesson in respect as they have done with the Trinovantes."

"Then get as many volunteers as you can between now and when we ride. Do it quietly though. I don't want the Tribune, or anybody else for that matter, to become aware of the size of our force. Wait till the last moment to tell our men and the volunteers precisely where we are going, and make it very clear to all of them they answer only to y and me."

*

Julius had spent part of the morning after his visit to Londinium briefing Tribune Marius Lanatus about his meeting with Decianus.

"Do you think he will do what you want? He's not a man who normally has regard for anybody else's wishes or opinions."

"At best I have put enough doubt in his mind for him to hold off claiming the full estate until we are at full strength once again. If I'm wrong we shall need all the men we can bring together to keep control of the tribes."

"There may not be enough. Can't we do anything to contain him?"

"On my journey back I considered raising what force I could that would be strong enough to go back and arrest him."

"We could easily provide the men to do that."

"I've decided against it. I agree we are more than strong enough but he would put up fierce resistance with his large army of thugs. Many men would be lost, his and ours, men who may be needed. Such a battle between ourselves could also be seen as a weakness and an opportunity to attack us by those very same enemies we are trying to contain."

"I take your point."

"I've decided to ride to Lindum today to speak to the Legate of the 9th Legion. With his help I think we just might be able to hold back any force Boudica might raise."

"Agreed."

"She might just be wise enough to recognise what a formidable task it would then be for her to defeat us here in battle, or how many of her warriors she would lose if she could overcome us before meeting our main army."

"What are you going to ask that pompous Legate of the 9th to do? Quintus Petilius Cerialis Caesius Rufus - have I missed any of his names out? - is not a man to be instructed by a mere tribune. That includes you, even if you have the ear of the Governor."

"Thanks, but I know what he's like," replied Julius. "I shall merely ask him to place his Legion on the highest state of readiness and to come to Camulodunum when needed. Wish me good luck, my friend. I'll be back in three days at the latest."

CHAPTER 19

Bestia had spent his time effectively since arriving in Camulodunum. To add to his own men, he had recruited more than 160 local citizens who could provide their own mounts. He was able to give Decianus the large force he had promised. Unfortunately, this presented him with the difficult task of avoiding unwanted attention, particularly from Iceni spies.

His solution was to divide the men into six groups. These were to assemble just after dawn at different places inside and outside the town and head off in different directions. They would then circle round to ride north again, meeting up at a small settlement on the southern Iceni border.

Decianus, who had spent the night in Camulodunum headed south as if returning to his base in Londinium. He met Bestia who was waiting with a small group of riders, a short distance outside the town.

"By now we have 300 men riding north. It's time for us to join them?" Bestia suggested.

"Well done," Decianus replied. "I think we are going to have a rewarding day in more than one sense."

"We must ride hard to make up time on the other groups," Bestia added as he signalled to his men to move off.

*

The day had begun like any other for the families who lived in the settlement by the river-crossing marking the boundary between their land and that of the Iceni. For many years life there had been peaceful and prosperous, unlike that for those living nearer to Camulodunum. There would be no reason to suspect the horror which was to befall them this day.

Most of the people who lived in the settlement were in the fields and only a few, mainly women and children, were left to prepare for the market taking place the following day.

The children were doing what children did everywhere. The younger ones were playing noisily outside the houses. The older ones were reluctantly carrying out tasks for their mothers.

The first group of horsemen came thundering at a gallop from the darkness of the nearby forest. At first the people stood and stared in surprise before realising the danger fast approaching. When they did, they ran chaotically in panic. The first to die was a little girl trying to reach her mother. The leading horseman trampled her frail body into the dusty ground which had been her play area shortly before. One very old man who had been enjoying watching the children at play moved to try to help her, leaning heavily on his stick to steady his stumbling steps. He was cut down from behind before he could get to her, the blade cutting deeply into his shoulder and neck. His blood, cascading down, drenched the side of the horse of his executioner.

It wasn't long before all the rest of the terrified men, who were trying to escape the slaughter had met a similar fate. The women and children were spared. They were rounded up and put into one of the larger houses.

Being the first group to arrive had had some advantages. What little items of value the people had cherished were quickly looted. Some of the men amused themselves with the younger women and girls while they waited for the other groups to arrive. Fortunately for some of the women that wasn't too long.

Decianus and Bestia had been in the third group and were growing impatient by the time the last one arrived. The full sacks which were tied to some of the saddles of this last group showed why they had been delayed. The opportunity to loot other settlements on the way hadn't been missed.

Bestia moved to the leader of this group who had dismounted. He'd unfastened the sack from his saddle to show the rest of the men the booty inside.

He was struck to the ground by the fist of a furious Bestia. Standing astride him he took out his sword, holding it high for a moment. Reluctantly he lowered his arm slowly to his side.

"If I thought we might not need every man later today you would be meeting your Gods by now," he roared. "I told every one of you we have one task today and only one. You can all be certain that I'll kill the next man who forgets what I've said. Get on your horses. We need to ride. Now!"

*

Justig and Limris had been on duty at the main gates since just after dawn. They were waiting to be relieved to allow them to take some food. Before that could happen their attention was drawn to what appeared to be a small group of riders in the distance, heading towards the settlement.

"Can you see who they are?" Justig asked his companion.

"Not yet. They appear to be riding in formation, probably four abreast, which suggests they're Romans."

"I think you're right," Justig agreed. "We must warn Boudica."

"Hold on for a little while longer. We need to give her more information. Look! At first I thought there were only a few of them. Now I can see there's a large column of riders stretching back a long way."

Moving through the gates Justig called back to Limris.

"I'm not waiting any longer. Close these gates after me."

Decianus kept the column moving at a trot before slowing to a walk and then halting just a few paces short of Limris.

"Stand aside and open those gates," Decianus ordered. "I have come to talk with Boudica."

Limris made no response or movement. He was a tall heavily-built man and he had planted his feet wide apart to increase his massive appearance. He drew his sword and held it by his side. In his other hand he held a spear, one end firmly planted on the ground with the other pointing threateningly towards the horsemen.

"Did you hear what I said? I am the Imperial Procurator on official business. Nobody stands in my way to prevent me carrying out the Emperor's bidding and lives."

"I heard you," Limris said dismissively.

He raised his sword and pointed it directly at Decianus.

"I obey only my Queen. You will stay where you are until I'm told what she wants me to do with you. If you approach any further you will be the first to die."

His large body tensed as he spoke. It was as if he knew his words wouldn't be accepted and he was expecting to have to carry out his threat.

His tension was eased slightly when he heard the gates open behind him and he turned to see Justig coming out to address the Romans.

"I've spoken to our Queen. She demands to know why you are here and why you have brought so many riders. You will not be allowed to enter until you have answered those questions to her satisfaction."

He didn't get any answer. Bestia, seizing the opportunity presented by the half-open gates, dug both his heels into his horse and sped forward. He forced the slightly off-guard Limris against the timber wall to one side of the opening before he had time to respond. He fell senseless to the ground. Justig fared still worse. The rest of the column followed Bestia, surging through into the settlement. One of the riders pierced Justig in his side with his spear when he rode past. It caused him to stagger half a pace backwards. The next rider to pass finished him with a wide slashing blow of his sword to the top of his head.

Decianus moved forward slowly, letting the column go past him. He pointed at Limris.

"Seize that one and bring him with us."

The noise at the gates had been heard by Linona and Marac who had been alerted to the arrival of the column. They had taken up a position outside Boudica's house. Others were running into the square to join them. Some had managed to pick up weapons. However, since most of the men were in the fields there were only a few, probably 30, who were able to arm themselves. There was no sign of Boudica.

The square was filling quickly, mostly with Decianus's men. They surrounded those already there and prevented anybody else from entering.

Decianus moved his horse slowly through his men. Without any instruction they moved aside to give him an impressive honour guard as he approached Linona and Marac. Riding high in his saddle, he moved his head from side to side. It allowed him to glare menacingly at those Iceni who were being restrained and disarmed.

"I suspect, looking at the size of this house, I've reached the sumptuous palace of the dead King Presutagus," he said mockingly. "And if I'm not mistaken I would wager that you, young woman, are one of his offspring. Am I correct?"

"Who asks, and by what right do you force your way into the presence of Princess Linona and her people?" demanded Marac.

His face was flushed with anger.

"My, my. Is this any way to welcome guests into your little community? Before I answer any of your questions I would like to know who asks them so aggressively. What's your position in the tribe?"

"My name is Marac. I'm not from the Iceni tribe. I am Prince of the Trinovantes and an invited guest here. I ask you again. Who are you and what do you want? Have you been sent by Tribune Julius Agricola?"

Decianus laughed dismissively.

"If you aren't Iceni I have nothing more to say to you. So, you won't utter another word. Do you understand me, you insolent son of a dog."

Marac moved half a pace forward only to be stayed by Linona's hand on his arm.

"I am Linona, daughter of Queen Boudica and Princess of the Iceni. You will answer My questions."

"Now we're getting somewhere," said Decianus

"Who are you and what business brings you here uninvited? Even your leader, Suetonius Paulinus, had enough respect to seek an invitation from us before entering our settlement."

Her cool dignified manner and words caught everybody's attention, including Decianus. His expression, stern from his scornful comment to Marac, slowly softened. An easy smile accompanied his next words.

"Well spoken young lady. I will willingly reply to one who is as charming and beautiful as you. My name is Catus Decianus, as I explained to that insolent creature over there."

He pointed to Limris. He had been trapped between two horses with his arms bound behind his back.

"I am the Imperial Procurator for the Province of Britannia. The taxes and other contributions which you so generously make to the Empire are collected by my men."

"But why are you here today?"

"I've been ordered to come here by the Emperor Nero. I don't need an invitation from any king, queen, prince or even a beautiful princess. Do I need to say more or have you already guessed why I'm here?"

"Please carry on. Explain yourself and do it loud enough so that all my people can hear what you have to say."

"But of course. After all, what I have to say will affect all of you."

"Including me?"

Boudica's late appearance from her house had the intended effect, grabbing the attention of everybody in the square.

She had dressed to impress. Her long, short-sleeved grey gown reached to her ankles. It was gathered at her waist by a long red sash. On her shoulders she had draped a heavy dark blue cloak joined at her breast by a large jewelled brooch. Her right arm bore a large golden bracelet between her elbow and her shoulder. Around her neck she wore a large, heavy golden torc signifying that she was the rightful queen and leader of her tribe.

Her long red hair, which had been carefully combed, fell neatly around her shoulders and down her back, almost to her waist. Dressed as she was, it was apparent the visit of Decianus or some other Roman official had not come as a complete surprise to her.

She moved to stand alongside her daughter. Once there she turned to her right to signal to Bodran. He had been partially hidden in the crowd until then. He emerged to walk the few paces to take his place beside his Queen.

"What I have to say is especially for you if, as it appears, you are Boudica. And who might the old man be? Don't tell me he's one of those nasty druids."

"I am indeed Boudica and this is our guide and healer, Bodran. If you've something to say then do so. But first tell your men to release Limris."

"That man treated me with disrespect and I will keep him tied until we leave. I shall expect you to punish him severely for his behaviour towards the Emperor's representative."

"Never. He is a brave and loyal warrior and we have thousands just like him."

"Enough of these distractions. Let's get on with what I'm here for. My patience is wearing thin."

Decianus dismounted, quickly followed by Bestia and the men closest to them.

"I'm here to claim what is due to the Emperor on the death of King Presutagus. By the laws and traditions of Rome, the Emperor can..."

"What exactly are you trying to say?" interrupted Linona before he could say anything else. "Don't speak to us of Roman law. Tell us in simple terms what you intend to try to do."

"Roman law," Decianus continued, ignoring her comments, "requires estates of a king to be passed on to a male heir. Where there's no such heir the Emperor can confiscate the estate, if he so wishes. I'm correct in my understanding that Presutagus had no sons, aren't I?"

"And under Iceni law we don't distinguish between sons and daughters when estates are passed on," countered Linona. "My sister and I are the rightful heirs to our father's estate. We aren't part of your Rome or covered by your laws."

"You are very naive if you believe that, young lady. Your father was allowed to remain King by us. At any time we could have got rid of him and absorbed his tribe as we did with the Trinovantes. We chose not to. Don't let this fool you though. You are still as much a part of the Province of Britannia and under the rule of Rome as any of the other tribes."

"I've heard enough" said Boudica. "You and your men must leave immediately."

"Look around. I think you might have difficulty forcing us to go." Decianus replied scornfully.

"The things you've been talking about are to be discussed very soon. Tribune Julius Agricola has told me Paulinus is to return from the North shortly, intending to give consideration to my husband's will. There's nothing more to be said. Go."

"And I've spoken with Julius Agricola in the absence of the Governor. He accepts that my authority to levy taxes and confiscate estates comes directly from the Emperor."

That much was true. He then added what he knew was a lie but added weight to the point he was making.

"As Paulinus's military representative he has given me his support for my work here today in taking whatever action I see fit. So let's get down to business."

His remark about Agricola was enough to provoke Linona into taking action. It was a hasty move which she would have reason to regret for the rest of her life.

"I knew that man was deceiving us and so are you. You must leave now."

She drew her sword and moved towards Decianus.

She didn't have time to see Bestia move swiftly from her right and bring his fist sharply down on her forearm. The shock and pain forced her to drop her sword. His other arm circled her neck from behind, violently drawing her body against his.

Marac leapt to help her but Bestia used Linona as a shield. Marac's hesitation for fear of harming Linona was his undoing. He failed to anticipate the spear which was thrust from behind him by one of Bestia's men. It entered him below his shoulder blade and continued deeply into his upper body.

"No!"

Linona's cry was followed by her long piercing scream as she saw Marac fall bloodied and lifeless at her feet.

The mayhem which followed didn't last long. Decianus withdrew to the protection of some of his men. The rest disposed of anybody who attempted to come to the aid of the Queen and Linona.

Boudica and Bodran had been forced to their knees with their faces in the dust. Their arms were being forced upwards and backwards, making it impossible for them to move.

"Let Boudica stand up," Decianus ordered.

He moved to stand close to her as she regained her feet.

"I think we start our collection with these."

He removed her brooch and golden arm band. When his hands moved towards the golden torc around Boudica's throat she struggled in a vain attempt to stop him.

"I understand that this lets us all know you are Queen."

His hands tore it away from her.

"This is now mine and you are no longer Queen. Look, as I put it around my throat this will make me the new King of the Iceni."

He turned round to his men to show them. As their laughter died down he turned back to face her again, only to be met full in the face by a mouthful of Boudica's saliva.

The back of his hand instinctively hit her across the side of her face with such force she fell backwards into the arms of her captors.

"Strip her to her waist," screamed Decianus, "and bring all those of her miserable tribe who are here in the square to the front. They should have the best view when I punish this witch. Make sure every one of them watches what is about to happen. Get me a whip or rope, anything that will let me remove the skin from her back."

"What shall we do with the druid?" Bestia asked. "The old fool might try to start something."

"Strip this one naked and let him watch his Queen suffer. Let us see how much respect they retain with those who are watching after we've finished with them. And where is the other little Princess? Find her and bring her here to watch our spectacle."

The soldiers brought a cart from a side passage leading off the square and bound Boudica tightly to one of the wheels. As each stroke tore into her back Boudica winced but remained silent. Cailan who had been brought to the front was shaking violently and sobbing uncontrollably. Linona only stared in total shock and Bodran stood, head bowed in complete shame. The crowd reacted the same way sobbing and wailing in horror and disbelief.

By the time Decianus had had his fill he was breathing heavily and sweating profusely. Boudica had slumped to her knees, her back covered in her blood. He moved to Linona who was still being held by Bestia's arm tightly clasped round her neck.

"Still want to be the Queen like her?" he asked, a cruel smirk crossing his face.

He was so close to Linona the sweat moving down his face and onto his lips was being sprayed onto her as he spoke.

Her knee caught him in the crotch before he had time to move away, forcing him to his knees. Painfully he growled his next command.

"Strip her to her waist also. We shall teach her the same lesson as her mother."

The soldiers did as ordered and were moving her to the cart when Decianus stopped them.

"No wait. I have a better fate for her in a moment or two."

He moved to Boudica who had slumped to the ground. Her arms, still bound to the top of the wheel, prevented her from collapsing fully into the dust. He grabbed her hair and pulled her head back. It forced a pained groan to escape her gaping mouth. He kept hold of her as he shouted to the crowd.

"I'm not foolish enough to think that all of the King's wealth was left here following his death. We shall take what is still here today, returning later for the rest. I will take your precious Princesses with me to make sure you bring it to me. If you fail to do so I will crucify the pair of them in front of a cheering crowd in Camulodunum."

He let Boudica's head fall before moving back to Bestia and Linona. He spoke to Bestia, continuing to speak loudly for all to hear.

"I have a problem, however, do I not Bestia?"

"What's that, Sir?"

"It's against Roman law to execute a virgin. I must assume our

Princesses are still intact. If I'm correct in my belief we would have to make them ready for execution should it be necessary."

"There's one way to be sure," said Bestia with a broad grin.

"I agree. To spare their dignity," he joked, "take them into the Queen's hovel and put things right."

"If you insist in ordering me to do it, Sir," Bestia joked, "I shall just have to obey."

The two Princesses, too shocked and tightly held, were unable to resist. They were dragged into the house by Bestia and several of his willing men.

Decianus together with the rest of his men laughed and joked as screams from the house pierced the air. The Iceni stood in silence, their faces still showing pained disbelief at the tragedy that was befalling them.

Before long the soldiers began to emerge, Bestia coming out first. He was laughing as he comforted one of his men, his arm placed around his shoulder. The man's face was covered in blood.

"This fool let his face get too close to the mighty Princess Linona when he was performing his duty. She bit his ear off."

His remarks were greeted with laughter by Decianus and his men. Bestia caused them even more merriment by throwing the detached piece of ear into the crowd.

"Let this be an offering to your Gods," he cried.

A strip of cloth was tied tightly around the man's head to stem the flow of blood.

"Now go and find gold for the Emperor," Decianus shouted excitedly to his men.

*

As soon as the Romans had left the square taking Linona and Cailan with them, Boudica was released from the wheel. Supported by her two sobbing maidservants she was helped to move towards her house. Reaching the entrance she made them pause at the doorway before giving an instruction to those gathered around her.

"Send out riders to all our clan leaders and to Frigionus with a message describing what has happened here today. Summon them to come to see me first thing in the morning. I will have recovered by then. Tell them we have important decisions to make."

With great care she was taken into her house by her helpers to let Bodran begin to treat her wounds.

CHAPTER 20

Julius had met Petilius Cerialis, Legate of the 9th Legion, only twice before and then only briefly. Paulinus, he knew, considered him to be a fearless, if not tactically brilliant military man. As Tribune Lanatus had reminded him, he could be dismissive in his treatment of junior officers lacking experience. This resulted in the reputation he had for relying too much on his battle-hardened centurions.

This reputation didn't cause too much concern for Julius, despite the warning from Lanatus. He had a job to do and he would do and say whatever was necessary to impress upon Cerialis the important role that his Legion needed to play. His own position of staff officer to Paulinus should give him an advantage that other tribunes lacked.

Cerialis had been made aware of Julius's arrival. He had given instructions for him to bathe, eat and rest before reporting to him. It was something that Julius had appreciated after his long ride from Camulodunum.

It was a refreshed Julius, therefore, who approached the clerk seated outside the Legate's quarters.

"He is expecting you in his private office. Please follow me," said the clerk.

Julius entered a small room to see Cerialis working at his desk. He was thumbing through a series of documents making alterations to a number of them.

"Ah! Julius Agricola I think," said Cerialis, raising his head only briefly to acknowledge him before returning his gaze to the documents.

"Please take a seat. I've almost finished. Pour yourself some wine if you wish."

He pointed, with a casual wave of his hand, to the chair to the right of his desk.

Julius sat in silence for a while. It would have been understandable if he had begun to think that he was deliberately being kept waiting. However, Cerialis's concentration on the documents in front of him suggested otherwise. Eventually, he finished writing and moved the documents to one side. His clerk, who had remained in the room, moved forward and collected them before leaving the room.

"I had to finish a task which I do not relish, but one that I fear is necessary if my Legion is to function effectively," explained Cerialis apologetically. "I understand you have ridden hard to see me which means you have something important to say. Given the reported unrest in the south I'm not surprised. However, before you start, let me join you in a drink of wine."

Drink in hand he leaned back in his chair.

"You'll be interested to know that I was expecting a visit from you. The Governor wrote to me from Mona explaining that you've been sent back early to monitor the health of the King of the Iceni and the mood of his tribe. He's asked me to provide you with whatever assistance I can, although it seems to me that events have overtaken you with the death of Presutagus."

"Circumstances have certainly changed rapidly," Julius conceded.

"You should also know that he was very complementary about you. He described the role you played in a crucial part in the invasion of Mona. Before you leave you must describe to me Paulinus's strategy in the battle to gain a foothold on the island."

"I'll be pleased to do so, Sir. At the time that I was ordered back I'd have preferred to stay to continue with the campaign. However, with the way things are changing quickly here, I think we will all have a vital role to play in what is developing into a very dangerous situation."

Julius was beginning to relax more with the Legate, sitting more easily in his chair. Hearing Paulinus's favourable comments about him would have helped.

Cerialis on the other hand was showing increasing tension and concern at what he was hearing.

"Please tell me more."

He was given a full explanation of what had happened before

Paulinus left to go north and his plans at that time for dealing with any unrest he might experience in the tribes on his return. Julius went on to describe what he'd found on his own early return, stressing his concern at the role Decianus might play.

Cerialis listened intently, asking detailed questions throughout.

"And what then do you think the Iceni Queen and her tribe are capable of if she decides to challenge us?" he asked when Julius had finished his briefing.

"If they are contained until our army returns from the north then the answer to your question is that she would not pose a problem that couldn't be dealt with by our four combined Legions. However, if she is provoked into actions before the return then she could be very dangerous to us all."

Julius halted, giving Cerialis an opportunity to make a comment. None came.

"What is certain," Julius continued, "is that the 9th Legion will have a crucial part to play in what may follow. Apart from your Legion, we have only half of the 20th based in the area, although they would be supported by a mixture of the Procurator's mercenaries and the retired legionaries at Camulodunum. That amounts to less than 5000 men."

"Not a very inspiring group either," said Cerialis. "What action do you see Boudica taking if she's foolish enough to try?"

"There's every chance that the Iceni would be joined by the Trinovantes. As a combined force they are likely to make some sort of gesture involving perhaps a siege of Camulodunum. They might think this would give them an advantage in negotiating a new treaty and understanding with us to replace the one that we had with Presutagus. If she attempted to target the people of Camulodunum, the intervention of your Legion would be essential to defend the town."

"I thank you for your report," said Cerialis. "Your assessment is obviously the result of a great deal of thought. However, I think you may have overestimated the ability of the Iceni rabble to raise a force capable of defeating our legionaries. They've tried in the past and failed, and they will fail again. Nevertheless, I shall make preparations to be ready to move quickly if required. Keep me informed."

Julius appeared to be wanting to reply, but was prevented by Cerialis.

"I suggest you retire early tonight and rest here with us for a day or two. You appear to have spent a lot of time in the saddle in recent times. That will give us time to talk about Mona,"

"I will be pleased to accept your offer, Sir," Julius added, and rising to his feet he saluted and left.

Cerialis leaned back in his chair and stared thoughtfully at his desk.

CHAPTER 21

"I have asked my warriors to prepare to attack the Romans as soon as I return. They are ready to avenge the death of Marac. Will you join us?"

An agitated Frigionus was talking to Boudica. Although she would be in considerable pain, she didn't show any sign of it to the many who had come to her as requested. Filling her house, they included all her clan chiefs. Frigionus had brought his own war council with him.

"Not only will I join you, I shall lead both our tribes into battle."

A loud roar of support greeted her decision.

"I now know we have only one course of action open to us. I've much to say to you all. Please listen carefully so that you can carry my words to all our people."

"We must rid this land of these lying, murdering, barbaric animals. If you, Frigionus, or any amongst the rest of you here today, Iceni or Trinovanti, oppose me, or if any of you would prefer somebody else to lead you, you have the right to speak without fear, in the way our traditions allow."

Silence fell as she waited for any dissent. She chose not to wait very long before continuing.

"Good. Then we are united. My painful, sleepless night hasn't been wasted. I have decided what we must do. We shall attack those savages who live in Camulodunum. We must act quickly before their Legion at Lindum hears about our preparations for war and marches to their defence. We will destroy the town, killing them all before we go on to defeat Paulinus."

The united cries of support filled the room. It took a while before she could continue.

"Show them no mercy. Our Goddess Andraste will demand their blood when we ask her to give us victory."

Frigionus couldn't contain his own emotions any longer.

"We shall avenge all those sons, daughters, husbands and wives who have died at the hands of the Romans during these many years. We shall get the Corieltauvi and the Catuvelauni to join us. Later other tribes in the North and in the South will see our victories and rush to our side."

"I agree we would be stronger with the other tribes fighting alongside us," said Boudica, "but we can't rely on them in the beginning. The Corieltauvi have been greatly weakened, and fear the strength of the 9th Legion controlling them."

"There are still the Catuvelauni."

"They are led by their cowardly king who can't be relied upon. When we have won our first battle, he will have a decision to make. He can join us or get out of our way."

"He's only one man. His people will join us," an excited clan leader shouted.

"I don't think so. They have become too Roman. However, when we move to destroy their town, Verulamium, it's for them to see the error of their ways and join us to defeat Paulinus in battle. If not, they can go into hiding with their King."

Frigionus continued to let his views be known only this time his remarks were made more quietly and with deep emotion that got everybody's attention.

"I've already lost my beloved son Marac. Your daughters may still be alive, Boudica. Before we do anything else we have to negotiate to bring them back so they can join us in our fight? Linona must be given the right to avenge herself and Marac in battle."

"My daughters are lost."

"Why do you say that? Why have you given up hope for them so quickly?" demanded Frigionus.

"That monster Decianus would never release them alive. I only hope they are dead by now and no longer at his mercy. I am the mother of you all. Our two tribes are one. I fear I shall have to mourn the loss of many more of my children before we gain our victory. But we will be victorious. We have Andraste with us and she won't betray us."

She quickly quietened the ecstatic shouts of support to make more of her carefully considered plans known. Turning to Frigionus, she placed her hand on his shoulder.

"This is what we must do. You can attack immediately as you wish but it must not be an all-out assault at first. We need you to attack the Romans in their many small outlying homes and villages. Destroy as many as you can to strike fear and panic in the rest so that they seek safety in Camulodunum. Do you think you and your people will be able to hold back and control your desire to march on the town for the time being?"

"We will, but not for too long. If we're ready and strong enough we'll attack. I don't want to restrain my people's desire for blood."

"We understand, but our success in battle depends on attacking at the right time in overwhelming numbers. In that way we will kill them all but with fewer of our own dead and injured."

"We'll do as you ask."

"I trust you as a brother. I know you won't fail us."

She turned to talk to the rest of those in her house.

"The destruction of Camulodunum will send a message to Paulinus and his other Legions. It will tell them they will be defeated and slaughtered as they have done to many people of this land. Some of us will die but this time we will be fighting to be free. Our march to freedom starts today!"

She sat down, clearly exhausted by her efforts and the ordeal of the day before. Her maidservant brought her a drink to refresh her.

Bodran had been standing close to her throughout, maintaining a dignified silence. He had only to raise his hand for the frantic discussions which were taking place to cease and for everybody to give him their attention.

"You've heard our Queen. What she's had to say must be put into effect without any delay. However, there's a sacred duty we must perform before you all go to start your preparations for war. We must sacrifice to Andraste to ask her for victory."

A ripple of excited chatter spread throughout the room.

"She has already blessed us by providing us with those she wishes to be sacrificed. Some of those who brought their evil here yesterday were foolish enough to break their journey to rob and destroy some of our villages. We were able to capture two of them. They're waiting for us to release their spirits to Andraste. Let's not keep her waiting."

There was no uncontrolled uproar, rather a quiet anticipation of what was to happen.

Bodran, taking Boudica's arm, helped her to rise from her chair. He asked Frigionus to take her other arm. The three of them led the rest out of the house.

The people had gathered outside. Aware of what was happening inside the Queen's house, they were waiting for her to come out to give the call to war. Their waiting finally ended. Boudica and those with her emerged into the bright light of day. A shocked hush descended on those in the crowd when they saw their exhausted violated Queen walk falteringly to stand before them. Their silence didn't last long. The many emotions of sorrow, anger, grief and shame were given release in an enormous cry of support for her.

She responded by raising her sword defiantly above her head before lowering it slowly to her side, an unspoken signal for quiet to allow her to speak.

"My children," she began. "You've suffered long at the hands of the Romans despite the great efforts of our King to keep them out of our land. They have shown us what the future will bring now he's no longer here to protect you. They intend finally to enslave us just as they've done with every other tribe in this land. We shall not let that happen."

A roar like the challenge of a mighty ferocious wild animal greeted her remarks.

"They will feel the full force of our hatred and anger. We will drive them from our land forever."

Again there was a mighty roar. This time Boudica let it last for some time as she struggled against her pain and fatigue. She didn't need to say anything more about her plans. Her earlier words to her war council would soon reach their ears.

Finally she raised her sword once more to shout out her last defiant words to them. After each word she paused to allow it to be triumphantly echoed by the crowd.

"War! Victory! Freedom!"

She lowered her sword, letting Bodran move immediately in front of her to gain the attention of all those present.

"We cry to Andraste for her support. Bring them before me."

He was speaking to nobody in particular. He didn't need to. From the right two, naked men, hands bound behind them, were escorted into the square. They walked with difficulty, their arms and legs tethered like cattle and with ropes tied loosely round their necks. Their bodies, bruised and bloody, showed the treatment they had already received since their capture.

They were forced to their knees in front of Bodran, facing away from him and towards the crowd. The smaller of the two had begun to shake with fear. The other attempted to resist, showing his contempt for his captors.

"Andraste," Bodran began. "We ask for your protection in the battles to come. May our enemies tremble and panic at the sight of your mighty warriors. With the victory you will grant us we will bring you many sacrifices in the coming days to honour you. Our enemy is strong but not as strong as we are with you by our side. Fill their hearts with fear and horror of the pain and agony-filled death we will bring to them."

He stepped forward towards the smaller of the two men kneeling with his back to him. He took hold of his hair in one hand, forcing his head up and back. In his other hand he held a large knife which he placed against the man's exposed throat. He placed his knee firmly in the middle of the man's back.

"This sacrifice I bring to you in all humility."

He was looking skyward as he spoke. His hand drew the knife slowly across the man's trembling throat. A red trickle began to flow downward and over the man's chest.

"These Romans I give to you today are merely the first of many who will follow with our victory."

He continued, using a sawing action with his hand until the knife had done its work. The body fell forward onto the floor, the head still in Bodran's grasp. He held it aloft momentarily, to the delight of the crowd. Casting it onto the ground he moved behind the second man. Again he held him ready for his death.

"I ask one more thing of you today mighty Andraste. Grant us in victory the capture of those two leaders of our enemies who came to us on our feast day with their lies and false promises. If we take them alive we shall offer them up like these two wretches today. Their blood will be offered to you as an act of homage."

The crowd erupted in approval. Bodran swiftly disposed of the second man. The cheering lasted for some time before order was restored by Boudica.

"Bodran by these sacrifices has secured us victory. Go now to prepare for the fight."

She turned and withdrew, leaving behind an ecstatic people who were confident their Goddess was with them, and defeat in battle impossible.

CHAPTER 22

Julius was disappointed with the difficulty he'd met in getting Legate Cerialis to accept his analysis of the threat posed by the two tribes and the role to be played by the 9th Legion in the defence of Camulodunum. His journey back there from Lindum had been uneventful. In approaching the town he'd become aware of more than normal movement of people on the road, heading in the same direction.

Inside the town there was an air of urgency and disquiet amongst the people in the streets. Normally, the pace of citizens going about their usual activities was leisurely, the swell of bodies slowing even the most impatient. Today was different. Nobody appeared to be stopping to pass the time of day or to gaze at goods being sold by traders.

What he saw disturbed him. He began to suspect what the likely cause was, though he hoped he was wrong. As a soldier he had come to recognise fear in groups of people, almost smell it. That's what he could sense now.

He kicked his horse's flanks to ride through the ranks of people in his way. One young man was unfortunate not to see his approach in time to be able to jump to one side. He was knocked to the ground as the horse sped past. Julius thought little of any harm he may have caused, his thoughts being dominated solely by the danger they could all be facing.

Dismounting, he handed his horse to a sentry outside the Governor's headquarters. He had to force his way through the not inconsiderable crowd which was milling around the square in front of the building.

In the room being used by Marius as his public office, Julius could barely see him through the large gathering of citizens talking animatedly to the tribune and each other.

Marius caught sight of Julius and demanded silence from those filling the room.

"I need to talk with Tribune Agricola. You must all leave immediately. Guards, clear the room."

He turned to Varus and spoke to him quietly.

"Varus, would you please stay behind for a while? Your advice as Magistrate will be necessary, I need to discuss with Tribune Agricola the threat we're now facing."

It didn't take long for the guards to do as ordered. Julius took the opportunity to sink down into the nearest chair to rest from his journey.

"Please don't confirm what I suspect has happened," said Julius. "You're going to tell me the Trinovantes have finally found their courage and taken up arms against us."

Julius was moving his eyes between the two men eagerly awaiting an explanation.

"I wish that was the extent of our problem. You couldn't imagine what has actually happened," Marius replied.

He proceeded to relate the deeds of Decianus and his men in the whipping, the rape, the hostage taking and the subsequent triumphant horror inflicted by them, pillaging villages as they left Iceni land.

"Do you know what's happened to Linona and her sister since this outrage? Has he taken them with him to Londinium?" Julius asked carefully, hiding the panic beginning to grip him.

"The two sisters were brought to me by Decianus's centurion Bestia, who told me to place them under close guard."

"Where are they now? Take me to them immediately. They must be returned at once to their people."

Julius's mounting anger and agitation at the realisation of what Linona and her sister must have endured was causing him to pace around the room.

"Give me some credit, my friend. Even a simple tribune is able to recognise a catastrophically provocative act when it presents itself. I released them at once in front of Bestia."

"Did he try to stop you?"

"He saw my anger at what he and his band of thieves had done and didn't dare. He wouldn't have considered it worth risking his life over."

"What did you do with him?"

"I sent him back to Decianus, who had returned to Londinium by then, to tell him what I'd done. I also told him to tell the traitor I believe he could have brought disaster to us all and he would be held to account for his actions by Paulinus."

"What's happened since to the two Princesses?" asked Julius, returning to his seat.

"I sent them to their mother and their people in the slight hope that this would help to calm the situation. They had an escort back to their land and were handed over to the first members of their tribe they met."

"No wonder Paulinus places such faith in you," a relieved Julius offered. "We're going to need leaders like you when the storm which is heading our way eventually hits us."

Varus had listened to the two officers without comment, but he could hold back no longer.

"Given that the storm is almost upon us, Julius, what do you propose to do to ensure the safety of our citizens here and those farmers in the surrounding land?"

"What's been happening? Has there been trouble already?"

"We have reports of attacks and slaughter of our people in those farms furthest away from our protection. People are flooding into the town with rumours that the Trinovantes are moving to attack us."

"I've seen the crowds in the town. They're not much safer here at the moment, with your poor defences. They couldn't withstand an organised attack. Our plan must be a show of force outside the town, to make them think twice about attacking us too soon."

"I agree," said Marius. "We've more than a thousand men. In addition Decianus possibly has up to another thousand. The 9th Legion, thanks to you Julius, has been made aware of a possible uprising and would provide close to 5000 more."

"I, like Marius, have already sent a message to Decianus," Varus added. "Mine was to remind him of his promise and the need to send his men urgently to help us, particularly since it was his actions which has caused this trouble."

"We cannot rely on that mad man," said Julius, who began to take control and give instructions to the other two men.

"You, Varus, must bring order to this town and organise what defences you can. As of now every man not already a legionary of the 20th Legion is a volunteer under the overall command of Marius. This obviously includes you."

"That isn't a problem. Do you think we can hold out if the Iceni and Trinovantes join together to attack us?" Varus asked.

"If, as Marius has suggested, we can pull together something like those numbers, particularly with the 9th joining us, then we could just hold out for Paulinus, even without most of Decianus's men. The Iceni and Trinovantes have large numbers but they're not all warriors."

"That's true," Varus added. "They include farmers and women and children. The whole tribe will fight together in large numbers. It's their strength."

"It's also their weakness and one which we'll exploit," said Julius. "In comparison our men are all trained fighters and will be organised to fight and defend our position. The enemy must be persuaded that we are capable of holding on until the arrival of the Governor."

"What are you going to do, Julius?"

"I will be riding to Londinium to see Decianus. If I can resist the urge to have him crucified on the spot, I think I'll take him to the Iceni and try to convince them that what he did was not in the name of Rome. There's a chance Boudica, if not Frigionus, will think twice and hold back."

"What if they don't believe you?"

"That's why you're in command of our forces. If they don't believe me I'll be a dead man, but I may have bought us some more time."

"Time is what we need most," said Varus.

"Send a messenger to Paulinus to urge him to return as fast as he can, Marius. I would go myself to bring him back but I'll be otherwise engaged with Decianus."

Marius stood and moved to Julius placing his hands on his friend's shoulders.

"I will do that as soon as we've finished here, and I'll send for the 9th Legion to come immediately to defend us. May the Gods go with you. I'm sure the God Claudius will be watching over us to protect his town and temple."

"Let's hope so. I need an escort of 200 of your best horsemen. Decianus might not welcome my visit and certainly won't be willing to embark on the journey I've got planned for him."

All three men laughed briefly, though the weight of what lay ahead quickly ended their amusement.

*

The same air of hurried, fearful confusion he had left behind was evident once again to Julius as he rode into Londinium at the head of his escort. His group, although too small in number to bring about an end to their concern, received welcome smiles and greetings from those hurrying about their business.

This time when he climbed the steps to Decianus's house there were no guards outside the closed door to greet him. He took his sword and banged several times with the hilt.

After a short time the door opened slightly. The face of the clerk who had dealt with him on his last visit appeared in the space provided.

"I want to speak with Decianus urgently," Julius shouted sharply.

"He's not here. He has ..."

The clerk didn't have chance to finish his sentence. Julius, accompanied by a large group of his men with their swords drawn, thrust the door and the clerk to one side and marched past.

"Decianus, where are you hiding? We have things to discuss."

Julius was moving quickly up the stairs to the private rooms.

"You can't hide from me for ever."

The room where he had been received last time was empty and he found the rest of the house to be the same - abandoned in a state of disarray.

"Bring the clerk to me," Julius barked.

"I tried to tell you at the door," the clerk pleaded when he was dragged into the room to be thrown onto his knees in front of Julius.

"What were you trying to tell me?"

"Decianus is not here. He has left."

"Left! Explain yourself. Where has he gone? When will he return?"

"He's not coming back in the near future, Sir. I've been ordered to stay to look after his house and office until he eventually returns."

"I asked you where he's gone. Don't play games with me."

Julius's voice displayed his anger. His suspicion remained, that Decianus was attempting to deceive him by hiding somewhere in the house.

"He left on a ship for Gaul with some of his men. He's gone to report to the Emperor on the situation in the Province. He said he will return later."

"What situation are you referring to?"

"That the Governor has lost control of some of the tribes around Camulodunum caused by his prolonged campaign in the north. They have taken advantage of his absence and a rebellion has started."

"Is that what he told you?"

"Not only me, Sir. He has told the whole of Londinium."

"Where's Bestia? Has he gone with him?"

"No, no! Sir. Bestia is still here in the town even though many of his men have left. His house is very close by. He should be there now."

Julius went quiet for a few moments, pondering on his next moves.

"Centurion! Take half the men and bring Bestia to me. If he's reluctant to come you can tell him that because of Decianus's departure from Britannia he now reports to the Governor through me. Drag him here if necessary."

By the time his men returned with Bestia Julius had decided the course of action he must take. When Bestia entered the room Julius wasted no time.

"Your cowardly leader has fled and gone to Rome. Do you now recognise my authority over you and your men given the situation we face?"

Bestia continued his approach across the room coming to a halt before answering.

"Until Decianus returns it seems I have no choice, Tribune. I accept what you say, for the time being."

Bestia was not a man to be intimidated easily. He feared no man, not even one with the influence Julius obviously had with the Governor.

"You are a wise man. Still, you do indeed have other choices. You could choose death, or to spend the rest of your life on a slave ship."

"As I said, I have no other option at this time but to do as you order."

"Good. My orders are this. You will gather together as many of your men as you can and report to Tribune Marius Lanatus in Camulodunum. You'll assist him in the defence of the town. Should any of your men refuse to go, execute them. If you fail to do so I will do it for you and you shall join them. How many do you think you can take with you?"

"I'll be lucky if I can find 400. Many have taken the opportunity of the departure of Decianus to desert so that they can return to protect their families."

"Then get lucky as you describe it. Don't fail me. Now leave at once. You have an urgent journey to make."

Julius dismissed Bestia with a wave of his hand.

"One other thing, Bestia," Julius added, making him pause before he reached the door. "When our difficulties are over I will be taking time to find out what your role was in the outrages in the Iceni settlement. In the meantime I need you and the men you command to help defend this Province."

"If we both survive the coming battles I'm sure we'll have an interesting conversation," Bestia replied.

With a broad grin he left quickly before anything more could be said.

Julius fought back the urge to bring him back to resolve the matter there and then. He reluctantly allowed Bestia to live for the time being. He looked towards the centurion in charge of his escort.

"I'll stay the night in this place. In the morning gather the important leaders of this town together and bring them here. I want to tell them the truth about the uprising of the Trinovantes and the Iceni. When I've finished with them I want you to take control of as many of the legionaries based here that can be spared and return with them to Camulodunum."

"What about you, Sir? Where will you be going?" asked the centurion.

"I'm going to take a troop of some of your best men to escort me. I need to ride northwards to meet the Governor."

"I'll tell those in Camulodunum where you've gone."

"Report back immediately to Marius Lanatus when you get there and tell him everything that has happened here."

"I shall do as you order, Sir. May the Gods speed your horse and keep you safe."

*

Later that night, Julius, despite his exhaustion after the day's journey and events, got little sleep. His mind was in turmoil at what he had learned from Marius about the horror faced by Boudica, Linona and Cailan. He couldn't remove from his mind the sight, as he imagined it, of Linona being raped by those men. He knew she was a very strong woman, but she must have suffered a great deal. How much had her will been broken because of it? Her dislike of everything Roman, which was evident before, must have been turned into intense and raw hatred.

His last thought before drifting off into exhausted shallow sleep was of his own burning hatred for those involved in her shame. It must nearly match hers. He hoped the gods would spare them from the fighting ahead. He could then be responsible for their slow, tortured, painful deaths.

CHAPTER 23

Linona ran through the mass of people towards her mother. She was standing outside her tent in their temporary camp talking to some of the clan leaders. Breathlessly and with obvious excitement in her voice she forced out her words.

"They are coming to us! Coming to US!"

"Calm down! Who are?" Boudica asked.

"The Romans of the 9th Legion aren't going to Camulodunum as we've been led to believe. They're coming here."

"What do you mean, coming here?"

"The scouts we sent to observe them have reported back. We won't have to march later to try to prevent them from reaching Camulodunum or meet them in battle there. They are coming to attack us!"

Linona stared wide-eyed at her mother and the other clan chiefs.

"Are they indeed. Then they are trying to strike at our heart before we are ready and our numbers are still small. We mustn't wait for them to arrive," said Boudica.

She was speaking to all those who were surrounding her, not just her daughter. Typically, she had quickly assessed the situation and made her decisions.

"Pass the word on to everybody. Prepare to strike camp. We march to meet them immediately. Those who have still to arrive can be redirected to follow on to join us."

Frantic activity followed amongst the tents except those near Boudica's. She had ensured that all five clan chiefs of the Iceni had pitched close to her. They were the main part of her war council for the battles ahead. She had begun to discuss with them what tactics were to be used against the approaching Legion.

"We can't afford to let them choose the battle ground to wait for us to attack them. There will be many legionaries and horsemen."

"It would appear, from what the scouts have reported to me, that they've sent nearly a full legion," Olsar explained.

"If we allow a force that size to get close to us," Boudica continued, "they will choose their ground and get their heavy battle weapons in position. We would suffer many losses which we can't afford if we're to defeat the main Roman army in a later battle. Nor must we let them reduce our numbers only to retreat to Camulodunum to fight us again. It must be total victory on ground of our choosing."

"We all agree," said Elidar, Olsar's father. His was the second largest clan, smaller in number only to that of Boudica herself. "What do you propose we should do?"

"They must cross the river to the north-west of here. They will be most vulnerable there. That's where we shall surprise them and attack."

Boudica had to convince them all that her tactics were acceptable. Any dissent now would cause delay and confusion.

"There will be more than one crossing point," Elidar suggested. "How can you be sure of the place they will choose?"

Bederus, the chief of the north-western clan didn't wait for Boudica to reply.

"The river is ours and I know it well. There's only one place which their scouts and vanguard will choose in the short time available to them. It's a wide ford, and not too deep. It will allow such a large force as theirs to cross. They can do so without the use of boats, but it will be deep enough to make their crossing slow."

He looked directly at Elidar, a man with whom he had had differences in the past. He appeared to need convincing of the wisdom of the Queen's plan.

"However, to make sure, we can send horsemen to meet and draw their vanguard in the direction we wish, to that particular ford."

"I know the place" said Boudica. "The Romans used this crossing when they put down the last rebellion by our people many years ago. It has forests on either side of the river. Therefore, there isn't much cleared ground for a Legion to manoeuvre, particularly on the western bank of the river as they approach it."

The rest could see Boudica pausing for thought as she finalised her plans in her mind. She made her final decisions.

"We shall divide their force and fight them on either side of the river. To do this, we must allow them to begin their crossing, letting them think they can fight us on the eastern bank where we will appear to be waiting for them. When they've split their force while crossing the ford we shall attack their flanks from the forest on the western bank. That's enough discussion for now. We will complete our planning when we are there. Bederus you can lead us to the river."

The group broke up without another word being spoken, and the clan leaders headed to where their warriors waited to be told of the race to the river.

*

Boudica stood on the eastern bank of the river watching a small group of her own horsemen make a crossing to the other side The river was not at its fullest at this time of the year, but it still had enough water to reach more than half way up the legs of the horses. So, she could see that the water would be at least at knee height, possibly up to the waist of the legionaries, who would be making their way through it. This would make the movement of a large body of men through the water a slow one. Moments earlier, she had finished forming her plan of attack with the plan chiefs. They had withdrawn to prepare to carry out their allotted tasks.

After taking a final look up the road on the opposite bank she turned her war chariot to move to her chosen position for the coming ambush of the 9th Legion. On this side of the river a large area of open raised land had allowed Boudica to place a large force of her warriors in challenging view of the enemy. Standing there with Frigionus and Linona, the Romans would see her clearly and be drawn to their fate.

"Our revenge begins today, my daughter," Boudica said while climbing down from her chariot.

She took a few steps to stand in front of Linona, placing her hands firmly on her shoulders. She continued with her words of encouragement,

"It will not end today, but we shall have a sense of it. It will end when we spill the blood of Paulinus, Agricola and Decianus. Hopefully, we will have the chance to watch them die slowly at our hands."

"You can have Paulinus. I want Decianus and Agricola," Linona added coldly.

"As you wish," replied Boudica. "However, that's not going to happen for either of us in this fight. So, for now, you must stay with me on this bank. As the legionaries approach we shall parade before our warriors, exciting them for the battle and taunting our enemies. We'll let them see that you and I are ready and eager to do battle. They will not be able to resist their desire to capture or kill us and put an end to our bid for freedom."

"I agree. I will do as you ask, today," Linona spoke with a hint of potential future defiance in her voice that wouldn't have been missed by her mother.

"Those I hate most will not be here," she continued. "Even so, once the fighting begins you won't be able to prevent me from taking part sooner or later."

"Nor do I wish to. Andraste will protect you so that you can carry out her work."

*

The battle had not lasted very long. The 9th Legion had been caught as Boudica had planned, fording the river. Only the cavalry and a few of the legionaries had managed to escape. Slowly a temporary camp began to form on the banks of the river as bodies were removed and the ground cleared. Fires were lit and groups of excited but exhausted warriors gathered to exchange tales of the day's bravery. Many were more subdued, mourning the loss of family members and friends.

Boudica and Linona were alone, talking quietly. They were seated on the ground, staring into the soothing flames of a large fire.

"Marac and your father would have been proud of the way you fought today."

"Perhaps so, but after I had killed two or three of them I felt my hatred ease. I began to feel nothing."

"Well, it didn't show in the way you dealt with them."

"Still, I hope my hatred returns when we meet Paulinus, Decianus and Agricola I want to face all those animals who came to our home to violate us. I need to hate so that I can enjoy their slow deaths."

"It will return, my child. When you look into their eyes again it will return. In the meantime continue to fight like the she wolf you are. Tomorrow we begin the march to join Frigionus at Camulodunum."

Linona allowed herself to give one brief smile to her mother before lying down to find the comfort of sleep.

CHAPTER 24

The Army was approaching the regional headquarters for the western part of the Province in the large fort at Viroconium. The relentless torrential rain which had accompanied the legionaries in their march south through this stark, misty land had not only slowed progress, it had exhausted everybody. Rest would be needed before the next part of the journey home was undertaken.

Paulinus, riding at the head of the column, recognised the figure standing at the gates to the fort, but couldn't quite believe what his eyes were telling him. Though the rain was still heavy and the figure wore a large, heavy cloak for protection, there was no mistaking it was Julius Agricola.

"It's good to see you, Tribune, but why does your presence here fill me with such foreboding?" Paulinus asked, halting his horse and looking down at him.

"My news isn't good, Sir. So I'm sure you'd like me to tell it to you alone in the first instance. For now, all I would say is that I'm relieved you've already reached this far south."

"If we're to talk alone, I suggest we meet in the bathhouse within the next hour. I've ridden this poor animal for days in this incessant downpour. My old bones are in need of some warmth."

He didn't wait for a reply. He moved past Julius and on through the gates into the fort.

*

Paulinus had wasted little time in taking refreshment before making his way into the large sequence of baths. Having reached the hot room in the centre of the building, he'd sat down with his back against the wall, trying to relax and enjoy the heat as it cleansed and soothed his aching body.

Julius had delayed joining the General to allow him time to

recover, and for the heat to ease his pains and improve his mood.

"When did you arrive, Julius?"

Paulinus's curt manner in greeting him suggested there was still tension in the General as he waited for his report.

"Late yesterday afternoon. I was greeted by the fort commander with the welcome news that he'd been told to prepare for your arrival with the army today and tomorrow."

"What have you to report then? It can't be pleasing if it requires you to bring it personally."

Paulinus's face, bright red from the exposure to the weather of the last few days and the heat from the bathhouse, was taut with concern.

"As I said earlier, the news is not good I'm afraid."

Julius took his time to relate the events in Camulodunum and the Iceni settlement. As Julius expected, Paulinus didn't sit quietly while he gave him a complete summary of the events as they had unfolded. He repeatedly interrupted with questions and curses as the seriousness of what was being told weighed heavily upon him.

"Have you finished?"

"I have, Sir, as far as I know it. Obviously I don't know anything of what has happened since I left. I can only assume events will have moved forward. We can only hope that Marius, helped by the 9th Legion from Lindum, will contain them."

"Let's move into the cold room where I can cool my body and my temper."

Seated again he went back over the report until he had almost exhausted his questions.

"Finally, do you know why Tribune Marius Lanatus failed to prevent Decianus from gaining access to the King's will? Had he done his job Decianus wouldn't have had cause to move before my return?"

"I don't think Marius or his librarian had any choice. Decianus took advantage of your absence and in his arrogant, pompous way he ignored the protocol requiring him to approach Marius in your absence. He'll have known that Marius would have denied him any request to see the will without your permission. So he went straight to the library."

"You say Decianus has fled to Gaul. There's no doubt he's making his way to Rome to tell his lies to the Emperor. When this is over I shall have to counter those lies and see to it that he's put to death for his treachery."

"If he returns here from Gaul when we've restored order you'll have to place me in irons," countered Julius. "If you don't I will kill him with my bare hands before you have chance to place him on trial."

"Whatever. We are where we are. We need to eat and get some sleep. Tomorrow we'll meet again in the morning with our two Legates. We need to plan what we have to do to claw our way back into total control of our Province. Afterwards we must ensure this can never happen again."

*

"Good to see you, Sir. Congratulations on our successful campaign on Mona."

Julius was welcoming Legate Pontius Lubellus into the room where they were to be briefed by Paulinus.

"Thank you Julius," Pontius replied, "but your news has shattered any feelings of self-satisfaction I had because of our victory."

"Indeed," added Legate Sempronius as he joined them. "As you can imagine the news has spread amongst the ranks of the men who've already arrived from Mona. The mood of celebration has quickly evaporated."

"I hope Tribune Camillus has survived and is uninjured?" Julius enquired.

"He has indeed. Like you, Julius, he was born to be indestructible."

Pontius's answer caused all three of them to laugh briefly.

"He's asked me to send his regards. I was told to tell you he expects you to join him in his quarters later, bringing plenty of wine."

Their lightened mood soon disappeared as Paulinus entered the room. He walked briskly to sit in his chair which had been placed at the head of a large table.

"Take your seats, gentlemen," he commanded with a stern expression on his face. "We have much to discuss and time isn't our friend. I have a great deal to say. So, as you might expect, I want you to leave any comments until I've finished."

"For the sake of our discussion we must assume that Petilius Cerialis has reached Camulodunum. With the citizens of the town, they stand a chance, if a difficult one, of resisting any siege or attack the Trinovantes and Iceni can engineer. So, the sooner we can go to their aid the better. I've already given the matter some thought as you might expect. I've spoken to each of you individually to get your views on the condition of the army. This is what I've decided to do."

"Firstly, the 14th Legion will leave tomorrow and march to Verulamium. When you arrive you will have one of two courses of action to take. If you hear that Camulodunum still survives, you'll carry on without waiting for the 20th to join you. Alternatively, if you find it's too late to save that town you must wait for the 20th Legion to join you in order to defend Verulamium from any attack."

"Boudica will try to get Cadellin and his people to join her. Let it be known to the Iceni spies in the town that the rest of our army is coming. They need to believe we are expecting to do battle with her there. Cadellin won't join her, particularly if we get to him first."

"Sempronius, you will march to Verulamium also and follow the lead set by Pontius. You must leave here as soon as you're able, but no later than the day after tomorrow, to join the 14th."

"I will head to Londinium with a large force of our cavalry to see what support and strength I can gather to increase our numbers to withstand any attack there. I might also learn more of the size and intentions of our enemy. I've already sent a message to Cogidubnus, the King of the Atribates, asking him to meet me in Londinium. He's been our good friend for many years. He should be willing to supply men to swell the ranks of our auxiliaries when we finally meet Boudica in full battle. His lands to the south of Londinium contain many fighting men who would be willing to join us. Julius will come with me and I'll require Camillus to command my escort. Do you have any objection, Pontius?"

"None at all, Sir. However, is it wise for you not to be in command of our army at this time? You'll also be placing yourself in greater danger?"

"There's little danger from tribes between here and Londinium, particularly if I take enough of our cavalry," Paulinus answered dismissively. "Besides with Camillus on one side of me and Julius on the other, what barbarian would ever get close enough to harm me?"

The three men laughed at his joke but still looked less than convinced at this final part of the plan.

Paulinus moved to reassure them.

"My decision to leave you is also a measure of the confidence and trust which I have in you both to lead our men into battle as I would. In order to complete my plan we shall send our fastest horsemen to take a message to the 2nd Legion at Isca. They will be told to march immediately to join me at Londinium."

He stood up straight, indicating to them he had finished outlining his plans.

"Any questions, gentlemen?"

He paused only briefly.

"Good. Go to prepare your men. Give them the heart for the coming fight. Tell them we go to secure this Province for the Empire and Rome."

CHAPTER 25

Marius Lanatus had summoned Magistrate Varus and Bestia to join him in his office in the Provincial Headquarters. He had a document grasped in his shaking hands.

"I asked you to join me so that I can give you the grave news I've just received. I have here a document which bears the seal of the Legate of the 9th legion, Petilius Cerialis. I'll summarise for you what he tells me. Firstly he says that the 9th Legion was ambushed yesterday as it was coming to our aid."

"How could this happen?" interrupted Varus.

"He goes on to say the attack was led by Boudica and consisted of many thousands of her tribe. The Legion was attacked whilst fording a river in Iceni territory. Despite their courageous efforts a great number of the legionaries with him at the time have been lost."

He put the document down, looked up in despair and added his own comment.

"I estimate that perhaps 2000 men may have been killed, wounded or taken hostage, Varus."

"This is a disaster if you're right."

"He goes on to report that most of the cavalry and those legionaries who made it back to the nearest fort with him will return to Lindum to recover. They will maintain a presence there to prevent the tribesmen in that area from joining the revolt. He thinks he will still be able to do so despite his losses. We're no longer to expect any help from him in the defence of our town."

"What was he doing crossing a river anywhere close enough to the enemy?" asked a despairing Varus.

"As you'd expect, he doesn't say."

"It would make him vulnerable to attack. His route directly to us should have been well clear of any major river crossings, particularly in Iceni land. I'm amazed. He shouldn't have been anywhere near Boudica and any force she could have gathered to her by then," Varus argued. "How could he think any differently than to join us here as quickly as possible?"

"I don't know. Maybe we shall find out one day," answered Marius. "I suspect Legate Cerialis was on an adventure to try to defeat her on his own. The pompous fool would be trying to gain all the glory to further his political career when he returns to Rome."

"If what you say is true he is insane. He must have realised the great risk he was taking."

"Whatever his thinking was, it isn't relevant to the even more desperate position we now find ourselves in. We have to decide how our plans to defend the town need to be changed."

"There's no possibility of defending this town without the 9th Legion," argued Bestia. "We must evacuate the town immediately."

"And where would you advise us to flee to?" asked Varus scornfully. "Verulamium perhaps or Londinium? Neither town has a force large enough to protect us. Their defences aren't much better than ours either. In any case Boudica's horde could run us and our families down as we fled. No! We stay and we fight and somehow we hold on until Paulinus returns."

"I agree," said Marius. "We've a duty to stay and fight. The Governor would accept nothing less."

"You may have a duty. My men and I don't," replied Bestia. "Despite what Tribune Agricola would like to be the case, my men and I are mercenaries still, in the service of the Procurator. Some of my men who have homes and families here may stay and fight."

"And the rest?" Marius asked.

"Others like me will return to our families in Londinium and elsewhere to wait for and fight with Paulinus. I wish you good fortune, gentlemen, but you are wrong to stay here without the 9th for protection. You are going to die needlessly."

He rose from his chair and walked quickly from the room.

"Aren't you going to stop him?" asked Varus, who had also risen from his chair and appeared to be about to chase after and confront Bestia himself.

"Sit down, Varus," Marius said firmly. "He has reacted no differently from what I expected after the loss of the 9th Legion. I won't lose any of my men or yours in trying to stop his band of villains from fleeing."

Varus returned to his chair, his face displaying a mixture of anger and despair as he looked for guidance.

"What are we going to do?"

"We're on our own. So we must make this town as much of a fortress as we can. We must block the roads into the town with carts, furniture, anything at all which we can use as a shield against the attack."

"Work has already begun building a barrier but it will be very difficult to block all the gaps between the buildings all around the town."

"We must if we're going to have a chance. Don't let me delay you any longer. Go, and let's hope the Gods are watching over us."

The two men shook hands and Varus left to make his way back to spend time with his family.

*

Frigionus had finally come home after many years, although he hadn't yet reached the house where he'd been born. In his heart he had known the building would have long been destroyed, lying buried under the stone buildings of the Roman town.

He was kneeling with his hands on the ground in front of him, his forehead close to the earth. He had stopped by the side of a small stream which flowed through this little copse at the edge of what was once his family's land and home for generations.

Tears flowed freely down his face. He'd long ago resigned himself to the idea that he would die without ever returning to regain his home and his honour. Then the Gods had looked kindly upon him and he muttered his gratitude to them. By his side was his only surviving son, Morfan. With the death of Marac he would be expected to become his tribe's leader one day. At the moment, though, he was only 17 years old and still to prove himself to his father and the tribe.

Morfan had placed his arm awkwardly across his father's shoulders, appearing not to know how to react to his father's sobbing. He knelt down by his side trying to comfort him.

"Don't be alarmed, my son. You haven't seen me cry like a woman before and I dare say you never will again. I never thought I would live to see this day after the years of suffering and humiliation we've all had to endure."

He moved to his feet and faced his son.

"Do you remember this little wood and stream? You and Marac would play here every chance you got."

"I'm sorry father, but my memory of this place is very dim. I can remember Marac telling me stories of the demons that lived deep inside what to me was an enormous forest."

"I forget at times how young you were when we were forced from this land. It was Marac's favourite place in the entire world. I just wished to honour his memory here with you and to make a pledge to his spirit and the Gods. Never again as long as I live will a Roman set foot in this land of ours, once we have driven them out. Will you join me in making this vow, my son?"

"Willingly, father. Our people are rediscovering their pride and self-belief. After we've taken and destroyed this town they'll fight to the death to keep it."

"Well said. Come on, let's go back to join the rest in preparation for the destruction of these Romans and their town."

He placed his arm around his son's shoulder and the two men followed the stream as it broke out of the trees to flow into the green fields surrounding the town.

*

For the last few days many thousands of Trinovantes had been arriving from all parts of their tribal lands. They had camped in the fields within sight of the Roman buildings and eventually they encircled the town. Those citizens who hadn't fled had become besieged with no hope of escape.

Through the chaos of tents and carts a group of Iceni horsemen was being directed to Frigionus. They'd brought a message from Boudica which they were to deliver personally to the King.

"Queen Boudica sends her greetings to you, King of the Trinovantes. She is one day's march from here. She asks for your patience and for you to wait for her to arrive to join you in the attack on the Roman town."

"I hear what you say, but Boudica has already had the chance to strike the first blow, destroying one of their Legions. Now it's the turn of my people."

"What should I tell the Queen?"

"Tell her this. Iceni blood has already been spilt. Many have been sacrificed on our path to freedom. We demand the right to do the same, to rid us of those who've destroyed our homes and stolen our farms. We are ready and so our attack will begin today. The Queen can join the battle when she arrives."

"I'll leave immediately if you can provide me and my men with fresh horses. I will report what you've said."

When the messenger had left, Frigionus turned to those by his side and issued his final instructions.

"Ride back to your clans. Tell them we are going to attack. When I think enough time has passed for all of you to reach your positions I shall signal with a single blast of the horn. Let that signal be repeated throughout the camp so every one of those Romans will know death and destruction is coming."

*

Marius and Varus had climbed the steps of the Temple to give them the best view across the fields to the enemy's camp. They could see it completely encircling the town.

"You can see the defensive perimeter we've built around the town," said Varus.

"You've done well with what we have."

"But there are so many weak spots. I'm afraid we can't rely on it for too long."

"That's why my legionaries have built a second defensive line around the Temple. You must hold out for as long as you can and only fall behind this second line when you can hold them back no longer."

"Once we are behind the second line how long do you expect it to last?"

"Who can tell? But it must last as long as we need it to. Our last refuge will eventually be the Temple. It's a strong building and will hold those of us who have managed to survive their attack."

"That may not be many."

"My one hope is that Boudica will lose interest after a few days."

"Why should she, when she hates us so much?"

"Because a small group resisting is not important to her. She wishes to meet Paulinus and the army as soon as she can. She'll eventually continue her march north to meet him, leaving only a small force to besiege the temple and try to finish us."

"May the God Claudius look kindly upon us and protect us."

"How many citizens have you managed to get to man the defences?"

"I can't give you a number. Some fled the town when they saw Bestia and his men leaving. Most will have remained. Like me, they believe it's better to fight and die defending your home and family than to be slaughtered without a fight somewhere on the road to Verulamium or Londinium."

"And a fight to the death it could well be for all of us," added Marius. "I hope the Gods make Decianus rot forever in the next life."

Their conversation stopped abruptly as a single blast from a horn sounded in the distance. It was repeated by many more all around the town. The two men just looked at each other, realising no further exchange of words was needed. They knew the attack was about to start. They ran down the steps to take up their positions with their men.

*

Morfan had thought he would die from excitement as he stood beside his father, who was staring stone-faced towards the buildings in the distance. He was so tense that, even dressed as he was with only a loin cloth, he was bathed in sweat. The paint on his body ran down and soaked into the top of the cloth.

Morfan had watched his father give the signal for the start of the attack. It had been met by a thunderous cry from the people and a mass movement forward towards the town.

Despite the King's instructions to start slowly at first before gathering momentum gradually as they approached the defences, many began to run immediately. They were the young warriors like himself who were eager to show their bravery and readiness for the fight. He almost joined them in his excitement but his father's hand grasped his arm and kept him by his side.

"I've lost one son already. I don't want to lose another. Our tribe will need you in the future. There'll be many more days of battle for you to show your courage and fighting skills before we're finished."

Morfan obeyed his father reluctantly, the expression on his young face showing his frustration at not being able to join the battle alongside his friends.

Very quickly those who were leading the charge came up against the defences, such as they were. Many at the front were speared or run through with swords by those behind the barriers. However, their deaths didn't deter the mass of men and women pressing forward from behind them.

It didn't take long for the first breakthrough to occur and for it to be repeated all around the town. The fighting moved into the streets and before long the slaughter was taking place in virtually every building in the town except the Temple.

*

Towards the back of the headlong rush into the town a small, ragged-looking elderly man joined the attackers. His steps, in contrast to most of the others, were heavy and slow. Gamellus Tullius had shed his Roman clothes, and changed into those worn by the poorer tribesmen of the Trinovantes. He had chosen ill-fitting and threadbare clothing so as to appear to others to be a pathetic old man wishing to play his part in the assault.

He picked his way through the bodies and debris now filling the streets. He wasn't a brave man and his privileged role during all those years as Librarian had sheltered him. It hadn't prepared him for the unfolding horror of which he had now become a part.

The bodies which he saw at first were those of the young warriors and legionaries who had died in the initial attacks. As he climbed over them he heard the screams of women and children coming from further into the town. He moved forward and saw the horror of women being dragged from houses by their hair and cut down before him. As they fell they were set upon by men and women who mutilated and disembowelled their lifeless bodies. He felt the vomit building in his throat and it burst from his mouth as he saw a baby dragged from its mother's arms and smashed against a stone building with such force that blood and brains splattered over the wall. The mother was stripped and her body slashed and cut to pieces.

Gamellus had been a slave of these Romans himself. He'd once hated those who had denied his freedom to live his life as he wished. But in his darkest moments he'd never contemplated such revenge. He felt sure his life was about to come to an end in slaughter and chaos. He moved forward nervously heading towards the Governor's headquarters. He still felt the guilt and shame, which a while ago had overwhelmed him, for letting the Procurator have sight of the will written by the Iceni King. It seemed to him that all these horrific events had followed on from that single act. He had to try to restore his self-respect, to do something, anything which would give him some kind of peace before he met his death.

He climbed the steps and entered the main entrance to the headquarters building unchallenged. The doors were wide open and the bodies of the guards who had attempted to hold back the screaming horde lay cast to one side.

He made his way along the corridors, stepping over more bodies until he entered the large reception room which the Governor had used to receive his many visitors. He stopped abruptly, desperately wishing he could withdraw unseen. Ahead of him was a large group of bloodied warriors. They were surrounding an elderly man who was giving them instructions. He stopped talking to them, his attention drawn towards Gamellus.

"Come in, old man," said Frigionus. "All of you look at what we have before us. Here is a brave man, who even with his many years has chosen to join the fight for freedom."

This time the vomit was helped on its way by the raw terror he was feeling. Soon he would be discovered and very likely disembowelled alive like many others he had seen. He bent forward and unintentionally emptied the remaining contents of his stomach towards the feet of those who had turned to face him. They began to laugh at the pathetic old man until Frigionus showed his disapproval of them.

"Go, old man, and leave us. You've done your duty today and it's beginning to take its toll. This town is now ours. There's no need for you to suffer and put yourself in harm's way any longer. Go back to your camp and remember you were part of our great victory today."

Gamellus bowed and left the room. Never before had he been grateful for having a weak stomach. If he'd had to speak to them his accent would surely have aroused questions and suspicion. He wouldn't have withstood examination about his presence in this building for very long.

He descended the stairs to the Library, again avoiding the bodies which were strewn everywhere. Unfortunately, he thought, none of them appeared to be his assistant, that scoundrel Gaius. If only he could find him and end his miserable, useless life. The room had already been looted and his beloved documents cast from the shelves onto the floor. The table at the end of the room had been overturned. The locks on the chests beneath had been broken. They lay on their sides, the contents spread across the floor.

His face lit up in relief. It seemed as if none of the documents had been considered worthy of looting. He withdrew briefly to search the nearby rooms until he found a piece of cloth large enough in which to wrap the documents. He slung his bulky bundle over his shoulder before making his way back up the stairs and along the corridors to the main entrance. Holding his breath, he was desperate not to meet anybody coming in or going from the building. Fortunately, the looting of this building had finished and the fighting had moved to the Temple.

He descended the steps outside and moved back into the town. To his relief he could see the streets were full of looters who had lost interest in the fighting. Their attention and efforts were fixed on taking possession of the many items from the homes. There were prizes most of them had never seen before or could even have imagined. Twice he was stopped by much younger, stronger looters who had opened his bundle, only to lose interest in the contents which were of no use to them.

He passed the last house on the edge of the town and moved on into the open fields. Darkness would soon be approaching. Many of the attackers were withdrawing to their camps for the night. He joined them, melting into the crowd to disappear once again.

*

"The second line is holding," whispered Marius.

He was kneeling by the side of Varus who was lying on the blood stained floor of the Temple. The large wound in his side had been attended to and the bleeding had stopped.

"They're withdrawing for the night to see to their dead and injured. They're sure to return after dawn tomorrow. I can see your wound has been treated. How do you feel?"

"How I feel isn't important. I lost my sword when I was struck down. Can you get me another one? I don't want to die without taking a few of them with me. When the time comes can you make sure I'm helped to my feet?"

Marius nodded his assurance.

"Where is your family?" Marius asked.

"I was going to ask you the same question. I was wounded early in the attack and wasn't able to get to them."

"I haven't seen them but they may still be safe."

"If you don't know where they are, they didn't make it inside the second line and they are dead. Please get me a sword!"

His face grew taut, showing a mixture of grief and pain.

"I'll see to it immediately."

Marius touched Varus lightly on his arm and stood up. Smiling cheerfully to make light of the situation they were in, he moved on to talk to the others who'd been wounded. They too had been brought inside to escape temporarily from the mayhem outside.

Later, Marius was walking along the line counting the numbers manning the defences. He decided that there were no more than 500.

They would not be able to withstand an all-out attack on their line. He thought it would come soon after dawn. From then on their survival would depend on how long they were able to hold out in the Temple.

He was wrong in one respect regarding his analysis. When the first light of dawn arrived the expected attack didn't come.

*

Boudica had made a triumphant entrance into the camp soon after dawn. Accompanied by her escort she had brought her war chariot to a halt close to Frigionus. Warned of her arrival he was standing with Morfan outside his tent. He had reluctantly, but only temporarily, delayed the next attack.

The Queen climbed down from her chariot and approached the two men, her arms outstretched towards them. Linona who was leading the escort dismounted and joined her.

"Tell me how the attack went? Did they put up a good fight?" she asked. "Have you lost many of your people?"

A stern-faced Frigionus didn't reply to her questions immediately. He clasped the two women to him and stood back to introduce his son.

"You've met my younger son Morfan before, I think, if only briefly."

Both women indicated they had.

"He will be my constant companion in the days ahead. Now that Marac is dead he'll succeed me as leader of our tribe."

"You've grown into a fine young warrior, Morfan," said Boudica.

Linona was silent as she stared at Frigionus. The pain caused by the mention of Marac's death was only too obvious on her face.

"But what about my questions? Please tell me what's happened."

Frigionus spoke proudly of the events of the previous day.

"I take it from what you say, with the exception of the Temple, the whole town has been stripped of its contents?"

"Correct. It's no more than my people deserve. Those thieves and murderers have stolen our land and our wealth for many years."

"Please don't misunderstand me, my friend. I agree with you. It's just that my people having fought bravely to destroy the 9th Legion were expecting to enjoy the spoils of war with you when we joined forces to attack this place."

"There will be other opportunities when we attack Verulamium and Londinium. These Romans are wealthy and their homes are full of riches."

"That's true."

"Your warriors will get their share."

"Again I agree. I won't let a matter of booty become an issue which could divide us and divert us from our main task."

"Then it's time for me to release my people once more."

"Hold them for a short while. The first group of my warriors will be arriving shortly ahead of the rest of my people. They will join in the second attack."

"So be it," Frigionus agreed. "But while we wait for them let's ride together in your chariot to visit the camps around the town. We shall let my people see the Queen who is going to lead us to victory. While we're doing so, these two young people can get to know each other better."

Linona gave no indication that she had heard what was said or even cared.

*

Marius had taken up a position on the Temple steps at dawn waiting for the final attack. It hadn't come. He peered through the early light, trying to pick out any sign that his enemy was about to strike. He relaxed slightly, but still didn't move from his vantage point. From there he would be able to see the first movement of warriors across the fields.

It was a bright, fresh morning and the sun had begun to rise in the sky when he eventually became aware of the movement of horses coming from the left. Unexpectedly, the direction wasn't towards the town but across the fields in front of the tents and carts of the barbarians. They were led by a chariot, which was being driven hard by a figure with long red hair flowing freely behind.

"It's Boudica," he said to the centurion who stood beside him.

Neither man had ever seen her before but the description Julius had given him left Marius in no doubt.

"The attack may not have come at dawn, but it won't be delayed much longer. The Queen is preparing to attack. Tell the men on the barriers to be ready, but don't mention Boudica is here."

He moved back into the Temple to talk to the wounded, eventually reaching Varus.

"As I told you last evening I'm well enough to fight when the time comes," said Varus. "What's happening outside? Why haven't they attacked?"

"I don't know why, but I've just seen Boudica riding her chariot across the massed ranks of her followers. I'm sure we won't have much longer to wait."

"What are our chances now?"

"If we have the Gods on our side we might hold out. They may outnumber us, but only so many of them can fight us against the barriers at any one time. It will depend on how quickly our men are picked off and how fatigued they become."

"At least we know that those of us remaining are not fearful cowards. We're all prepared to fight to the death. The men who are left are likely to be our best and strongest for them to have survived so far."

"Let's hope so. If only we can just hold on until she loses interest in us and goes to seek booty elsewhere, and her battle with Paulinus."

"They are moving towards us, Sir."

It was the Centurion who had been with him earlier. He was standing in the open doorway, his sword drawn.

"I have to leave, but I will be returning to join you later."

"Not too soon, I hope."

Marius walked to the steps to take a look at the fields. His heart sank. He had hoped the fighting the day before and the losses which the enemy had suffered would have reduced their forces considerably. On the contrary there seemed to be many more as they ran at full pace across the fields, trying to outrun each other.

The town was soon full of yelling, screaming near-naked warriors heading for the Temple. As Marius had expected, not all of them were able to stand at the barriers to fight at any time. He could see that the barriers so far were standing up to the pressure of the enemy numbers. The fighting continued for the rest of the morning. Attack after attack had been repulsed, although there had been the expected heavy losses.

Eventually the inevitable happened and the first break in the defences occurred. Before long it became a wide gap through which the attackers poured.

Marius gave the command to retreat. The remaining defenders began to fight a rear-guard manoeuvre to withdraw while still fighting off the attackers. Brave men were dying trying to hold back the flood so others could make it to the doors of the Temple. For his part Marius had organised enough legionaries to form a strong line in front of the doors at the top of the steps to allow as many men as possible to gain the safety of the inner Temple.

It was to be his last act before a spear entered his stomach. It was quickly followed by a mighty blow from an axe which knocked his helmet off, and fractured his skull.

Behind his body the large oak doors of the Temple slammed shut and were secured.

The noise from outside gradually died down and this gave Varus and the two remaining centurions time to reflect on their position and what might happen.

"It was Marius's hope that if we could hold out for a day or two the enemy might move on," Varus began. "Fortunately there are no windows in our Temple and the doors are made of thick solid oak. We may yet achieve it. See to our wounded and rest for now. We've earned it."

*

The fires against the doors of the Temple had been burning for some time. The heat had been intense and yet they still stood.

Frigionus was showing his frustration as Morfan approached.

"You look as if you don't have the patience to let the fire do the work for us, Father. Let me take some of my men onto the roof and lower ourselves onto the Romans inside."

"No! There must be more than 100 men in there and many of you would be cut to pieces as you descended."

"We could still overcome them. My men are ready and waiting."

"We will have use of your courage, and that of such brave men who would go with you, in the days to come. No! We shall be patient and wait a few hours more. Then we'll batter down what remains of those doors."

It was late in the evening before the doors finally gave way to allow the killing to begin again. The fighting didn't last long. The last few defenders who were still able to fight were gradually overwhelmed and hacked to death. The few who laid down their arms were spared only to be used as sacrifices later. The badly wounded were put to the sword.

The last Roman to die was leaning against a wall at the far end of the Temple. Varus had been protected by men who had served with him for many years before they had retired. They died defiantly one by one in front of him until only he remained. With a sword, given to him by Marius, he was urging his enemies to come to him.

Gradually the noise in the room died away. Those in front of him parted to allow an elderly warrior to approach and stand before him just out of reach of his sword.

Frigionus's cold eyes fixed on Varus's face before moving to look at the broad red patch on his side. A smile crossed his lips briefly as he took a spear from a warrior standing next to him and pushed the tip a short way into the wound. Varus winced with pain but managed to swing his sword to break the spear in two.

Again Frigionus smiled, holding out his hand to receive a second spear. This time he thrust the spear much harder into the upper part of Varus's arm forcing him to drop his sword in pain. Varus still managed to stay on his feet, though he appeared close to collapse. In a final, defiant, contemptuous act he spat into the face of Frigionus.

The last spear thrust went straight through his throat with such force the point broke against the wall behind his head. When Frigionus let go of the spear Varus's body slumped lifelessly to the floor. It signalled a final ecstatic, triumphant roar from those crowded inside the Temple.

*

The following evening King Cadellin arrived and was taken by Linona to see the still smouldering ruins of Camulodunum. If he was impressed by what he saw, he didn't show it. He would make his views known to Boudica in private.

He didn't have to wait very long before he was shown into Boudica's tent. She had been joined already by Frigionus and Morfan. The involvement of Morfan and Linona was intended to impress upon Cadellin that what was decided this day was to last long into the future when the Romans had been defeated and sent back to Rome. It was a message which wouldn't be lost on Cadellin when he joined them. He would have expected to meet only Boudica and Frigionus, but he was shrewd enough to understand why the young heirs to the kingdoms had been included.

"Welcome, Cadellin," Boudica announced, rising slowly from her chair and clasping his arm with her own.

Cadellin didn't speak immediately. He merely nodded in acknowledgement of her greeting.

"Thank you for answering my call to join us on this day of celebration. It's been a great victory by our two tribes."

"Firstly let me thank you for your welcome."

Frigionus shuffled impatiently. Cadellin continued.

"I've already seen the result of your victory and can understand why you might wish to celebrate. Celebrate while you can, that is."

"What do you mean by that?" asked Frigionus, rising to the not too subtle challenge by his old enemy.

"Before you answer, why don't you sit down, Cadellin," Boudica suggested, anxious to prevent the two men's obvious dislike of each other from killing off any discussion before it started.

"Let me explain why we've asked you to join us today. Frigionus and I have spent many hours in the last few weeks discussing and sharing our thoughts. Often there have been conflicting views about the future of this land and our tribes. Soon we shall become masters of our own destinies once again."

She gave a quick smile to Frigionus to indicate her gratitude for him recognising her attempt to calm things, and that he had been able to control his temper. It allowed her to continue to do the talking as they had agreed.

"The timing of our uprising wasn't decided upon by the two of us. The Romans by their actions have brought this upon themselves."

"I heard of the atrocities which you and your daughters suffered and I was appalled. I too share the outrage all of you must feel. It was the act of barbarians."

Boudica thanked him for his words of support, but a stone-faced Linona kept silent.

"However, this adventure which you have embarked upon can have only one disastrous ending. It will bring death and destruction to both your tribes."

"Haven't you taken in the scale of our victory here?" demanded Frigionus.

"From what I've seen and heard you've defeated an ill-prepared collection of legionaries, farmers and mercenaries."

"We have ripped out the heart of this monster which the Romans have created in our land."

"You had vastly superior numbers. The town had no defences to speak of or leaders with any significant experience."

"They fought us fiercely to the death."

"Still, you couldn't fail. It will be a different matter when you eventually meet Paulinus and his seasoned Legionaries."

Frigionus finally got to his feet, his hand moving to his sword.

"Your words dishonour the brave men and women who died taking this town."

"Please sit down," said Boudica firmly. "What Cadellin says is mostly true, although he could have chosen his words more carefully."

She placed her hand on his arm to gently draw him down by her side, and continued talking to Cadellin.

"I accept that our future battles will be considerably harder if we're to rid ourselves of these invaders. That's why we've asked you to come here today. If the Catuvelauni join us we shall be so much stronger to meet and defeat them."

Cadellin ignored the implied request that was being made of him.

"If by chance you were to defeat them, do you think they wouldn't send more legions to replace those which had been destroyed? Their Empire is mighty, its resources limitless. Their defeat here would send a message to the rest of the Empire which they could not afford. They would send even more than now to destroy you and ensure they were never threatened here again."

"On the contrary, if we crush them and destroy their Legions it will make them consider that the little they gain from our land isn't worth the price which they have to pay."

"You are taking a great gamble against an army led by an experienced and clever General. He won't be an opponent who is easy to crush. If you're defeated your tribe will suffer as never before."

"We cannot suffer any more than we already have," said Frigionus.

"Paulinus will have only two, maybe three legions available to him, since we destroyed the 9th Legion," Boudica added. "That's a force of perhaps only 12000. Our two tribes can bring nearly ten times that number. With the addition of your tribe we could make our victory a lot easier."

"I've made my views known to you before and they haven't been changed by your arguments today."

"You still won't join us?"

"Even if I believed as you do, I wouldn't be able to persuade my people to join you in a battle against the Romans."

"They must yearn for freedom from these murderers, these rapists?" said Frigionus, getting to his feet again.

"My people don't hate the Romans as you do. Yes, we would prefer it if they were to treat us as equals, as a valued part of their Empire, not controlled by it. The difference between us and you is that we feel it will happen one day without going to war."

"You coward," shouted Linona. "You're a king of slaves, willing through fear to accept the Roman boot on your necks."

"And you are a child who is ruled by her emotions, not by her head. You'll bring disaster upon those who follow you."

"Enough of this," commanded Boudica. "You've made your views clear to us, Cadellin. You say you won't join us. Then don't be tempted to do the opposite. I warn you against standing against us with the Romans. Victory will be ours, and if you have chosen to join them we will deal with you later."

"I'll do what I have to do to ensure my people survive and prosper in these troubled times."

"So be it. Now go!"

"I think this is the last time we will meet as friends, Boudica. Let's hope, if there is to be a next time we meet, it's not as enemies."

*

The four sat in silence for a while after he had left. It was Frigionus who spoke first.

"Until today we had to come to an agreement about where we should take our people and who to attack next. This coward has made the decision for us. I say we do the same to Verulamium in Catuvelauni land as we've done to Camulodunum. Londinium can wait."

"I agree," said Boudica. "Paulinus might think he can force Cadellin to join him. He will head for his town on his journey back from the North. We shall wait two days for our numbers to swell and to allow us to recover from the fighting. Then we march."

They left the tent to spread the news throughout the camps. Verulamium, a town as rich as Camulodunum, with plenty of booty, would be the next to fall and be destroyed.

CHAPTER 26

Bestia, together with the other leading citizens of Londinium was standing in the meeting room of Decianus's house, summoned there by Paulinus. He was remembering that the last time he had been in the large meeting room in the house of his employer had been on the day Decianus had told him he was leaving to go to Gaul. Bestia had long held the man in contempt, but he had been paid well by him. It had been sufficient compensation.

Previously he'd been successful in disguising his true feelings, but on that last day he couldn't hide his disgust. Before him stood a trembling, terrified, pathetic coward who, in his panic, was about to leave without giving any clear instructions to his men.

"What's going to happen to me and our men in your absence?" Bestia demanded.

"Don't bother me with such trivialities."

"How will they receive payments which are due to them? What about the future?"

"They'll be paid what they're owed whenever I choose to do so. At the moment they have no future, not, that is, until I return."

"And when will that be?"

"It will be when the Emperor sends a new Governor to replace that fool Paulinus. The man has brought this upon us with his foolish adventure in the north."

"You're a coward. You've no intention of returning. If you ever do, there are many among my men who'll want revenge for this betrayal."

"You insolent pig, I could have you flogged for making such a remark."

"Please call my men in and tell them you want me flogged. Tell them you're leaving and they won't be paid the money you owe them. You just might be lucky if I decide to kill you myself before they have chance to drag you outside to be tortured into telling them where you've hidden your money."

Decianus didn't reply. Realising the great danger he was in, he fled from the room. Shortly afterwards he was in the ship which he'd ordered to be prepared for him, and on his way to Gaul.

"Some of you aren't paying full attention to what I'm saying. Stop your murmuring and listen carefully."

The raised voice of Paulinus quickly brought Bestia's thoughts back to the present.

"You'd better listen because I have some harsh words to deliver. I've ridden hard to be here and I'm tired."

Paulinus was talking to a large group of the citizens of Londinium, summoned to meet him on his arrival. Tribune Antonius, Commander of the town garrison, had done his work well, collecting them all, although some had been brought at the point of the sword.

"I want you all to understand what I have to say. We don't have a great deal of time so you must answer all my questions carefully. Tribune Antonius, what is the current size of the garrison here in Londinium?"

"I can provide 300 men at the most, Sir. The rest went to Camulodunum to fight there and won't be coming back."

"I'm told that that's more than your cowardly mercenaries did, Bestia. Have they all run for their lives like Decianus? Explain yourself."

Bestia was experienced and wily enough to know his life today depended on his next few remarks. He had no intention of being made an example of in front of the citizens of the town. Most of them hated him and would relish his death.

"The last instruction I received from the Procurator was to keep the situation in Camulodunum under review while he was away. If it became hopeless I was to concentrate my men in Londinium to protect the citizens here until the army returned," he lied.

"A man of courage and honour would have stayed to defend all those women and children. Why didn't you do as I ordered?" demanded Julius.

"I did as I was told by the Imperial Procurator. If I'd disobeyed him in such a matter not only my life but the lives of my family would have been forfeit when he returned."

"What about Marius? He was in command at Camulodunum. What orders did he give you?"

"When the tribune informed me that the 9th Legion had been defeated I told him things had changed and the town and anybody who stayed to try to defend it would be destroyed. I told him I had to return to protect the citizens of Londinium, including those in this room, as ordered. He didn't try to stop me and my men from leaving."

"Is that all you have to say?" Paulinus asked.

"There was no hope. I did as I was ordered and so I can provide as many as 400 men to help to defend these people here today."

Paulinus stared at Bestia, but made no immediate comment on his reply. Bestia suffered as he waited to learn his fate. Eventually the Governor looked to the main body of those standing before him and spoke slowly and deliberately.

"All of you listen carefully to what I have to say. Don't interrupt. I don't consider that it's possible to defend this town. I'm told by Tribune Antonius that Camulodunum has either fallen or will do so shortly. We have all learnt of the defeat of the 9th Legion. My army is marching to Verulamium as we speak. I shall be joining them when I leave here."

"What happens afterwards will depend on Boudica's next move. If you are about to ask me if she will attack you here next, rather than Verulamium, I will reply truthfully and say I don't know. My guess is she won't. Verulamium has plenty for them to loot for her thieving horde. She will also hope to meet my Legions near there on their return as soon as she can, before her makeshift army starts to tire and many begin to lose interest."

"After I've assessed the situation in Verulamium I'll decide whether or not to call for the garrison here to join me. If I do, any citizen who wants to do so can leave the town and accompany them."

"I don't intend wasting my time with questions. You've heard what I've had to say. Go and make your preparations for what lies in store for us all."

He waved them all away and a relieved Bestia, joining the rest, turned to leave.

"Not you, Bestia! You wait. I have more to say to you when the others have left."

The room was taking some time to empty. Those present were moving out slowly, exchanging their worried views on what they had just been told. One man had held back and approached the Governor.

"My name is Tarquinius Marellus and I have in the past been Magistrate of this town. You and I have met before, Sir."

"Yes we have. Why aren't you leaving? I made it very clear I didn't want any questions."

Paulinus made it obvious by his sharp reply that he wasn't in the mood to discuss anything with a former magistrate or anybody else.

"I wish to complain most strongly about the actions of the young tribune who stands behind you. I've been told that he is Julius Agricola. He's the man who, without your authority, had my son Gaius brutally flogged. It left him in great pain for many days."

"Good," Julius cried.

"You may not have been told that my son had merely been carrying out his duty as a clerk in your service. I ask for this arrogant tribune to be punished severely."

"Your son is lucky I wasn't the first to hear of his treachery. I would have had him crucified. If you don't wish to follow your son's fate for wasting my time you'd better leave now."

Paulinus contemptuously waved him away.

The man, mouth gaping wide open in shock, almost broke into a run as he left the room.

Paulinus turned his attention to Bestia.

"From today, you and your men are part of the 20th Legion and will be under the command of Tribune Antonius. If a single one of them deserts again from the Legion I will hold you responsible and have you executed. So you had better command them with an iron fist. You promised me 400 men earlier. I shan't accept one man less from you. Leave my sight."

Bestia slowly descended the steps and made his short walk to his home. He thought he had a choice to make after what he'd just been told. His instinct was to collect his wife and children, flee the Province and go to join Decianus. The problem was the last conversation he had had with him, and he didn't know for certain where he had gone. If he eventually found him in Rome, would he be welcomed or would he have him killed because of what he knew of events in Britannia?

He needed to take more time to think it through. He could benefit later if he was able to gain the trust of the Governor and his staff in the coming battle. He still had a few days remaining to decide what he would do.

*

"I've received a message from the land to the south of the river, from King Cogidubnus."

Paulinus was talking to Camillus and Julius as they were finally able to relax from the day's exhausting journey to Londinium.

"He pledges his loyalty to us as I expected he would. He says he will be able to bring a sizeable force later but not immediately. What do you think?"

"I may not be popular for saying this," said Camillus, "but without the 9th Legion we are going to need the 2nd Legion to join us and the support of one of the larger tribes to be sure of victory. If King Cogidubnus cannot join us at Verulamium we will need the Catuvelauni if we decide to face Boudica north of Londinium."

"I support that assessment," said Julius, "and what's more I think Boudica will be aware of that as well. That's why she will attack Verulamium next. If she takes their town she could try to get the Catuvelauni to join her cause, or at least neutralise them."

"I agree with both of you," said Paulinus. "We will be in Verulamium tomorrow. The first thing I must do is to call on King Cadellin to see if he's with us. Only then can I decide whether or not Verulamium is to be our battle ground. But enough of these deliberations. More wine, gentlemen?"

*

True to what he had said the night before, on his arrival in Verulamium, Paulinus immediately made his way to King Cadellin's palace. His day had started badly. It had been confirmed finally that Camulodunum had been overrun and destroyed with no survivors. Then his spirits had been lifted by a message sent from the 14th Legion to say they were making good progress. The legionaries in the vanguard had already arrived.

Cadellin's palace, the largest building in the town, had been built for him by the Romans. Most of his clan chiefs and others had followed his lead, building houses of their own there in addition to their tribal country estates.

Julius was accompanying the Governor, whilst Camillus had gone to supervise the arrival of the 14th Legion. As the two men rode to the royal palace Julius could not help noticing the bustle in the crowded town. He was reminded once again of what he had seen on his arrival in Camulodunum when Boudica's attack was expected.

They dismounted and entered the building escorted by several of the King's smartly dressed staff. It was the first time Julius had been there. He was struck by the obvious luxury on display. He could have been in the house of a wealthy nobleman in Rome. It contrasted sharply with the basic, rustic surroundings of Presutagus and Boudica's home.

"Thank you for seeing me unannounced," said Paulinus.

"Welcome, Governor. I have been expecting you." said Cadellin. "I'm relieved to be told your army will be arriving here shortly."

"It's good to hear it gives you some comfort. May I introduce my staff officer Tribune Julius Agricola. He has come with me today because he's had recent contact with Boudica."

"You are welcome, Tribune. I too have met the Queen recently and I feel we shall see her again shortly. I'm told she's moving to attack this town."

"Do you know when?" asked Julius.

"She's no more than three or four days away."

"Will you oppose any attack by her?"

"We need to know what you intend to do, Governor. Are you going to stay and fight her here?"

"Without the 9th Legion, and with the 2nd Legion many days away, I don't think I will have the numbers to meet her here at this time with just my remaining Legions."

"I've heard of the fate of the 9th Legion and it is to be mourned."

"However, if I have the whole of your tribe to support me, we could defeat her together. That's why I need to know what you intend to do about her."

"I didn't realise until this moment that the 2nd Legion was so far away. Does it mean you've only one and a half Legions at your disposal? They are the men who have marched to Mona and back, are they not?"

"You're correct in what you say and I know what you're hinting at. However, the men I have will be ready to fight. They're the best soldiers in the whole Empire."

"I have no doubt what you say is true but I feel I will have great difficulty in persuading my people to fight Boudica here if your numbers are as limited as you say. They might fear that you're not strong enough to defeat her."

"Surely you could order them to fight with us, couldn't you?" Julius asked.

"You may know Boudica and her people, but you don't know mine, young man. They will fight if they choose to, and not just because they are ordered to. I will do my best to persuade them. It's all I can offer you."

"And what about your precious palace and this town if you don't persuade them?" Julius continued. "She would destroy it and everything in it."

"If my people decide to leave there'll be little left for her to loot. She will destroy our houses but we have elsewhere to live away from here until you have defeated her in battle, Governor. When you return to provide your protection once more we'll rebuild the town. We'll make it bigger and grander than before."

"That will depend on whether I choose to continue to provide that support and protection to a tribe which chooses not to help Rome in her time of need."

Cadellin didn't respond to the obvious threat from Paulinus. Instead he continued to avoid giving any clear guarantee of his active support against Boudica.

"Once Boudica is defeated, we shall continue to be your faithful allies, making our full contribution to Rome. What plans do you have to meet her if not here?"

Paulinus, showing signs that he was losing patience with Cadellin's obvious attempt to excuse any decision not to fight by his side, rose to his feet and glared at the King.

"I think it's time for you to go to join the rest of your frightened people in seeking safety. With regard to my plans, I shall keep them to myself in case you are taken by Boudica. Should she capture you as you flee, she'll torture you into revealing what you know, before she sacrifices you to her Gods. Good day, Cadellin."

"It's as we always knew it would be," growled Paulinus.

He was talking to Julius and the two Legates, Pontius and Rufius, back at the fort.

"He hopes to sit and wait until Boudica and I destroy each other. He thinks it will give him the opportunity to regain the lost power and the control the Catuvelauni had over the other tribes before we came here. We shall deal with him later. For now gentlemen we need to finalise our plans to move south."

*

The following morning the two legions began their preparation to march south to Londinium. Those citizens, men, women and children, who wanted to stay under the protection of Paulinus, were to be allowed to follow the army. For now at least, they would escape the horrific fate which had befallen those in Camulodunum.

CHAPTER 27

Olsar could see that the main gates to the town, controlling access through the defensive wall which surrounded it, had been left open. It was either a friendly invitation or it would make an attack on him easier. He took no chances and drew his sword.

His eyes were unblinking, staring to see beyond the gates. It looked to him as if Verulamium had been abandoned or he wouldn't have ventured this close. He knew he still couldn't completely rule out a sudden attack at any moment. He was keeping ahead of Linona and his small reconnaissance force to draw any first attack onto himself. It would allow Linona the chance to escape.

He moved his horse forward slowly to approach the gates. With all his senses heightened as if stalking a prey in the forest, he moved cautiously through into the street beyond. A movement to the right caught the corner of his eye. He gave a signal to Linona and the rest to halt. They were a short distance behind and moving warily towards him.

Linona immediately halted the column. Quietly she gave orders that she and Morfan were going to join Olsar. She instructed them to retreat and inform Boudica what had taken place, should an attack begin. They were not to try any rescue of them.

Olsar became aware of an old man a short distance from him. Stick in hand for support, he had moved out of a house fronting onto the street. His grey shoulder-length hair and his style of dress suggested he wasn't a Roman who had come from one of the far reaches of the Empire, but a member of the Catuvelauni tribe.

Acutely aware of the danger he could be in, Olsar moved carefully forward towards the old man. As he did so, he pointed his sword at him to warn him not to act foolishly. By the time he reached the stranger, Linona and Morfan had ridden to join him.

Olsar's face showed his anger at Linona choosing not to remain outside the town as his gesture had indicated. Nevertheless, his annoyance quickly disappeared allowing him to concentrate again on the old man.

"Where are the rest of the people of this town?" Linona demanded. "Where are they hiding? Do they plan to attack us? How many are there here with you? Speak while you still can."

Olsar raised his left hand slowly, with a shake of his head towards Linona to indicate the need to restrain her aggression. The old man stepped back. He appeared to be startled and afraid at the forceful way Linona had fired her questions at him.

"If you intend no treachery you don't need to be afraid," said Olsar. "Tell us what you know about what's happened here."

His quiet words had the desired effect as the man appeared to relax and speak freely.

"Some of the people living here have left with the Roman General and his army, heading south to go to Londinium. Most have followed King Cadellin and headed north, deep into our lands. They didn't want to join you. Neither did they want to fight you here, defending this town."

"How many are left here?"

"A few like me have stayed to welcome you, but I'm too old and frail to join your cause and fight."

"Is that everybody?"

"There are others who have stayed because they're too old and ill to leave. They'll beg you for mercy. Then there are some who won't welcome you and may be prepared to die rather than surrender their houses."

"You would be wise to join your kinsmen and leave to go north," suggested Olsar.

"I thank you for your kind words but I don't think my old legs and heart would get me very far."

"When thousands of our warriors arrive here there are many who won't distinguish between friend and foe. Go now and you may yet survive the hell that's coming to this place."

"I hear what you say, but I've chosen to stay here and take my chances."

The arrow flew silently and struck Morfan in his left arm just above his elbow. His scream momentarily caused Olsar's horse to rear, which in turn caused the other two horses to back away in alarm. With great skill Morfan had managed to cling to his horse's neck with his good arm, but he had dropped the reins.

Olsar was expecting more arrows to follow, but with less accuracy since they were no longer stationary. He fought back his instinct to head for the gates and safety. Instead he managed to steady his own horse. He reached down to grab the loose reins from Morfan's horse to gain control. Raising his head he was dismayed to see Linona riding after the old man, who had hobbled down the street in the direction from which the arrow had come. He was frantically waving his arms high and wide above his head, signalling to an unseen bowman.

To Olsar it was clear the old man was trying to prevent any more arrows from being shot in their direction.

Linona apparently saw it differently. Her sword slashed down onto the old man's head killing him instantly. Expertly, she wheeled her horse sharply to her left and lay forward on her horse's neck reducing the target for the bowman to aim at. Her swift, skilful movement saved her life. The next arrow sped over her body and thudded into the building behind her.

The riders outside the gate reacted instinctively. Ignoring the last instructions from Linona, they raced to cover the short distance to surround their three leaders. With so many targets the next two arrows brought down two brave men before the rest could reach the gateway and escape into the fields beyond.

*

Morfan's wound was not as bad as it could have been. The bone in his arm hadn't been struck. Once the arrow had been removed, a tight bandage applied to the flesh wound had stopped the flow of blood. Pale-faced, he had belatedly joined Boudica and her war council in time to hear Linona and Olsar complete their report about what had happened earlier.

"We mustn't waste any more time on an empty town," said Boudica, when they had finished. "We can't be too far behind our enemy. We have to move on."

Most nodded their heads or gave their audible agreement to what she proposed, but not all. Frigionus leapt angrily to his feet at Boudica's words.

"I've lost one son already and today I nearly lost my other one to those treacherous dogs in this town."

"I understand your anger, but those few still left in there can't be allowed to divert us."

"You may choose to go to Londinium tomorrow, but I won't join you," Frigionus insisted.

"At dawn we will destroy that town and all those in it. It has been the refuge for our Roman and Catuvelauni tormentors alike for too long."

His decision prompted cries of support from some of those present.

"Our aim, must I remind you and everyone else here, is to defeat Paulinus and drive all Romans out of our lands forever," Boudica insisted.

Frigionus countered what she was saying with a further challenge to her.

"We'll defeat Paulinus whenever we meet him. In the meantime we need to put the town to the torch after we've killed every single one who was foolish enough to have remained."

"I ache to destroy all they stand for just as you do, but we gain nothing by delaying our move in order to kill the few remaining old and sick merely for revenge."

"We'll have everything they haven't been able to take with them," Frigionus continued, ignoring Boudica.

"You'll find very little. They've had plenty of time to take or hide anything of real value."

"We won't be denied our revenge. Even if we only destroy their empty stone houses we shall regain some of the pride we lost many years ago."

"And risk what we have dreamed of for the future?"

"I've spoken my last words on this. You can leave tomorrow if you want to. We'll join you later, when we've destroyed this place."

He turned and left, followed by those from his tribe.

"Traitor," shouted Bodran.

"No, no, don't!" Boudica said quietly but firmly. "We can all see there will be no persuading Frigionus to change his view of what he feels he needs to do."

"But he has shown you great disrespect," Bodran added.

"He's blinded by hatred and his grief at his great loss."

"We should march without him. Let him follow on later," Linona added.

"For us to follow Paulinus without the Trinovantes would weaken us greatly. I won't take the risk and leave without them. We must stay together, but we won't take part in their attack. Frigionus doesn't need our help to sack an empty town. When he's finished, we will need him as we move south. A day's rest for all our people is perhaps no bad thing after our days spent travelling to get here."

"He's putting our cause at risk with his blood lust," said Bodran.

"I hear what you say, but remember that he and his family have suffered greatly, particularly in recent times. He still needs to calm his blinding hatred before we meet Paulinus."

"You and your family have also suffered, Boudica," Bodran added. "But your guidance as usual is measured and wise. Because of that, with the help of Andraste, you will lead us to victory."

The meeting ended without anything more being said. The mood as everybody left was sombre, reflecting the tension which had grown between the two tribes.

*

"Your mother is as wise as she is strong and determined."

Olsar was talking to Linona as they made their way to their tents.

"Of course she is."

"She controlled her emotions in there in the way all leaders should when provoked. In comparison, she was challenged by a man who was being ruled by his hatred."

Linona looked blankly at him and didn't respond.

"You've a lot to learn from her in the need for self-control in times of challenge and danger if your hatred isn't to make you become more like Frigionus."

She stopped abruptly to confront him. Her expression had changed to one of angry surprise.

"What are you saying exactly?"

"You are still young and you react too quickly, without thinking, to satisfy one emotional need or another."

Olsar knew that he was sure to get such an unrestrained emotional reaction by using such harsh words. He had reflected on what had happened earlier in the day. If he was ever to win her he decided he must begin to engage her as an equal and not as an obedient aide to her and her mother.

"How dare you speak to me like that? Explain what you mean."

Her eyes were wide open and glaring at him. She placed her hand on the hilt of her sword.

"You make my point," he said, fighting back a strong urge to burst out laughing at her flash of indignation. "Look at you, ready to draw your sword in anger against me, someone who has trained you since you were a girl."

"Will you shut up. I've heard enough."

"You fight so well now because of what I've taught you. You believe in yourself because I gave you that belief. You can stand up to any man because I demanded you do so."

"Have you finished?"

"What you've not yet learned is to temper your determination with caution and wisdom. There were signs you were beginning to learn these things, especially when you came under the influence of Marac. Sadly that ended when he died."

"And you're a fool who seems to have lost all reason. You don't appear to have any control over your tongue any more. I can't begin to think what's caused this outburst other than to assume you've become exhausted. I'll forgive you this time, and this time only."

She turned and stormed away.

Olsar took several long strides and grabbed her arm. He spun her round, bringing her to a halt, facing him.

"I can explain to you what I'm saying by giving you an example from today. What were you thinking when the arrow struck Morfan? Why did you do what you did to that defenceless old man?"

"You are continuing to act like an idiot and I warn you to stop." She replied with a voice which was beginning to shake with emotion.

"If you won't answer my questions then I'll answer them for you. You thought we'd been tricked into an ambush and he was part of it. You thought he was trying to escape. You were so filled with hate and anger your only thought was to cut him down."

"Correct! And if you had been nearest to him you'd have done the same," she countered.

"I would not and did not."

He softened and slowed his words to be sure she would remember them.

"Although I hate the Romans and those who support them just as much as you do, I don't let the hatred cloud my judgement. I saw only a friend in the old man. I saw it in his face, in his smile, in his words. His behaviour wasn't that of somebody who knew arrows were about to fly in his direction. He was as startled as we were when the first arrow hit Morfan."

"Please stop."

"You've just seen in Frigionus a sudden show of unrestrained hatred. It is behaviour you are increasingly sharing with him. It has blinded him and his reason has left him. He's prepared to put our victory at risk to satisfy his hatred and a desire to spill blood. Do you want to become another Frigionus or do you wish to be a great leader like your mother?"

"I don't care what happens to me. There's no joy left in my life and never will be again. I live only to hate and kill Romans and their supporters, or die trying." She was fighting back the tears, swallowing deeply to keep control. "Who are you to speak to me of these matters in this way?"

"I need you to want to live and enjoy life again," Olsar replied. "I want to continue to bring out the complete woman in you. I want to take the place of Marac in every sense, to finish what he started."

Her face showed the shock of realisation of the feelings he had for her.

"No! Please, no," was all she could say as she fled, sobbing freely and deeply.

The sobs as she ran away made Olsar begin to regret his decision to bring her face to face, both with her failings and with his own need for her at the same time. He wished he'd kept his personal feelings from her at least.

*

The first of those who had gone to attack Verulamium began to return in ones and twos at first, carrying small bundles of the spoils looted from the town. They joyfully showed the contents to those who had stayed behind. The envy this created soon disappeared when it became obvious that they were not typical. The rest of the tribe returned to the camp empty-handed.

They'd left behind the buildings burning fiercely. The thick grey-black smoke from the fires rose high in the late afternoon sky.

"You were correct in your warning of what we might find, Boudica."

Frigionus spoke as he approached the Queen, who was talking to a group including Bodran and Linona. Olsar stood a little way off. Hearing these remarks, he moved to join them. The King continued to tell Boudica what he had found in the town.

"There were only a small number of our enemy left behind."

"You were told that would be the case," said Olsar.

"Most of them were the old and the sick but there were a few who had stayed behind to resist us."

"We told you that also," added Olsar, despite being ignored.

"We treated them all the same and not one of them has been left alive. I did get one trophy, though."

He gave a satisfied smile as he raised a small cloth-covered bundle which he had been holding by his side. He held it out in front of him at first at shoulder-height for a few moments, ensuring that all eyes were on it. With a flourish he spilled the object contained within it onto the ground where it rolled unevenly towards Boudica.

It was the head of a young man. It came to rest, not at her feet as intended, but in front of Olsar. Frigionus, roaring with laughter, gestured towards the head.

"I found this fat fool in one of the large houses in the centre of the town. He was standing sword in hand by the bed of his sick, pathetic hag of a mother. He was trying to protect her by killing us all."

Again he laughed loudly at his own sarcastic remarks.

"Unfortunately he was no warrior. He pissed himself in fear when I growled at him."

There was laughter in the growing crowd which was gathering to see what was happening. Boudica and those with her weren't laughing.

"At least he was prepared to stand and fight us to the death. Perhaps there's a lesson in that for us all when we finally fight our real enemy," Olsar warned.

"Fight to the death you say, Olsar. He was quickly disarmed and he began crying like a babe in arms. Perhaps that's the real lesson for all of us. When he knelt before me he was asking for mercy for himself and his screaming mother. I wanted her to feel the pain I felt when I lost Marac. She begged me to spare him and kill her in his place. I severed his head and threw it onto her bed. She nursed it as if it was her baby again. I let her suffer for a while before I slit her throat."

There was a mixture of laughter and cries of support again from the crowd. Frigionus circled slowly, arms raised in triumph.

Olsar turned his disgusted gaze from Frigionus to look at Linona. He found her staring intensely at the grotesque head at his feet before she raised her eyes to his. Olsar turned and left.

Frigionus continued his celebration.

"We shall kill many more Roman sons before we're finished. Isn't that so, Boudica?" he boasted.

"Tomorrow we march on Londinium," she answered coldly, striding off towards her tent.

Her command was greeted with a loud roar of approval soon to be repeated throughout the camp.

CHAPTER 28

The sumptuous home Decianus had built in Londinium was proving to be ideal temporary headquarters for Paulinus. In addition to the private quarters which were richly equipped with furniture and trappings, as good as anything in Rome, there were offices for himself and his staff to use in the short time he intended to stay in the town.

The Governor intended wasting no time in preparing to have a further meeting with the leaders of the town to tell them what he intended to do. He was seated at Decianus's desk making a mental note of the things which he needed to make clear to them. They wouldn't be pleased with what he was about to say.

"It's good to see you again, General."

Bestia had entered the room unannounced as he always had with Decianus when he occupied this building. Old habits die hard. However, what had been appropriate as the right hand man to Decianus was an unwise move in the presence of the Governor of the Province.

"It won't be if you ever come into my presence again uninvited," Paulinus fumed. "Now get out!"

"I apologise, Sir. I intended no disrespect."

Bestia was showing no fear but he stiffened his stance and stared straight ahead in a gesture of subservience. "I was very anxious to let you know that my men have taken a looter from Camulodunum into custody." He spoke quickly to stop Paulinus interrupting him before he'd got his words out.

"What are you talking about, you idiot? Do you think my time is taken up by dealing with looters myself? Get out and put him to the sword."

"We thought he'd be of interest to you, Sir. He was found with looted documents from your offices in Camulodunum. He admits he has many more hidden. I've had him beaten, but as yet he hasn't told my men where he's hidden them. He also claims to know you, Sir, and thinks you'll recognise him. He wants to talk to you."

Bestia had finally gained Paulinus's attention with these last remarks which made him relax his stance. It was a mistake.

"Stand straight, man! How dare you stay here when I've ordered you to leave? I need time to decide on the most appropriate punishment for your insolence. While I think about it, have your men bring this looter to me. In the meantime you can go to tell Tribune Agricola I want him to join me."

*

"You wish to see me, Sir?" Julius asked when he entered the room a short while later.

"Take a seat, Julius. I'm about to meet an interesting thief from Camulodunum. I thought you might be interested in enjoying a little sport before we deal with the more serious matters waiting for us."

Paulinus had a slightly mischievous smile on his face as he gestured for Julius to sit beside him.

Neither of the two men immediately recognised the old man who was brought before them. His face was bruised and so swollen that even his mother would have been excused for not recognising her own offspring.

His clothes were torn and filthy, displaying considerable blood-staining. Even so it was clothing which was still recognisable as that worn by the Trinovantes.

"You're clearly from one of the rebellious tribes," insisted Paulinus. "What do you have to say to me? Be brief or I'll allow Bestia's men to continue their work?"

The broken, trembling man stood head bowed. He muttered a few words through badly swollen and bleeding lips.

"What are you trying to say?" Julius asked firmly. "I think you need to speak more clearly. Say something which has relevance to us or your next words may be your last."

"If they are my last words, Tribune Agricola, at least I will have died trying to do my duty, like many brave men who died trying to defend Camulodunum."

The old man had winced in pain, struggling to stand up straight despite his injuries. He needed to be understood. His life depended on it.

"You know the Tribune's name. How?" Paulinus enquired, glancing at Julius.

"I've met the Tribune once before. It was some time ago when he came to the Library."

"Gamellus! Are you Gamellus Tullius?" asked a shocked Julius. "Come closer to me."

He was pushed roughly towards him by one of his guards, causing him to stumble. He steadied himself to stand swaying slightly before the two men.

"I am indeed, or more accurately what's left of him, Tribune. I wasn't captured. I came to this town willingly to meet the Governor."

"Why?" Paulinus asked.

"I was able to save your most important documents from being destroyed in the fires at Camulodunum. I got to them before the palace and everything in it was burnt to the ground. If I'm to die let me take you first to where I've hidden them."

"What documents are you referring to?"

"You insisted that those documents which you identified as the most important to you and the Province were to be kept in locked chests in the library. They weren't to be shown to anybody without your permission. Unfortunately the Procurator violated your instructions and got access to those documents. I couldn't stop him. Therefore, I failed in my duty to serve you. For my failure I expect to die."

"How did Decianus know of the chests and gain access to them?" asked Julius looking knowingly at Paulinus.

"That wretched assistant of mine, Gaius Tarquinius Marellus, told him and gave him the keys."

"It is Gamellus," Julius acknowledged. "From what I learned of this man from Marius I'm not surprised to see him here today."

"Before I decide what to do with you, tell us what you did and how you managed to survive the slaughter which was taking place," Paulinus ordered.

Gamellus told them about the events he had experienced. He described, not boastfully but proudly, how, through his determined efforts, he'd been able to carry out his rescue under the noses of Frigionus and his warriors.

"You've done me a great service," said Paulinus when he had finished his story. "Your reward is to become a member of my campaign staff until such times I can restore you to your rightful position as our valued Librarian."

Gamellus with some difficulty was smiling broadly at the Governor. Before he could express his gratitude Julius added his comments.

"I think it would be appropriate if such a valiant servant of Rome and a member of the Governor's staff were to be rewarded with the appointment of his own personal man-servant. He must be at his constant beck and call to attend to his every need and whim. I recommend Gaius Tarquinius Marellus as the most suitable person to perform that role. Would the Governor agree to my proposal?"

"Indeed I will. Before that, though, I want Bestia found and brought here. He can personally see to it that Gamellus has his wounds treated. In addition, he can be his servant until Gaius Tarquinius is found and reports to take up his new position. I think that will ensure that the young man is found rather quickly."

Gamellus smiled triumphantly at the kindness he was being shown.

Paulinus gave instructions to the men escorting Gamellus to take him to have his injuries attended to. They saluted and this time took careful hold of the old man to help him leave the room.

"I don't think that Bestia will be as content as we are at your decision to treat Gamellus with such generous attention," Julius joked.

"Perhaps not, but I'm beginning to like causing discomfort to the partner in Decianus's crimes."

Both men enjoyed this sentiment briefly before they returned to the serious business before them.

"Before you summoned me I had been in the meeting room. I would think that by now those in there will be eager to hear how you are going to save their lives and their great wealth."

"Then let's not keep them wondering any longer."

*

"Before the Governor addresses us I would like to make a request on behalf of all who are present here today. Will you reconsider your decision not to defend this town?"

The plea was being made by the town Magistrate.

"We have no wish to lose everything we've spent years building," he continued.

"Have you quite finished?" asked Paulinus impatiently. "Listen to me, all of you. I told you the last time I was here that this town is not defendable. It has no defences and I would have my back to the river without room to manoeuvre against Boudica and her thousands of marauding barbarians. When I meet her it will be on open ground. I won't be trapped in this town where her overwhelming numbers would give her an unbeatable advantage."

"We only have two legions. The 2nd Legion for some inexplicable reason has not yet left its fort to join me. It may be too late when it does eventually commit to coming to my side."

"Finally, you citizens are not trained or equipped to fight alongside my legionaries. You would all get in the way when the fighting starts."

"You could defend us by meeting Boudica on your terms before she gets here," added the hesitant Magistrate.

"I've made my decision," replied Paulinus, completely ignoring the suggestion. "We will cross the river tomorrow and head south to join King Cogidubnus. You should all go home and make your preparation to follow us. If you remain here you will surely die."

Tarquinius Marellus didn't give up so easily. He plucked up enough courage to take over as spokesman from the less than forceful Magistrate.

"I ask you again, on behalf of all present here today, to reconsider your decision. We came to this Province and have spent the last ten years or more building this town and making Britannia rich."

There were many in the room shouting their support. It encouraged him to continue.

"Our warehouses are full of goods which have been imported from all over the Empire. All our money has been invested in those goods. It will be impossible to save it all and take it with us if we have to leave."

"Burn it," Paulinus commanded angrily. "Burn it all. Destroy every warehouse and everything in them. Burn every home, and every ship moored by the river not capable of being sailed away. Kill every animal and burn those we cannot take with us. Make sure every other bit of food from the town and the surrounding farms and villas is destroyed or spoilt. Leave nothing for them to loot. Let them find nothing of any value, only an empty ruined shell of a town. Leave them not a morsel of food to feed their hungry thousands."

"But this is madness, we won't do it."

It was an anonymous cry from the back of the room and it was echoed by most of those in the room.

"You will," ordered a furious Paulinus, "and if any of you can't do it yourselves, my legionaries will do it for you. If you resist in any way they will have my approval to cut you down."

"If we do this we will have no future."

"The future of this Province is at stake and not just your fat, overflowing warehouses. I have only one objective and that is to defeat Boudica and bring to an end the idea of freedom her treachery has put into the minds of the people of these lands.

Most of her army are with her, not only because they hate us. Just as importantly, it is because they expect to be rewarded with vast amounts of booty. They see your riches as theirs. They will have been disappointed at Verulamium by what little was left for them. Imagine how they will feel when they get here and find nothing."

"They won't be the only ones with nothing."

Paulinus ignored the anonymous comment and continued.

"Many of her forces, far from home, will be disappointed and hungry. They will leave and go back to their pathetic hovels. At least there they will hope to find food. After the destruction of the three biggest towns in the Province there will be no more glittering prizes, no more promise of booty and food. Her numbers will be greatly reduced. Our numbers on the other hand will be increased by Cogidubnus and his tribesmen, who are eager to join us and face a weakened Boudica."

The room had gone quiet, listening to Paulinus forcefully make his position clear. He allowed the near silence to continue for a while giving his audience time to come to terms with the fact that he wouldn't change his decision.

"One final word of warning," he added eventually. "My army will march tomorrow and we will be marching at full pace. If you try to take all you own with you we won't be waiting for you. You will undoubtedly fall prey to Boudica's scouts and vanguard."

"When this is over we shall rebuild Londinium and it will be a greater town than before. Camulodunum will no longer be the administrative centre of Britannia. It will be part of the wasteland that the lands of the Iceni and Trinovantes will become when we have destroyed those tribes."

"At least, won't you reconsider the…"

"Enough! I have finished and will hear no more. Tomorrow Londinium burns."

CHAPTER 29

The bridge across the river, like the rest of the town, was a burnt-out ruin. The only timbers which were left standing were burnt black stumps rising from the placid expanse of water.

Boudica was standing in her chariot at the water's edge where the Romans had built a landing stage for their large seagoing ships. Paulinus had done a thorough job destroying the town and she was considering what her options were. Every single building had been razed to the ground in order to send a message to her that victory would come at a great price. It told her that her enemy was prepared to lose everything in defiance of her fight for freedom

Across the river, somewhere between the far bank and the southern sea many miles away, Paulinus was preparing to meet her. He would have plenty of time to choose his ground. Was he perhaps intending to reach the coast and take his legions to Gaul only for him to return later with a vastly greater and refreshed army? She couldn't hold her army together indefinitely. Her mind was in turmoil. Would they gain victory with great losses and then because of that lose their freedom again in the future as Cadellin had suggested? She had to destroy the legions completely to send a message and make sure that new ones were never formed to be risked in these islands again. Surely Andraste, having brought her this far, would not desert her.

Her thoughts were interrupted by the approach of a small group of horsemen led by Olsar. The last of the riders had a long rope trailing behind him. Tied to the end of it, with the rope tight around his waist, ran a stumbling young man dressed in Roman clothing. He was trying desperately to keep up by staying on his feet to avoid falling and being dragged in the dirt behind his captors.

"We've managed to take a few captives from this town and the surrounding fields," said Olsar. "We found this one who I thought would be of particular interest to you."

Boudica looked at the breathless young man who had been brought before her.

"I'm surprised you found anybody foolish or brave enough to remain here."

"You might consider he is both when you hear his story. It depends on whether you believe him or not. Tell our Queen what you've told me, Roman."

"I've told you what I am, and it's not a Roman. I'm one of their slaves," he began.

Before he could say anything further Boudica raised her hand to silence him.

"You sound like a Roman, dress like a Roman and look like one with your darker skin and hair. What's your name? I wager that's Roman also."

"My slave name is Draco," he replied. "I sound and dress as the Romans do with a Roman name because I was born a slave to them in Gaul. My ancestors had been forced into slavery when Julius Caesar conquered that land many years ago. I've known no other life."

"Why should I believe you? It would be easy to create such a story to save your life. In fact I think that's exactly what you've done."

Slowly Draco turned his back towards Boudica and drew down his tunic from his shoulders, baring his torso down to his waist. His back was criss-crossed with numerous scars from frequent whippings and beatings. Some were still in the process of healing. The gesture was not lost on Boudica.

"So, you have got my attention. I still don't believe you yet, but I will listen to what you have to say before I finally decide what to do with you. If I accept your story you can join us and fight for your revenge."

"My master was Tarquinius Marellus. I was his property and he assumed I was loyal and devoted to him and his family. That meant he thought nothing of speaking about secret and personal matters in front of me as if I wasn't there."

"What sort of secret matters?"

"He was an important man in the town. With others like him he was spoken to by the Roman General a few days ago. He was told what the army proposed to do."

Boudica raised her eyebrows showing her growing interest at the possibility of gaining answers to her many questions. She was also aware that this man could very well have been sent by that cunning fox deliberately to misinform her.

"Look me straight in my eyes as you tell me the rest of this story. If you're lying I will know it, and you'll wish you had never been born. Continue!"

"He returned from a meeting with the Roman General in a great state of panic. He told his family that he had been ordered to burn his house and destroy everything they couldn't load onto one cart to take with them. Nothing was to be left for you and your followers."

"That we can see for ourselves. Is that all you have to offer?"

"His daughters were greatly distressed and asked what was to become of them. It was at this point he revealed what the Roman army intended to do."

"Your life is hanging by a thread. This next part of your story, if it's a lie to deceive me, will be the last thing you ever say."

"The army is to meet the King of the southern people. He has promised to add his warriors to the Roman legions when they reach his lands."

"You are still telling me what I already know."

"Tarquinius Marellus didn't believe the Governor could defeat you even with such support. Even so he told his family he had decided they had no other choice but to follow him. He would have preferred to have fled to Gaul but there was no spare room on the few ships still remaining. Most had been destroyed by the army."

"Did he say why he believed the Romans would lose the battle against me?"

"He said the General had confirmed what had been rumoured here for many days. The 2nd Legion still hadn't left their fort in the West to join him. The General thought that it was too late for it to arrive in time, if at all, to take part in the battle to come.

My master thought two legions wouldn't be enough to withstand you even with the help of the southern tribes. If the Army were to be defeated he would flee with his family to the southern sea and escape to the safety of Gaul. It's what he thinks the General is preparing to do also, with what would be left of the Army. That is the real reason why the Governor is heading south."

"Anything else?"

"I decided to escape and wait for you and take my chances. I consider it a finer death to die at your hands a free man. It would be better than being put to the sword by your people in the coming battle, still a slave of the Romans."

"Your story has the ring of truth about it but I find it too convenient that you escaped and survived despite the mayhem taking place here."

Boudica was still deciding what to do. Olsar took the opportunity to intervene.

"Like you, I am inclined to suspect any man who has been tainted and corrupted by these heathens. Even so, if you allow him to live and he proves to be what he says he is he could prove a useful addition to us."

"I agree. I'll place him under your command. Make sure a careful watch is kept over him. Let's return to our camp. It's time to leave this burnt-out ruin."

Boudica felt some of her questions had been answered. She turned her chariot back in the direction of the camp which was being set up in the fields to the north of the town. Even if everything which she had just been told was true, the absence of the 2nd Legion may not last for very long. She could not believe they had ignored Paulinus's orders. There was no time for delay. She needed to engage Paulinus very soon. The less time he had the less support he could expect to gather to him, either from Cogidubnus or his missing 2nd Legion.

*

A large open area had been set aside at the centre of the overnight camp. The war council members had gathered in response to a summons by Boudica. While they waited they were already discussing the information which the slave had provided.

An excited air of celebration, which might have been expected to follow the fall of another Roman town wasn't evident. On the contrary, the faces of those present carried expressions of concern and unease. The discussions taking place quickly came to an end. All eyes had turned to Boudica and Frigionus as they emerged from her tent where she had been giving the King prior warning of what she was about to say.

She wasted no time on pleasantries but began her speech to tell them what she intended to do.

"The time is fast approaching when we will meet our enemy and defeat him. We know he's likely to have only two legions if we move quickly. He'll be waiting for us somewhere between the far shore of the river and the southern sea. It won't matter where he chooses when faced with our mighty army eager to crush him.

We are told Paulinus is going to meet Cogidubnus, hoping that he will join him and give him greater numbers. He will have thought the same about Cadellin and look what happened there."

Her remarks were greeted with laughter and insults for the absent King.

"When Cogidubnus realises how vast our numbers are he and his people will melt away just like the Catuvelauni did. Therefore, we must cross the river immediately and march with determination to give him as little time as possible to prepare for us. Do you have any questions?"

If she hadn't noticed the concern showing on some of the faces before, she was soon made aware of it by the intervention of one of her strongest supporters. It was Elidar.

"We're not as strong as we were, Boudica. You must be made aware of this if you aren't already."

"Speak freely."

"We are getting weaker as each day passes. Many of my clan, who have come the farthest with you are tired and hungry after many days on the march. As each day goes by we gather less and less food to replace what we brought with us."

"There will be plenty of food south of the river."

"Many, especially the children and the old, are beginning to fall sick."

He glanced around to see there were others nodding their agreement with what he was saying. It encouraged him to continue.

"We hoped, even expected, to have met Paulinus by now, either in Verulamium or further north of the town as he tried to return to protect it. He has managed to avoid that happening. This will greatly extend the time we need to keep our forces together and supplied."

"I agree."

"In addition there was little reward to be plundered from Verulamium. Many of those Trinovantes who were richly rewarded at Camulodunum took their leave and returned home rather than risk losing what they had already gained. Yesterday we found nothing in this town and little prospect of finding anything elsewhere. It has the potential of being disastrous for us and our cause."

Boudica, showing her annoyance at what she was hearing, raised her voice in reply.

"It is to be expected that a small number of the faint-hearted and those who are only interested in booty will betray us, but we can easily afford such losses. Remember, we have lost very few of our people in battle so far."

This time it was a different clan chief who chose to add his comments.

"If we don't lose any more, I would agree with what you have said. However, I've been warned that, as you march away at the head of our column tomorrow, many more who have lost the heart and the will to continue are likely to melt away."

"Enough," barked Frigionus. "I will hear no more of defeat from Iceni clan chiefs who seem to have come with us only to increase their personal wealth. Some of you have not forgiven us for taking most of the rewards from Camulodunum before you arrived late for the fight."

Elidar reacted quickest and drew his sword, pointing it at Frigionus.

"You and your stupid mouth go too far this time if you doubt any loyalty I have to our Queen, or my willingness to die for our cause. I speak for all the clan leaders here who you have just insulted. If you doubt my courage draw your sword and we shall settle this here and now."

"Control your tempers, all of you," Boudica ordered. "There will be no fighting amongst us now or at any time in the future. If we're divided disaster surely awaits us all."

She turned to address the two clan leaders who had told her of their concerns.

"I have listened to what both of you have said and I know you to be loyal and brave friends. I didn't like what I heard from you but I've listened and noted your concerns. Spend the rest of the day talking to as many as you can. Remind them again what our lives were like before these tyrants took control and conquered these lands. Give them some of the fire in your bellies, some of your aching desire for freedom."

"We shall do as you ask," said Elidar, "but when the battle starts I won't fight alongside this King of the Trinovantes. Keep us well apart in your battle plan."

"Don't concern yourself over that," Frigionus retaliated. "It won't happen. Some of the Iceni clans will only join in the fighting when the battle is already won like at Camulodunum."

This last provocation caused uproar as accusation and insult passed between the two tribes. Gradually the noise subsided as one by one those present became aware of Linona. She had moved into the centre of the ground with both her arms held high and her head lowered looking at the ground. It was a dramatic and exaggerated stance.

An expectant silence descended, leading to Linona slowly lowering her arms and raising her head. She began to move her fierce gaze from one person to another. After she had turned full circle she moved in front of Frigionus to address him.

"What would Marac have said if he were here today and saw what a rabble we are in danger of becoming? Did he die for nothing? He would have been ashamed with his father choosing to insult brave Iceni clan leaders."

She turned to face those clan leaders he had argued with.

"He would have been dismayed that those very leaders would need to be told by our Queen to go and encourage our followers to stay true to our cause. I was told very recently by a dear friend not to lose my focus. He told me that I have to control my selfish, personal hatred. I have to remember we have a very clever and mighty experienced army to defeat and we have to concentrate only on that. I beg you to take notice of this guidance too and to honour Marac's memory."

As she finished she looked towards Olsar whose face carried a broad smile of approval at her return to the Linona he so admired.

Boudica seized the moment and spoke before anything more could be said.

"My daughter has spoken the final words for today. At dawn tomorrow we break camp and cross the river to go to meet our enemy!"

She took her daughter's hand and together they walked back towards Boudica's tent.

When they were inside the relatively private space which their tent afforded them, mother and daughter began talking quietly of the events which had just occurred.

"The meeting ended quite well at least, with the words you delivered," said Boudica.

"You can thank Olsar for that."

"The differences being spoken of are real, though, and are beginning to show. We need to fight soon. We can't hold such a large number together much longer."

"Then we must ensure that we do everything we can to keep those differences under control," Linona suggested.

"I'll ask Olsar to spend what time he can with our clan leaders to convince them Frigionus is a good ally and still vital to our victory," Boudica offered. "He just doesn't know how to show it other than in battle."

"And I'll talk with Frigionus. We are still close because of our shared feelings for Marac. I'll remind him that when he insults our clan leaders he insults us all, including you, Mother. Despite his intolerance of those others he wouldn't want to do that to you."

CHAPTER 30

"This, gentlemen, is where I shall meet my destiny."

Paulinus was talking to Julius and King Cogidubnus. The three of them had spent the morning riding across the gentle rolling fields of short grass.

"Within the next few days I shall meet my enemy in battle in these fields. The decisions I'm about to take will be remembered by the people and Senate of Rome. Either I shall be lauded as a great conqueror of these wild and ferocious tribes of Britannia or I shall be remembered and loathed as a traitor responsible for the loss of Britannia and the destruction of our Legions."

"Together, with your legionaries and my warriors, we can't fail," Cogidubnus added looking slightly surprised at Paulinus's comments.

"Thank you, my friend. You are a true ally."

"Are you prepared to share your thoughts with me as to why you have chosen this place above the others we've seen, General?"

"Indeed I am. That is why I have brought you here. You and your people will have an important part to play in the battle if we are to triumph."

"What do you want us to do?"

"Let me explain. This place where we are standing, on this rise looking down the valley, is where I will put my command position. It gives me a clear wide view of the battleground as it slopes downhill away from us onto the broad plain below. The dense forests behind us and to our left and right give us protection from a mass attack to our rear and to our flanks."

"But you told me Boudica ambushed the 9th Legion by attacking from hidden positions in woodland," said Cogidubnus. "She could do that here, could she not?"

"On that occasion, she had had time to choose the place for her ambush and to decide where and how to position her warriors. This won't be the case this time. We got here first. In the heat and turmoil of the battle, she may still try to send some of her warriors to infiltrate those trees, harassing our flanks. That's where you and your warriors will serve me best."

"How?"

"You will fill those woods with your people. Place somebody behind every tree if you can," he joked. "That way you will make sure whoever she sends in there never leaves."

"But won't we be useful on the main battlefield?"

"Yes, but only later in the battle. She'll send her forces in an all-out attack on our front line formed just below us here. She will do so in the belief her numbers are so great they'll overwhelm us like a great tidal surge of water."

"That will be her mistake. Our battle-hardened legionaries will hold firm to withstand their assault. There'll come a time when part of her army's belief in their invincibility falters. That's when I will give you the signal and you can emerge in force all along their flanks to feed on that uncertainty."

"Until that moment it will keep her believing that you have chosen not to join us," Julius added. "If she sees only our legionaries facing her she'll assume that you, like King Cadellin, have chosen to run and hide as he did."

"Precisely," beamed Paulinus. "Julius reads my mind as usual. It will make her more confident that a headlong attack using all her forces at once must bring her a quick victory. That's what I need her to do."

"I will bring my warriors here and keep them hidden from Boudica as you ask. However, they will itching to join in the fighting."

Paulinus stepped forward one pace. Facing downhill, he spread his arms to point to the forests to his left and right.

"See how the edges of the forests come closer to us as they approach where our front battle line position will be. That will have the effect of funnelling their attack so that as they get closer they will become more compacted. The advantage of their superior numbers will be greatly reduced. Now all we need is for her to oblige us with her presence."

"She can't be very far away from us by now, Sir," Julius observed.

"I agree. We need to send out some of our scouts and cavalry to meet her. They must provoke her and guide her to the plain below. She will follow eagerly."

"I will liaise with the Legates and arrange for it to be done immediately."

*

On the ride back to the camp Julius began to dwell on those thoughts which had been increasingly troubling him in recent days as the final deciding conflict approached. His mood became increasingly sombre as he accepted that Linona would not only be fighting against him but probably leading the attack. He had been asking himself many questions. The answers to them were not easy to face.

Would she survive the battle? Her chances, if she led her warriors, would be virtually nil. The ballistas would be aimed at the leaders of the charge as they approached the defensive line. The bolts from those machines would hit their targets with deadly accuracy.

He would be leading the cavalry. What would happen if she too was given the task by Boudica of leading her riders to engage his cavalry? They would be no match for the experienced war-hardened men under his command.

Would he be able to carry out his duty if they should meet face to face? Would he be able to kill her without hesitation in a way he would with any other? If he were to hesitate it might endanger himself or his men. It troubled him that he couldn't be sure.

If she were to be taken captive, either unhurt or wounded, would he be able to leave her to her fate, particularly if it were realised who she was? It wouldn't be beyond Paulinus's political ambitions for him to take her back to Rome, with or without her mother. He would be lauded and she would be humiliated in front of the Senate and the people before some sort of ritual torture and execution was carried out. Would he try to rescue and save her? Would he even be prepared to help her to escape at the risk to his own future?

There was a still more troubling question to be answered. What if she lay mortally wounded on the ground in front of him? Would he be able to stop her misery and suffering by ending her life? Not to do so would leave her open to torture and mutilation before she died. This would certainly happen if it was known who she was. The legionaries and the auxiliaries took great pleasure in such acts of revenge for their fallen comrades, particularly against women.

"You look quite depressed, Julius," Paulinus commented. "I would have thought, knowing your wish for personal glory, you would hardly be able to contain your excitement and emotions. I'm expecting you to volunteer to be at the forefront of the fighting."

"Yes I am; both excited and eager to show my loyalty to yourself and the Emperor."

Julius quickly changed his expression to show his enthusiasm.

"I was serious for a few moments because I was going through your plan in my mind. I was wondering where I could be of greatest assistance to you."

"I thought this might be the case. I'll want you to command our cavalry with Camillus. When the enemy turns and tries to flee I want you to be merciless as you were on Mona. Take our cavalry, and wipe out as many as you can. We need to make this day memorable for all the tribes in Britannia. Those taking up arms against Rome can expect death and destruction."

*

The early-morning humid haze had quickly disappeared and the bright, sharp sunlight revealed the broad sweep of grassland. A few days earlier it had contained only a few cattle grazing peacefully in the summer heat. On this morning it was completely occupied by two mighty armies preparing for battle.

Boudica's widely spread forces had begun to arrive during those days. By now they had grown into a mighty gathering of men, women and children. A camp the size of a large town had appeared made up of tents, wagons and carts.

This camp was different from the many overnight marching camps which had been used in this long march to war. Those, in the main, had been merely places to rest for the night, haphazardly formed without any plan or control. This camp was being organised for the battle ahead.

At the front, a large area of open space, leading eventually up the slope to the Roman position, was being kept clear to enable those taking part in the battle to be marshalled and readied for the attack. Thousands of tents had been erected in the area behind. Finally, many carts and wagons had been placed at the rear.

The wagons had been arranged in a series of long lines facing the battlefield. Those who were unable to take part in the attack on the Romans would have a perfect view of Boudica's victory from the carts and wagons. They would be able to tell their story to future generations.

Both armies, having risen with the dawn, were preparing themselves and their weapons for the killing ahead of them. The constant low noise of activity in both camps was drowned out on occasions by an organised deafening, animal-like roar of challenge from one side or the other. Each time it was met immediately by a response from the opposing side.

In Boudica's tent she had brought her two daughters to join her as she prepared herself for the day ahead. Around her upper arms she had placed ceremonial royal golden torcs. They would demonstrate her authority over both her own people and the Trinovantes on this day of all days.

"Are you going into battle still wearing those when the time comes?" Cailan asked looking anxious. "Won't they make it difficult for you to steer your chariot and use your sword?"

Boudica and Linona exchanged a quick, slightly amused glance which didn't go unnoticed by Cailan, causing her to react a little sharply.

"What! I'm concerned for you, Mother."

"I know you are, my child. I don't wear them once the fighting starts, and I won't be needing my sword at the beginning either since I'm not leading the attack today."

"Why not? Won't our people expect it?"

"There are some clan leaders and many young men who want the honour of being the first to reach the Roman lines. Frigionus is insisting that he leads the charge when I give the order to attack."

"Where will you be, Mother?"

"If Frigionus is at the front, then I must stay in the rear to observe how the battle is progressing. Then I can make changes as necessary."

"What do you want me to do, Mother?"

"You were never meant to carry a sword into battle, Cailan. You must stay amongst the tents and wagons taking care of the sick, the children and our old ones."

"But Mother, I..."

Cailan was halted in her protest when her mother raised her hand sharply towards her.

"Do as I ask on this day of all days, Cailan."

She turned slightly to speak to Linona.

"Your sister doesn't like what I've ordered and neither will you, Linona. You'll stay at my side and won't join in the first attacks."

"I can't obey you, Mother."

"Don't challenge my decision."

"But our people need me to demonstrate how I'm prepared to die for our cause, particularly if you don't lead the attack."

"And I need you here with me. Clan leaders will be at the front giving all the leadership our people need. If things don't go as well as I expect, I will need your support to give fresh instructions to our people."

"Others could do that perfectly well."

"There will also be a need for you to be prepared to take over the reins immediately and continue our fight for freedom, should anything happen to me."

Linona began to argue her case even more forcefully but was stopped from doing so.

"I don't want to hear any more arguments from either of you. I've made my decisions. We must go to prepare for the battle."

*

Paulinus had arranged his two legions and their auxiliaries in ranks stretching most of the way between the two side forests. On either flank he had placed his cavalry as protection against any outflanking manoeuvre by the opposing forces. Julius was to command the right flank and Camillus the left.

The legates and their tribunes were to explain his battle plan to the men to be certain they knew what to expect. Although they'd fought for him before, they were likely to experience an initial assault the like of which most of them had never faced. The pressure of the huge number of opponent's being funnelled by the forests onto the shield wall would test their strength and discipline to the limit. Paulinus had placed two thirds of his legionaries in these front ranks, line after line to absorb this initial onrush and impact. The remaining third he kept a little way behind to be fed into any area of the front ranks showing signs of being forced backwards.

Julius was amongst the last to take up his command position with the cavalry on the right. He had taken a final opportunity, in full view of the whole army, to ride across the front ranks of legionaries to the cavalry on the left to exchange a few last words with their commander, Camillus.

"At least everybody here today will have just seen and noted Julius Agricola taking a prominent and fearless part in the battle for Britannia," Camillus teased Julius, who brought his horse to a stop alongside him.

"You do me a disservice," Julius countered, "I came merely to pay homage to my friend, the mighty Camillus. I'm hoping some of the limitless courage and cunning granted to you by the Gods will be passed on to me."

"I wasn't aware you thought you needed assistance from the Gods to make you brave. You didn't appear to, when we crushed the druids of Mona together."

"You're right. We really don't need the Gods to help us today? Just look at these magnificent men behind us. How could that mass of farmers, women and children below possibly defeat us?" Julius pointed down the slope to the massed Iceni horde.

"Agreed. However, since you're here, there's one last thing to say before you return to your men. I've greatly valued your friendship and loyal service in the short time I've known you. It was a privilege to have you alongside me on Mona."

"And I've benefited from your leadership and guidance," replied Julius. "I'll always be in your debt. Allow me to ask one more favour of you, however?"

"And that is?" Camillus asked.

"When the enemy break and turn in flight, hold your men back for a brief time to allow me and my horsemen to be the first to join the chase and get all the glory."

Both men broke into laughter. Before Camillus could deliver a suitable scathing reply he was prevented from doing so by the sudden deafening noise which broke upon their ears.

Paulinus had given the signal to begin the challenge to war. Thousands of legionaries began to strike their shields in unison, with the blades of their swords. It was a sign and a taunt to Boudica to let her know they were ready and thoroughly prepared for her to attack.

Julius gave one last fierce grasp of Camillus's arm. Any further words by either man would go unheard. He turned his horse and sped back to his men to take up his position.

The noise from the massed ranks of legionaries carried down the slope and across the fields to where Boudica was slowly guiding her chariot across the front line of her many followers. They were eagerly awaiting the battle, only being held back with some difficulty.

She rode past those clan leaders at the head of their warriors shouting her words of encouragement. They weren't needed. Gradually a mighty roar accepting the final challenge to war began to build in volume in response to the drumming of shields opposing them.

As Boudica reached the end of the line she turned and gave the final signal to Frigionus. The headlong rush for victory began.

*

The legates had arranged a long line of ballistas loaded with their bolts, just in front of the defensive front line. With deadly accuracy they began to bring down those leading the charge up the slope. Frigionus was amongst the first of them to fall. He and the many like him in the front of the charge died when they were still a hundred paces or more from their objective. Nobody paused to see to those who had fallen. Their bodies lying in the way were trampled into the ground by the thousands of onrushing feet. There was no stopping the headlong stampede.

With many already slain and their work done, the ballistas were picked up and carried back to the defensive line. It parted briefly to let through the legionaries carrying the machines, only to close quickly again.

The rampaging horde continued to move forward despite being temporarily hampered by the slaughter of so many of those leading them. Inevitably, as the ground started to rise and the approach between the two forests narrowed, the momentum of the onward rush began to falter.

Leaving little to chance, Paulinus had given the order for markers to be placed in clear view at a distance of 40 paces from the front line. When the front of the wave of attackers reached and raced beyond this point the legionaries in the front ranks released a devastating volley of a thousand javelins. This was followed almost immediately by a second volley from those ranks a little further behind.

It was as if the front wave of attackers had hit a stone wall as hundreds fell to the ground and others stumbled over their bodies. Still, those behind came on as they recovered, only to be hit by yet another volley of javelins.

Boudica had intended that the initial contact with the shield wall would smash forcefully and overwhelmingly through the defences. With all this carnage the advance was almost at walking pace along most of the front line by the time the shield wall was reached.

Even so, the eventual surge of numbers from behind began to build up pressure against the shields. In places legionaries were taking a pace or two backwards, but the line was being held.

The legionaries, equipped as they were with their armour and large shields, were taking a heavy toll of those poorly protected, some even naked, painted attackers. In a wild frenzy the front row of those attacking the shield wall were desperately trying to force spears, swords and axes upon those hidden behind.

Many brave men and women were dying in large numbers at the front. The crush from behind was so strong that those who died or had been wounded were prevented from simply falling to the ground.

Because of this the front lines became increasingly congested with the dead and dying, making it difficult for either side to have an impact. The battle was reaching a stalemate.

From her position just behind her army, and well to the rear, Boudica couldn't see all that was happening at the front. The fighting had gone on for some time, with each side trying to gain the upper hand. The Romans hadn't lost many men but those at the front had been fighting continually throughout, and were showing signs of fatigue. The front line was perceptibly moving backwards in a growing number of places.

Paulinus acted quickly and decisively. At his signal the trumpeters sounded 'relief'. His force reacted immediately and with discipline. The men in the front few ranks gradually exchanged places with those behind them and moved in an orderly manner to the rear. They were replaced by those who were fresh and eager to join in the killing.

Order had been restored. The legionaries were beginning to push and press forward in some parts of the line. Bodies from both armies were being removed back through the ranks to clear the ground.

"Should we give the signal to Cogidubnus to join the fight, General?" asked Legate Lubellus.

"No. It's too soon."

"Surely, if Boudica had intended to use the forest to outflank us she would have tried it by now. We haven't heard anything to suggest the forest has been infiltrated to any extent."

"I said not yet!" Paulinus snapped. "The battlefield is already congested. We have contained them. Now we must push them back upon themselves and cause confusion. The lower down the slope we can go before we throw all our forces at them the more room we shall have to kill them. I shall release Julius and Camillus first when the right moment comes."

*

Olsar had been given command of the horsemen from both tribes. His second-in-command was the eager but inexperienced Morfan. Despite his desperate pleading, he had been ordered by his father to stay in the rear and not to join him in the front of the attack. He had put his frustration to one side, when he proudly watched his father become the first to lead the line and run headlong at the Romans. He saw him hold high his family's royal banner to allow all his people to see him and follow his lead.

Linona had been ordered to stay with Olsar by Boudica, who had raced her chariot away from her command position to join the back of her army. She continued to move along the line urging them to press forward.

Olsar had persuaded her to take a squadron of his riders as protection, but he and Linona could see they were having difficulty in keeping pace with her.

"How do you think the battle is going?" Linona asked.

She was speaking to Olsar but she was looking at the frantic efforts of her mother.

His concentration, however, was not on Boudica but on the two groups of Roman cavalry.

"We should know before too long. If and when those horsemen on the left and the right make a move, they will have chosen to go onto the offensive to try to defeat us. We must stop any such movement."

"I'll come with you, and don't try to stop me. If we lose the battle today there won't be any Iceni tribe to lead."

*

The next signal delivered by the trumpets saw three tribunes take up positions directly behind the front ranks of legionaries. One stood in the centre and the other two were either side of him at about 30 paces away.

They began to bark their orders and those legionaries in the centre gradually began to increase their efforts and drive those opposing them backwards. As they slowly started to make progress the tribunes saw to it that more men were fed across and behind them. The effect was to apply more pressure, driving into the centre of Boudica's warriors. They were also giving commands for reserves to be brought forward to plug any gaps.

Gradually a wedge of legionaries began to form. It was splitting the opposing mass of packed fighters into two groupings.

Julius from his raised position on the back of his horse could see the move forward taking place at the front. He had been waiting for this to happen. The time for his crucial decisions was fast approaching. He ordered his officers to keep the pressure on their opponents' flank, to squeeze them back into their faltering centre.

"Some at the back are feeling our movement forward and are leaving the field," cried Legate Lubellus.

"They are merely the faint-hearted and camp followers," growled Paulinus. "There are many determined warriors out there still fighting. They won't easily desert. Send a message to Camillus to mirror what Julius is doing and squeeze inwards from the left."

*

The first sign of panic at the rear had been quickly dealt with by Boudica. Her cries thundered at those she had seen turn to begin to make their way back towards the camp.

She hadn't hesitated to draw her sword and cut down two young warriors who she deemed to be leading the withdrawal. She continued her drive through those heading to the camp waving her bloodied sword. The retreat was checked allowing her to come to a halt to catch her breath. One of the horsemen who had been helping to keep the fearful from leaving the lines came galloping over.

"There's movement in the forest to our left. We haven't sent any of our warriors into there."

"Then let's go to have a look," Boudica ordered.

Olsar, who had been watching the action in front of him closely, noted with concern the sudden movement of Boudica as she headed towards the trees.

Boudica brought her chariot to a halt ten paces from the edge of the dense forest.

"Three of you move into the trees and see what you can find. The rest of you..."

She didn't complete her next command. An arrow flew from the trees and hit her just above her left breast causing her to fall backwards from her chariot, to lie dazed on the ground. One of the horsemen jumped from his horse to shield Boudica from any more arrows. Another took control of the horse which had been pulling her chariot. The rest of her escort had been joined by many who were on foot. They raced into the dark interior of the forest. At the same time Boudica was helped onto her chariot and taken back, at a full gallop, towards the camp.

"Follow me," Olsar shouted, racing with Linona to meet them. They led them through the tents to the rows of wagons and carts.

Boudica was carefully placed onto the flat surface at the back of a large cart. Linona could see her mother's right leg had been badly broken in falling over the side of her chariot. She was barely conscious but she managed to motion her daughter to come close to her.

"We now know why Cogidubnus hasn't joined the battle yet," she whispered. She winced in great pain and coughed and spat out the blood filling her mouth.

"Try not to speak just now, Mother."

"He and his people are in the forest, probably on both sides. He's waiting until we've been weakened enough for him to dare to join in with Paulinus."

"Mother, Mother, what's happened?"

Cailan had seen the commotion and rushed to her mother's side.

"Don't upset yourself, Cailan. I'm not dead yet. Olsar! You mustn't remain here. Take your riders to protect our flanks. If Cogidubnus's people leave the forest, cut them down."

"I shall take my horsemen to the forest on the right where my people are fighting," said Morfan.

He left immediately without waiting for agreement from either Boudica or Olsar.

"Stop him," Linona cried.

"Let him leave. He knows what he must do," Boudica whispered to Linona. "You stay close to Olsar." Her voice was beginning to falter. "Cailan will look after me here."

She turned once again to Olsar, fighting against her pain and growing weakness.

"Drive your horsemen up the flanks to protect our people. Meet and destroy their cavalry. If you can do this and get round behind their lines to kill Paulinus, we can still defeat them."

*

Paulinus observed the mass of Boudica's horsemen taking up positions on their left and right at the rear. He saw them beginning to move up their flanks.

"They've found out we've got people in the trees," he snarled. "I'm still not ready to release them, though. Send riders to Julius and Camillus to tell them to push harder down through the flanks and engage their horsemen. When they've overcome them, they can start to attack the rear of those fighting on foot. Cogidubnus will then be released. We shall have them on all sides."

Julius received the message and responded instantly, thrashing into the ranks of his enemy.

Olsar could see that Julius had made his move. He was forcing a way down the slope towards him. He drew Linona's attention to what was happening.

"I've decided we won't go any further to meet them. We can't leave our rear unprotected from those hiding in the trees. We'll wait until they reach us and then we can fight them on open ground where our greater numbers will be in our favour."

Eventually the fearless efforts of Julius brought him very close to Olsar and Linona, although they didn't immediately have chance to cross swords. The sudden clash of riders and the resulting chaos produced fighting both savage and bloody. All three were distracted as they fought to defend themselves.

Fighting off a feeble attack from his right Julius had chance to see Linona defending herself expertly from an attack from one of his men. She nimbly whirled her horse to avoid the first thrust of his sword. Julius allowed himself a look of admiration at the speed with which she countered the attack, almost severing the man's arm just above his wrist. For a short while he lost sight of her as he fought off challenge after challenge.

Gradually the Roman cavalrymen, battle-hardened in recent times, were gaining the upper hand against the fierce but inexperienced horsemen.

Olsar had fought his way slowly but determinedly towards Julius until he was able to shout to him above the noise of battle.

"I told you the last time I saw you that our next meeting would be our last. Are you ready to die and meet your Gods, Roman?"

"Not yet, you savage, and certainly not by your hand."

Olsar kicked his horse hard, crashing it into Julius with such force it unseated him, throwing him to the ground.

Linona could see what was happening from a short distance. She fought fiercely to join them to be able to get to fight Julius. She'd seen him fall from his horse. What she saw next came as a complete surprise to her. Instead of acting immediately to trample him to death under his own horse, as she would have expected, Olsar paused. He had taught her always to strike without hesitation if she was to win in battle. To her horror he leapt from his own horse to fight the Roman on foot.

Her warning cry went unheard by him in the deafening noise of the struggle going on around them. For a few brief moments the two men fought with difficulty amongst the mass of whirling horses closing in on them.

Linona didn't quite make it to Olsar's side to do what he himself should have done, to trample the Roman to death. She gasped as she saw Olsar stumble, kicked sideways by another rider's horse. He clutched helplessly at thin air, only to land forcefully onto his back in the churned-up earth. She winced in despair as Julius moved to stand above him. Without pausing he thrust his sword into the side of the defenceless Olsar. A desperate cry left Linona's lips when she saw Julius strike his blow and withdraw his sword to stand astride Olsar. He raised his arm to strike again, a smile of triumph lighting his face. It was the last she saw of Olsar, the man who had played such a large part in her young life. She wheeled her horse and reacted just in time to parry a slashing blow aimed at her head. Suppressing another overwhelming feeling of personal loss at Olsar's death, she had to fight hard for her own life as the Roman cavalry sought to gain the upper hand. She could see some of her fighters gradually giving ground.

Soon after, she saw the long line of her army begin to crumble all along its length. It wasn't yet a full retreat and she turned her horse to do as her mother had done, riding along the line to scream at those fleeing. She desperately ordered them to turn and be prepared to fight.

Despite the noise all around her she still managed to hear loud blasts from the trumpets behind the Roman positions. Cogidubnus's hidden warriors emerged with a loud roar from the trees on both sides to attack the flanks of her people. She could see the whole of her panicking tribe begin to race away from the battle in the direction of the camp.

She rode to join her mother and sister to tell them the battle had been lost and to give them all the protection they would need when they tried to escape. The cart, where her injured mother lay, was surrounded by a large crowd, some crying and wailing, while others were standing in shocked silence.

She leapt from her horse, fearing the worst, and forced her way through. Her mother lay cradled in Cailan's arms. The arrow was still deeply embedded in her chest, although the shaft had been broken off. Bodran stood at the side of the cart, his old craggy face pale and drained of any obvious emotion.

"Quickly! We must make arrangements to leave and regroup," Linona ordered. "Our warriors have lost the battle and the camp will soon be overrun. Once I know you are ready and able to leave, Mother, I shall organise a protective force to make sure you are taken away to a safe place."

"I'm going nowhere, my child." Boudica spoke very quietly and weakly. "I can feel the life draining away from me. I won't be able to leave this place. I've failed Andraste and she wishes for me to join her."

"Please Mother, don't leave us," Cailan cried.

"Don't be upset, my dear child. Please look after our little Cailan, Linona. You mustn't fight on, even to avenge me. Promise me you'll try to escape to keep both of you alive. Our people will need you more than ever. Promise me! It's my dying wish."

"I promise."

"Louder! I want Andraste to hear your sacred oath."

"I promise to do as you ask," Linona shouted. Tears streamed down her face. She had great difficulty in believing what was happening all around her.

"Good! We have little time left. Where's Olsar? He will protect you."

"Olsar is dead. He was brought down and killed by Julius Agricola."

Boudica's face winced in pain.

"I mustn't be taken by those barbarians either alive or dead. Bodran, you must remove the arrow from my chest. It will let the blood and my life flow from this body more quickly. Afterwards you must set fire to the cart with me in it to make my body unrecognisable to my enemy. Remove anything from me that might give me away."

"It will be done," replied a solemn Bodran.

"Thank you my friend. Now all of you must save yourselves."

Bodran bent to do what was asked. With some difficulty he removed the arrow head, causing the blood to gush out of her chest. Linona and Cailan, holding tightly onto each other, sobbed and said their final farewell to their mother, whose life quickly ebbed away.

*

The slaughter continued on the battlefield, in the carts and in tents throughout the camp. During the battle Camillus had quickly disposed of Morfan and his men. Seeing the enemy flee, he had chosen to take his cavalry around to the rear of the carts and tents. He was ensuring that as few people as possible would escape the battlefield.

Julius had broken off from the killing of the retreating Iceni to move amongst the dead. He headed straight to where the cavalry duel had taken place searching in vain for Linona's wounded or dead body. He began to fear the worst.

CHAPTER 31

By the time darkness approached, many of those who had fought against them in the battle, had either been killed during the fighting or wounded and put to the sword later by the jubilant Romans. Those who had been spared had been secured and placed under close guard. The women and children likely to bring a good price as slaves or who could be given to Cogidubnus and his people the following day had been rounded up and placed in hastily erected holding pens. They had little chance or desire to escape, with nowhere to run to in this land so far from their own homes. The very old and those seriously sick, like the badly wounded, were considered a liability in the aftermath of the battle and had been disposed of.

Julius, physically and mentally exhausted, hadn't taken part in this tidying up. Once victory had been assured, and having rested for a short while he'd spent most of the time since with Paulinus. With all the other senior commanders they had been reviewing the battle and exchanging stories of personal experiences.

When their discussions had ended he began walking aimlessly in the growing gloom of dusk. He had realised he was unlikely to find the relief of sleep early that night. The events of the day kept playing and replaying through his mind.

After the fighting had ceased, his partial search of the battlefield for Linona had produced no sign of her, dead or alive. Eventually, he had given up, overwhelmed by the sheer number and state of the bodies lying all around. Hoping she had survived but was perhaps injured, he had spent some time amongst the wounded, who were being attended to by the surgeons. Later he had gone to look amongst the captured women, thinking he might find her there. Overwhelmed by the huge number in the holding areas, he finally admitted defeat. He was left with the hope that she had somehow managed to escape.

He moved to the temporary camp where he thought he might find Camillus again, intending to spend the rest of the night in his company. He paused, recognising a figure approaching him. It was Bestia, a man he would rather see dead than speak to at that moment.

"A moment of your time, Tribune Agricola," Bestia said, making it sound more like a demand than a request. "It could well be to our mutual advantage."

"Be quick, man. I've little time to waste."

"Earlier, I was rounding up captured women in the camp helping to ensure they were placed under guard in holding areas. It wasn't easy, believe me."

"Why are you trying to annoy me with this useless information?"

"I assure you it's not useless. I've discovered things which you'll find very interesting."

"So? Get on with it."

"As you know, a while ago I was commanded by Decianus to order my men to punish Boudica and her daughters. That was despite my strong objections."

"You're trying my patience to the limit."

Julius was about to explode, reminded as he was of Bestia's role in supporting Decianus. He was having great difficulty in controlling his urge to cut out this man's lying tongue. He held back and spoke again.

"You need to reach the end of what it is you have to tell me, and quickly."

"Well, Sir. Two of these captured women are Boudica's daughters. They were heavily disguised when I found them, but I eventually recognised them beyond any doubt."

"What are you saying?"

"I thought you would want to know so that you could be the first to take this information to the General. He'll be very grateful. You could expect to be rewarded in some way."

"And what reward are you looking for?"

"I want to be released from the Army. I would also like to be granted a large farm near Camulodunum now the war is over. There's bound to be a lot of land to spare there from now on."

"I see. I'm grateful to you for coming to me," whispered Julius, moderating his previous aggression. "Take me to see them. We've no time to lose if we are to benefit from this."

*

Julius looked over an upturned cart which formed part of one of the simple pens containing a large number of female captives. Many of them were sobbing quietly in the gloom.

"There they are, leaning against that wagon over there."

He pointed to a wagon some distance away to the left.

"I've had them tied to the wheels to separate them from the crowd and to ensure they don't escape. Do you want to enter the compound to take a closer look?"

Julius peered through the darkening gloom and was nearly overwhelmed with relief. He would recognise her anywhere.

"That won't be necessary at the moment. Who else have you told about them?"

"Not a soul. I'm not a fool. I've told only you. I would have gone directly to the General but he's ordered me never to approach him without being summoned. I also think you'll want to show your gratitude for what I've done for you. Your support will increase my chances of getting the reward I want."

"At least you're being frank with me. You've done well and acted wisely," Julius lied. "Let's take a short walk while we discuss this. We must think this through and work out how we can both gain the maximum advantage. If only we had their mother or could find her body if she's dead. Show me where you captured them."

"Come this way."

"Wait! One last question before we go. How well have you left them guarded?"

"They won't escape."

"Why do you say that? It just might be possible for them to break free and melt away in the night."

"I have a man watching them closely. But, if by chance those pathetic creatures did manage to get away they wouldn't get very far on foot. The cavalry will be sent out in the morning to round up any stragglers who managed to escape today. They would be brought back to me and taught a lesson."

He gave a little chuckle of self-satisfaction. Julius was finding it difficult to stop himself from striking him to the ground. He nervously shuffled about in front of Bestia.

"You don't look convinced, Tribune. Don't concern yourself. My man can be trusted to keep a close watch over just those two."

"How good is he?"

"He's not very bright but he fears me more than any other man alive. He has been with me a long time and is somebody I always use and rely on."

"I suppose then he was one of those who you took with you on that visit to the Iceni settlement with Decianus."

"He was indeed. He'll obey my every order without question. They won't escape."

"If he's seen them before couldn't he recognise them as you've done? He might go to tell somebody else in your absence?"

"They have tried to disguise their appearance and dress. Not being very clever or alert, he hasn't recognised them so far in this darkness."

"How can you be sure?"

"If he had I would be the first and only person he would have told. Besides we'll shortly be telling the General, won't we?"

"Of course. Now, show me where you found them."

"They were standing next to that when I first recognised them."

Bestia had taken him to a burnt-out cart.

"Were they alone?"

"They were standing with their holy man, the druid. They had thrown away their weapons. I can only think they hadn't been able to get away because the cavalry had blocked all the escape routes."

"What were they doing?"

"I assume they were discussing their options. If I'm honest with you I might not have spotted the two females if he hadn't been there. I immediately remembered him. Because of his size he couldn't easily disguise himself even if he had tried. It drew my attention to them, if you know what I'm saying."

"Carry on. What happened to Bodran?"

"Ah yes! That was his name! I remember now. I just ran my sword through him."

"Why do that? He was a good prize as well."

"I may have taken him prisoner if the idiot hadn't tried to stop me from grabbing hold of those two."

"What did you do with his body?"

"It's probably still lying around here somewhere, if it hasn't been collected yet."

He began to search, crouching low in the darkness.

"Yes, here it is, half hidden by this cart," he added, sounding pleased with himself.

He stood up and turned to face Julius. The sword entered his body at his waistline just below his armour. Julius moved it upwards with a quick thrust.

Bestia's expression changed into one of pained surprise. He staggered a step forward, placing his hands on Julius's shoulders to prevent himself from falling. He opened his mouth as if to speak but could only let out an agonised gasp.

Julius's hate-filled eyes stared coldly into Bestia's questioning face as he slowly pushed the sword upwards seeking the man's heart. He found it.

Bestia fell backwards and lay lifeless alongside the body of Bodran.

Julius's mind raced as he considered what options he had. He decided he had three and began to consider each of them in turn.

He could leave Linona and Cailan to their fate. At least they would stay alive. If they remained unrecognised they would be sold into slavery once the legionaries had had their fun. It was more likely they would be given to Cogidubnus tomorrow. Either fate would eventually destroy them.

Secondly he could take them as his personal slaves and try to hide them from Paulinus until he could release them. The risk of this would be too great. Sooner or later Paulinus would come into contact with them and recognise them. He would consider it an act of betrayal to hide Boudica's daughters. Their lives and his would be forfeit.

Finally he could help them to escape. At least they would have a chance, but only if he could provide them with horses. Linona was very resourceful and would have a good chance of survival. His problem would be to try to convince them that he sincerely wished to let them escape. He had spent the day killing many from their tribe and fighting off those trying to kill him in return. He didn't have the time to try to build any trust in them. He had to act that night, whilst it was still dark.

*

Much later, as the camp had settled down for the night, he made his way to where the horses had been tethered. If he was seen and recognised, it would be quite natural for a tribune to be carrying out a security inspection on a night such as this. Earlier he had noted only a few guards covering a large number of horses spread over a wide area. He moved in the dark and quietly released two horses. He led them slowly and calmly round to the burnt carts where he could secure them.

Next, he walked back to the pen and approached the lone guard, who had taken a position sitting on top of one of the carts. His head was hanging down onto his chest as if he was having difficulty keeping awake. He saw Julius at the last moment and jumped fearfully to his feet.

"Relax, Legionary. After what we've all experienced this day I'm surprised to find you awake."

He smiled as he placed his hand on the legionary's shoulder.

"Thank you, Sir," the relieved man replied.

"Now, there's something I want you to do for me. Come this way."

Julius walked a few paces to where he could point out Linona and Cailan.

"I can't sleep tonight either, and I need something to amuse and relax me. Do you see those two young females tied to the cart wheel over there?"

He gave a nod.

"I want you to take them to the back of this holding pen. There you'll find carts which have been burnt out."

"I know where you mean, Sir."

"Good man. Wait for me there. I've other things to do before I take them off your hands."

Julius moved off into the dark as if he was making his way to the temporary camp. He hid in the shadows and watched the legionary do as he had been instructed.

After waiting a few moments he followed them at a distance until they reached the cart. He moved closer but kept far enough away in the dark so that the two sisters couldn't recognise him.

"Legionary! What do you think you're doing with those savages? Leave those two and come here immediately."

"But, Sir, you..."

"Don't question my order. Do as I say if you value your life."

The man ran to Julius and stood trembling before him. Linona saw her chance as the two Romans were talking and she grabbed Cailan's arm.

"Quickly we haven't a moment to lose. There's a chance for us to be free."

She pushed her sister and they stumbled towards the horses. The soldier turned as he heard the horses moving away.

"They're escaping, Sir. I must report to Bestia quickly. There's something important I need to tell him about those two."

Julius clasped the young man to him, roughly turned him around with his back towards him and slit his throat.

"That's for the pain and shame you, Bestia and those others brought to Linona and Cailan," he murmured.

He let the man's body sink slowly to the floor and walked quickly into the dark interior of the camp.

He had no doubt now that he would sleep easily for the rest of the night.

*

A jubilant Paulinus was spending the following morning touring the whole of the battlefield reliving each moment with Cogidubnus, his two legates, their senior tribunes and Julius.

"Soon all Rome will hear of my victory here."

"Never again will your enemies dare to threaten you," said Cogidubnus.

"That's certainly true of the Iceni and Trinovantes. We shall end this by destroying their settlements. They no longer need them. Their lands will be given to the true friends of Rome," an excited Paulinus added.

"And what about Boudica?" the King asked. "Is she among the dead?"

"There are thousands of bodies out there already starting to rot. I won't waste too much time looking just for her."

"What if she's escaped? She could still be trouble."

"Even if she isn't dead, her cause certainly is. If she managed to escape she has nowhere to go, no-one left to lead, no life ahead of her. If she's out there and we're fortunate enough to capture her, I shall take her to Rome. Otherwise, she's no longer relevant."

"Come, gentlemen, we have much work to do. We shall begin to restore and rebuild Britannia without delay. When we've finished here we'll return to Londinium."

CHAPTER 32

Quintus Tiberius Saturninus was standing with his head bowed in the courtyard of his house in Londinium trying to identify any blessings he might still have left. He was having some difficulty, and was coming to the conclusion that the Gods had become indifferent to him and his family. They seemed to have ignored his many sacrifices and pleadings. While they hadn't chosen to have him destroyed by this war, he hadn't been left untouched by it either. On the contrary he felt he'd lost a great deal that was dear to him.

He had spent the last few days in Londinium trying to come to terms with what he'd found. Every building had been destroyed. Initially damaged by fire, many had been razed to the ground by those savages in their frustrated rage at finding the town already put to the torch by their enemy. He had wandered through the ruins of his own house and warehouse, reflecting on the years of work that had been obliterated in a day.

Friends he met when he came back into the town had told him Paulinus had returned and set up camp to the north of the town. He'd let it be known to all those returning that the victorious army would now be put to work rebuilding the town. Londinium was to become the new centre of his administration of the Province instead of Camulodunum. This would bring new wealth to the town and those citizens like him who were prepared to work with him.

He began to think perhaps things weren't so bad after all. It wasn't long before he had seen enough. He decided to leave the town to return to his villa and estate, only a short ride to the west.

When he arrived back in the early evening in late summer he became acutely aware of the lack of activity in the fields. His mood darkened again. At this time of the year he should have been busy in his fields from dawn until dusk, as would everybody else who would have lived and worked on the estate. Nearly all of them had gone. He recognised the size of the task ahead of him here and in Londinium.

He eased himself off his horse and secured it for the night. Slowly, he made his way back to his silent, almost deserted villa.

"You don't look as if you're happy with what you've found, my love," said his wife Julia, walking towards him with her arms held out in greeting.

"Things could have been worse, but if I'm being honest, not very much. At least we still have this villa, and Paulinus has promised to help us."

He kissed her on the cheek and described to her what he had discovered.

"But how are we going to survive here?" asked Julia with tears in her eyes. "There are only the five slaves remaining, those who went with us when we fled to your brother's villa in the west. The rest who ran away are probably dead by now."

"Please don't upset yourself again, my dear."

"Don't upset myself? Of course I'm upset. How are we going to work the fields without slaves?"

"Let's go indoors. I need to recover from my journey. We need to talk about the things we can do and not those which are beyond us."

"Who will help you to restore and look after your interests in Londinium? Who will help me to take care of our home and our daughters?"

She buried her head in her hands and sobbed.

"At least the Gods have spared us," he said. "We'll make offerings to let them know we need their assistance like never before."

"We need slaves not Gods."

"Don't forget you still have faithful Caris. She will help you with the household, and I have Portos to help me. He can control and train the new slaves when we purchase them."

He took hold of her and cradled her to him for a few moments before carefully guiding her up the steps and inside the silent building.

*

The following morning hadn't started well for Quintus. His wife had refused to rise. Still tearful from the evening before, she had chosen to stay in bed refusing to join him for the first meal of the day. He was concerned at her state of mind. Normally, she was a gentle, sensitive, caring woman and he loved her deeply. She wasn't strong or in good health anymore because of the trauma of the war. Somehow he had to help her to get well and find enjoyment in life again. He needed her.

The heavy, humid air was still present from the previous evening. The rain had continued to pound against the roof of the villa when the first light came. The sound of it wouldn't have encouraged her to change her mind about staying in bed all day. Neither had it lightened Quintus's mood. He stood at the front of the villa staring out across the rain-soaked fields. The depressing downpour finally ceased and the sun began to break through the rapidly thinning clouds. He was trying to persuade himself it would make good sense to ride around his estate to see what had survived the war.

On his return from the safety of his brother's estate a few days earlier he had found the villa had suffered only minor damage in his absence. They had been able to set up home again very quickly. It had allowed him to make it a priority to go straight to Londinium to assess the situation there.

He was gazing at the fields, wondering what cattle and crops had survived Boudica and her rapacious followers. His thoughts were soon interrupted.

To his mild surprise he saw a group of four wagons leave the main east-west road which ran past his estate. They joined the short track leading up to his villa. He withdrew into the villa to find Caris and Portos. Instructions were given to them to gather together the other three remaining slaves. They needed to prepare a welcome meal for the approaching visitors.

*

"The war may have changed many things, Quintus, but not your famed hospitality," said Lepidius.

The words coming from his mouth were followed by a dribble of red wine. It fell down the front of his gown, which had already been soiled at previous meals.

"This wretched weather has been with us off and on for weeks since the great battle. It's as if Boudica's Gods are crying in sorrow at her great loss. But her loss is our gain. Isn't that so, my friend?"

"I find it difficult to see any gain or take any comfort in the war and the devastation it's caused," Quintus replied.

He'd dealt with this slave trader before and he had some difficulty hiding his distaste for the man. His charm and manners were those of a pig and he smelled almost as bad.

"I know you've had property in Londinium, which was destroyed, and like many others lost a great number of runaway slaves. At least I can provide you with replacements for the slaves."

"I could see that by the number in your wagons as you approached the villa."

"The war has produced many already and we're still capturing those who escaped the battle. You can have a wide range to choose from."

"Where have these come from?"

"From the west, where I've been collecting those captured recently. I can let you have first choice of them and at a very reasonable price."

"Let's go to have a look at them then."

"Paulinus and his staff will never know, or even care, if I arrive with one or two fewer prisoners to be shipped out to Gaul. That's where these captured fugitives from the war are being sent. Just let me finish with this wine first."

He gulped down the last of his wine, once again spilling some of it down his clothing in his haste.

*

Quintus had chosen three of the strong-looking young men from the tribe of the Trinovantes. They seemed on first inspection to have survived the fighting without any serious injuries. Satisfied with his purchases, he'd been about to end his dealings there for the time being. Portos, being the size of an ox, would have little difficulty in quickly taming and controlling these three. Together they would be able to begin to restore the estate.

He was turning away from the wagons when his attention was

drawn to the one furthest away.

"What's wrong with these?" he asked, pointing to two young females who were slumped in the corner of the wagon, clutching each other.

"Those two were only captured and beaten into submission in the last few days. They are skin and bones. They must have been hiding in the forests for weeks."

"They look in need of attention to me."

"The oldest, the one covered in vomit, is ill for sure and the other may be also. I doubt they will survive until they reach Londinium. I've no spare food to give them and even if I had I'd prefer to give it to my horses. They're worth more."

He looked carefully at the curious Quintus before he made him an offer.

"You look interested, Quintus. I'll do a deal with you if you want."

"What sort of deal?"

"If you buy two more healthy slaves and give me a better price for those you've already chosen, I'll let you have those two pathetic bitches for free."

Quintus looked at the two poor wretches. He couldn't help thinking that had things turned out differently it might well have been his two precious daughters cowering in an Iceni wagon. They were about the same age, perhaps a little older. They would have been on their way to being delivered to Boudica instead of Paulinus.

"I'll buy one extra slave at the prices already agreed and will take both those females off your hands as a gift."

"If you can improve your offer I'm sure we can do a deal."

"I won't have any further discussion or argument, if you want to do business with me in the future. You know very well I will need more to replace all those I've lost."

Julia had been alerted to what was happening outside and joined Quintus on the steps of the villa. He was watching the wagons leave the courtyard to head down the track. She looked down to see the new slaves which her husband had just purchased. They were crouched in the courtyard just in front of her.

"What's been happening, Quintus?"

"I told you we would soon be able to replace our slaves and make a start to rebuild our life. Already, we have bought these four strong young men to help in the fields."

"And what about those two?"

"The two females can help Caris although she may have to wait a short while before they're fit and able to work."

Julia moved down the steps and crouched to touch and gently stroke the heads of the two young females.

"You poor things," she sighed. "I wouldn't see my animals in the fields suffering and treated as you've been. Caris! Portos! Come here and bring these two indoors where we can treat their wounds and feed them."

PART III

CHAPTER 33

LONDINIUM, 70 A D

Following his arrival in Londinium, Julius hadn't had time to absorb all the changes which had taken place since his recall to Rome nearly ten years previously. What he had seen had surprised him. He hadn't expected the transformation which had taken place in such a short time.

When he arrived by boat from Northern Gaul he was impressed by the new docks which had been built in front of the replacement warehouses. He recalled the view he'd had from the far bank looking back to see the town in flames ten years earlier. The docks, like the new bridge and most of the substantial newer buildings which he could see, had been built with a bright, almost white stone. They couldn't fail to impress citizens and visitors alike. The lesson of how easily the earlier, mostly wooden town had been utterly destroyed in one night by the fire had been learnt by those who'd set about the task of rebuilding.

It was also a demonstration by Paulinus and his successors that Londinium was now the heart of the Province. Rome and its powerful army were there to stay. It had become a monument to the victory over Boudica.

His time after stepping ashore, apart from attending the Games, was taken up settling into his new official residence. He'd acquainted himself with his junior officers and legionaries in the 20th Legion, before his attention turned to familiarising himself with the deployment and general condition of the other legions throughout the Province.

The task ahead of him, bringing greater discipline to the whole of the army, was very much in his mind when he walked the short distance from his quarters to the Governor's new palace in the centre of the town. He noticed the amphitheatre which for much of the day of the Games had been a cauldron of tumultuous noise. Today it stood in silent homage to those who'd died there.

The sight of it reminded him of his astonishing meeting with Linona as he'd called her ten years previously. Now he must remember to refer to her by her new name, Lucia.

At first he'd felt relief at seeing her alive. He'd often hoped, occasionally imagined, that she'd survived, but he'd never considered they would meet again after so many years.

The shock of seeing her alive and stunningly beautiful after her victory had caused turmoil with his emotions. Her beauty was not that of the gentle well-bred, languid gentlewomen of Roman society. Rather her attraction came from her smooth, lithe and taut body combined with a skin which gave off a radiant glow.

Not for her the easy life of long lazy days in the bath houses, and hours spent applying creams and perfumes to her face and body. She had spent the last ten years maintaining her physical fitness and readiness for conflict in the arena.

He'd been overwhelmed by an aching need and a curiosity to learn how she'd survived after her initial escape. Had she recognised him in the shadows the night of her escape? How had she become the favourite of the crowd in the Arena? Perhaps most importantly, how had she kept her identity secret and avoided discovery?

There had been a feeling of sadness and regret, watching her expression change from shock at seeing him again to one of fear and defiance. Should he tell her later how he'd tried to avoid the war with her mother and her tribe? Would it be safe even now to confess to her that it was he who had saved her and her sister that night from immediate cruel slavery or death? If he did tell her would she believe him? She had gone through so much and lost almost everything dear to her. If she did believe him would she use it against him in the future?

He reached the Governor's palace and began to climb the steps past the saluting guard. His final thoughts before he entered the building were to ask himself why he felt such a great need to seek her out and explain what he'd done, what he'd had to do and why. Why couldn't he just behave as if he hadn't recognised her? There was no obvious need for their paths to cross again. Soon he would be marching north, not returning for months, perhaps years. Why not just let her escape again and disappear into the background once more?

Forcing his thoughts back onto military and political matters, he reached the large private office of Governor Vettius Bolanus. He did so without pausing for his presence to be announced. He didn't wish for Vettius to assume any more authority over him than circumstances required. He was superior to him only in official status and title, not in personal authority. Because of the freedom Emperor Vespasian had given him to sort out the military failings of the Governor he didn't feel the need to behave in any way that would give Vettius the idea he intended to play a subservient role.

Vettius looked surprised at Julius's unannounced entry into his office. Nevertheless, he made no comment about it. He merely stood and held out his arm in greeting to him. The large, rotund man he had been talking to also rose from his chair and stood stiffly, as if to attention. He lowered his eyes submissively to stare at the floor.

"Welcome, General. I trust you've settled into your new quarters and they are to your liking?" Vettius enquired, taking Julius warmly by the arm.

With his free arm he pointed to a large couch in an invitation to him to take a seat.

"I will remind you of what I said when you first arrived. If there's anything you need in your quarters you must let me know."

"Thank you, Governor. If it was necessary I certainly would. However, I find everything that you've already provided completely satisfactory."

"That's good. Nothing will be denied you in making your stay with us as comfortable as possible."

"I can see that by the ample supply of that special red wine which you've provided for me. It's a generous welcoming gesture which is very much appreciated."

Julius had responded generously and diplomatically. He'd also copied Vettius's lead and addressed him formally by his title rather than with personal names. Perhaps the presence of the other man had prevented a more informal greeting from him. This thought made him look more closely at the man who still hadn't relaxed his stance.

Julius's quick assessment put him at about 30 years old, although his ample chins may be adding years to his appearance. He thought he looked vaguely familiar but couldn't quite think why.

"I see you're looking closely at Gaius. Forgive me. I need to introduce him to you. He's my secretary, Gaius Marellus."

"Welcome, General."

"Thank you, Gaius."

"Perhaps you recognise him. He was telling me just before you joined us that he'd met you before. It was ten years ago I believe, when you were here as a young tribune. He says it was only once and briefly even then."

Julius wondered if the reference to him being only a "young tribune" was an attempt to establish his own maturity and hence some sort of personal authority over him. He quickly decided not to respond. He reminded himself not to be over-sensitive at this early stage to what was probably an innocent if mildly provocative comment.

"Is that true? And when was it?" Julius asked, directing his question at the young man.

"You won't remember me, Sir. I was part of Governor Paulinus's administrative staff. We only met briefly on one occasion."

"You do look familiar, but if we only met once it would explain why I don't recognise you."

Julius turned his attention back to Vettius.

"Let me explain why I've called to see you. I believe you're about to hold a more formal business meeting with some of those who you invited to the banquet before the last Games."

"That is correct. It's a group of the town's elected officials together with the wealthiest businessmen and largest landowners. I hold these meetings on a regular basis."

"I'd like to attend this one. It will help me to get to know them better. I can also add to the reassurances I gave to them before those Games."

"But naturally you must be there. Perhaps you and I could take a while to discuss the matters I want to place before them. None of them are military issues I hasten to add."

He turned to Gaius and smiled.

"Would you please leave us, Gaius? We can continue our discussion later."

The secretary rose and hastily left the room with only a slightly hesitant nod towards Julius.

"A bright young man, that Gaius," said Vettius. "His father is Tarquinius Marellus, who is probably this town's richest and most generous citizen. He has interests in everything and has funded many public works here in recent years."

"From what I've already seen he should be very satisfied with the results."

"It's no surprise that he has considerable influence in the town. I like to keep him on my side. I'm sure he could prove very useful to you and the army in meeting your need for supplies and equipment."

"It sounds like a suggestion that I would do well to make a friend of both father and son."

"Indeed! It could prove a great advantage to you. The son particularly has proved a great asset to me. He's lived most of his life in this town. He knows everybody and he has an ability to get to know what's going on in every aspect of public and private life."

"How so?"

"He's developed a wide network of contacts and he employs them to great advantage to keep his finger on the pulse of what is happening in the Province. His father's wealth helps with the funding of this network. I often use Gaius as my eyes and ears. As a military man I'm sure you appreciate the need for good information about the mood of the people."

"I note what you're saying and will give your advice some thought. For now, let's concentrate on what is to be the business of this meeting."

*

Julius had spent his time during the meeting observing those present and the contribution each of them had made or indeed had not made. He had been particularly interested in the secretary's father Tarquinius Marellus because of what Vettius had said.

It hadn't taken long for him to recognise the son, once the reference to Paulinus's administrative staff had been made. He was ten years older but he remembered the miserable wretch who had done Decianus's bidding, and that he had been well and truly flogged for his crime. Julius had contented himself with the thought that it was no wonder the man had appeared nearly to wet himself when he saw him.

The formal meeting had been drawn to a close by Vettius and the wine and delicacies brought in to allow more relaxed informal discussions to take place. It allowed a free exchange between Julius and those curious to talk to him about his role ten years previously, and what had happened to him since. It also gave them an opportunity to catch up on the latest news and gossip from Rome.

"Ah! Here is a distinguished senior citizen for you to meet, General," said Vettius.

Taking Julius's arm, he guided him to a small, balding old man.

"I'm sure you will be pleased to meet each other. This is my good friend Quintus Tiberius Saturninus. I'm sure you have much in common to talk about, particularly the events of the Games."

Vettius gave a little knowing chuckle as he winked at Quintus.

"Before you two begin, however, may I say that you don't look at all well, Quintus."

"I'm fine, perhaps a little tired."

"You look pale. I hope you aren't suffering an illness of some sort. The climate in these islands doesn't make it easy for us to stay healthy. Do you want to sit down?"

"Please don't concern yourself, Vettius. I didn't sleep well after the Games. Unfortunately at my age you very easily and clearly reveal your lack of a good night's rest."

"I'm not surprised you didn't sleep after such a unique event. The performance by Lucia was magnificent, as I knew it would be. I also knew she was never in any danger of losing. None at all. You must be very proud of her?"

"As you know, I didn't attend. I didn't share your total confidence in the outcome. I can only say I'm grateful the Gods were watching over her and chose to favour her."

Quintus was talking to Vettius but looking closely at Julius.

"You must be beginning to realise that indirectly this man cost you a great deal of money, Julius," said Vettius. "His daughter Lucia was the victorious gladiator you bet against, but I'm sure you hold no grudge."

"Indeed not. The young woman was extremely impressive. Her name is Lucia, you say. It was a delight to watch her skilful display of the art of combat. It's most unusual, maybe without precedent, to find a woman of Rome who is capable and willing to fight in the Arena. She must be an extraordinary woman and you must be very proud and honoured to have produced such a daughter."

"She is my adopted daughter as Vettius knows," said Quintus, his gaze not leaving Julius's face. "But she is no less precious to me for that. I would willingly die for my children if their lives were threatened. That's why I couldn't watch the contest and didn't attend."

He turned back to speak to Vettius.

"Given the nature of the contest, I hope the unique spectacle of yesterday will remain just that, Vettius, unique? I wouldn't wish for Lucia to be involved in any such future event."

"I can understand your concern for your daughter's safety entirely," said Julius before Vettius could reply.

Quintus looked sideways at him, a slightly surprised look on his face.

"Do you have children of your own, Julius?" he asked

"I have a wife and a young daughter, who has already developed a stubborn, independent streak."

"Have you brought your daughter with you?"

"No. I have purposely left her in Rome where she can be tutored properly in my absence. Whatever sort of woman she eventually develops into, I can only hope I will be as supportive and understanding as you undoubtedly are with Lucia, Quintus."

There followed an awkward silence as Julius and Quintus each waited for the other to speak next. The silence was broken by Vettius who, aided by Julius's interruption, had ignored Quintus's anxious question about Lucia's future in the Arena.

"You must pay a visit to Quintus either at his house here in town or at his country estate and villa. He's renowned for the hospitality which he and his daughters provide."

"I would welcome an invitation, but did you say daughters? You have others like her?"

"There can be only one like her. I do have another daughter living with me, but she is completely different. She would never raise her hand to harm another, not even to defend herself."

Vettius had been looking around the room and could see that others were anxious to meet and speak to the General. He politely brought the discussions to an end, excusing himself and Julius.

"This is Tarquinius Marellus," said Vettius. "He..."

"We've met before," interrupted Tarquinius. "It was a long time ago when we last met. They were painful, chaotic times then."

"Indeed they were," Julius agreed. "It was in a meeting much like this I recall, but in completely different circumstances. We had to make difficult decisions in those days affecting us all. From what I've heard, you made a magnificent recovery from the war and have prospered as well as anybody in this land."

"That may well be true but not without a great deal of difficulty considering the losses we had to endure, and nobody more than me."

"Many lost a lot more than money and property," said Julius. "On both sides."

"Well, we are where we are. My son tells me you met earlier today. You didn't recognise him, although you had dealings with him in the past."

"No, I must confess I don't," Julius lied, "but it was a long time ago. Much has happened since then to erase for ever so many memories. He looks to have made a success in his role on the

Governor's staff."

"He has indeed. Perhaps we can both be helpful to you in your work."

Julius didn't wish to get into any premature discussion on important matters, military or otherwise.

"I'm sure we will have some mutually beneficial dealings in the future. Would you excuse me for now, though? I have many more of your friends to talk to."

*

Eventually Vettius and Julius were able to move to one side of the room to talk quietly in private.

"Well, Julius. You've met the great and the good of this town. What do you think of them?"

"I think they're very much like those I left ten years ago, which isn't surprising when a good number are the same people. Despite you calling them the great and good I suspect they're a mixture of the good, the bad, the energetic and the lazy, the devious and the naive. They will be much like any gathering of publicly spirited men, including our Senate in Rome."

"True. However, did anybody impress you particularly?"

"Quintus appears to be a man of substance and character. I think I'll pay him a visit as you suggested, if his food and wine are as good as you say."

"And it will enable you to study his daughter a little bit more, no doubt," Vettius teased.

"What do you mean?" Julius asked, slightly nervously.

"I noticed your interest in her at the Games. Be careful my friend. Her reputation suggests she's a man-hater."

"Hasn't Quintus found a suitable marriage partner for her?"

"Not yet, and from what I hear he wouldn't dare. I see where your interests are heading. I can understand if you might be missing the comforts of family life already. I shall arrange for your needs to be attended to tonight by the best in women the town can provide. Maybe your interest in what might be unattainable will diminish."

"I can see you are a very shrewd observer of men," Julius said, choosing to take the opportunity to apply a little flattery. "I think we shall work well together."

*

Much later in the evening Vettius, Tarquinius and his son were taking a late drink of wine as they often did, reflecting on the day's events.

"I think I may have some difficulty with my new General," Vettius suggested. "From what I've heard, he won't be a man who will be easy to control, or to persuade to join us in our little arrangements."

"All men have their price or their weaknesses," murmured Tarquinius.

"Maybe that doesn't include this one. He comes with a reputation of being incorruptible, just like his beloved sponsor Vespasian. They served together, you know, before he became Emperor."

"I disagree. Give me and Gaius a short while to dig a little and I'm sure something will come to light. Don't forget we will never forgive him for what he did to my son."

"So be it," said Vettius. "It might be advisable for you, Gaius, to brief your spies to pay close attention to Quintus and his daughter. He showed a lusty interest in her. If anything were to develop, his wife and family in Rome might be interested. It could give us an advantage."

"It will give me great pleasure," Gaius snarled. "I never thought I would have a chance at revenge for what he did to me."

CHAPTER 34

The solitary large oak tree cast a broad area of welcome soft shade from the bright early afternoon sun. It offered Portos a good vantage point from which to peer into the gloom of the thick forest which lay in front of him.

He couldn't detect any movement from his enemy but he knew he was lurking somewhere in there, waiting for the right moment to strike. He mustn't let him get the chance to break free unexpectedly, catching him at a disadvantage.

Cautiously, he moved his horse out into the glare of the sun. Drawing his sword, he barely blinked, waiting for his prey to break cover. He thought he would either try to escape suddenly, emerging at a distance from him, and flee across the open fields, or he would choose to try to surprise him close by. That way he would gain the crucial initial advantage in any ensuing contest.

Portos moved to within a few paces of the edge of the forest. Turning his horse, he trotted slowly along the line of the trees. Was that movement he could see a short distance ahead? He stopped. Shielding his eyes from the glare of the sun with his hand, he was able to stare into the thick growth of trees. Too late he realised he had made a mistake.

Behind him his opponent gave a loud triumphant war-cry. At the same time, he forced his steed out from the trees, heading at full speed to attack him.

Portos had just enough time to turn his horse and hold his sword to parry a mighty slashing blow aimed at his body. The clash of weapons was so great the attacker's sword broke in half.

As the broken end of the sword flew harmlessly through the air, the two of them, Portos and his young student, burst out laughing.

"I think that's enough war games for now," Portos ordered. "Let this be the lesson for you for today, Marcus. Make sure your weapon is made from the finest materials and not inferior to the one used by your opponent. Obviously the wood from the tree which produced my sword was stronger than yours. It was much bigger as well."

Marcus laughed and threw the rest of his broken sword into the forest.

"What are we going to do next, Portos?"

"It's time for us to return to the villa. Your grandfather should have returned by now."

"Race you to the gates," cried Marcus, forcing his heels into the sides of his pony to speed across the open field.

"Take care, young Marcus."

Portos looked concerned that this nine-year-old boy was casting caution to the wind as usual.

"If you're seriously hurt, we can expect your grandfather to sell me to the first slaver that calls on him," Portos shouted after him.

"You know that's not true," Marcus yelled back. "He wouldn't dream of it. He treats you like my father. Perhaps you are, even if you look as old as Grandpa himself."

"You rascal. Just you wait until I get my hands on you."

The race was on.

As was often the case the boy won the short race before Portos had the chance to catch him. He jumped from his pony and ran straight to the outstretched arms of Quintus, who was waiting on the villa steps.

"I won, Grandpa."

"I see old Portos is getting slower each time you challenge him. Or are you getting quicker? You'll soon have to let him have a start if he's to have any chance of beating you."

He winked at Portos who was walking towards them.

"When did you get back from Londinium, Grandpa?"

"Not long ago."

"Portos tells me there's a new General. Did you meet him? Were you frightened of him? Did you buy me anything?"

"Too many questions, young Marcus. Take a moment to catch your breath. Then you might want to go to see what I've just asked Caris to look after for me."

Marcus sped off without another word and dashed up the steps and into the villa. He was followed more slowly and sedately by the two old men. They exchanged a knowing, affectionate smile.

"Caris! Caris! What's Grandpa brought me?"

"Not so loud," Flavia cried from the kitchen. "You'll make my ears burst."

"Sorry, Auntie F. Where's Caris?"

"I'm here," said Caris walking towards him with her hands teasingly hidden behind her. "What can I do for you?"

"You have something behind your back that Grandpa has brought for me, haven't you? What is it? It is for me, isn't it?"

With a sharp movement she brought her hands in front of her to reveal a brightly multi-coloured horse blanket. It was just the right size for a small pony.

"Just what I wanted, Grandpa," cried an excited young boy. He grabbed the blanket from Caris. "I can't wait to show it to Mama."

"I can see it," said Lucia, walking into the room. "But do you think you've earned it?"

The boy didn't bother to answer. He ran and jumped into his mother's arms. Lucia returned his caress before holding him away from her at arm's length.

"And have you thanked Grandpa for his kindness?"

"Of course I have, haven't I, Grandpa?" He looked at Quintus, nodding his head to try to get his support.

"Your delight is thanks enough, Marcus. You must promise to take good care of it, though. It's very rare. Blankets like this one are hard to find these days. They're only made by some special people who live a long way away, far beyond Londinium, to the north-east."

He looked first at Lucia, and then at Flavia. Both knew why he had deliberately mentioned the north-east. He gave them a gentle but sad smile.

"Now, Marcus. I would like to talk to your mother and auntie, so run along with Portos and try out your new blanket on your pony. He won't have cooled down yet."

After the others had left and the three of them were alone, it was Flavia who spoke first.

"Does the gift of the blanket and what you said about our people being 'special' mean you've begun to forgive us for hiding the truth from you for all these years?"

"It's a gesture of some sort, my child, but I'm not sure what. In any case it's my way of saying I still love you both dearly. It will take me some time to fully understand and accept all the things you've told me. But you're still very precious to me."

Not for the first time since their confession, Flavia could hold the tears back no longer. She rushed to Quintus, burying her head in his chest. Lucia took more measured steps to join in, wrapping her arms around the pair of them.

*

A short while later, when emotions had calmed, the three of them were talking quietly about Quintus's meeting with Julius Agricola.

"He's an impressive, confident, charming man. In fact he is a much more sophisticated man than I was expecting, given his reputation as a ruthless military commander."

"Yes, but did he know who you are?" asked Lucia, showing her tense impatience.

"He certainly knows I'm the father of the victorious gladiator from the games of a few days ago. Governor Bolanus made sure of that."

"Did he tell you he knows who we are? Has he told you to surrender us to him? You aren't telling us something are you? How much time do we have?"

Flavia was firing her increasingly desperate questions, showing the state of panic which she had reached.

"If he has recognised Lucia he still didn't acknowledge it. We must try to stay calm. Perhaps he was testing me to see if I would betray you both in the hope of saving my own skin, though I doubt it."

"There is one thing we can assume," Lucia added. "Whatever he was doing, it would appear he hasn't said anything to Governor Bolanus yet. What do you suggest we do, old man?"

Quintus had always known that when Lucia called him 'old man' it was her way of showing her deep affection for him.

"We behave normally. We carry on with our lives. I'm not without influence and you, my dear Lucia, are a favourite of the citizens of Londinium. He's a powerful man, but from what you've told me, added to what I heard and saw at the meeting, I can see he's a shrewd and cunning politician as well."

"And devious, and unscrupulous, and…"

"Therefore, Lucia," said Quintus, interrupting her, "he won't act in haste unless he feels threatened or has a pressing reason to do so. He has no need to feel threatened yet."

"Don't trust him, whatever you do," snarled Lucia.

"I also have one other thing to tell you. He has more or less invited himself to pay us a visit in the near future."

"I could have guessed as much," said Lucia, with a slight curl of her upper lip. "He is playing games with us all. Just don't expect me to be present and to take part just to humour him."

"Please, let's not take those sorts of decisions today," Quintus begged. "There's plenty of time for us to plan for his visit when it happens."

Flavia nodded in agreement

"In the meantime, as I rode back from Londinium, I thought about the long story of what has happened to you. I have many additional questions to ask. The more we talk, the more I will be able to understand."

CHAPTER 35

The initial shock and confusion caused by seeing Linona alive and well, and transformed into a Roman citizen called Lucia, had soon abated. It allowed Julius to return to being his normal self, the efficient, determined, single-minded military commander, qualities that had brought him much success in recent years.

The courageous tribune of ten years ago who recklessly helped the two sisters to escape would have made it his priority to approach Lucia immediately. He would have acted to resolve their unfinished business, not allowing any further delay, to confront her about the tensions that had existed between them from the start all those years ago. Not now. He could bide his time. The General of today was a different, more circumspect man.

In the meantime he would make it his priority to carry out an inspection of the peaceful parts of the Province. Outstanding issues with Lucia would be resolved eventually. Time would help to calm the raw emotions resurrected by their first unexpected meeting and allow a second, less tense, meeting to give them the chance to talk to each other.

He decided to undertake a tour of all the military installations of any significance, having discussions with all his commanders. So far he had covered the far West and the North-West as far as Viroconium. He'd been reasonably comforted by what he had found. The tribes were totally subdued and at peace, apparently content with the prosperity Rome had brought to them. The downside had been that the legionaries based in those lands had become soft and ill-disciplined.

Eventually he made his way back southwards to Verulamium to meet King Cadellin. The last time he and Paulinus had spoken with him, the King had confidently predicted that the Romans would be victorious over Boudica and would return to rebuild his town and his palace. He hadn't been completely genuine but he had been correct on both counts.

*

"Is Paulinus well?" Cadellin enquired. "We haven't heard of him for some years in this far outpost of the Empire."

Julius, after a few words of greeting had been exchanged, had sprawled across a couch in the King's new luxurious palace.

"He's retired and I've not heard of him since his retirement. Then again I've had no reason to."

"Why is that?"

"For many of the years since my last time in Britannia, I've been in Rome immersed in politics and administration there. It was either that or my time was spent with the Army, far away from the city and all the politics and gossip. So I'm not aware of where he's living or if he's well or not. However, I'm sure he's experiencing the fruits and pleasures peace has brought, just like you."

"Let's hope so."

"But what about you and your people? I trust that you're still content with the rule of Rome, and are an effective ally of Governor Bolanus?"

"Indeed I am. I promised Paulinus I would continue to respect the wishes of his successors when he returned to Rome."

Cadellin had responded easily, unprovoked by Julius's rather obvious taunt.

"I can see you've become very prosperous again."

"Indeed, as has the whole of my tribe. Add to that, we have become strong again. In fact we are the strongest tribe in the whole of the Britannia. I'm certain you and I can continue to work well together."

"I'm sure we can. In fact that's why I'm here. I want to be reassured that I can count on your support later when I move to quieten those troublesome Brigantes and others further North. What forces will you provide when I decide to take action?"

"Naturally, you can expect my loyal support, General. I understand this is now the correct way to address you. It's a promotion you no doubt richly deserve. Did you receive a welcome reception from those citizens of Londinium on your return?"

"Does your loyal support include providing fighting men to join my auxiliaries?" Julius probed, ignoring his other comments, designed to avoid answering his question directly.

"But of course. As to how many, I'm sure we can come to a mutually acceptable arrangement should the need arise."

"The need has arisen. In preparing for my campaign I will need to add your men to my numbers. Let me be clear about what I require. I shall expect you to provide 2000 of the best fighting men from your tribe, one half of them with horses."

"That's a large number of men," Cadellin replied with a deep frown.

"Any of those which you send, that I find are unsuitable, will be returned and replaced by double their number. Will you provide them willingly? Yes or no?"

"What you're asking me for would have a serious effect on my tribe's ability to pay our taxes."

"Yes or no?"

"Of course my answer is yes. But I'm sure you and Governor Bolanus will use your influence to ask the Imperial Procurator to look favourably on any future request for an appropriate reduction in our level of taxes."

"You can talk to the Imperial Procurator yourself. You will no doubt receive the same sympathetic and supportive treatment you would usually get when making such a request."

Julius stood up. He had got what he came for.

"That concludes my business. I've been travelling more or less continuously for a number of days and I'll be leaving early in the morning. I'll take my leave so I can bathe and retire early."

Julius had made it clear to the King that he would not countenance any failure to meet his demands. He wasn't in the weak position Paulinus had faced the last time Cadellin had chosen not give his support to Rome.

*

The last part of his tour of inspection was to be through the lands of the Iceni and Trinovantes. He would have the opportunity to see for himself the continuing effect of the desolation of those tribes.

Julius discovered that Camulodunum, unlike Londinium and Verulamium, had only recovered to a small degree in the past ten years. A few of the retired legionaries, who had escaped from the town and survived the war, had returned to farm the land. Only a small force of his own men from the 20th Legion was now needed to be garrisoned there, commanded by a young inexperienced tribune.

He had deliberately chosen to arrive without warning and found a relaxed, untidy fort. Those legionaries present outside the tribune's headquarters looked at him with disbelieving eyes at first, before nervously standing to attention to salute him. He stormed past them without a word.

The tribune rose from his chair, showing the same disbelief and fear as his men. Julius stood in the doorway of the young man's office, his legs wide apart and his hands on his hips. His face showed the anger that was building inside him.

"Why was I allowed to enter the fort without being challenged?" he growled. "Why are there no guards at the gates?"

"We've no need to be fearful of any attack, Sir."

"And why have you come to that conclusion?"

"There are very few Britons left in these lands. Those who are here are farmers interested only in crops. They have no military ambitions against us."

"The history of this Province and indeed of all our conquered lands teaches us we must never lower our guard. As a soldier of Rome you must never assume our subjected peoples see us other than as conquerors, or that they will never rise up against us."

He moved to stand menacingly close up to the youthful tribune, their faces almost touching. The tribune was shaking with fear, no doubt expecting the worst. Julius spoke quietly, almost in a whisper.

"I shall take light refreshment." His eyes searched the young man's trembling face.

"Certainly, Sir."

"It will help me to recover from my journey and allow my temper to calm down."

"Yes, Sir."

"Afterwards I will decide what to do with you and your miserable band of untidy layabouts."

"Yes, Sir. I'll arrange something for you immediately, Sir."

"Don't move yet! By the time I've finished refreshing myself I will expect you to have every single man in the fort on parade in full military dress. They will have the opportunity to demonstrate to me that they and you are worthy to continue in my army. Now you can send for food and drink. Get on with it!"

*

If the garrison at Camulodunum had been a surprise and disappointment to him, it was a much greater shock as he toured the lands of the Iceni. Eventually, he arrived at the site of Boudica's settlement.

He found the extensive fortification and buildings had vanished. They had been ploughed out of existence, covered in a full crop which would soon be ready for harvesting.

At this point he decided to end his tour, having seen enough to know the Iceni people no longer existed as a significant proud tribe. Those from the tribe who were still occupying the lands were small collections of individual families bent only on survival. It could explain why Linona had never returned to her tribal lands, and instead had somehow been able to become Lucia.

*

The tour of inspection had confirmed to Julius what he had strongly suspected. Firstly, the Legions were in need of a sharp lesson in his kind of discipline. Secondly, he need not be concerned about absenting himself to conduct a campaign in the north. There wasn't a threat anywhere he'd visited like the one facing Paulinus when Presutagus had been King of a powerful and difficult people. Cadellin and his tribe were thriving and more content than ever with the wealth that Rome had brought.

Vettius and Julius were meeting to let the Governor receive an initial report to this effect.

"It's good to see you again Julius. I'm sure you found everything more or less as you expected? There must be plenty of improvements that you with your wide experience of such matters will be able to make. You can tell me all about it later. Fortunately, you've arrived in plenty of time to enjoy our next games in ten days."

Julius thought it typical of this man and his sense of priorities that he obviously wasn't eager to hear any details of the mood of the army or the tribes in his Province. He preferred to dwell on the pleasures provided in the arena. He quickly decided that he wouldn't waste any of his own time or energy explaining what he'd found and intended to do about it. He didn't need any authority from this man to get on with the task he had been set.

"What sort of gladiatorial contests might we expect?" Julius enquired.

"I thought you might ask that. Anxious to win your money back, eh?"

"Exactly."

"I thought you may have another interest as well," Vettius teased.

"Such as?"

"It doesn't matter. Regarding the events being planned, I can't give you all the details. Tarquinius Marellus is arranging and paying for them."

"He'll have to spend a lot of money if he's trying to compete with those you provided," Julius suggested.

"I don't think he will consider doing so. They don't have to be as prestigious mine were. Circumstances are different. Even so, he'll be offering a good variety of events."

"Anything unusual this time?"

"He tells me there should be a fight between two females again. If there is, I'm sure it will be arranged so that Quintus's daughter is included. That would please you, would it not?"

"It doesn't matter to me."

"Perhaps you would like to bet against her again or have you decided to support her this time?" Vettius continued with a smirk.

"Maybe so. I will have to give it some thought."

He had avoided answering the questions more directly. It was more difficult to disguise his unease at the possibility of a fight to the death again.

"Will your friend Quintus have great cause for concern like the last time?"

"No! No!" Vettius explained. "That contest was unique as was the occasion. It may be a long time before another warrants it. Perhaps a glorious resounding victory against the Brigantes and the complete absorption of the whole of the rest of the tribes in the north might be an appropriate time."

"I understand."

"This time we shall revert to a contest for exhibition and ceremonial display only. Any blood which is spilt with intent will only be by men. I'm sure at least one of their contests will be to the death. Marellus is rich and can afford the cost."

"I shall look forward to it," said Julius. "And now if you don't mind I would like to spend the rest of the day recovering in the baths."

Despite his last comment, Julius, instead of heading for the comfort of the baths, returned to his office. He spent some time preparing a document, which he sealed before summoning his staff officer.

"Come in, Titus. Take a seat."

Julius didn't wait for him to be seated before starting to give him his instructions.

"I've decided that we will move against the Brigantes sooner rather than later. But there is much work to be done in preparing our forces. I found the 20th Legion to be poorly trained and manned, so I need you to draw up plans to rectify that. We shall be building up our auxiliary forces. I must give some thought to how they will be absorbed into my command structure."

"What you have found is no different from what we expected, Sir. I shall draw up suggestions to put to you as quickly as possible.

"Good man. At the same time I want you to look closely at how the army and navy are being provisioned."

"I will start right away, Sir."

Julius smiled a sincere smile of appreciation at the tribune's enthusiastic response. Taking the young man as his staff officer had been a gamble when Titus's father had asked for him to be appointed. Satisfying requests from old family friends could sometimes lead to difficulties and disappointment, even embarrassment. Not so in this case. In the two years in which he'd served him Titus had proven to be efficient, courageous and totally trustworthy.

"However, that's not what I want you to do for me immediately. I have an important task for you to carry out in the next few days. I have here a sealed document which I've prepared for you to take to Northern Gaul."

He noted the look of surprise on the young man's face. He was amused at the thought that he himself wouldn't have expected or welcomed the role of a simple messenger, a document carrier, when he was his age and a proud young staff officer.

"I can see you're wondering why I'm asking you to carry out this task."

"It does seem a bit unusual, Sir."

"I shall explain. This document is to be taken to Camillus Pecius who is Legate of the 5th Legion based in the land of the Belgae in Gaul. He's an old friend of mine and I need his help. I've told you before he was my commanding officer for a short while when General Paulinus led the campaign against the druids on Mona. He's a man for whom I have the greatest respect."

"I've heard you talk of him often, Sir. I'll be pleased to meet him."

"It's vital that this document is for his eyes only, which is why I'm sending you rather than anybody else. There's nobody I trust more."

"Thank you, Sir. I'm honoured that you place such trust in me."

"I've arranged with the Commander of the Fleet here in Londinium to take you."

"When do I leave, Sir?"

"First thing in the morning on our fastest ship. For now I would like you to join me at the baths, where I might just bore you by telling you once again about my time with Camillus."

They rose from their chairs and walked to the door.

"Come to see me before you leave in the morning. I've some small gifts for you to take to him, gifts of red wine and a special cheese from the south west which he was always partial to. You might also tell him I was wondering if his feet are still a problem to him and his staff, but only when you think he's in a good mood."

CHAPTER 36

"Come in and take a seat. Please don't be alarmed, Laric," Gaius said reassuringly. "I realise you must be wondering why the Governor's Secretary has arranged for you to be brought to me by my men."

"I was, Sir. What have I done wrong?"

"Nothing at all. I assure you I will explain fully, but first make yourself comfortable. Would you like something cold to drink to refresh you?"

Laric nodded and with a quick, nervous step, moved forward and sat in the chair, which had been placed in front of Gaius's desk. He was a small, child-like, stick-thin man. He sat with a rigidly straight back and placed the basket which he carried onto his lap, gripping it tightly with both hands.

"Let me repeat what I just said. I don't believe you've done anything wrong. Neither are you in any personal danger. So please try to relax. The sweat on your brow suggests you're still quite anxious. Perhaps you should place your basket on the ground and settle back into your chair."

Laric did as was suggested, trying to relax his shoulders and look less fearful.

"I've asked for you to be brought here because I think you can be of service to me."

"I think you may have mistaken me for somebody else, Your Honour," Laric mumbled. "I'm a slave belonging to Quintus Tiberius Saturninus. I was in the market buying some spices and herbs for my master's kitchen when your men arrested me."

"No! No! Not arrested. As I said, you aren't in any trouble. My men were asked to invite you to come here to see me. If they didn't make that clear to you and handled you roughly, I shall punish them later."

Laric kept his gaze firmly fixed on his lap where his fingers played with the hem of his tunic.

"I can't see how I can be of service to you, Sir."

"Then let me explain it to you."

Gaius spoke softly and continued to show his pleasure with a broad, fixed smile.

"I'm told you often talk in the market of your wish to be able to buy your freedom from Quintus. I believe you want to return to Gaul one day. Is that correct?"

"Please believe me, Sir. I'm not planning to run away from my master, if that's why you've brought me here."

Panic had returning to his taut little face and voice.

"I know you aren't. I think it's praiseworthy to have the desire and ambition to work so hard and loyally so you can earn the right to be freed. In fact I have friends who were once slaves."

"Really? You have people who were once slaves as your friends?"

"Of course. Having been set free because of their loyal service, they have become citizens of Rome. What do you think of that?"

"I am amazed that you have former slaves as your friends," said Laric, his mouth wide open in astonishment at the mere thought of it.

"I can see we are going to get along fine. But let's pause for a moment. Here's the drink which you asked for."

Gaius waited for Laric to take a slow, careful drink of the milk.

"I think I may be able to give you some tasks to do for me, for which you will be well rewarded. Maybe, if you perform exceptionally well, I will be minded to buy you myself from Quintus and give you your freedom as a reward. You would be free to return to your home in Gaul as a proud Roman citizen. How does that sound?"

An astonished Laric moved forward in his seat.

"I'm honoured if you consider me worthy enough to serve you, Sir. But what would Quintus say. He needs me to help Caris in the kitchens and…and… and to serve him and his daughters in the villa and town house. He might not like it."

"I won't be taking you away from those duties, but I agree it would be unlikely he would want to allow such a valued member of his household to serve another master in any way. It might be better if he knows nothing about it for the time being. Do you understand?"

"Please don't be angry, Sir, but I really don't understand. How could I hide it from him if I'm called upon to serve you as well?"

"Because I need you to do so," replied Gaius, his voice developing a slightly impatient edge to it.

It was enough to frighten Laric again. He sat back in his chair, his fingers returning to the hem. Gaius no longer bothered to try to calm him but continued to explain what was required of him.

"What I am about to tell you must remain a secret between us. I've received information which suggests Quintus, and maybe his daughters, may have become engaged in activities that could be harmful to the Governor. I will say no more at this stage because it may all be untrue and the work of their enemies."

"That must be the case. My master is a good and honourable man, who treats his slaves well, including me."

"Which is why I've chosen you and why you're going to be very useful to me," said Gaius, easily slipping into a more reassuring manner once again. "I know you will be faithful and honest in reporting back to me."

"Reporting what, Sir?"

"I want you to observe Quintus and his daughters very closely, together with anybody who pays them a visit. It includes the new General Agricola. But, and I stress this, not the Governor. Watch them and tell me anything you consider is unusual and may be of interest to me. Record in your memory what you see and especially what you hear. Do you understand what I'm asking you to do?"

"I do, Sir, but how will I give you my reports and how often? How can I do it without Quintus discovering me?"

"Good questions. I can see I've chosen well in asking you to carry out this most important duty. You will ask to see me only when you have something to report. I suggest you do so only when you are in Londinium visiting the market as today."

"How will I get a message to you to let you know I've got something to report?"

"Don't concern yourself with that. I have here a red ribbon for you to take away with you. When you have something to report, tie the ribbon to the handle of your basket. My men will be there. They will see to it that you are brought to me. Do you have any more questions?"

"What if I've been seen today being escorted from the market? What do I say to Quintus if he should ask me about it?"

"Tell him I asked you to pass on a message saying I would be delighted if he could join me at my father's side at the coming Games as guest of honour. You can tell him you forgot to pass on my invitation. He may flog you for the delay in giving him the message but it will be worth it in the long run, don't you agree. If he comes to the Games and sits next to my father rather than going to another seat I will know you have been questioned about today."

Gaius rose and came from behind his desk.

"I have pressing matters to attend to. I want you to return to your master. Act as if nothing has happened unless you are challenged. Remember, I'm a generous man to those who are loyal to me. On the other hand, I destroy anybody foolish enough to betray me."

Gaius was towering over Laric, grasping his arm tightly to guide him out of his chair. They walked over to the door where Gaius gave his final instruction.

"Remember what I said. Only you and I will know our secret. Not even the Governor must be told of our arrangement. You must only give your reports directly to me. Do you understand the importance of secrecy in this matter?"

"I do, Sir. You can rely on me."

"Good. Now go about your business."

CHAPTER 37

"He's coming up the track, Grandpa. It's the new General," Marcus shouted.

He came running into the stone-cooled interior of the villa from the courtyard, hardly able to contain his excitement.

"His army is riding with him. Do you think he'll let me ride his horse?"

"You mustn't ask him," Quintus warned, trying to look threatening to the boy, "especially when he's accompanied by his men. He's a very busy and important man. In any case his horse will be twice the size of your pony and it's trained for war. You wouldn't be able to keep him from charging off, taking you with him."

"Yes, Grandpa."

"And there's another thing. There will be no challenges for him to join you and Portos in a race across the fields."

"No, Grandpa."

"I want you to be on your best behaviour. Do you understand, young man?"

"Yes, Grandpa."

"Now! Thank you for letting me know he's coming. You can go back to welcome him, but remember what I've said."

Marcus turned with a sulk to go back to the courtyard.

*

"Halt! Who shall I say comes to visit Quintus Tiberius Saturninus?"

Marcus had taken up a position at the top of the villa's steps, his stance broad, his back straight. He had half-drawn a wooden sword to show how fierce he was.

"Would you tell your master that General Julius Agricola has come to visit him and his family? Naturally, that would include any children or grandchildren he may have."

Julius tried to hide his amusement behind one of his severest faces.

"I'm not a slave to do your beckoning. I have no master. I am Marcus, grandson of Quintus."

"Thank you, Marcus," interrupted Portos, appearing behind him. "I will see to our visitors. Would you please go to tell your grandfather that General Agricola has now arrived with a troop of cavalry. I shall be accompanying him into the villa shortly."

Marcus replaced his sword, stood to attention and saluted Julius before running back into the villa.

"You are well protected by a fine sentry," Julius shouted, intending for the boy to hear him before he disappeared inside.

"Indeed we are. I hope his greeting wasn't too severe, Sir. We rarely have a General and his cavalry escort approaching the villa these days, and he seemed to be a little excited."

"I fully understand. I assure you no offence has been taken."

Julius dismounted and began to climb the steps towards Portos. He commented on the impressive size and splendour of the villa and how Quintus and his daughters must be very proud of it.

"Indeed, Sir. I have arranged for your escort to be given refreshments. They will be attended to shortly. Would you follow me please?"

"You've kept your word to visit us, General. You are welcome and we are honoured," said Quintus, extending his arm a little awkwardly in greeting.

"Please call me Julius. Despite having my usual escort of cavalrymen I didn't come here on official business. I came with the intention of continuing our earlier brief discussion so that we might get to know each other better. The Governor obviously values your friendship. I would hope we too can become true and long-lasting friends."

"As do I, if it proves to be possible. Would you like to have a tour of my home before we take time to talk at leisure?"

"It would be a pleasure, although I must warn you that I will have some difficulty hiding my envy and jealousy at the beautiful, luxurious home you've built here."

"I understand you've met Marcus already. I hope he greeted you respectfully."

"He was very - how shall I put it – very disciplined in carrying out his duty."

"He didn't mention anything about horses or racing did he?"

"Not at all. Should he have?"

"No! No! I'll explain later. First let's take a stroll so you can enjoy my little reminder of Rome in this distant land."

A short while later they had returned to the large reception room. The tour had helped them to relax slightly with each other. They sat down on well-cushioned chairs to continue their conversation.

"Your villa is magnificent, and a credit to you and your family. I remember from what was said when we met before that you entertain guests with the help of your two daughters. I would very much like to meet them. Are they here today?" Julius asked as casually as he could. Quintus stiffened slightly.

"They're around somewhere. They'll come to join us later. In the meantime I've had Laric bring us some wine to help us to relax more. Thank you Laric. That will be all for now."

He waited for his slave to leave the room before addressing his guest again.

"Isn't it time for us to stop avoiding the questions we both have of each other, Julius?"

His voice was soft and non-threatening, while his face showed his nervousness at what might follow.

"What sort of questions? To what effect?" Julius replied.

"Why do you want to see them?"

"I am intrigued. I've already met one of them and found her fascinating. I'm sure the other is no less interesting. By the way, I've recently learnt that you have two other daughters. I understand they've married and no longer live at the villa."

"Please, Julius, we could play games like this until it's time for you to leave and my daughters won't have put in an appearance. I don't think that would be to your liking."

"I don't know what you mean."

"Oh, I think you do. As of this moment, they have no wish to meet you. I won't order them to do so, even if I thought they would obey me. I can take a guess at why you've come here today, but I need to know what you intend to do after your visit."

Julius could see the anxiety growing on his face as he was almost pleading for his questions to be answered. He decided the time had arrived to be more direct.

"What have they told you?" Julius asked. "They've obviously told you something of the past, so you must understand why I've acted with circumspection."

"I'm sorry but I don't understand at all. On the contrary, I fear your failure to be frank and open."

"Why do you say that?"

"We can't understand why you didn't immediately disclose her identity when you recognised Lucia. She recognised you even though it has been ten years, and you recognised her. Please don't deny it."

"I'm not going to."

"Are you playing some sort of game with us? Do you want them to suffer more than they already have? Are you going to choose a moment which gives you the greatest satisfaction? What can I do to save them? They and my grandson are my life."

Quintus's questioning was becoming increasingly frantic and emotional. He had risen to his feet to make these last comments, and began pacing the floor in front of Julius.

"Please take your seat again," murmured Julius, trying to reduce the tension which had grown between them.

"I'm too concerned to sit down."

"You have nothing to fear from me. I shall stay here and answer all your questions. I'll take as long as is needed to reassure you. Please do as I ask and retake your seat. Take a little wine and I'll try to give you an explanation."

Quintus paced a little more but eventually sat down and waited.

"I've no wish to expose your Lucia and Flavia to Governor Bolanus or anybody else for that matter. I had thought that Boudica and her daughters, Linona and Cailan as I knew them, like most of their tribe probably perished at the time of the revolt or in the aftermath."

"To the rest of the world they had, even to me, until you came back."

"I did hold on to a faint hope that maybe they had survived. I wanted to think they were living out their lives in some remote corner of this land."

"Why? I find that difficult to believe. Didn't you play a large part in the defeat of their mother and what happened to her tribe?"

"I did my duty as a soldier and played a part in our victory over them, as you would have done. However, I'm not proud of the action taken against the Iceni and Trinovantes that took place after the war. For a short time I played my part in restoring order to ensure the future security of the Province. I soon considered we had taken it too far. For my objections I was recalled to Rome not long after the war. Recently I went back to Lucia and Flavia's home and it no longer exists. Their tribe is only a pale reflection of what it once was."

"So now you know they have survived what are you going to do about it?"

"There's nothing to be gained in adding your daughters to this devastation. I know there's not the remotest possibility of a second Iceni revolt."

"Anyone in Londinium could have told you that. We don't have an enemy here threatening us today."

"I agree. However, Rome does have an enemy elsewhere in this land. It's the Brigantes and I will soon be heading north to concentrate on bringing them under our control."

Julius's admitted he had much more to say, particularly about the past, but preferred to say it when Lucia and Flavia were present. He owed them that. Quintus was watching Julius closely, particularly his softening expression His own face had become less drawn, and his agitation had ceased as he stared across, not at a General but at an ordinary man beginning to bare his soul.

"How can I be sure what you are saying is the truth?"

"Please believe me when I say I know they're not a danger to Rome any longer. Therefore, nothing is to be gained by disclosing their true identities."

"Lucia and Flavia may not be a threat any more. However, you would gain great credit in Rome if you were to expose them and take them there to present them to the Emperor. He could make a great display of humiliating and eventually executing them."

"Vespasian is not a maniac like Nero. He has no interest in crude gestures of that kind. He has only instructed me to establish order in this Province. If our new Emperor were to see it differently I wouldn't want to be here doing his bidding. But I know he would not. He is a great man, which is why I decided to join him in his bid to become Emperor."

"There's much in what you say that I want to believe, but I'm not convinced yet. Your reputation suggests I should be very careful in accepting what you say too readily."

"I fear I won't be able to persuade you of my sincerity until I have done so with your daughters. I can't begin to do so until I've met and spoken with them."

"Why is that so important to you?"

"I have so much to explain and share. It won't be easy to convince them, and I may never succeed, but I need to try for the sake of us all. If I fail it won't alter the position that you have nothing to fear from me. Only time will prove this. Will you help me?"

"I won't force them to speak to you, nor can I resist you if you use your power to insist. If you want me to I shall ask them if they will come to meet you."

Julius nodded and Quintus took hold of a small hand bell from the table at the side of his couch. With a short sharp ring he summoned his slave.

"Laric would you go to my daughters and ask them to come to join us."

"Do I need to tell them why you wish to see them, Master?" Laric asked.

"Do as I say without questioning my instruction and be quick," snapped an angry Quintus.

Obviously startled and fearful at the unexpected aggressive response by Quintus, Laric rushed from the room, only to return after a brief time looking even more frightened.

"They... they told me to tell you they have no desire to see or speak to the General," Laric stammered. "They won't be joining you as requested."

"Leave us," barked Quintus before turning to Julius.

"I shall go to speak to them myself to see if I can change their decision."

Quintus had barely left the room before a little face peered around the door.

"Is your horse the fastest in the land?" Marcus asked, moving cautiously into the room.

"Of course. What general would allow anybody else to have a faster horse which would let the enemy escape from him in battle?"

"Have you fought many battles? Have you killed lots of people and taken many prisoners?"

He had reached the centre of the room and, pushing the fruit bowl to one side, sat down on the low table. He stared in awe at Julius and continued with his questions.

"If I decided to join your army would I be given a horse of my own and be provided with a real sword like yours?"

"Slow down. Slow down," said Julius with a chuckle. "For a small boy you have asked a lot of big questions."

Julius realised his mistake immediately.

"Sorry, Sorry. Don't be angry with me. I meant young warrior."

Marcus was still bristling with offence. He let his feelings be known by frowning furiously at Julius.

"I will answer your questions if I can remember all of them. Yes! I've fought many battles against many barbarians in many lands. That's what generals do. What was next?"

"Have you killed lots of barbarians like Julius Caesar did?"

"Yes. I've killed many warriors in battle and sometimes they have nearly killed me. I have been wounded many times. But like the best gladiators I've always been able to carry on fighting and be victorious."

"Can I join your army one day?"

"If you did you'd be provided with a fine steed which would run like the wind. Like all my legionaries, you'd have a full set of armour and a sword so sharp and strong you could chop down trees with it."

"I shall ask Mama and Grandpa when I can join you."

Julius stifled any urge to laugh to avoid causing any further offence.

"I think you're needed here to help them for the time being. What would they do without you here to guard them? You talk only of your Grandpa. Don't you have a father?"

"Mama has told me my father was a great warrior who died bravely before I was born," Marcus replied proudly. "I shall be as brave as he was and one day prove myself in battle. Please tell me more about the battles you fought. Did you fight in Germania? Grandpa says they are the fiercest of all Barbarians?"

*

"I know him! He's lying to you," Lucia snarled. "He has a plan and we're in great danger."

"I didn't see a man in there who's trying to trick us," Quintus countered. "He has no reason to. I believe he's a man who has a story he needs to tell, for whatever reason. He could order his escort now to come into the villa if he so desired and kill or take all of us prisoner. He needs no other authority from the Governor or anybody else. Why has he chosen not to? He appears to be sincerely interested in your welfare."

"We should do as Quintus asks and go to speak to him." Flavia suggested. "What have we to lose?"

"We have everything to lose," Lucia warned. "Like before, he can take away our freedom, our dignity, everything we have rebuilt in our lives."

"I repeat myself when I say he could easily do that, Lucia," Quintus added. "Even if you don't speak to him. At least if you see him you will have the knowledge that you met him and tried to save not only yourself but your sister, your son and probably me. Do it for us all, my child."

*

"Mama. The general says I can join the army one day," cried Marcus running to Lucia as she entered the room ahead of Quintus and Flavia.

Lucia didn't respond immediately. She placed her arm around his shoulder, avoiding eye contact with Julius. She took him over to the small table and used the bell to summon Laric, who was standing just outside the room in the corridor.

"Go with Laric and find Portos. Tell him that I've said its fine for you to go to meet the General's men and look at their wonderful horses. Who knows, you may even be allowed to sit on one."

Marcus took hold of Laric's hand and dragged him out of the room.

The silence seemed to last forever. It was Julius who broke the tension by speaking first.

"It's good to see you both again."

The silence returned. Quintus looked from Julius and back to his daughters repeatedly. Flavia looked firmly at her feet. Lucia stared at Julius, every muscle in her face taut and motionless. Julius broke the silence again.

"I'm very happy you've found a contented life here with this good man. I've no wish to put it in jeopardy. Please believe me."

"Then prove it. Go now and never return," Lucia snarled. "We've nothing to say to you."

Flavia shifted nervously, forcing herself to look at Julius for his reaction.

Julius didn't react immediately. At least Lucia had spoken to him. It was a start. He moved his eyes from one to the other several times before he spoke again, slowly and quietly.

"I shall leave shortly, but there are things you need to know if the two of you are ever to live the rest of your lives free of the hatred burning inside you."

"What does it matter to you if I hate you and all your kind in this Roman Empire? We lost all we had because of you." Lucia's voice trembled as feelings long hidden began to surface. She glanced at Quintus.

Flavia took hold of her sister's hand and spoke quietly.

"You must realise that your return has altered our lives once again. If you have any kindness in your heart you will accept what we are saying. What made us the people we were has been destroyed and has gone forever. We have found peace and a new life. Don't destroy it, I beg you."

Julius seized on the change in the tension which her calm words had brought about.

"I have absolutely no intention of doing you harm. Please let us all sit down and enjoy a drink of wine and reflect upon the situation we find ourselves in. I'll talk only of one incident from the past. I promise you that if you don't accept what I tell you I will leave and never speak to you again unless you wish differently. I swear this to you by all the Gods I worship."

He stared at Lucia unblinking. She in return looked deeply into his eyes.

"We accept," Flavia replied, to the surprise of the other three. She didn't look for support from Lucia or appear to require it.

"There are conditions, however," she added.

"Name them," said Julius gratefully.

"Firstly, you must agree that we can stop you at any time to ask questions and you'll answer them honestly."

"Of course."

"Secondly, if at any point my sister and I agree we've heard enough, can bear no more and want you to leave, you will do so."

Julius swallowed hard before replying.

"If you in return promise to try to give me a fair and full hearing, even if some of what I say brings back some painful memories."

"Agreed," said Flavia before Lucia could say anything to object. Even if Lucia had wanted to, her obvious surprise at her sister's uncharacteristic behaviour had stopped her.

Quintus took advantage of the intervention by Flavia to speak to Julius.

"Please proceed."

Julius rose to his feet and began to pace the floor slowly.

"I would like to take you back to the night after the battle when the fighting had ceased. Try not to say anything while I set the scene. I know it will hurt to recall those events but it will help me to explain what happened.

You had originally been captured and as darkness began to fall you had been placed under guard. I had..."

"Where?" interrupted Flavia, already unable to contain herself.

"You were placed in a make-shift fenced-off area."

"So were all the other women, placed there by you."

"On the contrary, you were captured by others. I didn't leave the battlefield or Paulinus's side until darkness fell, by which time the roundup of prisoners had been completed."

"Please continue," Quintus urged, while raising his hand to try to restrain Flavia.

"You were placed there and tied together to an upturned cart. You were separated from the others for a reason."

"You must have seen us there, so what are you saying?" interrupted Flavia again.

"I saw you there because you were drawn to my attention by Bestia, the man who had recognised you. He was the centurion who had supported the Procurator when they visited you and brought about the whole catastrophe which followed."

Lucia winced and took a deep breath, her nostrils flaring with the memory.

"I would have expected him to do just that, to expose us to you." said Lucia. "He must have known it was important, and it was his duty to do so?"

"Indeed he did. He wished me to tell Paulinus so that both of us would gain the credit for his discovery. He had been barred by

Paulinus from approaching him directly."

"This doesn't have the ring of truth," said Lucia looking at her sister.

"It does if you know, as I do, that Paulinus hated the man because of his former allegiance to Decianus the Procurator."

"Is this all you have to say?" Lucia asked impatiently.

"I've only just begun. He took me to the place where he'd captured you and killed Bodran in front of you when he tried to protect you. It was there where I killed him."

"Why would you do that?" asked an astonished Flavia.

"Because at this point he was the only person who knew you were there. He was also partly responsible for what happened to you and Boudica in front of your people. I was punishing him for his crimes against you and for helping to cause the disastrous war."

"But why did you have to kill him then?" Lucia demanded. "You aren't making any sense. I've heard enough."

"Wait Lucia," interrupted Flavia. "Please continue. I want to hear what you did next."

"At this point, I was again the only one who knew who you were. I had to decide what to do. I couldn't see you executed or given to Cogidubnus. So I let you escape."

"Now we know you're lying," said Lucia. "We escaped while we were being taken elsewhere in the camp. We did it without anybody's help. I've heard enough."

"You escaped because I tethered two horses close to where Bodran died. I ordered the lone guard to untie you and to escort you to where the horses stood. I came out of the darkness to order the legionary to leave you and approach me. I was standing some distance away in the dark. You took your chance and escaped as I knew you would."

He stopped, waiting for a reaction from any or all three of them.

"That was you?" asked a disbelieving Lucia, her brow wrinkled in confusion. "Why would you do it? If Paulinus had found out he would have had you executed. He, and you for that matter, hated us and our mother for leading the revolt?"

"On the contrary, dear Lucia. I was a young man who greatly admired you. More than that, I think I was fascinated by you, even falling in love with you. Young men in love sometimes do crazy things. What I did was foolish and disloyal to the Emperor. I would have been considered a traitor if what I'd done had been discovered. In fact it would still be considered an act of treason if it were to become known now. So you have been provided with a weapon against me should I belatedly reveal your identity."

Flavia began to weep slowly at first and then to sob uncontrollably. Lucia put her arms around her, comforting her, but kept looking at Julius. Her wrinkled brow, and the shaking of her head from side to side, showed she was still confused and disbelieving.

"You don't believe Julius do you, either of you?" Quintus asked.

"I don't know what to believe," was all Flavia could say. Lucia remained silent.

"And please don't cry so, Flavia," Quintus pleaded.

"I'm crying with relief. For days and days I've thought our world was about to come crashing down again. Now I have hope. I want to believe him. I need Julius to carry on - to tell us more, Quintus."

"Then Julius should stay the night with us," Quintus suggested. "There's much to talk about. I also have many questions to ask. What do you say Lucia?"

She was still staring at Julius, occasionally shaking her head as if she was willing herself not to accept what she'd heard. Although she didn't reply, she waved her arm to one side in resignation, as if to indicate that she didn't have the energy to object.

Quintus took it to mean just that and nodded towards Julius. Had his suggestion met with her disapproval she would have told him so quite clearly to avoid any misunderstanding. Julius, for his part, acted quickly at what he could assume to be her grudging agreement

"I accept," he said, smiling appreciatively. "I shall order my escort to return to Londinium. Except, that is, for the Tribune and two others, but only if it causes you no difficulty."

"None at all," Quintus replied, "I shall ask Portos to arrange for them to be taken care of. Let's all take a stroll in the garden and try to gain control of our emotions. There will be plenty of time to continue later, after we've all eaten."

*

"Laric! Just listen to me! Whatever Portos has ordered you to do, you can forget it," barked Caris. "I need you to help me."

"But he's ordered me to prepare rooms for our unexpected guests. I can't be in two places at the same time, can I?"

"You'll do as I say. I will talk to Portos. We have extra food to prepare and it must be our best. When did we last have a general to stay with us?"

"It may be the first and last time if you ask me."

"I didn't ask you, but what gave you such an idea?"

"Earlier the Master sent me to invite his daughters to join him so that they could meet the General. He was very nasty to me when he did it. He's hardly ever been like that before."

"What are you talking about? Quintus is never nasty to any of us."

"He was this time. Anyway, that's not my only point. The Master didn't look very pleased with the General either."

"Would you please get on with it and explain yourself."

"Lucia and Flavia refused to join them and looked quite concerned that they had been asked to do so. The Master had to come himself to take them to see the General."

"You're mistaken. I'll have no more of your mischief. Go to the larder and bring me the suckling pig."

"What mischief?" asked Portos, who had just walked into the room. "Bring me some cheese, Laric. I'm feeling hungry."

"His imagination is running wild," Caris explained. "He thinks Lucia and Flavia are refusing an invitation to meet the General."

"Whatever you think you saw or heard, you're mistaken," said Portos. "I've just seen them walking together in the garden. Now please get some cheese, my good fellow."

*

"I've told you of my part in your escape. I would like to know what happened to you after I watched you disappear into the night."

The meal had gone reasonably well despite the tension in the air. All four of them had avoided continuing to discuss the painful past. Most of the conversation had been between Quintus and Julius about the recent state of affairs in Rome. Quintus was particularly interested in Julius's role in the ever-changing political scene before Vespasian had become Emperor. They had also gossiped about the social scene, discovering a surprising number of family connections between the two men.

Lucia sat tight-lipped as she had throughout the meal. She didn't react to Julius's question. It was left to Flavia to begin to describe what had happened to them after their escape.

"We rode through the night until daylight when we found a forest to hide in throughout the following day. We quickly decided not to attempt to go home by using river crossings near to Londinium for obvious reasons. Instead we headed west and started on what we thought would be a long detour. We lived off the land, working our way slowly back. Just what we were going back to we dared not think. We had no other choice."

"How did you come to live with Quintus?"

"After many days we were exhausted and hungry. We made mistakes and were discovered by local tribesmen who were loyal to Paulinus. We were beaten and abused, but we had a value to them greater than becoming their own slaves. We were sold to Roman slavers searching for others like ourselves."

"I bought them soon afterwards," said Quintus, taking over the telling of the story. "They were in a desperate condition. My wife soon became aware that Lucia was pregnant and before long Marcus arrived. Within a few years my wife died, and soon afterwards I formally adopted the three of them, although in reality it has always seemed rather the other way round. Without them I too would have died, of grief. My other daughters by then had married and left. Replacing my family with Lucia, Flavia and Marcus and making them citizens of Rome, was the most natural thing to do. It has been a blessing from the Gods. We've become very close since and are very happy and content. At least, we were so until you arrived from nowhere and put us all in danger."

"It's surprising you've never been recognised in all these years."

"Not really," said Flavia. "Our appearance and dress quickly became Roman. We were part of a Roman family, particularly after we ceased to be slaves. Last of all there were very few Iceni left alive who had ever met us and would know who we were. In any case, they would have been elsewhere, most likely in Gaul."

"What part did you play at the side of Paulinus?" Lucia whispered, her anger no longer evident. Her expression had changed to one of deep sadness. "I want to know everything you did after you left our feast and went north with your army."

Choosing his words very carefully, Julius briefly explained what had happened in Mona until he had been sent back by Paulinus.

"We'd heard of your father's illness and Paulinus feared how your mother would react if he should die."

"I undertook a tour of our forces after I got back to Camulodunum. I took steps to warn Decianus that if Presutagus died he must take no action regarding his will until the Governor returned. At the time I got back to Camulodunum after my tour, word of the death of your father hadn't reached us. I attempted to visit you to let you know Paulinus would be returning soon."

"I arrived at your settlement to find he had died. Unfortunately I was quickly sent on my way by Boudica with a little help from you, Lucia."

Her expression didn't alter, nor did she react to his last comment.

*

"I felt she might not want to go to war then if it could be avoided. However, I knew she wouldn't be as easy to deal with as your father had been. I then went to Lindum and when I returned to Camulodunum again it was too late. Decianus had carried out his evil and we were all set on a course of destruction."

"Decianus told us you knew of his denial of the legitimacy of Father's will. More than this he said you supported him in what he was doing when he came to see my mother. Are you trying to deny that?" Lucia asked.

An angry Julius got to his feet.

"I wasn't aware until this moment he'd said that to you. No wonder you've hated me so much. He lied for his own twisted reasons. The opposite is the truth. I had specifically told him not to provoke your mother in any way. He was to wait for Paulinus to meet Boudica to discuss the will. Between them we felt we could avoid a disastrous war. When I learnt what he'd done to the both of you and your mother I went to Londinium to arrest him. That was if I could resist killing him first. I wanted to take him either to you or Paulinus. I hadn't decided which, but I didn't get the chance. He'd anticipated me and fled to Gaul."

"You have no proof of this have you?" Lucia asked.

"I haven't. You will either believe me or you won't. The rest you know. We fought our battle. Many died then and afterwards. Paulinus lost faith in me when I began to differ from him in what he was doing to your people. I was recalled to Rome and spent the next few years in different parts of the Empire. I eventually went back to Rome, joining Vespasian in his bid to become Emperor. I was sent back here by him because of my knowledge of the land and people. Now you know what has happened to me."

"You will understand if I ask you to leave it there for tonight, Julius," said Quintus. "I think we are all drained of any emotion, and we'd prefer to reflect on what you've told us. Your room has been prepared."

"Thank you, Quintus and the both of you, Lucia and Flavia. I have released a heavy weight from my shoulders. I shall leave in the morning and not raise these matters with you again. I will never reveal your former identity. I give you my solemn word."

"The word of a Roman," Lucia spat out contemptuously.

"Yes! The word of a Roman citizen," Julius countered. "A Roman like Quintus, like his grandson Marcus, and like you Lucia and Flavia. Good night!"

*

Much later Julius stood by the window in his room staring up at the partly-clouded sky. Deep in thought, he watched the full moon disappear and reappear repeatedly as the short showers came and went. He couldn't sleep even though his mind was at peace. The villa had long since fallen into silence.

The knock startled him even though it was barely audible. Whoever had knocked was most anxious not to disturb others.

He had nobody to fear, yet he held his foot hard against the door as he opened it slightly to see who was there. His mouth opened in surprise but no words came out. He stepped back slightly so as not to block the doorway.

"I have more to ask and things to say," said Lucia.

"Are you sure this is the time and place?"

"I don't care," she whispered through clenched teeth as she placed her hand on his chest and pushed him backwards into the room.

"What gives you the right to conquer other lands and other peoples, to destroy those who oppose you? How do you justify what you've done to me and all my people?"

"Do you want to sit down?"

"Don't avoid my questions. Answer me!"

"We are Romans. We are no different from any other people, merely stronger, more powerful, and more efficient in everything we do."

"That doesn't excuse what you do."

"Before we came to your land you had spent countless years fighting wars, one tribe against another. If we weren't here no doubt you would be engaged in or planning yet a further war against another tribe either to dominate them or to be free of their domination. It's the same throughout the world."

"That is no justification."

"We have the right because we can, as you would if you could. We suppress those who oppose us because not to do so would be seen as weakness and threaten our whole society."

"What you have done to my people goes beyond mere suppression," said Lucia, her voice shaking with emotion. "You've destroyed them, not suppressed them. You've wiped them out!"

"I told you earlier that what we did ultimately was wrong and unnecessary. I came to understand this and tried to oppose it before it was too late but without success. We serve our Emperor as you and your people served their Queen when they killed and slaughtered women and children in Camulodunum. You were party to those brutal acts, were you not?"

"Those horrors happened because of what you had done to the Trinovantes for years."

"Ultimately we bring the peace and prosperity of Rome to the world and it will happen throughout the whole of Britannia. It already has happened for many tribes who have accepted us and now seek and enjoy the wealth and protection we bring."

Her eyes opened wide and she drew her lips tightly together. He thought she was about to strike him with her bare hands but she didn't move them from her side. In her anger she had moved to face him standing very close so that he could feel her hot breath as she breathed quickly and forcefully. He waited for a moment or two but she didn't speak. He continued.

"I didn't and never would seek to harm you. I know you lost Marac and the future you had planned together. There was no need for that to happen. You lost your mother, but it was her decision to lead her people to war."

"A decision forced on her by your cruelty and brutality to us all."

"You lost many friends. So did I. Many were cruelly tortured and mutilated by your people. At least I played a part in saving you and Flavia and ultimately Marcus. In him you have something of Marac to remember."

She lowered her gaze, not replying.

"I told you earlier that as a young man I was fascinated by you, probably begun to love you. Today, I realised that nothing has changed after ten years."

"The child is not Marac's. I was a virgin when Decianus came to our home that day."

"But Marcus told me you..."

"What was I to tell him? That his father was really a Roman rapist and murderer? I will tell him one day when he's old enough to cope with it, but only when Quintus is dead. The old man must never know the child he loves so much was conceived in violence and hatred."

Her lips were no longer taut, but were trembling. Her eyes were no longer wide open and staring. They were half closed and full of tears. Her breath now came bursting out of her as she started to shake and sob.

"I don't know what to believe anymore. I've hated you and what I thought you stood for, throughout all these years, and now I'm not so sure."

"Then let me continue to explain what took place and answer any of your questions."

"I still find what you have told me today hard to believe. I don't want to believe it. Are you the monster I've always thought you to be, or have I misjudged you."

She lowered her head and Julius instinctively and hesitantly raised his hands to caress her cheeks gently and stroke her hair. He closed the small gap between them and gently pulled her tear-stained face into his chest.

If he expected her to pull away she didn't. He lifted her tear-sodden face so that he could look down at it. Her eyes were closed when he gently placed his lips lightly against her forehead, moving on to her cheek. Finally he let his lips touch hers, not demanding but lightly, just to join them tenderly together as one.

For a long lingering moment she neither accepted nor returned the kiss. Still not pulling away, she thumped him lightly against his chest with one hand. The next blow was a little harder. So was the next before she pulled her mouth away from his and hit him forcefully several times with both hands together. She moved her head from side to side in denial of something. Finally, she ran to the door to get away, closely followed across the room by Julius.

He stood at the door and watched as she moved down a dark corridor full of shadows.

*

Laric had risen early with Caris to help her to prepare the morning meal.

"Stop yawning," she cried. "You have a long day ahead of you today or have you forgotten? You are to accompany Lucia to the house in Londinium to help her to prepare for the Games. The

Master and I will join you in two days. Is that clear?"

"Yes Caris. It will be a pleasure to go to Londinium again."

"You'll be in charge of the others attending the young Mistress until I arrive with the Master. Have you understood everything I've said?"

"Of course I have. Why do you keep asking me, treating me like an idiot?"

"Because you are one! When we've finished preparing the meal you are to get ready to join Lucia. She'll be accompanying the General on the journey back to town."

*

Lucia gave Marcus a long lingering tight embrace and lifted his sulking little face to hers.

"I'll be back in a few days when we can go down to the river for the day to see if you can improve your swimming. How does that sound?"

His face lit up.

"Can Portos come?"

"Of course," she said, relieved that she'd taken his mind off her departure.

She mounted her horse and took up a position at the side of Julius in silence. Marcus moved into the comforting arms of Caris.

Moving out of the courtyard they had been joined by Julius's men. A small cart full of provisions and Lucia's belongings, needed by her to meet her next challenge in the arena, was driven by Laric.

CHAPTER 38

The daily market in Londinium had grown considerably in recent years. A worried Laric, surrounded by a large crowd, began to wonder if he had misunderstood the Governor's Secretary. Perhaps, since he hadn't gone to him quickly with information, he had lost interest. He played with the ribbon with his right hand, partly because of his nervousness. It could also be because he may not have been noticed in the crush by whoever was supposed to see him. Maybe he needed to make it more obvious.

A sharp tap on his shoulder startled him and made him turn round. His doubts were about to prove unnecessary.

"What's your name?"

The man who asked the question wasn't much bigger than himself and certainly not somebody who would stand out from the rest in the crowd.

Laric had expected to be met by the burly thugs from last time. This man was different. He asked politely if he would be pleased to follow him, and Laric liked that. Obviously, the Secretary had listened to his complaint from the last time and had done something about it. His confidence grew and he began to think his information would be well received.

With the walk to the Governor's palace soon completed he was shown into the same office as before. This time it was empty. His escort asked him to take a seat and informed him the Secretary would join him shortly. He was grateful for any delay. It would give him extra time to rehearse his story.

As expected, the delay didn't last long before he heard footsteps approaching. He stood up, his heart beginning to pound.

"Please take your seat again, Laric. We are friends and there's no need for formality when we're alone. It's good to see you. Have you something to report?"

Laric waited until Gaius had taken his seat behind his desk and was leaning forward expectantly.

"I'm not sure if it's the sort of information you're looking for, Sir, but some strange things have been happening at the villa. Caris doesn't think so but I do."

"That's why I chose you. You'll be able to see things others not as clever as you would miss. Take it very slowly and tell me what's happened. And remember to tell me everything, not missing anything out. It could prove to be very important to me."

Laric began to tell what he had seen and heard.

"What do you mean – refused to meet the General?" Gaius interrupted. "Perhaps they were frightened because of his status or shy or just teasing him. I'm sure you know what I'm getting at if I say they might have been playing a game with him."

"I do indeed, Sir, and I'm sure it was none of the things you suggest. Lucia especially was angry because she was being asked to go to be introduced to him."

"She's a difficult one, that Lucia. She doesn't have time for simple pleasantries, does she, Laric? I know because I've met her often. She's even been rude to me, would you believe? Flavia on the other hand is a gentle, sweet person. She wouldn't have refused surely?"

"Oh yes she did, Sir," said Laric beginning to realise he really was reporting something which was important. "She was the first to refuse and she became quite agitated."

"What happened next?"

"I went back to tell the master and he wasn't pleased. He went to see them himself. I'm sorry I couldn't hear what was said but their voices were raised. Eventually they did what was asked of them by Quintus and they went with him to meet the General."

"Thank you. That's very interesting. There's more, I hope?"

"Oh yes!"

"Please continue."

"For a while afterwards everything seemed to be fine. I served them at the meal. The General and the Master particularly seemed to be getting to know each other. Whatever had been the problem earlier appeared to have been resolved. But it wasn't."

Laric took a few deep breaths. He could see he'd really got Gaius's interest and he began to imagine how much money he would get as a reward.

"Go on. What happened next?" Gaius asked impatiently, not appreciating any pause.

Laric described how he'd heard raised voices after the meal but not what was being discussed. He then had to concentrate on attending to his other duties. Nevertheless, it had seemed very strange to him that the General should change his plans so late in the day to stay the night. He'd decided he had to stay awake to see if anything happened. He had been rewarded much later. He began to describe what he had seen.

"Stop! You're telling me she went to his room, and in the night? What for? Was it for obvious reasons? Did she stay the night?"

"No, Sir. She wasn't there for very long. After I saw her enter his room I got as close as I dared. Even so, I still couldn't make out what they were saying, only that she seemed to be crying. Soon afterwards she ran from the room very upset. I only just avoided being discovered. In any case no mention of me being seen was made the following morning."

"Good man. You have done a great service for me. Is that all?"

"Yes, except perhaps for one other small thing. I accompanied her the following day when she came to the house here in the town to prepare for the Games. I didn't see them exchange one word during the whole journey. I thought it was very strange."

"I agree. It's most intriguing. I'm glad you and I are investigating this. It could be very important for the safety of the Governor. Your reward for this work is going to be great indeed if you continue to provide reports of this quality."

"I'm sure I can. We shall be in the town house for the next few days. Because of the Games there'll be many visitors. The house is a good deal smaller than the villa. So maybe I will be able to observe more closely what's said and done."

"Let's hope so. Now, would you like a drink of wine?"

*

Laric walked back to the Market feeling the effects of too much wine. He was happy with himself and his life in a way he hadn't experienced before, certainly not since he became a slave all those years ago. Finally he had hope. He had a new powerful friend in Gaius and a way of working towards his freedom.

"How much are those oysters, my good fellow?" he asked the man who was almost hidden by huge piles of fresh fish. He could feel his new-found confidence making him sound much more important than a mere slave.

"It depends on how many you want to buy, young Sir."

CHAPTER 39

The stone house which Quintus had built to replace his former wooden building was not as grand as some which had been rebuilt by others in recent years. Nevertheless, it was big enough for him and his family to use when they needed to be in Londinium.

When Lucia participated in the Games she was able to relax there and prepare herself, away from the distractions at the estate's villa. It allowed her to concentrate on the coming contest. Not this time. She couldn't escape the turmoil in her mind. She would have preferred not to be fighting but she had accepted the challenge some time ago and withdrawal now was unthinkable. Apart from the shame that would fall upon Quintus as well as herself, she would forfeit the magnificent purse which was being provided to the winner of the contest by Tarquinius Marellus.

She had been told she would take part in two demonstration contests. The second of them would take place immediately before the final gladiator contest, which alone would be to the death. The Master of the Games had explained that she and her opponent would be expected to display skill and aggression just short of delivering fatal blows. It was essential they excite the crowd in readiness for the contest which would follow.

It was the afternoon of the day before the Games. Tired after spending the whole morning exercising and practising her skills, Lucia had bathed before taking to her bed. She could rest her body but not her troubled mind as she continued to reflect on her encounter with Julius.

He had sounded so plausible and yet he was the man who had helped to destroy all the people she had cared for with the exception of Flavia. In his presence, listening to his words, she had begun to believe he might not be the monster she had considered him to be. She had also been devastated to realise she was still physically attracted to him despite what he had been and what he had done.

Why had she gone to his room? Why had she let him touch her? She still disliked him and hated all that he stood for. If he'd been telling the truth, he would keep his distance from now on and they were all safe. The story of their escape had sounded as if it could have happened the way he said. On the other hand he could have been told all the details of how they had taken the horses when their guard was distracted and invented a role for himself to hide his real intentions.

She hadn't recognised him that night as the Roman tribune who spoke to their guard. Then again it had been very dark and her concentration had been on the need to escape the horrors of the battle and its aftermath.

She was also facing a question she had resisted asking herself for a long time. What had she become? She had been shocked at his declaration that she too had become a Roman. Yes, she had accepted freedom and the right to be called a citizen of Rome. But she had done it to survive, hadn't she? She took part in the Games merely to earn money to secure the future for Flavia, Marcus and herself, didn't she? She had played the role of Mistress of the Estate, waited upon by slaves as Quintus's daughter should be, to hide her real identity as Boudica's daughter, hadn't she? And she had gone to his room late at night only to challenge his Roman arrogance, hadn't she?

"Lucia, where are you?" The cry from Quintus brought her away from the whirlpool of doubt and repeated questioning, and she rose to answer his call.

"I'm here in my room, resting."

"May I come in, my child?" he murmured through the door.

"Please do, old man, but I warn you I'm in a foul mood."

"It may well get worse," he said, sitting on the bed next to her. "Julius has sent word with one of his soldiers that he'll shortly be paying us a visit."

"As I thought, his intention to leave us alone didn't last long."

"He says he's no intention of staying long. He merely wants to bring you a present and then leave."

"Why on earth would he do that? What trickery can he be trying now?" she asked, not really expecting an answer. "When is he coming? At least Flavia has stayed at the villa and isn't here to have to face him again."

"I don't think she would have been as disturbed as you by his visit even if she was here."

"Why do you say such a thing?"

"Because it's true, my child. I have spoken to her since you left and I think you should do so as well when you see her next. She wants to accept that what he's said is the truth. However, she needs to talk to you first, as you might expect."

"But he's coming here again to cause mischief. I can feel it."

"He'll be here shortly. Let's see what he wants. I'll let you prepare yourself to meet him while I go to give instructions to Laric and the others."

*

Lucia and Quintus were seated in the reception room and heard the sound of a soldier's booted footsteps on the marble floor outside. Lucia prepared her sternest expression and held it until Julius entered the room.

"Thank you both for seeing me at such short notice," he said. "I shall take only the briefest amount of your time, Lucia. I've no wish to disturb your preparation for tomorrow. But I couldn't wait to present you with a gift as a demonstration of my sincerity and truthfulness in what I said to you in all our discussions the other day."

She didn't miss the slight emphasis he placed on the word "all" even if it wouldn't be particularly significant to Quintus.

"Where is it then?" Quintus asked. "I don't see anything in your hands."

"It's a heavy gift and I've left it in the reception hall. I didn't want to bring it in before I'd had these few brief words with you. If you'll excuse me I shall go to get it. Afterwards I'll leave immediately and not disturb you any longer."

After he left the room, the two of them sat there in silent wonder looking quizzically at each other. Very soon they heard the sound of his approaching footsteps again. Lucia was the first to break the silence before he arrived.

"How extraordinary. What can he be bringing us?"

"Shush. He's here."

"Oh, No!" screamed Lucia, bringing both hands to clutch the sides of her face as a tall soldier in full Roman military uniform entered the room.

"Who are you, Sir," demanded Quintus "and where is Julius?"

"My name is Olsar, Sir. Julius has left."

*

Julius had left the house to make his way to the home of Tarquinius Marellus, only to find that the Governor and his secretary were also there. They had enjoyed a rather sumptuous feast, judging by the remains, before moving on to drinking freely from a large container of wine.

"Welcome Julius," cried Vettius, smiling broadly. "Come and join us in a drink of wine. These two have eaten all the food, I'm sorry to say. If you're hungry though, I'm sure Tarquinius can quickly arrange for something to be prepared for you."

Julius didn't respond. He was still taking in the scene he had been presented with, wondering what he'd interrupted. Vettius started speaking again, ending an awkward silence.

"We've just been discussing the Games and Tarquinius has been telling me what contests we can expect. Do come and sit down. You make me nervous standing there."

"I came to see Tarquinius on official business but it can wait until a more appropriate time. Unfortunately, I have pressing matters and must decline your offer to join you. Perhaps some other time."

"Rubbish! Relax man. The two of you can do your business while Gaius and I have some more wine. Is that not so, Tarquinius?"

Julius didn't wait for any agreement and turned to address Tarquinius.

"In which case I shall tell you what I came here to say to you. It's clear to me that you are by far the main provider of the army's and the navy's supplies."

"That's correct and have been for years."

"I've studied the prices you have been charging. In virtually all items bought there has been gross overcharging. It will not continue."

"Excuse me! You're mistaken," Tarquinius objected. "Please explain what you're saying."

"Not now. I'll meet with you in my office the day after these Games. We shall discuss a completely new arrangement. Good day, gentlemen. I look forward to the Games and hopefully I can win some money back, Governor."

Julius, not requiring a response or agreement from Tarquinius regarding a meeting, turned and left.

"The man is an arrogant, preposterous egomaniac. He is still the insufferable bully he was ten years ago," said Tarquinius, who had turned a pale shade of purple caused by a combination of the effects of too much wine and his anger at what Julius had said.

"He is indeed, but he's also a favourite of the new Emperor and he's in charge of our army," Vettius reminded them. "So we must be very careful. It looks as if our very lucrative arrangement may have to come to an end for a while. But things may change to our advantage again eventually. So please stay calm and do as he asks for the time being. Have you come up with anything yet that will help us, Gaius?"

"No Governor," he lied. "Nothing at all."

"It's early days yet, I suppose. Keep trying."

*

"But I saw him kill you," said Lucia.

"Obviously not," said an amused Olsar. "Badly wounded yes, and surrounded by a forest of flying horses legs and hooves but I survived."

"How?" Lucia asked. She had overcome her initial shock and continued to embrace him.

"Before you say any more can I please be introduced?" asked Quintus.

Lucia did as she was asked. She briefly reminded Quintus of her story and the role Olsar had played in her life.

"It would seem to me we owe you very much," said Quintus.

"I'm sorry, Olsar," Lucia continued, "but I am totally confused, as well as elated, by you just suddenly walking into the room, walking back into life. For me you've been dead for ten years."

"Julius is responsible," replied Olsar. "In fact he's responsible for many things which you may have difficulty believing, but I can assure you that what I am about to tell you is the truth. It's perhaps better if we all sit down. This is going to take some time."

Lucia led him to a large couch, refusing to let go of his hand. She sat close to him and continued to shake her head in confused amazement.

"I survived in the first instance because Julius stayed on his feet after I'd been wounded. He stopped himself half-way through delivering a final blow while I lay at his mercy, and stepped back. Despite being buffeted by the surrounding frantic horses, somehow he was able to drag me clear so I wouldn't be trampled to death. He left me in a safe place at the edge of the forest before he re-joined the battle."

"Was he leaving you to bleed to death in pain?"

"Quite the opposite as it turned out. Later in the day, when he could, he came to search for me among the many dead and wounded. I must have already appeared dead to others who had passed by me earlier. I was very weak but my memory is clear about what happened next. He had me taken to be seen to by his healers, insisting I be treated as if I were a Roman. I survived and he claimed me as his personal slave not to be sold to any other."

"Weren't you recognised by anybody else?" Lucia asked. "Surely somebody must have known who you were?"

"Not at first. However, as I recovered in the following days it was inevitable that Paulinus did."

"And? And? What happened then?" she demanded, thumping him playfully against his chest.

"He thought it was most amusing that Julius had chosen to humiliate one of Boudica's trusted aides by making him a slave. He even paraded me in front of his senior officers after he'd discovered me. He took great delight in pointing out to them that Boudica's great warrior had become a staff officer's personal slave."

"So Julius saved you only to make you his slave, and for him and his General to use you as sport," Lucia suggested, her face beginning to darken again. "I might have known it."

"Why do you say this?" Olsar asked.

"Because we know what he did to us all. We recognise what sort of man he was. He was there to do Paulinus's bidding."

"Perhaps I was of the same mind and would have agreed with you in the early days of my recovery, but not for long."

"What happened to change your opinion?" Quintus asked.

"I gradually felt the unspoken respect we had felt for each other before the battle, the respect two warriors have, was still there. His behaviour in those early days seemed to be demanding me to recover fully. He ensured I received constant care from his surgeons."

"I'm not a soldier," Quintus added, "but it must have been unusual to treat your enemy in such a way."

"I agree. Eventually, and once I had fully recovered from my injuries, he objected to yet another attempt by Paulinus to ridicule me. I think from this time onwards his relationship with his General was never the same again. In fact the relationship between Julius and me also changed from then on."

"You haven't explained yet why a proud man like you could just accept becoming a slave and not resist after you recovered?"

"Why didn't you? You became a slave for a while. In my case it was because there was nothing left and I thought only of surviving for as long as I could. I thought that one day I would escape. I know I never felt hopeless. That was because of Julius."

"Why do you say that?" Quintus asked.

"I was witnessing a change taking place in him. Differences he had with Paulinus began to occur and grow in number during the next few months, particularly over what was happening to our homeland. This eventually resulted in his recall to Rome. As his slave I went with him. I say slave, although he treated me more as an equal."

"You're no longer a slave though, are you?" Quintus asked. "How can you be, wearing Roman military dress if you still are?"

"Please let me finish, there's more to tell. Before long he was ordered to a series of postings in different lands, taking command of armies fighting tribes like ours. In one very difficult battle, at a critical moment, he ordered me to take command of some of his auxiliaries."

"And you couldn't resist the challenge could you?" Lucia teased.

"Perhaps that was the reason I obeyed without question. Then again, maybe it was because of the great respect I had for the man. In any case, from that time forward I served him as a commander of a large group of auxiliaries. In time we became good friends and eventually he was confident enough in me to admit his role in your escape."

"He told you that as well? Do you believe him?"

"Of course, although I think by the expression on your face you don't or are still not sure."

"I'm very confused."

"I'll explain why I do. He had no need to tell me about it, years after the event. We were reminiscing one night. Perhaps we were a little drunk. I can't remember. We eventually confessed to each other the feelings we both had for you. I was surprised at what he admitted. I told him of my grief at your loss and how I still mourned your death. It was then when he really shocked me. He described how he had behaved disloyally to his Emperor with the role he played in your escape. By doing what he did he felt he had given you your only hope of surviving, slim as it was. He had no regrets at what he had done. Since that night, realising you were still alive after the great battle, I hoped you had been able to continue to survive. I began to believe I would see you again one day."

Lucia let go of his hand briefly, first to wrap her arms around him. Then, as she pulled away, she wiped away a tear from her eye.

"But if you are part of his army why have you only reappeared today?"

"I was no longer part of his command when he returned here. Let me explain. Julius granted me my freedom a long time ago. Despite my part in the great battle against Rome, Julius was able to persuade the Emperor to go further and grant his request to make me a Roman citizen.

Two years ago Julius's great friend Camillus Pecius was involved in a difficult military campaign and asked Julius for any assistance he could give him. That's how I became the Commander of all Camillus's legionary auxiliaries. I have been content in this role ever since. Having witnessed the devastation of our tribe and our tribal lands after the war, I continued to feel there was nothing here to return to, until now."

"Lucia has a lot to tell you," said Quintus, "and since I know what she has to say, I will leave you two alone. You're welcome to stay here as a guest of this house for long as you wish, Olsar."

"You still haven't explained why and how you have come to be here," said Lucia when they were alone. "Why has he brought you to our house today?"

"It's simple. Julius cares about what happens to both of us and Cailan. Sorry! I've been told her name is now Flavia. I will be more careful not to repeat that mistake. He decided you and I have unfinished business. He wanted you to be happy again in your life. He told me today to tell you he hadn't destroyed 'all' the things in your past which you cared for. He asked Camillus if he would release me back into his command and he agreed. And so he brought me here."

He watched as she was absorbing the impact of what she had been told. She was staring at the floor. Her grip on his hand had become soft and limp.

Eventually Olsar spoke again.

"There is one more thing to tell you. I married some years ago only to lose my wife in childbirth. I now have a beautiful small daughter. She will be joining me when I'm settled and can send for her."

"I'm sorry about your wife, but pleased you have someone to love with your child. I have a son, Marcus, and he has become my life. He and Quintus, and Portos for that matter, have become inseparable. Seeing you alive again has completed my newly found happiness."

"I wondered after all these years, having had a wife and daughter, how I would feel when I met you again. My feelings for you haven't changed."

Lucia took both his hands in hers and held them tightly, holding his gaze.

"The last time you told me this I ran away in tears. I won't do it again. My feelings will always be the same for you, though. You are my true friend and teacher and I love you dearly, but not as you would want me to. I'm sorry."

She stood up, tears beginning to fill her eyes, but she remained controlled.

"This has been an extraordinary afternoon. There's so much to tell you about my life during the last ten years. Has Julius had a chance to tell you I fight in the arena? Come and look at the equipment and weapons I use."

CHAPTER 40

The Games were not going well. At least that was what Julius had whispered to Quintus, who wouldn't have known if they were or they weren't. He didn't often take a seat in the arena, even before Lucia had begun to participate in them. He considered he'd been witness to enough spilling of blood during his long life, without seeking out yet more, especially where pleasure was the excuse.

Quintus decided Julius must be correct by the concerned look on the face of Tarquinius Marellus. He had spent a lot of money only to hear a growing number of those in the crowd shouting their disapproval.

Even Lucia and her fellow gladiator were jeered at in their first contest. Between them they had easily disposed of a rather tame 'wild' bear. The woman fighting alongside Lucia had received a graze to her arm from the animal, producing a roar from the exited crowd. However, Lucia had swiftly dispatched it, strangely oblivious to the wishes of the crowd for more sport to take place with the animal.

Quintus had accepted the invitation from Julius to sit next to him. He in turn sat next to Vettius. On the other side of the Governor, Tarquinius Marellus had been given the most prominent and prestigious seat as the sponsor of the Games. Alongside him sat his son Gaius.

Even the event taking place before the return of Lucia had not pleased the crowd. An execution of two thieves, which was normally greeted with great excitement, had gone badly wrong. The first had managed to break free and run towards the exit gate in a terrified futile attempt to avoid his fate. He'd been brought down by an arena guard's spear and many in the crowd hadn't noticed the kill had taken place. The second had been executed as intended but it had been carried out in a clumsy, unskilled manner. It had taken the axeman several attempts to remove the man's head. The jeering from the massed terraces was interspersed with not very favourable shouted comments directed towards the executioner. This had caused widespread laughter from the crowd watching the thieves' remains being placed on carts and quickly taken away.

Tarquinius leaned over to tell Quintus that Lucia would be next to appear, causing him to sweat heavily at the thought of what could happen. Julius, who could see his agitation, gave a comforting tap on his thigh.

"Don't worry. Your daughter is the best there is. In any case her life isn't at stake in this contest."

"I know, but she could still receive a serious injury," Quintus countered. "I only came because you invited me to sit with you. I was most reluctant to accept your invitation because I really don't enjoy these occasions. That's definitely the case when Lucia appears."

The Master of the Games gave his introduction to the next contest. Greeted by a deafening chorus of cheers, Lucia and the other gladiator walked to the centre of the arena. At first they stood, heads bowed, with their swords and shields by their sides.

Neither moved except for raising their heads slightly to look at the Games Master. He waited for the crowd to grow quiet. A trumpet blast saw the two contestants spring into action to take up their initial stances, swords and shields raised. The noise from the crowd erupted again and the contest began.

At first, the exchange of blows and the display of skilful defensive movements had gone as might have been expected. Nevertheless, Julius moved more and more restlessly on his seat as the contest progressed. Without realising it, he was showing his agitation at what he was watching.

"Something isn't right," Julius whispered to Quintus. "She's slow and too passive. Her opponent on the other hand is very keen to demonstrate her superiority. She's lucky this isn't the final contest to the death. Let's hope this will soon be over."

The words had hardly left his mouth before a fierce blow was aimed at Lucia's head. She was slow to raise her shield in the expected manner to ward off the sword. It forced her to stagger backwards for a few paces. Her opponent seized the opportunity and moved forward quickly. A second similar strike followed and Lucia was forced down onto one knee.

The crowd applauded this display of aggression. The knowledgeable amongst them would be expecting Lucia's opponent to withdraw to allow her to gain her feet. According to the rules of the arena, she had won this part of the contest. Instead she took one step further forward to deliver a third menacing blow aimed at her head. Lucia fell to one side at the same time moving her shield to protect herself as the sword fell. With some difficulty she was just able to deflect it harmlessly. At the same time she drew her own sword tip across her opponent's leg above her knee, causing a gash which began to bleed freely.

She could have delivered a more telling blow but it would have been inappropriate in the circumstances. Nevertheless, it was sufficient to force her opponent to take a few steps backwards giving Lucia time to recover slightly.

She got back to her feet and shouted to make herself heard against the noise of the crowd yelling for more blood.

"What are you doing? The Games Master has explained the limits applying to this contest and you just went beyond them. What's the matter with you?"

"I've just changed the rules," she replied.

Another fierce swing of her opponent's arm brought her sword crashing down again. It was parried, but Lucia let out a cry of pain. Her shield fell to the ground and she brought her arm limply to her side. The cheering crowd, sensing something had changed, began to cry for more blood. Lucia backed off, using only her sword to defend herself.

"It would appear we have a real match to watch, Julius," said Tarquinius. "I believe you've placed a wager on Quintus's daughter with the Governor. Are you prepared to repeat your gamble with me? I shall be pleased to accept it."

Julius ignored his taunting. Quintus couldn't.

"Something is wrong with my daughter, Vettius. I ask you to give the order to end this contest immediately."

"The Master of the Games is in charge of proceedings. Is that not so, Vettius?" Tarquinius asked.

"I'm afraid that's correct. But please don't concern yourself,

Quintus. Your daughter's opponent is clearly winning the contest and a halt will be called soon."

The conversation was interrupted by a loud response from those in the crowd. They seemed to cry out with one voice. Lucia, without a shield, had finally succumbed to a sword thrust into her side. She dropped her sword and sank to her knees again. The wound was not deep, but it was sufficient in normal circumstances for the contest to be declared at an end. Lucia's challenge was over. There would be no purse for her today.

Her opponent, however, didn't consider it had ended. She lifted her foot, placed it against Lucia's breast and pushed. Lucia had relaxed, not expecting such a move. She fell backwards, her uninjured hand covering her wound to try to stem the flow of blood. She was now pinned to the floor by a sword tip pressed against her throat.

A hush came over the crowd. Most of those on the terraces would know that what was happening was unplanned. It didn't matter any longer. The question was about to be asked. Should the defeated be allowed to live? Uproar followed. Some screamed for the kill whilst others called for Lucia to be spared.

"Can you do something, Julius?" Quintus begged.

"You must stop this farce immediately, Vettius," Julius demanded. "This is not what we came to see and it's contrary to the rules of the Games,"

"It's for the Sponsor of the Games to take that decision," Vettius replied. "Whatever the previous intention, and despite what might be considered correct procedure in these circumstances, we have a crowd that wishes to see a contest concluded in an appropriate manner. We have one gladiator at the mercy of another. They would not welcome interference, even by me. It appears to me that the crowd is split on whether the defeated deserves to live or die. Order needs to be restored. They are waiting for you to give your answer, Tarquinius."

"Thank you Vettius. What do you have to say, Julius? Why do you think she should live? The crowd is becoming very impatient for my decision."

Tarquinius had stood up so that he could be seen by the crowd. All eyes were upon him waiting for his decision – life or death.

Julius had changed his position on his seat to allow him to draw his sword quickly if he needed to. He exaggerated the movement ensuring it was noticed, and deliberately placed his hand on the hilt.

"If the decision is yours I suggest you make it with great care. You can see there are clearly many in the arena who don't want the defeated gladiator to be put to death, particularly in the circumstances of this contest. They just might take action later if you were to displease them by choosing to end the life of one who is a clear favourite of theirs. In a town as small as this you could be in great danger, particularly at night."

"But I have you to protect me, General. Perhaps we could talk about protecting me and my interests when we meet to discuss my continuing business with you and the Army. Do you understand what I am saying?"

"I can assure you I shall take into account the wisdom you display today whenever we meet next. Do you understand me as I understand you? It's very important for you that you do."

"Indeed I do. I think we shall have a good future together that will prove to be mutually beneficial."

He turned to Vettius.

"I think they have both fought well. The daughter of Quintus deserves to fight and entertain us again on another day. Such a clear favourite of the crowd, and apparently the General, deserves to live on this occasion."

He moved forward slightly and raised his arm, palm upward to give the signal for Lucia to be allowed to gain her feet. Mayhem broke out again with a few fights taking place on the terraces. To restore order, The Master immediately ordered the trumpets to be sounded to let the crowd know he was about to introduce the final contest of the day. It brought the crowd's attention back to the arena, awaiting the imminent entrance of the gladiators. Lucia in the meantime was being carried off into the murky depths beneath the terraces.

Julius and Quintus rose from their seats and left without waiting for the last contest to begin. Vettius watched them leave before turning in his seat to face Tarquinius. He gave a broad, knowing grin, patting him on his thigh several times. With a satisfied sigh he returned his attention to the activity in the arena below.

*

Julius thrust through the turmoil being created by the many attendants who were busying themselves in the poorly lit corridors below the terraces. Quintus was breathing heavily, trying to keep up. They were directed to the room where Lucia had been taken.

"Lucia, what are they doing to you?" cried Quintus when he saw his daughter laid out on a crude table. She was being attended to by two of the Games Master's surgeons.

"We must close the wound if she is to recover quickly," one of them shouted. "It must be done before she can be moved again."

"Are you trained in such matters? I'm General Agricola. I can call upon the services of my own men, experienced in looking after those wounded in battle."

"And I'm Cornelius Drabo. I served in that role in the army for many, many years before I retired. So will you please let me get on with treating this woman?"

*

Lucia, her wounds treated, had been carried the short distance to Quintus's house and placed in the welcome luxury of her own room. Quintus had explained to her how Julius's strong words, particularly with Tarquinius, had probably saved her life.

"I hear what you say, old man. Now don't fuss so much."

Lucia was beginning to get a little impatient and annoyed with the attention she was getting from him.

"The wound isn't much more than a flesh wound. I'll recover in a few days. I'm suffering much more from my sprained wrist and I don't recall anybody ever dying from that."

"I understand," Quintus said by way of an apology. "I'll take a seat and not disturb or annoy you anymore. I'm feeling very tired. Today's events were too much for an old fool like me."

"You can do more than that. You can retire to your own room and rest," she ordered gently. "I have Julius here if I need anything and Olsar has been sent for. I shall be fine. So please go away and stop worrying about me."

He returned her warm smile and, giving Julius's arm a last grateful squeeze, he left the two of them alone.

"If you want me to, I can leave also. Laric is around somewhere. I can send for him to look after you."

"There's no need for you to go. I want to say a few words while I have the opportunity. I lost today because of you."

Julius stiffened. Perhaps anticipating a need to explain himself and his past yet again.

"Not in the way you might expect," she continued. "I lost because I wasn't fully prepared. I wasn't concentrating totally on the woman, who I now think was directed to be prepared to kill me for some unknown reason. I was foolish. My mind instead of being fixed on her was continuously being taken over by thoughts of what Olsar had told me about you. It seems I've misjudged you by not being fully aware of what happened in the past or of the way you changed then and since."

"It was clear to me you weren't fighting as you could. I couldn't understand why."

"You do now. I want you to know that I've changed the way I think about you and will welcome your company in the future."

"That is what I was hoping for but more than I was expecting."

"It won't be easy for either of us. I can't forget the tragedies of the past, but I think I can become the friend of the man Olsar has described, in the way he has."

"I'm pleased to hear that. You won't regret it. Olsar has told me that the two of you talked about me at some length but I didn't expect his words to have had such an effect."

"Well they have."

"He is indeed a good friend and a fine man. I'm sure you can find happiness together. I shall do what I can to protect you as I did with Olsar."

"Whatever Olsar has said, I think you may have misunderstood our relationship. He and I are true friends, but that's all. You appear to assume there's something else between us. I assure you there's not and Olsar knows that now."

"I see," said Julius.

"Since I've made that clear, I have many more questions to ask you, but not at the moment," she said, her voice beginning to sound tired. "I promise to try to be less confrontational in asking them in future. For now, I think I need to rest."

*

The following morning Quintus said his farewell to Lucia.

"It's better if you stay here until you're fully recovered. I'm going back to the villa but I'll leave Laric here to make sure you're well taken care of. I'm certain you'll get constant visits from Julius and Olsar to see you get everything you need."

"Thank you, Quintus. I'm pleased you're going back to Flavia and Marcus. Tell them I'll be back soon, fit and well. You should rest too. You don't look at all well."

"I'm fine," he said, trying to reassure her. "I'm just a little strained after the traumatic events of the last few days. I think things are going to be much calmer again. We can perhaps return to concentrating on the running of our estate and living our lives in peaceful contentment. We have our new friends to help us."

CHAPTER 41

Laric had been taken prisoner in Eastern Gaul when he had been a youth of only 13 years. In those days he hadn't fully developed physically. Very small, he wasn't considered worthy of being put to heavy work in the fields. He would have succumbed very quickly in the cold and the damp. It would have been a waste of good money to lose a slave in such an unnecessary way.

Instead he was trained to become a slave for the household, working in the kitchens at first, and later throughout the rest of the villa and bathhouse. Even so his natural lethargy had given cause for him to be beaten often by his owners. Consequently he had been bought and sold often until finally he was acquired by Quintus and his daughters.

In time he grew out of much of the lethargy of his youth. He had given good service to them, only occasionally receiving a beating from Lucia. It was no surprise he developed an intense dislike of her. He still had mixed feelings about Quintus though. These thoughts were in his mind as he tied the red ribbon to the handle of his basket and headed for the market. He felt sure he would soon be set free by Gaius when he reported to him what he'd heard and seen. However, he wondered what would happen to Quintus.

Hurrying to join the bustle of the market place, he was reflecting on how fortunate he'd been to get the information which would lead to his freedom. He'd learned at an early age that the Romans considered their slaves to be objects. It was something he had gradually grown accustomed to. His owners were only aware of him when they put him to use. Otherwise he would go unnoticed, part of the rest of the background features in the villa. He became invisible to them until needed.

Although it could still be irritating at times, he was able to take advantage of this treatment from time to time. This had never been truer than in the last few days, with the hectic comings and goings by the family and their friends. This turmoil, together with the unguarded, emotional conversations which had taken place throughout the house, had worked to his advantage when going about his duties.

The result was that he had pieced together a story which would amaze Gaius. Walking towards the Palace he began to wonder if he wanted Gaius to buy freedom for him directly from Quintus. The alternative would be to ask for a financial reward from Gaius. Then he might be able to persuade Quintus to let him go for a much lower price. He would be able to keep the rest of the reward. Perhaps not. He had realised Quintus may not come out of this very well and he may refuse to free him whatever the price, as an act of revenge. He thought it would probably be better to let Gaius make the arrangements.

*

For the first time he entered Gaius's office without fear. He was excited and confident about what he was about to report. Gaius could see the difference in the little man who strode confidently into his room. He rose with a broad, warm smile and moved from behind his desk to welcome him.

"By the look on your face you have something very interesting to tell me. Let's withdraw into my private rooms rather than this office. We don't want to be disturbed or overheard," said Gaius, pointing to a small door behind him.

Laric lounged on a low couch, taking in the luxury of the room he had been taken to. The first beaker of wine had been drunk by him without pause, unlike his earlier hesitant, nervous sips. This was the life he could look forward to. Good wine was something he occasionally had access to, but only if Caris wasn't around to see him take it. Even then it could only be in very small amounts.

"I can see you enjoyed that. Let me give you a refill, but please begin your report."

Laric told of the General's unusual short visit with a fellow soldier who Laric had never seen before. He explained how tense the General had appeared and how he had left alone, leaving the stranger behind. It had prompted him to pay particular attention to what was happening.

He continued to tell his astonishing story as events had unfolded over the following few days.

"Have some more wine while I absorb what you've just told me," said Gaius, pouring him yet another full beaker of wine.

Laric took a firm hold of it. His head had begun to spin a little but he felt so clever at what he'd done. He was so proud of the obvious pleasure his story had given his good friend.

"Let me clarify what you are telling me. It's so staggering that I need to be sure I've understood your words properly."

"Firstly you are saying Lucia and Flavia are the daughters of that long-dead witch, Boudica?"

"Yes! Yes!"

"Please let me finish my summary without interruption. It's for the best."

"Secondly, the General hasn't just learned of that. In fact he recognised Lucia from the moment he first saw her on his return to this province."

"Thirdly, you even believe it was with his deliberate assistance that they were able to escape the battle scene after the defeat of their mother?"

Laric kept his mouth shut but nodded his head vigorously in agreement before taking another large gulp of wine.

"And finally, he's repeating his treachery. Rather than surrender them to the Governor and the Emperor he intends to help them to continue to hide their identity."

A broad contented smile had settled on Laric's face.

Gaius went silent for a while. He began to pace around the room, his brow wrinkled, his hands crossed behind his back. He returned to his couch and smiled at Laric.

"Don't misunderstand me, Laric, but how do I know that what you tell me is the truth? I don't think for one moment that you're lying, but could you have misheard or misunderstood them?"

"No Sir. There are other things I could tell you but I don't know what they mean. I wasn't here at the time of the revolt."

"Such as?"

"Well, I heard Lucia talking about somebody called Decianus, whoever he may have been, and that the father of Marcus, her son, was in fact one of his men. We've often wondered what happened to his father."

Gaius rose sharply from his couch and returned to pacing back and forth, deep in thought.

"I have decided that what you've told me is entirely true. You have done me the greatest service and you will be rewarded accordingly. However, before we talk some more about that, I need some more information. I have to decide what is the appropriate action to take and when. The General is a very dangerous and ruthless man. Who is staying at the house in town at the moment?"

"Only Lucia. She's made good progress but is still not well enough to travel. She'll be there for two more days. My master has returned to the estate."

"What of this Olsar. Where is he?"

"He has gone to Ratae and Verulamium with the General. They won't be returning until the day after tomorrow at the earliest."

"How can you be sure of the whereabouts of General Agricola? It's a confidential matter and isn't disclosed to those outside the Military, not even to me."

"Because he told Lucia he and Olsar were going to change their plans to go to these two towns. They wanted to stay with her. She told them in no uncertain terms to carry on with their visits. She didn't need their presence for her to recover from her injuries."

Gaius uttered a contemptuous grunt, followed quickly by a reassuring smile for Laric.

It gave him the confidence to speak again.

"Is this the sort of information you were looking for? Does it deserve the reward you spoke of the last time I was here?"

"It couldn't have been better. What reward do you suggest is appropriate?"

Emboldened by the wine Laric decided to ask for what he felt his bravery warranted.

"You promised me my freedom if I pleased you. From the look on your face, I think you will be pleased to give me what I yearn for above anything else."

"Well put, Laric," said Gaius, moving towards him to grasp his hand. "It's the least I can do."

Towering above Laric, he pulled him like a child towards him, wrapping his arms around his upper body to hold him close. It was so close Laric's face was nestled firmly against his chest.

"There's one last thing I need to know. Have you obeyed me and spoken to nobody else about what you've told me today?"

"Nobody, Sir. I swear it."

"Good! Very, very good."

Pressed as he was against Gaius, Laric was feeling very dizzy from the effects of the wine. He began to find it difficult to breath. He made to pull away but found he couldn't move. One of Gaius's hands moved up to the back of his head to press his face a little more firmly against his chest. Laric thought this show of affection must really be proof of his gratitude.

Nevertheless, he needed to pull away, to catch his breath. He tried, only for the grip to tighten. It caused him to feel faint and he began to panic as his breathing became very difficult. Very quickly darkness began to envelop him.

Gaius waited until long after the pathetic little man's arms and legs had stopped twitching. Only then did he lower the frail lifeless body onto the floor.

"Now you have your freedom as I promised."

He called his trusted personal guard to his room and pointed to Laric's still body.

"It would appear that the slave died of shock when I chastised him. It will be best to avoid a fuss if you deposit his body in the river tonight. If and when his body is found it will be one more slave who drowned attempting to run away while his master was absent."

CHAPTER 42

The area of land between the west wing of the villa and the large bathhouse had been turned into a small garden by Flavia. Nobody was allowed to work in it but her. She didn't need the help of slaves, or an over-eager clumsy nephew. It was where she found peace and comfort, where she sought refuge if she was troubled. Here she could gather her thoughts if she had decisions to make. It was also where she went if she just wanted to be herself for a while.

Quintus had his bathhouse. Lucia had her training area and the arena. She had her precious garden and plants. There she met and spoke quietly with her Gods, and remembered her father and mother.

She was sitting on one end of her little bench, looking up into the sky, letting the sun warm her face. The quiet of the moment let her mind wander onto how her life had recently been put into turmoil once again.

She was no longer depressed at the thought. She was convinced her life had finally been changed for the better. It seemed to be set on a course towards a settled happiness, even though she would always carry the mental scars from all that had happened in the past. Agricola's reappearance had brought back those dark memories, which she had learnt to suppress. In the telling of her story to Quintus she had relived the brutal rape, the death of her mother and so many of her people. There had been the agony of the futile attempt to escape with her sister and their inevitable capture, before coming to rest in the haven provided by Quintus.

Her thoughts dwelt on the time when she reached the depths of despair after her mother's death. She recalled thinking of taking her own life when she and Lucia had suffered so dreadfully in the forests, trying not to be discovered. She was so grateful she had been able to fight through all her misery, helped by Lucia's strength.

The reappearance of Julius, at first threatening, had become a blessing. She had the most powerful man in the land wishing to protect her and Lucia. Those terrible years would never be repeated.

Quintus had returned and told her Olsar was alive and had returned to Londinium. He had confirmed what Julius had told them. Perhaps it might help Lucia to rid herself of some of her demons.

A shout from Caris at the open kitchen window interrupted her daydreaming. She pointed to Dena the young slave girl who had recently been purchased to help in the kitchen. She was making her way along the path towards her.

"Caris has sent me to ask you to come inside, Mistress. We have a visitor, but the Master is not here to receive him."

"I've told you to call me Flavia, not Mistress. Where is Quintus?"

"He's gone to inspect the crops in the fields."

"And where is Portos?"

"Portos is with the grain merchant in Londinium. He won't return until this evening."

"Who is the visitor?"

"I wasn't told."

Flavia rose from her seat, picked up her basket of flowers to give to Caris and hurried indoors.

"Gaius. What a surprise," she said, only partially able to hide her astonishment. "Quintus is not here at the moment. Can I help you?"

"You can indeed. It isn't Quintus I've come to see. It's you. Is there somewhere where we can go so we can be alone? I don't want the important things which I need to say to you to be heard by anyone else."

Flavia was intrigued and slightly concerned at the same time. She had met Gaius Marellus in Londinium on a number of occasions and to some extent had enjoyed his company. However, this was the first time that he'd paid a visit to the Villa.

"Of course. We have a reception room which will do perfectly well. Can we get you any refreshment?"

"There's no need, thank you."

"Then please follow me."

"I know who you are," said Gaius when they were alone and the door was closed behind them.

"Excuse me? I afraid I don't understand what you mean," said Flavia, her heart missing a beat.

"You and your sister are the daughters of Boudica. Please don't try to deny it. I know much more and I have a witness who is ready to swear it's true to the Governor."

Flavia let out a long, deep groan and fell to the floor in a dead faint. A short while later her eyes fluttered open again.

"I'm sorry if I caused you to faint and fall. I hope you haven't hurt yourself. I would never knowingly harm you. Please believe me."

Flavia had gained her senses to find herself lying full length on a couch. He was kneeling beside her, holding her hands. She couldn't control her trembling or the growing sense of dread.

"What is it that you are saying you know exactly?"

"As I said, I know who your mother was and I know Julius Agricola is aware of it. He saved you and helped you to escape after our victory over your tribe. What is more, I know he has no intention of telling the Governor who you really are."

"No! You must never tell anybody. I beg you."

The panic she was feeling was almost unbearable. She could scarcely breathe as she made a feeble attempt to rise. He moved his hands onto her arms and easily prevented her.

"Now you've admitted it and I know for certain, I will still promise you I'll never tell another person. But there is a condition."

"What is it?"

"You must marry me. Please tell me you will."

"What?" she gasped. "What could you possibly expect me to say? What do you mean?"

"I mean exactly what I say. I have wanted you and tried to show it to you for longer than I can remember, but you have never seemed to notice it. I'm not comfortable in the company of women and have never had the courage to tell you what I feel. I don't care if you don't love me at the moment. I will teach you how."

"Please stop," she begged.

"Don't you understand what I'm saying and what I am offering you? What I've discovered will change your life forever if it becomes known. You have to make a decision now. I'm about to return to my office in the Governor's Palace, either to tell him what I know or to tell him the good news that I am to marry Quintus's beautiful daughter."

"I can't marry you, ever," she sobbed.

"I'm sorry to hear it. You have just condemned yourself to death, together with your sister and Quintus. Julius Agricola will have to answer to the Emperor Vespasian."

He started to rise. She grabbed his hand as she attempted to stand. Still very unsteady, she had to sit down again. Gaius showed his concern and knelt back down beside her.

"I swear by my deep love for you that I will keep your identity secret. All you need to do now is to allow me to court you for a short while. I will ask Quintus for his permission to allow us to be married. Nobody will ever know your true identity."

"What about the person who told you about us? He could tell others."

"Don't worry about that. I will silence my informant before he can tell anybody else. I swear nobody else knows or will ever know if you do as I ask. As the Governor's Secretary I would be the first to hear and silence any other rumours which might arise."

Somehow she had to buy some time. Then she could tell Julius before this evil man could do any harm. He would know what to do. She made her decision.

"I agree," she whispered, "but you must swear to save all of us."

"I do! I do!"

He sat down and placed his arms around her, pulling her roughly to him kissing her firmly on her lips. She flinched as his mouth covered hers. He touched her breast and she froze, instinctively beginning to resist. He forced her back onto the couch. Before long his strength and weight ended any resistance left in her.

"By the Gods, Gaius, what are you doing to Flavia?" Quintus yelled.

On his arrival back at the villa he had come to the reception room without delay and walked straight in, intending to welcome his guest. He came to a shocked halt.

Gaius stood up abruptly, rearranging and straightening his clothing.

"It's unfortunate that you have found us in these circumstances. Nevertheless, I can tell you Flavia and I intend to be married. I would have preferred to ask you for your agreement at a later, more appropriate and convenient time. However, events have overtaken us. We need to look to the future. I'm sure you realise she will be marrying into the wealthiest family in Londinium."

Quintus, his mouth half-open and a pained expression on his face listened to the man's hurried and embarrassed explanation. He spoke in a whisper with his head bowed.

"What do you have to say, Flavia? Why are you crying, my child?"

She was fighting back her feelings of utter shame at what Quintus had seen. Resisting a desperate need to tell him what had really happened, she lowered her head to give her trembling, tearful reply.

"I'm sorry you've been embarrassed in this way but it's true. I've agreed to marry Gaius and my tears are because I'm happy."

"So there you have it," said Gaius, his nervous embarrassment still very obvious. "I must go to attend to the Governor. I'll return in a few days to begin the preparation for the wedding."

Gaius headed for the door. He walked cautiously past Quintus, who made no movement to get out of the way to make it easier for him to pass. At the doorway he turned to speak to Flavia.

"Farewell for the time being, my love. I look forward to the time soon when we can tell the Governor of the future we've agreed to share together. I wouldn't want him to learn of our little secret from anybody else."

Quintus remained very still, head and shoulders still bowed.

Flavia's pretence began to crumble as soon as Gaius had gone. She let out a loud sob of despair, unable to keep the horror inside.

"Gaius has raped me, Quintus. I've been raped again. I am nothing, nothing."

"What are you saying, my poor chid?"

Walking slowly towards her, he tried to reassure her by placing a comforting hand on her shoulder, only to withdraw it and place it forcefully on his chest.

"I... I...Please help me, Flavia!"

*

Caris heard Flavia's cries for help coming from the reception room. She told Marcus to stay where he was in the kitchen with Dena until she returned.

She entered hurriedly to see Flavia cradling Quintus's head in her arms. He lay on the floor, his face grimacing with pain.

"Quintus," she yelled, "what has happened?"

His reply was weak.

"Don't be concerned about me. Take care of Flavia. She's been raped by that monstrous Gaius."

Caris looked at the distraught Flavia who was staring blankly at Quintus.

"Help me to lift him onto the couch," Caris insisted.

*

Portos arrived as he had planned, just as dusk was falling. He was carrying the payment from the grain merchant in Londinium and didn't want to be on the open road at night.

He made straight for the kitchen and the usual warm welcome from Caris, only to find it empty. The prepared meal which usually greeted his late arrival, something he had been looking forward to, was nowhere to be seen. It wasn't the only thing causing his surprise. There was no sign that the kitchen had been used at all that evening.

Calling out Caris's name he heard her faint reply coming from Quintus's room. Curious to find out what was happening, he grabbed a piece of cheese and walked quickly down the corridor. What he saw when he entered the room brought him to a sudden halt.

Quintus was lying on his bed, apparently asleep. Caris and Flavia were crouching down on either side of him. Caris lifted her tear-stained face to look at him.

"What's happened? Is he dead?" he whispered to her.

"Not yet, but his time is close."

Flavia let a muffled groan escape. Unusually for her, there were no tears to be seen. Her eyes, deeply set in her pale face, stared vacantly at Quintus's still form.

No further words were spoken. Caris's prediction proved to be correct. Quintus's breathing became increasingly shallow until his long last breath left his body. His face gave a tight final grimace before becoming still and relaxed.

Flavia didn't react as Portos might have expected. Instead of crying as Caris was at his final passing into the next world, she immediately stood up. Drained of any emotion she looked first at Caris and then at Portos. She calmly announced she was going to her bed and didn't wish to be disturbed until morning.

Portos took Flavia's place at the side of the bed and held Quintus's lifeless hand. After a long sad silence Caris was the first to speak.

"What will become of us?"

"We are still what we were when Quintus lived. We're part of this estate and will become the property of whoever receives it under the terms of Quintus's will. In that sense we're no different from the other slaves. At the moment though, I'm more concerned about Flavia. She acted very strangely."

Caris explained that Quintus had told her of the rape by Gaius. Flavia had confirmed what had happened while they sat nursing him later.

"She also asked me to send word to Lucia to tell her Gaius knows everything."

"Knows what exactly?"

"I asked her that but she just went silent. So I told her I would be asking you to return immediately to escort Lucia back home tomorrow and she could tell her herself. You must leave soon after dawn to bring her. Flavia needs her more than she ever did."

*

The following morning, Caris had been the first to rise when the first light of dawn appeared. She had prepared a light meal for Flavia and Portos and looked relieved to have his company when he came into the kitchen.

"Good morning. Come and have something to eat while I go to see Flavia to ask her if she's ready to eat anything."

Portos had just filled his mouth with a lump of bread and was holding a large beaker of fresh milk to wash it down. A shrill scream made him splutter the food across the table. He dropped the milk in a frantic movement to get to his feet. In the corridor, on his hurried way to Flavia's room, a second louder scream assaulted his ears.

Flavia lay on her back on the top of her bed as if she had just decided to take a short nap. She was dressed in her favourite gown and she appeared just to be sound asleep. Except, that is, for the colour of her face. Drained of any blood it had turned an almost translucent grey.

In her arms she held some of her beloved flowers, the ones she had picked from her garden the day before.

Caris had stopped screaming. She was trying to recover from the shock of her discovery. "The poor child is dead. She must have taken poison."

"I can see that. It must have been soon after she left us last night."

"The poor child," Caris whispered. "Why would she do it? Why would she be desperate enough to take her own life?"

"Whatever it was, it must have included the trauma of the rape. That and the shame of being discovered by Quintus while it was happening."

"Then, there followed the horror of seeing Quintus die," Caris added, "and the guilt she would have felt. It must all have been too much for her to bear. If Lucia had been here she may have been able to comfort and save her."

"Poor Lucia. What a message I have to take to her," Portos added. "Two of the three people she holds dearest are dead. I must leave immediately."

"You must also pass on to her what Flavia said of Gaius. Her exact words were 'He knows everything'. The message must be important for Flavia to have mentioned it at the time she did."

CHAPTER 43

It hadn't taken Gaius long on his journey back to Londinium to recover from the unfortunate intrusion by Quintus. The morning afterwards he could even see the funny side of it, especially the look of utter amazement on the old goat's face. At least he'd had just enough time to finish with Flavia before he had burst in on them. He knew his father would be amused by it when he eventually gave him the details, but that wouldn't be today. Before going to his office, he was on his way to explain to him his decision to marry and it wouldn't be easy.

"I have something good to tell you, Father," he said, finding him in the garden of his villa.

"Don't say anything. Let me guess. General Agricola has fallen from his horse and broken his neck?"

"Not that good, I'm afraid," Gaius chuckled. "It's something of a personal nature you've been hoping would happen for a number of years. I've decided to get married."

"At long last! Tell me who she is. Of course you'll have chosen someone who is from a family worthy to be associated with me and my name. You know if she isn't I won't permit it."

Gaius thought the warning was unnecessary. He'd learnt a long time ago about his father's essential requirements for his choice of bride.

"She is Flavia, daughter of Quintus Tiberius Saturninus."

"You can't be serious. She's an adopted ex-slave. Are you playing the fool with me?"

"Not at all father. I'm deadly serious. We care very much for each other. Adopted or not, she's still his daughter. I would point out that her father is well respected and really quite wealthy. I have made my decision and I'm determined to overcome any objection you may have. I will marry her."

"You will, will you? I would enjoy the novelty of seeing you trying to defy me. But perhaps you have no need to, thinking more about it. What you say about Quintus is true. He is very wealthy. He also has the advantage of being very old and not far from going to join the Gods."

"I knew you would see the sense of it."

"If you are determined to go ahead with this you'd better get on with it. Otherwise he will be dead and she will have very little to offer us."

"What do you mean?"

"Remember, he has two other daughters with husbands who will try to claim his estate. I shall have a word with Vettius and arrange for us to see Quintus's will. He will have it in his possession. With his help we can look to make changes to it so you get the major share. We don't have to have absolutely everything. We need not be too greedy."

"I shall leave such matters to you and Vettius. I'm eager to make her my wife but for different reasons from what you might think. I'm not interested in her estate, only in her."

Tarquinius didn't react, choosing only to give his son a dismissive wave before returning to work in his garden.

*

Not far away, and a little later that morning, Portos was being shown into Lucia's room.

"Good to see you Portos. I've been expecting you to come to get me, although I'm quite capable of riding home by myself. My wound is healing rapidly and I'm perfectly able to control my horse with one good hand if my injured wrist makes it necessary."

Portos didn't say anything in reply. He just watched as she busied herself with collecting the items which she wished to take with her. Because of his silence she paused and turned to look at him.

"Is there a problem?" she asked, looking at his downcast expression. "The look on your face suggests I won't like what you have to say."

She turned and joined him, taking his hand in hers. Her own face was beginning to show her growing concern at his silence.

"Please tell me Marcus isn't hurt. Has he been injured while riding and jumping with his pony?"

"Marcus is fine, not injured in any way," he replied. "But I'm afraid what I have to tell you will still be very painful for you to hear."

He swallowed hard, trying to control his emotions.

"There's no easy way to say this. Both Quintus and Flavia are dead."

Lucia took in a long, deep breath, stiffened and took a step backwards.

"No! No! You're lying. It can't be."

"You know I never lie to you, Lucia. Please forgive me for bringing you this news. They both died yesterday."

"How? What..."

"I would have given my life to have been there to save them if I could, but it happened while I was on my way back from seeing the grain merchant."

"What's happened? Was it an accident?"

Portos described what had taken place. He explained how Quintus had discovered the rape of Flavia. The shock had probably contributed to his death. The treatment of her by Gaius, followed very quickly by the death of Quintus, must have made Flavia take her own life.

"I can't believe what you're saying. It can't have happened."

"I wish it wasn't true."

She sat down on a small chair, suddenly drained of any energy.

"There's something else I need to tell you. Caris tells me that while they were attending to Quintus, Flavia asked her to give you a message."

In her state of shock she didn't immediately ask what the message was. He carried on despite her silence.

"Referring to Gaius she said you were to be told - he knows everything. Does that make any sense to you?"

She lifted her head sharply to look at him but didn't comment. She stood and walked to where she had been collecting her possessions. Her back was turned to him and she remained still and silent for some time.

Portos waited for her reply, respecting her silence.

She turned towards him, her face emptied of any emotion.

"I won't be returning with you today. I want you to go to the villa and take charge of Marcus. Keep him with you, always by your side, until I return."

"I understand. Please take great care of yourself. Is there anything I should tell the boy?"

"Tell him I love him dearly and will come to him as soon as I can. I have unexpected things to see to here first of all."

*

The guard outside the doorway leading to Gaius's office made a feeble attempt to block Lucia's determined entry into the room. Gaius raised his head and rose to his feet in alarm when she strode into the room, closely followed by the flustered guard. She came to a halt, feet apart and hands on her hips. She glared at him, her eyes wide open in anger.

"I see that Flavia has told you we are to be married," Gaius said nervously. "I expected you to try to oppose it, but I never imagined you would dare to force your way into the Governor's Palace in this way. I can have you taken into custody for this, but I won't do so if you leave immediately."

"You will not be marrying my sister."

"You can't prevent it. Quintus has already given his consent and my father will be speaking to him to draw up an agreement."

"Quintus will not be making any agreement."

"You can't stop him from doing so. You won't prevent us from getting married. I am Secretary to the Governor, and as such, I insist that you leave his Palace immediately."

"I don't have to stop either of them," Lucia snarled, ignoring his demand. "Both Quintus and my sister are dead because of you."

"Are you crazy? What are you talking about? I was with them both only yesterday when everything was agreed. I really don't appreciate this joke or whatever mischief it is you're planning."

"You raped my sister and the shock of witnessing it took Quintus's life. Flavia took poison, no longer wishing to live with her shame and the loss of our father. They both died because of what you did. For that you will die."

"Guard, seize her," he yelled, through lips trembling with fear.

In one swift movement Lucia drew her sword. Spinning round she crashed the hilt hard against the side of the guard's jaw as he was making a slow, hesitant movement to take hold of her. He crashed unconscious to the floor.

Casting her sword aside Lucia took hold of the dagger which Vettius had presented to her at the Games. She pointed it at Gaius's horrified face. He began to cry with terror.

"You are going to die but not swiftly," she said coldly and quietly, her emotions under complete control. "Never again will you be able to cause pain and suffering to another."

Gaius tried to push past her to seek safety elsewhere in the building but her forearm smashed into his face breaking his nose. He fell bloodied and dazed onto the marbled floor.

Lucia rolled him onto his back and, wincing slightly with pain, she placed her forearm with the injured wrist across his throat. Her knee on his chest pinned him to the floor.

"Who else have you told about me and my sister?" she demanded.

"Nobody, I swear by all the Gods!"

"Why would you keep such valuable information from the Governor? Who told you who we are? Don't lie and you may yet live."

"I was told by Laric. I killed him for his treachery to you and Flavia. I made sure I was the only one he told. I've kept your secret. I swear it."

"Why should I believe you?"

"I would have had to tell Vettius first, even before my own father. Do you think you would still be free if I had told him?"

He delivered his answers with difficulty. Her arm pressed down harder on his throat to force the truth out.

"I gave my promise to Flavia when she agreed to marry me, never to disclose what I know and I never will."

Lucia began to realise what had happened and how Flavia had been raped, unable to offer any real resistance, for fear of what he might do to them all if she did.

"Before you die I want you to suffer the pain and horror that should be felt by all the men who do as you did to my poor Flavia."

Her hand which held the knife moved slowly down his body. As the blade began to cut into his groin, Gaius screamed in terrible agony and terror.

His screams were heard throughout the building and Lucia could hear footsteps approaching rapidly. She withdrew the bloody knife and raised it high above her head. Gaius moved his bloodied hands from his groin in a feeble attempt to resist her. She brought the knife crashing down into his chest. She did this not once but repeatedly until a sharp blow to her head brought a black mist down upon her. She fell forward onto the mutilated dead body of Gaius.

CHAPTER 44

"Good day, Tarquinius. I've asked you and General Agricola to join me. I'm told by my staff that he will be arriving shortly," said Vettius. "You have my deepest sympathy for the death of your son."

"Death! That's too simple a word to describe what has happened to him. It was slaughter by that she wolf. She mutilated and tortured my Gaius. I demand that she be put to death. I can think of a number of ways she can be tortured and made to suffer terrible agonies in her beloved arena."

"I agree we must avenge him. Remember that while you have lost a son, I've lost a loyal and efficient secretary. You can also add the fact that the killing took place in my offices. It was an act of great dishonour to me and Rome. I want satisfaction just like you."

"I understand. But why have you asked for Agricola to join us? It's not a military matter, is it?"

"Not technically, I agree. However, there's considerable unrest in the town and surrounding areas after what has happened. We may need him to maintain control."

"How long will it be before he arrives?"

"He arrived in town this morning. I'm told he went immediately to Quintus's estate for some reason. I'm sure he'll be here very soon."

Vettius wasn't wrong. Julius, still dirty from his ride and red faced, stormed into the room a short time later.

"Release her at once!"

"Sit down and explain yourself, Julius," Vettius commanded. He gave a sideways glance at Tarquinius and shook his head slightly to prevent an immediate reaction from him.

"I've no need to sit down, since I won't be staying. Did you hear and understand me? I want her released immediately!"

"She has brutally murdered my Secretary while he was performing his duties here in my offices. May I remind you I am Governor of this province? I alone will decide on the fate of this woman."

"And I remind you that I command the Army. The legionaries will do what I tell them to."

Vettius ignored the implied threat in Julius's words.

"I have brought you here so I can remind you it's your duty to maintain order until I have investigated the matter thoroughly before deciding her fate. There's no doubt at all she did it. She used this knife on my desk. It's the one I presented to her at the Games."

"You have no need to tell me what my duty is. I am indeed responsible for maintaining order. It's for this reason that I shall take her from here. No harm must come to her in your jail or anywhere else."

"You can't possibly allow it, Vettius," Tarquinius pleaded.

Julius didn't wait for a reply from Vettius.

"From what I've heard today, I believe that Lucia's sister had been raped by your son Gaius. Quintus died after the shock of witnessing her being raped. This crime, committed by that miserable pathetic coward, your son, caused her to kill herself. Quintus was a much admired and respected man in this town. There could well be considerable unrest aimed at both of you when it's known what evil the Governor's Secretary has done."

"Those are lies. Who has told you these things?" Tarquinius demanded.

"Portos and Caris."

"I say they are liars. They are slaves in any case. Who will believe their word against mine?"

"I believe them totally, and who in this town will dare to prefer the word of Tarquinius Marellus to that of General Agricola?"

He addressed Vettius once again.

"If you don't want me to leave this room to call a meeting immediately of all the people of any significance in this town, to tell them what I've discovered, then I insist she is released to me now."

Vettius glared at Julius, but didn't answer immediately.

"You mustn't let this happen," Tarquinius shouted.

"Please be quiet!" snapped Vettius. "I shall do as you request, Julius, but on one condition. You must give me your word you won't free her or tell her she won't be held to account for her actions. You will return her to me later for my ultimate decision in this matter."

"Agreed. Don't disturb yourself. I'll see to this myself."

Julius turned on his heels and stormed out of the room.

"You've betrayed me. How could you do this to me?" Tarquinius roared.

"Because, you fool, if your son has done this we have a problem. Your standing in this town will be nothing for a long time. We shall have to end all our business ventures. I need to think this through."

*

Even in the dim light of the oil lamp in the cell where Lucia had been placed, Julius could see the poor state she was in. Snatching the key from the prison guard he released the manacles which secured her ankles to the floor. He placed his arms under her to lift her motionless body. Outside, the bright daylight fell onto her eyes, causing her to stir. A quick glance let her recognise Julius's anxious face. The slightest of smiles touched the corners of her mouth...

"Put me down, you brute."

She closed her eyes and rolled inwards in his arms, enabling her to grasp his arm tightly in case she should fall. He gripped her even more tightly, placed his lips gently on her forehead, and released her to his men to be carried away to safety.

*

Lucia awoke to find she was lying in a large bed in a small room. She had woken to see a face which she recognised from the town house.

"What are you doing here and, incidentally, where is 'here' for that matter?"

"I've been ordered by Portos to attend to you, Mistress," Dena answered timidly. "You are in the General's private quarters."

"How long have I been here?"

"You've been here two days, drifting in and out of sleep. You had a wound on your head. I've been treating that and your other injuries."

Lucia looked at the wound in her side to see it had improved. Now it only needed a small dressing. Her wrist had been wrapped very tightly and the pain had been replaced by just a dull ache. She moved her hand to the back of her head to discover a small cut but a very large lump.

"Have you done all this for me by yourself?"

"No, No! The General has helped me to wash and dress you and to treat your wounds."

Lucia didn't have time to reflect on what she had been told. She could hear quick short footsteps approaching her room. It was a sound she recognised instantly.

"Mama, Mama," Marcus cried. He dashed straight into her arms and clung to her with all his strength. "Portos has brought me to see you and he says the General has said I can go to see all the horses in the stables."

"That's wonderful," said a joyful Lucia. "I shall come with you once I'm dressed."

"I think not," said Portos, knocking lightly on the open door and walking into the room. "The General has insisted that you're to rest until he's happy for you to be allowed out of bed. And in this building everybody obeys the General without question."

"Do they indeed? We shall see about that. But perhaps what you say is right for today."

Mother and son spent some time discussing what had happened to his grandfather and aunt Flavia. The great sadness at their loss was only slightly tempered with joy at being together again.

"Time for us to go and feed the horses don't you think?" Portos suggested firmly to Marcus.

The boy got to his feet. He hugged and kissed his mother then ran out of the room as fast as he had entered it, followed by Portos.

"I'm feeling a little tired after that, Dena. I think I shall just lie back and rest my eyes again for a short while. Please leave me. I've no need for you to attend me for the time being."

The slave-girl did as she was asked after briefly tidying the room. She crept out quietly, closing the door gently behind her.

*

"Where are Marcus and Portos and the girl Dena?" Lucia asked.

She had woken again to find the room in semi-darkness lit by several lamps placed around the room. She was talking to Julius who stood up immediately from his chair at the side of the bed.

"I've told them to return to your house and to wait until you ask to see them again tomorrow. Apart, that is, from the slave girl. She'll return at dawn."

"It was you who brought me out of that dark hole, wasn't it?"

"Yes it was. I wouldn't let you rot in there until Vettius and Tarquinius decided what to do with you."

"I couldn't really have expected to be allowed to leave the building alive after I killed that pig."

"I simply persuaded them I would be better at keeping you under close arrest than their prison guards. I can be quite persuasive when I choose to be."

"I'm sure," she said, sitting up to adjust her pillows behind her back.

Julius moved quickly to help her and instinctively Lucia took hold of his hand to stop him interfering. She didn't let go immediately, though. Her grip tightened forcing him to look at her quizzically.

"You know what has happened to Flavia and Quintus, don't you?"

"Only what I learnt from Portos and Caris."

He made no attempt to loosen her grip or move away from her.

"Please sit down beside me. There's more to tell."

She told him of Flavia's last message to her and the need to silence Gaius quickly.

"I don't know for sure if he's told anybody else. He also told me his informant was Laric and that he killed him before he could tell anybody else. How can we believe him?"

"He couldn't have told his father or Vettius. They would have done something about it very quickly."

"That's more or less what he said to me, when he was pleading for his miserable life."

"Vettius would have tried to have me taken into custody when I went to rescue you if he had done so. If he didn't tell those two he wouldn't have risked telling anybody else before them."

"What about Laric?"

"If Laric has told someone else and is now dead - and he has certainly gone missing - we can ridicule his story. Really! General Agricola secretly allowed two of the most important prisoners to escape when he was here ten years ago fighting gallantly in the battle. How ridiculous!"

"I see what you mean."

"I will dismiss any suggestion that you are Boudica's daughters as the malicious ramblings of a deranged, lying, runaway slave. Who would dare to contradict me? If he is still alive and is captured I can soon persuade him to confess that Gaius made him make up the whole story, before I dispose of the wretch."

"I understand what you are saying and wish I could accept it. I want to believe we are safe, but I can't. Which is why I must take Marcus and get as far away as possible."

Julius took hold of her hand which was still gripping his arm. He drew it into both of his, gently stroking it.

"You're safe with me. Please stay here and let me take care of you. You disappeared from my life once before because I let you go. You're my prisoner again and this time I'll guard you very closely so you can't leave me, ever."

Lucia didn't reply but held his gaze during a long, tense silence. Eventually she gave a brief sigh.

"Perhaps it's a decision best put off for now. I've only just woken up and perhaps I'm still too tired to think too deeply to resist you."

"Agreed."

"I guess by the lack of any activity throughout the building it's late and time for bed," she said.

Julius, taking this as a sign to leave her to rest, slackened his grip and straightened his back to regain his feet. She tightened her grip on his hand and prevented him from standing. He sank back to sit on the edge of the bed, a puzzled look on his face. Leaning forward slowly he moved his face close to hers.

"Am I about to misunderstand you and embarrass myself?" he asked.

"Oh shut up," she whispered, her hand moving behind his head to draw his lips hard against hers.

*

They were woken by a girlish shriek as Dena dropped the morning meal that she'd been carrying and fled. They both laughed exchanging a light embrace before Julius rose from the bed to dress.

"What now?" he asked.

"Well! You go and do whatever a General does. I intend to return to the estate with Marcus and Portos."

"I want to come with you. We must talk about the future, our future."

"Do we have a future?"

"We can..."

"Don't answer that!" She said, before he could say any more. "I need time to think about what's best for Marcus. He's all I have left. Please don't pressure me, Julius. I'll come back here to the house in a few days and you can imprison me again." She paused, smiling broadly. "Like you did last night."

Julius laughed and held her close to him.

"Now, please go! I need to try to find that young girl and stop her from trembling to death.

CHAPTER 45

Marcus had been devastated at the death of his grandfather but with the help of Caris and Portos he had quickly begun to recover. Portos particularly had taken time to occupy him.

It was something Lucia had become acutely aware of and grateful for since her return from Londinium. It helped her to make one decision about the future at least. She would arrange for the freedom of both of them, whatever happened to the estate. With the help of Julius they could become Roman citizens. She would then ask them if they would stay with her and her son. It would be their first free decision to make.

Since her arrival home, Caris had helped her to clear the villa of all Flavia's clothes and belongings. They destroyed most of them, but placed her most cherished items beside her in the family mausoleum.

Quintus's two other daughters with their husbands paid a short visit whilst Lucia had been in Londinium. They left, intending to return later to sort out their father's written will once they had recovered it from the Governor's office.

Lucia was drifting through a time of great uncertainty. Could she rely on Julius to be able to help protect her and Marcus indefinitely? Did she want to spend her life with Julius? What of Olsar, her dear friend? Where did her future lie, and with whom? She was unhappy with her feelings of confusion and indecision. It was a state of mind she wasn't used to.

Despite her last words to Julius, she wouldn't be returning to him in Londinium. No doubt he would soon appear wondering why she hadn't done so.

She sat on Flavia's bench seat in her garden. It was already beginning to show the lack of her care. She had never known life without her dear, sweet, gentle sister. She ached to see her just one more time to ask for her forgiveness. If only she had been here on that day to protect her. The feelings of guilt swamped her. She stood up, tears in her eyes, and ran to the stables. She made her horse ready and raced out into the fields.

She rode mile after mile until the tears gradually slowed and then stopped. Out of breath she slowed her horse to a walk. She continued her journey aimlessly in a vain attempt to escape the turmoil in her mind.

Almost without realising it she came upon a small tribal village close to the river's edge, several miles upstream from her home. She moved slowly along the main track which led through the middle of the two rows of houses. The inhabitants going about their work became aware of her. They stopped what they were doing and stared as she passed by. To her surprise, some of them bowed to her and kept their heads lowered until she had passed them by.

After she cleared the houses her face broke into a gentle smile. She kicked her horse lightly at first to ease it into a trot. It was followed by a harder kick making the horse begin to run faster. The final kick produced the gallop which would last until she reached the villa.

She had made her decisions.

*

"Caris, I shall be going back to Londinium in the morning," Lucia explained.

"It's good to see you looking better," Caris observed. "The ride must have done you some good."

"It has. By the way, I wanted to ask you if anything had been seen or heard of Laric yet. It's been a long time since we last saw him. Has anybody on the estate had word of him?"

"Nothing. He just seems to have disappeared completely," Caris replied. "He often talked of his longing to buy his freedom. Perhaps he's taken advantage of the death of Quintus and fled to his home in Gaul."

"Perhaps he has. In any case, if you or anybody else should hear of him would you please let me know immediately? He will need to be punished for his absence, if he's ever found."

"I couldn't agree more."

"Would you please let Portos know my plans for tomorrow? I need to use the bathhouse after my ride. Then I'll want to rest afterwards. My side and wrist are still a little painful."

*

Caris rose a little later than normal the following morning. As usual she made her way to the kitchen. To her surprise she saw Portos seated with his back to her, resting his head on the table. It wasn't like him to arrive in the kitchen before her. Perhaps it was because she was later than normal. He had apparently fallen asleep again while he waited for her.

"You had better be asleep and not teasing me about my lateness," she said as she crossed the kitchen to get to the table.

When she got close enough to him she saw a small patch of blood on the table beneath his head. She bit her lip, fighting back a scream. Her hand moved his head gently to one side. Despite her efforts to control her growing panic a loud, shrill scream burst out of her. She could see his severed tongue lying at the side of his head.

Lucia, who had heard the cry of terror, met Caris running to her room.

"What is it? What's the matter?"

She got no reply from Caris, who could only make hysterical gestures in the direction of the kitchen.

*

Lucia took hold of Portos's body and moved it back in the chair, away from the table. His throat had been cut. Once the initial shock had subsided she realised there was too little blood for such a large wound. His death must have happened somewhere else in the middle of the night. Later he had been placed in the kitchen for some reason.

They went to look at his room and found his bed covered in his blood. Although the tears were still flowing down Caris's face, she had recovered enough to question what had happened.

"What sort of monsters would do this to poor Portos? Why would they kill him in his room before placing him in my kitchen? Why should they remove his tongue?"

"I don't know," replied Lucia, "but we're not stopping here a moment longer than we have to."

She found Marcus asleep in his room and held him tightly to her as her mind raced ahead. Leaving him to settle back in his bed she went back to the kitchen and Caris.

"This is what we must do, Caris. You prepare Marcus to be ready to journey to Londinium. I shall get some help to get the horses ready."

Having prepared her own horse and a cart for Caris, she moved to the small stable to bring Marcus's pony. The body of the poor creature lay on the floor. Its severed head was pinned to the wall by a short stabbing spear.

Returning to the main building she took hold of her son.

"Come on, Marcus. I've decided Caris is getting too old to drive the cart by herself. She needs your help."

Caris gave a puzzled look which was met by a silent shake of Lucia's head before she had chance to question what had been said.

"But Mama, I always ride my pony there. You can ask Portos."

"Do as I say, Marcus. We must leave now," Lucia ordered before then whispering to Caris. "I've given instructions to everybody on what must be done here until I can arrange for Julius's men to arrive later today to take care of the estate and all our people. Once I've told him what's happened here, he'll do what I ask."

*

Lucia raced straight to Julius, not daring to go to the house in Londinium. Once inside his headquarters, she paused only briefly to ask Titus to look after Marcus.

She entered Julius's office with Caris and told him about the bloody events which had taken place at the villa during the night.

Julius slammed his fist down upon the desk causing Caris to jump.

"I apologise if I startled you, Caris. Please go to catch up with Marcus. I want to talk with Lucia. No doubt you'll find him feeding the horses by now. Bring him back here."

He turned to Lucia.

"I will then have the three of you escorted safely to your house by a troop of my cavalry."

When they were alone Julius took hold of Lucia's hand.

"This is the work of Tarquinius's men. He's removing those who he thinks are witnesses to his son's crimes and threatening you at the same time. He's telling us he can get to you and have his revenge slowly, coldly, one step at a time. That includes harming Marcus."

"What can you do to stop him?" Lucia asked. "You have to do something or I'll be paying Tarquinius a visit myself."

"I'll stop him, but not today. I want to think about the options I have. You must promise me you won't do to him what you did to his son. Your thoughts must be for your safety and that of Marcus and Caris. My best men will be there at your house to protect you until I've acted."

"I won't do anything unless I'm forced to do so," she warned. "But I can't stand by for very long, waiting for this monster to hurt my Marcus or Caris."

CHAPTER 46

Julius had spent the following morning reviewing the detailed documents which had been presented to him by Titus and his clerk.

"Have you made copies of them all?" asked Julius, continuing to browse through them.

"Yes, General," replied the clerk. "In fact I've made two further copies."

"Where are they?"

"As normal, one has been made to be kept as a permanent record in my office under lock and key. In addition, as ordered by Tribune Titus, we've produced a further copy and placed it in the strong room."

"Excellent. You've recognised the importance of the information which is contained in them. It's vital that only the three of us, who know about the details, have access to these documents. I'll tell Olsar of their content shortly. Whatever the pressure that may be applied, you must never release any of the copies in case they should be destroyed."

"What about the Governor, Sir?"

"It applies to him more than anybody else. This is a military matter and my responsibility alone. Now leave us and return to your office."

"So these corrupt dealings have been going on for some time, Titus," said Julius when they were alone.

"Yes, Sir. They have been happening since well before Governor Bolanus arrived."

"And what about his involvement since?"

"It would appear that soon after the Governor took up his position he became involved, particularly with the major supplier, Tarquinius Marellus."

"What precisely has been going on?"

"In addition to the excessive over-pricing there are other cases of fraud."

"Such as?"

"There've been many instances of failure to deliver full quantities of supplies which had been paid for. Poor quality equipment and supplies which have been returned were not replaced or money refunded instead by the supplier. Bribes have been paid to record items as having been received when subsequently they were never delivered. There's more if you wish me to continue."

"That's sufficient for now. I intend to place this information before those two later today. I've asked them to meet me in the Governor's office. It's unlikely anything will happen to me to prevent my return after I've spoken to them. However, if it does, you should leave immediately to take a copy of these documents to Camillus in Gaul. He knows that I trust you fully and will know what to do. Thank you for your good work. Go now and ask Olsar to report to me."

*

A short while later Julius had given Olsar a brief explanation of what the documents contained, and what he intended to do about it. He told him he had sent word to the Governor that he was on his way to see him and it would be advisable to invite Tarquinius to join them.

"They will think it's about Lucia," Julius added.

"But I can't understand why you're only taking me with you to confront Vettius and Tarquinius. Wouldn't a troop of legionaries be more appropriate?"

"This is the Governor's official residence and a large military force entering his offices would be too dramatic a gesture. It would soon be known throughout the town. I prefer to handle this simply and quietly at first to achieve my objectives."

"Who knows what actions they may choose to take once they know their corruption has been discovered?" Olsar argued. "Because of recent events, Vettius will have made sure there are plenty of his men in and around the building."

"Which is why I need you to protect my back. You are equal to a troop of legionaries at any time."

Both men smiled at the exaggeration, but it was a demonstration to Olsar of the trust Julius had in him.

*

Vettius and Tarquinius were waiting in silence as the guard showed Julius and Olsar into the room.

"Leave us," Julius ordered, "and close the door behind you."

The guard looked to the Governor who gave a nod of approval to withdraw.

Julius stepped forward, throwing the bundle of incriminating documents onto the desk.

"Both of you read these."

Vettius, a little surprised at first, untied the cord which had been wrapped around the documents. He passed half of them to Tarquinius who was seated to the side of his desk. Vettius showed no emotion as he slowly read and took in the information before him. Tarquinius on the other hand looked increasingly agitated, the more he skimmed through his bundle of documents.

"These are the work of somebody's wicked imagination," said Tarquinius. "Why are you wasting our time? Is it some scheme to try to save your whore?"

Julius's lip curled and he stepped forward, not to assault Tarquinius who sat back in alarm, but to sit down in the chair in front of the desk. He slapped his hand down on the documents in front of Tarquinius.

"I've come to take this criminal into custody. I'm sure you'll support me in removing anything that harms the efficiency of the army, Vettius. We all know the Emperor has sent me to restore discipline in our forces and to eliminate anything, anything or anybody, who prevents me from doing that."

"He's trying to undermine your authority, Vettius."

"You are a criminal, Tarquinius," Julius countered. "With your associates you've been defrauding the army for years. You've corrupted and bribed many of our officers. Not surprisingly I've found an ill-disciplined, poorly led force. You'll be tried, found guilty and dealt with as the thief and traitor you are."

He turned to Vettius, addressing his next remarks at him.

"At the last Games he was the sponsor. He was the main point of attention. At the next he will be again. This time, though, it will be as the main criminal to be publically executed."

"Vettius! Stop this madman. Use your authority to have him arrested. My men are here and will assist you," cried an increasingly desperate Tarquinius.

Vettius said nothing. Instead, he concentrated on Julius's contemptuous grin. His fingers played with the corners of the documents in front of him. Julius took notice.

"I have another set which will be on its way to the Emperor, should I fail to leave this building."

"Please, Vettius," Tarquinius begged.

"Calm yourself," Vettius said sharply. Fixing his unblinking eyes on Julius, he continued.

"I think I would like to read these documents in a little more depth to see who is identified and what they are accused of. Perhaps you would stay, Julius. The two of us could then discuss the implications once I have read these documents?"

"No!" cried Tarquinius. "I will not be sacrificed in this way."

With surprising speed he leapt from his chair, seizing Lucia's knife from the desk. His forward downward lunge at Julius was only partly parried by him, and the blade entered the top of his shoulder. Tarquinius raised the knife to strike again. He didn't get the chance to deliver another more deadly blow. Olsar's sword penetrated the middle of his body with such force the point of the blade emerged from his back, spraying blood onto the desk behind him.

Olsar quickly withdrew his sword from the falling, dying Tarquinius and moved towards Vettius.

"No!" cried Julius. "We need him."

*

A short while later, the body had been taken away and the blood stains removed from the desk and floor. Julius's injury had been looked at by the Governor's staff. The flow of blood from the gash on his shoulder had been checked, and the wound dressed. It allowed him to continue with his demands of Vettius.

"These documents will be put away and we shall mention them no more. The people will be told that Tarquinius had become insane with grief and shame. You had told him of your decision not to take action against Lucia because of the rape carried out by his son. He had attempted to assassinate us both to hide his son's guilt. Thankfully the Gods - and Olsar - saved us."

"Agreed," said Vettius with a look of relief on his face.

"This ends the whole episode and Lucia and her son will be safe. Do we understand each other?"

"I agree. However, I warn you that you have laid down a marker today, Julius, which will set the tone for our relationship in the future. I'll take as much interest in your dealings and welfare, as you have shown in mine."

"So be it. Come along, Olsar. I think I need the Legion's surgeons to get to work on me."

CHAPTER 47

That evening Julius lay in his bed feeling sore. He was still a little drunk from the wine which had been poured into him as his wound was being treated. He had been propped up to allow him to take a light meal. Finding it was the most comfortable position, he had remained there.

"Come in," he called, answering a light knock on the door.

The door opened slowly and Lucia entered cautiously.

"I wasn't sure if you were sleeping," she explained.

"Not until I'd seen you."

"Olsar has told me what happened. You've been very fortunate."

She sat on the side of his bed.

"Fortunate, perhaps, but things went much as I planned. Tarquinius is dead and Vettius has been placed on his best behaviour. He won't be a problem to us in the future."

She took his hand in hers.

"I'm leaving tomorrow, taking Marcus and Caris with me," she said, a single tear appearing on the top of her cheek.

"What are you talking about?" he said in disbelief. "We've removed those who threaten you. Nobody knows of your identity and I can protect and care for you and Marcus for ever. I know you care for me. I can't allow you to leave and disappear from my life again."

"You couldn't stop me and I don't think you would even try to force me to stay. You are no longer that man. Let me try to explain. I owe you an explanation."

The day before Portos died I took a long ride, full of self-pity. Towards the end of it I rode through a small tribal village where the people lived much as I had a long time ago. It was there that I finally accepted that I have become a 'Roman'. I rode back, having decided I would see if we could find happiness together. I felt safe, even with the thought that for a long period you would be elsewhere in the north. I knew your work would one day be done and I would be waiting for you here in Londinium."

"All of which can still happen," he pleaded.

"Not any more. The death of Portos and the message sent in the slaughter of Marcus's pony showed me we could never be safe. Tarquinius is dead but he has brothers and he has other sons who will never forget or forgive me for killing Gaius. They will believe I was also the cause of Tarquinius's death."

"We can take steps to deal with the worst of those and keep you safe."

"Perhaps, but I also realise that living in Londinium will always carry the possibility, however unlikely, of me being recognised."

"So come with me on my campaign in the north. When I've defeated the Brigantes I shall ask the Emperor to return me to Rome. You will come with me."

"I couldn't join you to watch you conquer another people like my own. I accept what you are doing is your duty as the Emperor's General but I can't be by your side, helping you to defeat another tribe. And what would happen to your wife if we were to go to Rome eventually?"

"I will divorce her."

"There will be no need. Please forgive me but I really have no choice."

She leaned forward to kiss him gently. That kiss and more that followed became more passionate as her tears fell from her face onto his. And then those kisses became gentle again before she drew her face back a little and gave him a slight, sad smile. She drew back fully.

"I fear that those kisses were meant as a final farewell from you" said Julius. "Where will you go?"

"If I am a Roman, I should to go to see Rome. Maybe my destiny still lies in the arena. Then again, perhaps my future will take me on to other things. Who knows what waits for me there? Perhaps my future lies elsewhere."

"If I can't change your mind, then let me take care of you one last time. I shall send for my clerk and have him draw up a document to release Olsar from service in the Army. He can go with you to keep you safe for me."

She looked surprised at the suggestion.

"What if he prefers to stay with you? He's still a warrior."

"He would follow you to the underworld if you asked him to. You know that's so."

"You really are the man I've grown to admire," she said, and the tears came again.

"Shall we meet again?" he asked sadly.

"Who knows? The Gods brought us back together once. Maybe they will again. I would want it to happen if it's possible. Something inside me tells me we shall."

"Take this before you go."

He reached to the table at the side of the bed and took her knife in his hand.

"You may need it. I certainly don't."

He laughed, touching his shoulder with the point. She took it and rose from the bed.

"Goodbye, Julius."

She turned and ran without a backward glance.

*

Walking slowly back to the house she began to reflect on what had just happened. Was she throwing away a last chance of blissful happiness with a man she had begun to care deeply about? Wasn't everything secondary to that? Could she, even now, follow him and put behind her the abhorrence of what his coming military duty required him to do?

Without realising it she had nearly stepped into a rubbish pit as she walked towards the amphitheatre and its arena. She halted, looking up at the dark walls towering in front her and then down to the knife she still held in her hand. She realised the demands of the arena, which had once given her hope of building a future free of her past, were no longer what she needed. She was free to face whatever challenge came her way when she got to Rome.

She smiled and threw the knife into the pit and ran as fast as she could to see Marcus and Caris. Together, with Olsar, they would begin to prepare for the great unknown journey ahead of them.

AUTHOR'S NOTE

Did Rome really have female gladiators, particularly involved in contests to the death? Perhaps after reading this book there will be a few more who think it was likely, given the appetite of the Roman citizens for ever more exciting, thrilling and extreme forms of combat and display in the arena.

The generally accepted view is that the final battle between the Romans and Boudica happened somewhere north of London as the Roman army returned from Mona (Anglesey). My view is that it was just as likely to have occurred somewhere much further south and west of London. Perhaps we will never know. My view certainly allows for a more interesting tale to be told.

Allan Fox, 2015

Printed in Great Britain
by Amazon